The Doll Collection

Also Edited by Ellen Datlow

A Whisper of Blood

A Wolf at the Door
(with Terri Windling)

After (with Terri Windling)

Alien Sex

Black Heart, Ivory Bones
(with Terri Windling)

Black Swan, White Raven
(with Terri Windling)

Black Thorn, White Rose
(with Terri Windling)

Blood and Other Cravings*

Blood Is Not Enough: 17 Stories
of Vampirism

Darkness: Two Decades of Modern
Horror

Digital Domains: A Decade of
Science Fiction and Fantasy

Fearful Symmetries

Haunted Legends
(with Nick Mamatas)*

Hauntings

Inferno: New Tales of Terror and
the Supernatural*

Lethal Kisses

Little Deaths

Lovecraft Unbound

Lovecraft's Monsters

Naked City: Tales of Urban Fantasy

Nebula Awards Showcase 2009

Nightmare Carnival

Off Limits: Tales of Alien Sex

Omni Best Science Fiction:
Volumes One Through Three

Omni Books of Science Fiction:
Volumes One Through Seven

OmniVisions One and Two

Poe: 19 New Tales Inspired by
Edgar Allan Poe

Queen Victoria's Book of Spells
(with Terri Windling)*

Ruby Slippers, Golden Tears
(with Terri Windling)

Salon Fantastique: Fifteen Original
Tales of Fantasy
(with Terri Windling)

Silver Birch, Blood Moon
(with Terri Windling)

Sirens and Other Daemon Lovers
(with Terri Windling)

Snow White, Blood Red
(with Terri Windling)

Supernatural Noir

Swan Sister (with Terri Windling)

Tails of Wonder and Imagination:
Cat Stories

Teeth: Vampire Tales
(with Terri Windling)

Telling Tales: The Clarion West 30th
Anniversary Anthology

The Beastly Bride: And Other Tales
of the Animal People
(with Terri Windling)

The Best Horror of the Year:
Volumes One Through Six

The Coyote Road: Trickster Tales
(with Terri Windling)

The Cutting Room: Dark Reflections
of the Silver Screen

The Dark: New Ghost Stories

The Del Rey Book of Science Fiction
and Fantasy

The Faery Reel: Tales from the
Twilight Realm

The Green Man: Tales of the Mythic
Forest (with Terri Windling)

Troll's Eye View: A Book of Villainous
Tales (with Terri Windling)

Twists of the Tale

Vanishing Acts*

The Year's Best Fantasy and Horror
(with Terri Windling,
Gavin J. Grant, and Kelly Link)

*A Tor Book

THE
DOLL
COLLECTION

Edited by

Ellen Datlow

A Tom Doherty Associates Book
New York

THE DOLL COLLECTION

A Tor Book
Published by Tom Doherty Associates, LLC
175 Fifth Avenue
New York, NY 10010

www.tor-forge.com

Tor® is a registered trademark of Tom Doherty Associates, LLC.

The Library of Congress Cataloging-in-Publication Data
is available upon request.

ISBN 978-0-7653-7680-0 (hardcover)
ISBN 978-1-4668-5194-8 (e-book)

Tor books may be purchased for educational, business, or promotional use. For information on
bulk purchases, please contact the Macmillan Corporate and Premium Sales Department at
1-800-221-7945, extension 5442, or write to specialmarkets@macmillan.com.

First Edition: March 2015

Printed in the United States of America

0 9 8 7 6 5 4 3 2 1

Copyright Acknowledgments

Contents

✽

List of Photographs   9

Acknowledgments   11

Introduction *by Ellen Datlow*   13

Skin and Bone *by Tim Lebbon*   17

Heroes and Villains *by Stephen Gallagher*   35

The Doll-Master *by Joyce Carol Oates*   49

Gaze *by Gemma Files*   75

In Case of Zebras *by Pat Cadigan*   97

There Is No Place for Sorrow in the Kingdom of the Cold
   by Seanan McGuire   121

Goodness and Kindness *by Carrie Vaughn*   149

Daniel's Theory About Dolls *by Stephen Graham Jones*   167

After and Back Before *by Miranda Siemienowicz*   191

Doctor Faustus *by Mary Robinette Kowal*   215

Doll Court *by Richard Bowes*   225

Visit Lovely Cornwall on the Western Railway Line
   by Genevieve Valentine   243

Ambitious Boys Like You *by Richard Kadrey*   259

Miss Sibyl-Cassandra *by Lucy Sussex*   283

The Permanent Collection *by Veronica Schanoes*   295

Homemade Monsters *by John Langan*   309

Word Doll *by Jeffrey Ford*   329

Photographs

✳

Title page: *Ellen Klages*   3

Skin and Bone: *Ellen Datlow*   17

Heroes and Villains: *Ellen Datlow*   35

The Doll-Master: *Ellen Klages*   49

Gaze: *Ellen Datlow*   75

In Case of Zebras: *Ellen Datlow*   97

There Is No Place for Sorrow in the Kingdom of the Cold:
    Richard Bowes   121

Goodness and Kindness: *Ellen Datlow*   149

Daniel's Theory About Dolls: *Richard Bowes*   167

After and Back Before: *Ellen Klages*   191

Doctor Faustus: *Ellen Datlow*   215

Doll Court: *Richard Bowes*   225

Visit Lovely Cornwall on the Western Railway Line:
    Ellen Klages   243

Ambitious Boys Like You: *Ellen Datlow*   259

Miss Sibyl-Cassandra: *Ellen Klages*   283

The Permanent Collection: *Ellen Klages*   295

Homemade Monsters: *Construction by Richard Herman;*
    Photograph: Ellen Datlow   309

Word Doll: *Richard Bowes*   329

Acknowledgments

Thanks to Jonathan Carroll for sending me a brief excerpt from a book about the Bauhaus Group back in 2010 that he very likely has totally forgotten.

To Jim Frenkel for his enthusiasm for the project.

To Liz Gorinsky, my patient editor.

To Veronica Schanoes for her brilliant help with the introduction.

To Ellen Klages and Richard Bowes for loving and owning weird and creepy dolls as much as I do.

Introduction

Dolls, perhaps more than any other object, demonstrate just how thin the line between love and fear, comfort and horror, can be. They are objects of love and sources of reassurance for children, coveted prizes for collectors, sources of terror and horror in numerous movies, television shows, books, and stories. Dolls fire our collective imagination, for better and—too often—for worse. From life-size dolls the same height as the little girls who carry them, to dolls whose long hair can "grow" longer, to Barbie and her fashionable sisters, dolls do double duty as child's play and the focus of adult art and adult fear.

Some dolls were never meant for children at all. Voodoo dolls, for example, are created as objects of transference and loci of power; effigies of hated figures such as Guy Fawkes are created specifically in order to suffer violence; shrunken heads were used for religious purposes and as trophies; and Real Dolls, anatomically correct life-size models of women, are made for men who prefer their sexual "partners" lifeless and mute.

I myself collect dolls (including three-faced dolls—dolls that, given a turn of the head, will show a baby sleeping, crying, or smiling, as long as you don't mind twisting your doll's neck), doll heads, and other doll parts. That physical collection has led to this collection of dark fantasy and horror stories of dolls and their worlds.

Of course, I am hardly the first to see the connection between dolls and terror. Evil dolls are practically a subgenre of horror fiction and film: 1936's *The Devil-Doll* with Lionel Barrymore as the mastermind behind a set of murderous dolls; 1975's *Trilogy of Terror,* wherein Karen Black is menaced by a Zuni fetish doll (based on the short story "Prey" by Richard Matheson); the 1976 William Goldman novel *Magic*, an example of the ever-popular "evil ventriloquist's dummy" subset of doll horror; the 1960 *Twilight Zone* episode "The After Hours," in which mannequins long for lives of their own; and of course the *Child's Play* franchise, featuring the homicidal Chucky, which first saw light in 1988. More recently, 2013 saw the release of *The Conjuring*, featuring Annabelle, a possessed doll, whose own spin-off was released in October 2014.

With this venerable tradition in mind, when I approached writers about contributing to this anthology, I made one condition: no evil doll stories. While these writers could and did mine the uncanniness of dolls for all it's worth, I did not want to publish a collection of stories revolving around the cliché of the evil doll. Surely, I thought, there was horror and darkness to be found in the world of dolls beyond that well-trodden path. As you shall shortly see, I was right: the dolls and doll-like creatures within range from the once-ubiquitous kewpie dolls created by Rose O'Neill, which were often given away as prizes at carnivals and circuses; to a homemade monster created out of a repurposed Commander Kirk doll; to a Shirley Temple doll come upon hard times; to unique dolls and doll-like objects created from the imaginations of the contributors to punish or comfort humans, or placate the inhuman.

Sigmund Freud, in his 1919 essay "The Uncanny," noted that dolls were particularly uncanny, falling into the category of objects that look as though they should be alive but aren't. But he also suggested that uncanniness in general was the result of something familiar that should have been kept secret instead of being brought to light—the cognitive disjuncture produces that feeling of unease which we attribute to the uncanny. What do dolls bring to light? In these stories, what they so often highlight is the malevolence that lurks not in dolls—which are, after all, only poor copies of ourselves, only objects at our mercy—but in the human beings who interact with them. Not horrific in themselves, but imbued with horror by their owners or controllers, what the dolls in these stories often reveal is the evil within us, the evil that we try to keep hidden, but that dolls bring to light.

Theories of uncanniness have been elaborated upon since Freud's time. The "uncanny valley" refers to a theory developed by robotics professor Masahiro Mori in 1970: It posits that objects with features that are human-like, that look and move almost—but not quite—like actual human beings, elicit visceral feelings of revulsion in many people. The "valley" in question refers to the change in our comfort with these objects: Our comfort level increases as the objects look more human, until, suddenly, they look simultaneously too human and not quite human enough, and our comfort level drops off sharply, only to rise again on the other side of the valley when something appears and moves exactly like a human being. It is in this valley, the realm of the too human but still not human enough, that dolls have taken up residence, and it is this valley that seventeen writers invite you to visit.

Skin and Bone

by Tim Lebbon

After sixty-two days in the cold, the unexplored landscape where words hardened into solid shapes and every breath might have frozen his soul, Kurt's wedding ring fell off. He only removed his glove for a moment, needing the more dextrous use of his bare fingers to unhook frozen gear from the sled. And for a few seconds he didn't even notice that the ring had slipped away. It was like that sometimes down here, as if the cold could slow brain functions in the same way that it thickened oil and paraffin, made every movement three times harder than it was the day before. He saw it drop from his finger and sink into the snow, but it was several heartbeats before he said, "Shit."

He'd thought that metal contracted in the cold. Enough, at least, to keep it on his finger. But he supposed his loss of weight from starvation and excessive effort had finally superseded the ratio of gold shrinkage.

"Shit. *Shit!*" He had the good sense to put his glove back on before digging into the snow.

"What the hell?" Marshall asked. They were the best of friends, closer than brothers, but they had experienced strange moments on this expedition when they hated each other.

"My wedding ring," Kurt said. "Bindy will kill me."

"I doubt she'll even care," Marshall said, and he continued the laborious effort to set up camp. The sky was clear right now, a startling blue streaked with fingertrails of cloud high up. But a bad storm was coming, and they had mere hours to prepare.

"Can't you help me?" Kurt asked.

"Why don't you just—!" Marshall shouted, loud, breath glistening in front of his face and then drifting to the ground as a million tiny diamonds. He sighed. "Sorry. Yeah. Sorry."

The cold played strange tricks on the men. On day seventeen, Kurt had seen a line of camels on the snowscape to the east, walking slowly up the rocky ridge from the ice fields. He'd insisted that they were there, and even after Marshall told him he was hallucinating—and Kurt acknowledged that—the camels were still visible, slow and lazy. On day thirty, Marshall swore that his dick had fallen off. He'd tried stripping his layers to find it, preserve it in ice so that the surgeons could reattach it after the expedition. Even when it was exposed, his sad shriveled member turning blue in its nest of frost-speckled hair, he'd made Kurt grab it to make sure it was still attached. On day forty-seven, a day before they reached the South Pole, Kurt and his sled had slipped into a shallow crevasse, and it had taken Marshall four hours to haul him out. By then Kurt was trying to scream, but the cold had swollen his throat and frozen his pain inside.

The cold ate into a person. The physical effects were obvious, but the psychological impact was more insidious. They had hardly shared a harsh word in the thirty years they'd known each other before this adventure, but on day fifty-three Kurt had threatened to fucking gut Marshall if he didn't finish every last drop of his soup.

Such things were laughed about afterward. They were doing this by choice, and they knew that odd things would happen. That made it almost bearable.

"Here it is," Marshall said. "Stupid sod. Don't lose it again."

"Oh, mate," Kurt said, taking the small gold ring from his friend. "Marshall, thanks."

"Stupid sod." Marshall went back to unpacking the tent and equipment from the sled. "Now let's get a shift on. I don't want to freeze to death today."

"How about tomorrow?"

"Nah, not then, either."

Kurt smiled as he slipped the ring back on. "How about three days' time?"

"Help me with this."

"How about a week next Thursday?"

"Fucking prick!"

They finished erecting the small tent, and while Marshall zipped himself inside to light the stove and start melting snow for cooking and drinking, Kurt set about tying down the camp. He hammered stakes into the ice and tied the two sleds to them. Then he banged in more stakes and made sure the tent was secure.

Hands pressed into the small of his back, he stretched, leaning back and looking around. As always, it still felt like he was pulling that damn sled across the ice. It might be months before he *didn't* feel like he was pulling all that weight. But it was worth it.

The desolate Antarctic landscape was as beautiful as it was deadly, and he never felt more alive than when he was on some mad expedition or other with Marshall. And this was the maddest of all. It was one of the harshest places on Earth, and survival took every ounce of intelligence and strength, endurance and ruggedness. It was that more than anything that had brought them here. The rest of the world was an endless distance away, so remote that it felt like a dream. Here and now was all that mattered.

Marshall had probably been right about Bindy not caring if Kurt lost his wedding ring. They'd been drifting apart for years, and she'd effectively told him that "another fucking adventure" would cost him his wife. She wanted kids and security, a three-bedroom house and a Labrador. He wanted danger and challenges, the satisfaction of taking on the elements, the thrill of extremes. Jack London had written that "the function of man is to live, not to exist." Kurt was living as well as he could.

He tried to care about Bindy but could not make it happen. It was too cold, the incoming storm too terrible, to care about anything other than surviving the next few days.

"Toilet break!" he called, and Marshall muttered something from inside the tent. Kurt knew that they could well be confined in there with each other for days once the storm hit. He'd relish this one last opportunity to take a dump in private.

He tramped past the sleds, making a final inspection to ensure their equipment was tied down securely, then made for a rocky outcropping to the east. He knew from experience that it was farther away than it looked, and after a few minutes of tramping across the ice he reached it. Breathing hard, he turned around to make sure the camp was still in sight. The sky was mostly clear, the sun was dancing with the horizon, and the storm was several hours away.

Behind the sculpture of snow- and ice-speckled rock he found a tent.

Kurt gasped, breath stuck in his throat, his body refusing to react. Then he let out his held breath and took a step back.

"Bloody hell," he muttered. "Hey, Marshall." But Marshall was still inside their own tent across the snowfield. Maybe if Kurt shouted he'd hear, but . . .

But he didn't want to call out to his friend. Not yet. He wanted to see what he'd found.

The tent was old. Very old. Almost shapeless; he could only tell what it was from the struts protruding like the smashed rib cage of a dead giant. The old canvas was its skin, and the humped shapes its distorted insides.

Kurt's heart was hammering. He'd heard about occasional finds like this—explorers out on the ice discovering remnants of old camps, forgotten expeditions, sometimes even the sad remains of dead adventurers. But through all their adventures in Alaska, the Sahara, South America, and Nepal, he'd never seen anything like this himself.

He moved closer. A gust of wind blew a haze of snow across the scene, and he winced as it grated against the bare skin of his face. He should have covered up, worn his hooded coat and heavy face scarf. He was becoming clumsy; so many weeks into their journey the routines that could save their lives were too easy to let slip. It was the Antarctic summer, the cold a mere thirty degrees below zero. But frostbite could still strike, especially with the rising breeze adding to the chill factor.

He didn't have long.

The tent material looked many decades old. It was holed in places, and when he grabbed at it a chunk came off in his hand. He knelt and lowered his face close to the snow surface, trying to see beneath the fallen tent. Trying to see what might be inside.

"I should get Marshall," he muttered, his words made ice and stolen by another gust of wind. They sprinkled on the rocks beyond the tent.

Maybe it had blown here from elsewhere. Perhaps it had been buried for many decades, and some of the recent, deeper thaws had brought it back to the surface. Or it could have been nestled here all along, covered with snow one year, exposed the next, a yearly cycle of burial and exposure.

He stood and turned away, emerging into the open again and ready to go get Marshall. Then, looking back out across the ice fields toward camp, he blinked several times, trying to make sense of what he'd seen.

It was like trying to retrieve an old memory, rather than his most recent.

Something there, he thought, and he clambered back behind the rocks. *Something not part of the tent.* And there it was. He crouched down and tugged at a support spur. It snapped off and pulled a spread of canvas with it, and beneath there lay a leg. He worked quickly to uncover the body. The clothing confused him, so thin and slight for the harshness of even the best conditions this place might present. Then he realised that it was not clothing at all. The corpse was naked. It was leathery, weathered skin.

He worked faster, uncovering the whole form until he reached the corpse's head.

And he cried out in revulsion and shock, stepping back and catching his heel on something buried in the ice—a timber support, a rock, a bone—and sprawling onto his back, never once taking his eyes from that face.

The plainest face he had ever seen. A blank. He had seen dead people before, but never like this, never so *washed away*. It was like a person who was not quite finished. The face held the features of a normal human, but even in death there was something so vague, so incomplete, that Kurt could not tear his eyes away. He wanted to. He needed to. But like a child fascinated with a crushed rabbit by the side of a road, he could only stare.

The eyes were sunken pits. The nose was a bump, unremarkable, shapeless. There was hair but it had been styled by ice and time into a shapeless wig. Flat lips were drawn apart over yellowed teeth, the mouth a slit as if sliced by a knife.

The figure stared just over his shoulder.

Kurt stood again, slowly. His shock receded and his heartbeat lessened. It was only as he backed slowly away that he realised there was another shape next to the first, partially hidden beneath the rest of the old tent, yet just visible. Its face was flat and blank.

He turned and tried to run, but his clothing was too heavy and thick, his muscles too weakened by eight weeks on the ice. He sprawled into the snow. It stuck to his chilled skin, reaching cold fingers into his mouth and eyes. He stood again and ran on, feeling a warmth around his crotch. He'd pissed himself.

By the time he reached camp he was exhausted. Marshall was still inside the tent, and when Kurt opened the flaps and tumbled inside he received a torrent of curses.

He'd let out all the heat.

"Dickhead," Marshall said. "Get them off, get them dry. You stink. We might have another few hours of peace before the storm hits."

"What does the forecast say?" Kurt asked. He hadn't told Marshall about the old tent.

Marshall checked out the small laptop sitting on a warming plate to encourage the battery back to life. "Four days of freezing our bollocks off," he said. He said something else, too. A quip, a joke. But Kurt didn't hear.

He wanted to tell Marshall, but he couldn't. The longer he left it, the weirder it would sound. *Oh, and by the way, I found two dead bodies that don't even look like real people.*

"Hey!" Marshal nudged him softly.

"Yeah."

"Get those clothes off, Kurt. You need to get warm."

"I'm fine, I'm okay."

"Like hell. You're no use to me dead. All skin and bone."

While Kurt undressed and huddled deep into his sleeping bag, the words circled in his mind, and he realised why they sounded so strange.

The bodies he'd found were more than skin and bone. If anything they'd resembled shop mannequins.

"I need to get back out there!" he said, trying to unzip the sleeping bag. "I need to make sure."

Marshall moved closer to him, one arm around his shoulder and the other offering a mug of hot tea. "Drink. All of it."

The fight went out of Kurt just like that, and he realised that he'd probably been seeing things. He hadn't taken his snow goggles with him, and had left himself open to the cold. It was harsher than he thought. It did stuff to the mind.

"Marsh, I'm cold."

"Yeah. One guy I heard about on his last trip down here, he got so cold that his brain fluid froze. When they thawed him out he'd been reset as a six-year-old. All he wanted to do was get home and watch *Power Rangers*."

"You're so full of shit."

"You know it."

They drank hot tea together. Marshall rehydrated some spiced lentil and steak soup, and they hugged the warm mugs, spooning food into their eager mouths. They made small talk until the storm hit several hours later.

Then they hunkered down, listening to the wind, imagining the inches of snow piling up and blowing around them with every hour that passed.

They'll be smothered, Kurt thought, and the idea pleased him. *When we next get out of the tent they'll be gone, and it'll be like they never were.*

In places like this, the dead should stay buried.

✳

Huddled into their sleeping bags, they listened to the storm. They didn't talk much. They sat on either side of the stove, reaching out occasionally to adjust the gas up or down. Wet clothes hung around them. The small tent stank of sweat and piss from the drying clothing, but they were more than used to that. It was the odour of exploration, and they had been in a place like this together many times before.

Boredom rarely touched Kurt. He thought of his childhood dreams and how far he had come. And he thought of Bindy, waiting for him back home if he was lucky, gone if he was not. That was another strange thing about existing in such an extreme environment—right now, back home didn't seem to matter. London was as far away as the moon, and only the here and now was important.

A couple of hours into the storm, Marshall started brewing more tea. Kurt watched the blue flames kissing the pot, eyes drooping, blinking slower and slower, and then the pot and flames were gone.

The dead bodies appeared in their place. The storm was raging, scouring the landscape with ice fingers and teeth of frost, but around Kurt there was a circle of calm and peace. He approached the old, rotting tent and the things it might once have protected. They were moving. He could see that from far away, and though he had no wish to go closer his feet took him, tramping through fresh snow, ignoring the high winds and piercing cold that should be killing his exposed extremities. *No no no,* he thought as he walked closer, because one of the shapes he'd uncovered seemed to be sitting up, turning its blank expression and empty eyes his way, leaning to the side, ready to stand, shifting and quivering as if seen through a heat-haze, not a cold so intense that the marrow in his bones was freezing.

No no no, he thought again, and when he took in a breath to scream he tasted sweet steam.

"Here," Marshall said. "Kurt? You awake?"

Kurt's eyes snapped open. He looked around the cramped tent and nodded, leaning to his left, ready to sit up. "Yeah, fine. Nodded off." *And saw them,* he thought. *I saw them moving out there in the storm!*

"What's up, mate?"

"Up?"

"You're acting weird."

Kurt took a grateful sip of the tea. It burnt his split lips, but he relished the pain.

"Well . . ." He sipped some more and sighed, making a decision. "I saw something out in the snow, over by the rock outcropping to the east. Couple of bodies."

"Yeah?" Marshall was interested, not shocked. They both knew how many people had died in this vast place, and how many of those had never been seen again. Marshall had climbed Everest several years ago, and often told Kurt about the bodies he'd seen up there. He said they weren't spooky or sad, just lonely. They'd died doing what they loved.

"But they were weird," Kurt said. "They didn't look . . . normal. Human. It was like they were mannequins or something. You know, unfinished."

"Could've been really old," Marshall said. "Cold can do weird things to a body. Cold, dry air dries the corpses out, leaches all the fluids from them."

"But their faces," Kurt said, blinking and seeing that face staring at him. "Their eyes."

"Should've told me!" Marshall said. The revelation seemed to have cheered him up. "When the storm's passed we'll go and check them out together."

No way, Kurt thought, but he didn't say that. He didn't want to sound scared.

They finished their tea. The storm roared on. Neither of them spoke again for some time.

Kurt thought of Bindy, turning his loose wedding ring and trying to care.

❁

The tent grew darker as snow piled up outside. Kurt kept the stove burning, and the air remained musty and heavy. He didn't mind. He was so used to the burning touch of cold on his skin that it was good to feel something else. And he knew it would be over soon. The storm would pass, they would dig themselves out, and their journey home would continue.

They'd leave those things behind.

Marshall mumbled in his sleep. He shifted, kicked his feet in the tight sleeping bag, then shouted. Kurt sat up and stared, not used to his friend making such a noise. Marshall was always such a deep sleeper, and Kurt had always been jealous of just how quickly he managed to fall asleep.

Clear conscience, Marshall would say. Now he twitched and moved, and when he kicked again he came dangerously close to knocking over the stove burning between them. It had a cover, and if tipped over there was an auto shut-off. But it was still a risk.

"Marsh?" Kurt's voice sounded thick and heavy, as if the warmer air held it longer. It was strange not seeing his breath condense. Moisture dripped from his beard. "Marsh?"

Marshall rolled onto his back again, kicking his feet in the sleeping bag. Its hood had twisted and fallen to half-obscure his face, and in the poor light Kurt couldn't make out whether his eyes were open or closed.

"Marshall!" He spoke louder, fighting against a gust of wind that roared around their tent.

Marshall stiffened, grew still, then started breathing easier. Bad dreams.

Kurt settled again and passed the time by assessing his body, alternately tensing and then relaxing muscles from his toes up to see where problems might lie. The first two toes on his right foot had gone almost two weeks ago—they were darkened and stiff, and it was likely that he'd lose them. But the rest of his toes seemed fine. It was surprising that he hadn't suffered more.

They'd agreed that they would only call for rescue if one or both of their lives were in danger. Frostbite, weight loss, snow blindness, borderline starvation, these were acceptable risks for the adventure they had embarked upon. They'd spent two days at the Pole, recovering at the research station there, but they'd found themselves keen to continue, working their way back toward the coast, where they'd be able to pronounce their expedition a success. They'd both lost a huge amount of weight, and when Kurt looked in a mirror inside one of the huts he'd let out a startled cry. He'd not recognised himself.

Marshall had laughed at that. "Few people who come here and do the sort of thing we're doing go home the same person," he'd said. "This place changes people. Got to accept that."

There was not far to go now. But as Kurt sat wrapped in his sleeping bag, feeling how weakened he had become in his time on the ice, he was farther from home than ever before. It wasn't just distance and time, but remoteness. They were deeper in the wilderness than they had ever been, and closer to the pure unknown.

Marshall muttered again. Incomprehensible words, mostly, but then one phrase that stood out, harsh and stark: "My eyes are mine!"

Fear pulsed through Kurt's veins. He leaned across and shook his friend, rolling him back and forth in his sleeping bag, but Marshall would not wake. He stiffened beneath Kurt's hand, went limp, and stiffened again, and all the time he was whining and mumbling wretchedly.

Kurt sat back, watching his friend dream and fighting a sudden, overwhelming desire to close his own eyes. He blinked slowly. It was dark in there.

Wind groaned around the tent, the storm given voice. He held his breath, but doing so meant he heard Marshall's haunted mumblings clearer.

Breathing deeply, he felt tiredness sweep over him again.

What's wrong with me? Why can't I stay awake?

But there was plenty wrong with him, and he knew it. Exhaustion, both physical and mental. Weakness caused by calorie deficiency. Aching bones, pulled muscles, torn ligaments, shoulders and back rubbed raw by the sled straps. The excesses he had been subjecting his body to for almost eight weeks, the intense cold, the endless hours of pulling and shoving, hacking routes through ice ridges to advance three miles in a day, climbing and slipping, falling and standing again because to stay down was to die. *Everything* was wrong with him, but he could not sleep.

He did not wish to find the dreams his friend was having right now.

"I should never have told you about them," he muttered. He unzipped the sleeping bag and started pulling on his wet clothes. They were slightly warmed by the air inside the tent, at least. But he knew that would not last.

He'd freeze in minutes outside, but he couldn't stay in here.

※

The landscape was transformed. The horizon had been dragged in to dozens of feet instead of miles. The wide sky was hiding, the rolls in the land were swallowed by the snow, and all tracks and prints he and Marshall had laid down had been consumed.

He hugged his coat tight, pulled the heavy scarf over his mouth and nose, made sure his snow goggles were snug, and started out to the east. He tied the end of a cord to one of the tent uprights and played it out behind him as he went. It was his way back.

Kurt leaned into the wind, head down as he pushed onward. He seemed to get there quicker than before. Perhaps he'd drifted away while walking, mind wandering somewhere warmer and safer, but he could not remember where.

At first he thought they'd gone. *It can't have snowed that much!* he thought, struggling to fight down his excitement. Gone and buried again, they would be out of sight, out of mind. He could return to the tent and wake Marshall. He'd tell him that everything was all right. Then they'd wait for the storm to pass and make the final drive for the coast.

But then he saw a shape ahead between swirls of snow, tucked behind another ridge of rock, and he knew that he was in the right place.

Wind had raised a flap of the tent, uncovering the two bodies underneath. The storm whined between rocks, the wind so harsh that it was stripping old snow and ice from the corpses rather than allowing new snow to settle. Against every instinct he went close, because he had to see.

One of the bodies had been turned onto its side, the arm beneath it propping it up, its head dipped. Could the wind have done that? Perhaps fresh exposure to the elements had contracted dried tendons, or the frozen ground beneath the body had shrugged, lifted? The other corpse still lay on its back, but its face had changed. It was fuller, not so death-like. Its lips were thicker, its nose more sculpted.

Its eyes were open.

They stared unblinking as flakes kissed them and were lifted away by the wind.

Kurt needed to run, but he stumbled forward instead, dropping to his knees and lifting off his goggles so that he could see for sure. The blankness had gone from these bodies. They looked like death-sculptures close to completion, rather than rough, lifeless forms.

He wanted to destroy them. If he'd brought a knife or an ice axe he'd have set about them, smashing and hacking them into pieces that were nowhere near human, and held no resemblance to . . .

But could he really move that close?

"It's all in my head," Kurt said, and the storm rose as if to swallow his words. A corner of the old tent flapped, and he squinted, looking closer, wondering how canvas could be networked with shapes that looked like old, dried veins.

Its poles might have been bone.

He backed away, then turned and ran for the camp, pulling hand over hand on the cord as if to haul himself and the tent together. In a blinding surge of snow he tripped and was enveloped, cool dark digits fingering into gaps in his clothing, his ears, leaking through loosened snow goggles. He struggled to stand with one hand, the other still clasped tight around the cord. If he let go of that he would be lost, and then he'd die out here on his own. Perhaps Marshall would find him when the storm settled. Or maybe he'd be discovered in a hundred years by exhausted, terrified explorers.

He stood and moved on, his focus on the cord that was his lifeline.

Once inside the tent Kurt hurriedly zipped up, throwing off his coat and crawling into his cold sleeping bag. He turned up the stove and broke open a couple of chemical warmers. Their effect was vastly lessened through overuse, but they still took the chill from his hands.

"Not sure," he said, shivering. "Not sure what that was. Not certain . . . certain what I . . . I saw. Marsh? I dunno. But I think those bodies are moving." He looked sideways at the man lying motionless in his sleeping bag. "Marsh?"

Marsh whined. It began so low and quiet that at first Kurt thought it was the wind. But the noise rose, growing louder, harsher. As it became a scream Kurt screamed himself, trying to drown that terrible sound in his own fearful cry. But his own voice faded while Marshall's went on and on, and he reached out to shake his friend awake.

He would not wake. His eyes were wide, his mouth open, and when Kurt unzipped his bag he saw his friend's hands clawed in front of him as if grasping something unseen.

Marshall took in a long, ragged breath and started screaming again. But the scream did not touch his face. There was no frown and no grimace, little of Marshall there at all. His wide eyes reflected nothing.

Kurt kicked himself away from his friend, hand striking the stove and knocking it on its side. He felt an ice-cold touch across his palm, and when he looked he saw the burn, already blistering and bubbling yet feeling like nothing. He waited for the pain but it was quiet, subsumed, perhaps, beneath Marshall's endless scream.

"Shut the fuck up!" Kurt shouted. He pulled his fist back, ready to strike, but held back at the last moment. Something was so terribly wrong. If he had to hit someone or something it was not Marshall.

He felt so tired. Despite the noise his own eyes drooped. He felt reality drifting even farther away than it already was, and he reached up and gripped his cheeks between fingers, pinching himself awake.

It did not feel like resurfacing.

His eyes drooped again and he grasped the tumbled stove, waiting for long seconds before the searing pain finally scorched in. He opened his mouth, but Marshall screamed for him. The pain did not last long. It was as if someone else had been subjected to the burn.

Out in the snow . . . , he thought, and the idea of going out there and falling asleep was so enticing that he found himself unzipping the tent again, crawling outside, and slumping down in the fresh snow. Wind howled, but it was the usual emotionless scream that this continent was more comfortable with.

Marshall's screaming seemed even louder out here, and even more shocking because he was out of sight. He competed with the wind and won.

It's them, Kurt thought. *Something about them, their stillness, their lifelessness, and he didn't even see them.*

He scrambled over to the sleds and unhooked one of the covers, throwing it back to reveal the tool rack. He snatched up a long-handled ice axe and turned into the storm once again. The cord was still attached, and he followed it toward where he had dropped it so recently.

Marshall doesn't have nightmares. He's strong. He just sleeps and walks. The nightmares are from somewhere else.

Just before he reached where the bodies should have been, he realised that Marshall's screaming had stopped.

Behind the sheltering rock, just visible as gray silhouettes through the dancing, wild snow, he saw the two bodies standing with their arms by their sides.

⁂

It was his lifeline. His umbilical cord back to the tent, back to reality, the thin rope bubbled with icy droplets stiff in his hands, waving in the wind and snapping back and forth. If he let go and lost it he'd stumble into the nothingness. Lose himself and die. It didn't seem to matter, but each time he grabbed, the burns on his hands sang a short sweet song of agony. He grabbed hold of this, too, because it was real.

Maybe they were following him. Or perhaps they were lost as well.

Marshall remained silent, and crawling back through the tent entrance and inside, Kurt saw why. His friend was not there anymore.

In his place was something that looked little like his friend. The similarity was vague at best, a rough attempt at impersonation. The body in Marshall's sleeping bag was devoid of expression and anything that might make it human, yet it wore his clothes and hair, carried the old scar on his cheek and that scruffy, ginger beard. Other than that, he might have been carved from ice.

Kurt tried to shout, scream. His voice did not work. Maybe it was the cold, but he thought not. He was starting to feel more distant than ever before, not only from Bindy and home and everything beyond this place, but from himself. He was becoming a stranger.

But still he fled. There remained that part of him—a spark of hope amid wretchedness—that grasped onto instinct and believed in survival. He burst from the tent and fell, scrambling to his feet, running in the direction he thought was away from the bodies. He tripped again and went sprawling. The cold did not feel so cold anymore. The white was not so white. His senses seemed more remote, as if he were viewing his life through the wrong end of a telescope. He tried to call for his wife but no longer remembered her name.

He stood and ran. The storm swirled him around, sending him staggering into ice ridges and falling into drifts. Wind roared in his ears, a voiceless scream.

In the distance, two shapes approached through the whirling snow. They seemed to pass through the storm as if they were apart from it, and though Kurt tried to turn and run, his legs folded and he fell to his knees. He tugged the ice axe from his belt and held it up, ready to swing it, throw it, wield it in anger and fear.

The figures drew closer. They were naked but did not seem to feel the cold. One was Marshall, but his eyes were expressionless, no recognition there.

But Kurt recognised himself.

The figure stood before him, head slightly tilted as it regarded him with an emotionless gaze.

Kurt went to swing the axe but dropped it into the snow. He reached out with both hands to ward the figures off.

The figure that was him snatched off Kurt's glove, placed its thumb and forefinger around his wedding ring, and lifted it clear of his finger. There was no friction or resistance. It was as if he were no longer there at all.

The figure slipped on his ring, then the two of them turned their backs on Kurt and walked away into the storm, leaving him forever in the frozen white silence.

Heroes and Villains

by Stephen Gallagher

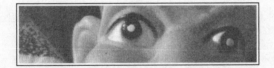

You can barely hear the bell from my office at the top of the museum. He must have pressed it four or five times before I went down and unlocked the door.

He was about twenty-five. Certainly not much more. He stood there in his parka with a parcel under his arm and a sad-eyed Hippie Jesus look, and I said, "The museum's closed on Wednesdays."

But he said, "I'm here about the ad?" in the manner of someone venturing onto untested ground.

"Which ad would that be?"

"The one in *The Stage*."

So I moved back to let him in. "I called first," he said as he stepped past me. "I thought I was expected."

"You probably spoke to Miss Pope," I said, closing the door behind us. "She isn't in today. It doesn't matter. I'm the one you need to see."

We went up the stairs, past the stuffed birds and the civil war armour and the grandfather clock. Ours is a small-town museum. Though we make the best of what we have, we don't have much of real importance. Our art collection is mostly minor Victorians and a few of the Cornwall Sunday painters from the 1920s. Our best Roman artefacts were taken by the British Museum, leaving us with a few clay lamps and one sandal.

My room is right up in the eaves, with a circular window overlooking the park. The door has an etched glass panel that's frosted and marked "Private." Beyond it you'll find exactly the kind of overcrowded space you'd expect of a curator's office. Things waiting to be dealt with, and things already dealt with but awaiting some inspiration for where they might go. I've been there ten years. I believe Miss Pope has been around for longer than the sandal.

I asked the young man his name and he said, "It's Wallace. Alex Wallace."

"Can I offer you a drink or anything, Alex?"

"Some water would be great."

"Take a seat. I won't be a second."

When I came back with the glass, he'd opened up his parcel. It was a Morrisons's bag wrapped around an inch-thick album.

"I brought my cuttings, in case you wanted to see them," he said, offering it to me.

"Of course," I said, taking the album and laying it to one side on my desk, but before I could go on he said, "I won't be able to leave it with you. Those are my only copies."

So then, feeling self-conscious under his gaze as he sipped at his water, I sat down and opened the book. It was a photo album rather than a scrapbook. The pages were of thick card with the cuttings behind a clear plastic layer. A few were from newspapers, but most were printed-out screen grabs from websites. Festival fringe reviews, mostly, all positive and some of them five-starred. In one photograph he looked about twelve years old, standing in front of a display of vintage puppets. The album was only one-third filled.

I was trying to give it my attention, just reading a line here and there, and after a few moments I was aware that he wasn't watching me at all. He was looking at the third chair in the office, the one where I'd placed one of our storage crates. The crate was wider than the chair, and sat across it like a child's coffin.

I closed the book.

"That's all fine," I said. "When you spoke to Miss Pope, did she explain what we're looking for?"

"Not really," he said.

"You've heard of Max Hudson?"

A nod of his head told me that he had.

"Next year we're holding a festival to celebrate five hundred years of the town's royal charter. The Council got hold of some Lottery funding and came up with a theme of 'Heroes and Villains.' For villains they're having a Highwayman Day with coaches in the market square and a sponsored Zombie Shuffle for charity. A Witches' Ball in the Winter Gardens and that's about it." I didn't add that for real villainy there had been a couple of quite nasty murders in the fifties, but no one was allowed to mention them.

"On the good-guys side, it's slim pickings. The British Legion's organising a parade to honour local servicemen and -women, which doesn't leave the rest of us much to play with. We've got an Olympic bronze medalist from the 1984 relay team and a merchant sailor whose family claims he served under Nelson but wasn't at Trafalgar. We needed a proper local hero, so we put out the word through the media. We were basically fishing for suggestions.

"Then the *Telegraph* printed a letter about Max Hudson. Seems he was more than just an entertainer. He was the hero of the St. Joseph's Sanatorium fire in 1952 when he was killed trying to save some of the children. The letter came from a pensioner named Alice Bridges. Her younger sister was one of those who died with him."

I stood up. Alex rose with me, and we went over to the chair.

"This was his dummy," I said, folding back a layer of tissue paper to uncover a shabby mannequin that fitted none too comfortably into the storage box. Two knotted linen strips held it secure.

"Square Bash Willie," my visitor said, reaching out to push back the tissue that was threatening to fold itself in again. The mannequin was dressed in army khaki. He added, "A vent would call it a figure, sometimes a doll. Never a dummy."

"I stand corrected," I said. "The doll was found in the building after the fire. Alice could remember attending a ceremony with all the other families where Max Hudson's parents presented Square Bash Willie to the Council. It was supposed to go on permanent display, but I couldn't find any record of that. I finally came across the doll itself, packed away and stored in the basement. I'm not sure it was ever shown at all. It had been mis-catalogued in the sixties and no one had seen it since then. You'll probably know more about it than I do."

"I don't know about the fire," he said, studying the figure without touching it, "but Max Hudson's a name in the business. He won a talent contest and worked in concert parties as a teenaged magician. During the Second World War he joined the army and ended up in ENSA. The unit he was assigned to already had a magician, so that's when he switched to a vent act."

ENSA was the Entertainments National Service Association, a wartime division of the military set up to provide live entertainment to the armed forces. It was a refuge for enlisted show folk who couldn't fight to save their own lives or anyone else's. I'd seen no record of Hudson the young magician, but Hudson the ventriloquist had developed an act based on army humour.

"Square Bash Willie," Alex said again, looking down on the figure with obvious affection and respect. With his big eyes and wispy beard he looked like some species of young urban male, the kind that's educated but aimless, yet here on his own turf I sensed some authority.

I struggled to imagine him as a performer of any kind, though, despite what his scrapbook might say. Onstage or in a crowd, you just wouldn't notice him.

I said, "We could just display the doll downstairs, but it's an opportunity to get local groups and children more involved."

"What have you got in mind?"

"We're looking for someone who can take Square Bash Willie into schools and interact with the kids. There'll be other events as well. It'll be a big part of the festival, and if it drives some traffic to the museum afterwards, we'll all be happy."

"You want a vent to put a voice into Max's figure."

"That was the point of the ad."

"That's quite a challenge," he said. "Can I ask, what's the fee?"

"We can't offer a fee," I said. "But you'll get publicity out of it. We're hoping to have someone film it and put it on YouTube. It's a civic event. A lot of people will be giving up their time."

I took his silence for agreement.

"And it'll look good on your CV," I added.

He looked at the doll again and said, "Can I . . . ?" And then, with care, he tugged at the first of the linen strips to undo the bow that secured it.

With the second strip untied, he carefully lifted the figure. I said, "The museum catalogue had it listed as a 'Cheeky Boy Figure.' That's why no one knew what it was."

"The description's accurate," he said. "The Cheeky Boy is a traditional knee figure style. Look at the face."

The face was the kind that you'd associate with most of the old-school ventriloquist acts; wide-eyed, apple-cheeked, alert, and equally capable of mischief or horror. At home on the body of a schoolboy or a toff or, as in this case, an unreliable-looking army private. The papier-mâché was cracked with a few flakes, but the head was intact. As to the works, I didn't know. I'd taken a careful look inside the body, but the complex mass of rods, ropes, levers, and rings had deterred me from investigating any further.

Alex said, "You need to be careful who you let handle this. A lot of modern vents use a soft figure, which is basically a glove puppet. A hard figure's a completely different proposition. This one has a control stick loaded with three different actions." He worked his hand into the back of the figure and spent a few moments in exploration. "Four actions," he amended. "We've got lower lip, upper lip, side-moving, self-centering eyes, and a blinker. The upper lip's leather. That can dry out, so I'm not going to risk it. Were you planning any restoration?"

"Just conservation. Can you say what it needs?"

"Don't let anyone touch it. I'll give you the names of some people."

He ran through the actions and the head came to life, swivelling and clattering with more noise than I might have expected. I have to say that this kind of handling went against all my instincts as a curator. But the people who pay my salary had ordered a civilian hero.

Alex said, "It's an Insull head. Len Insull was the top man for figures in England. This one's based on one of his stock designs." As he spoke he shifted position, settling the figure on his free arm so that their faces were almost on a level. Its own arms hung boneless, swinging with the weight of the figure's solid hands. "He supplied Lewis Davenport's magic store, back when it was on Great Russell Street. I think it's a Number One. On this model the blink would be an extra."

The eyes closed and the head rolled from side to side, and already it was eerie, like a bizarre little man working out the kinks after so long in a cramped position.

I said, "What kind of voice do you think?"

"Don't arsk him, he wouldn't have a farkin' clue."

Seriously, I jumped. Alex looked as surprised as I. The head swivelled to make it seem as if the figure looked back and forth between the two of us.

"What?" it said.

"We weren't expecting you to speak yet," Alex said.

The figure seemed to look him in the eye. *"Well,"* it said, *"he has a good excuse. But what's yours?"*

"That's very good," I said, and they both ignored me.

"Who's he talking to?"

"He's talking to you."

"Then why's he looking at you?"

"Because I'm the boss."

"What am I?"

"You're nothing."

"So you're the boss over nothing."

"That's a very old joke."

"I've been in a fucking box since nineteen fifty-two."

I said, "We'll have to keep it clean for the kids."

Square Bash Willie turned his face toward me and, with half-lowered lids, affected the accent of a stage cockney aping an aristocrat.

"Would these be the children wot I will be obliged to entertain with tales of other children being burnt to death and kippered and such like?" he said. *"Why, I can 'ear their merry larfter already."*

I'd been wrong about Alex. I could see it now. His diffidence was actually the key to his performance. It meant you paid him almost no attention while the dummy—sorry, the figure—was speaking. To my untrained eye his technique was good. He had the slightly mournful expression that many a ventriloquist has to adopt, but that was how his face looked all the time. The occasional slight movement of his throat was the only giveaway.

"*I can't gnoove ne lip.*"

Square Bash Willie had inclined his head toward Alex, who now had him speaking in a low voice, as if I wasn't to hear.

Alex said, "You mustn't move your lip. The leather's cracking."

"*That's not a crack, it's a cold sore.*"

"It's a crack."

"*It's a cold sore.*"

"How can *you* get a cold sore?"

"*I picked it up on a weekend pass,*" Willie said, at full volume with the plosives clear and perfect. "*While proposing to a petite young lady.*"

"Where?"

"*I kissed her under the aqueduct.*"

"There's no aqueduct around here. I think you're attempting a double entendre."

"*Like a fucking ballet dancer? With these legs?*"

"You know what I mean."

"*All right, it was a passenger bridge. But you try saying that with only one lip.*"

"Look," I said, "this is fine. Everything's fine. Except for the effing and blinding. That will have to go."

"*You sound like Mother Teresa's life coach.*"

I'm not proud to admit it. But I gave up and talked to the dummy. It was so much easier.

I said, "Have all the fun you like and make them laugh, but here's what we need to put over. Today's kids don't know anything about Max. After the war he kept the character and the uniform and made the act over into a National Service routine. He appeared on the BBC a few times, but none of the footage survives. It was the variety circuit and summer seasons back then."

As I was speaking, Square Bash Willie kept his gaze on me, but I was aware that his top lip kept trying to creep up, baring his teeth in a kind of sneer. Alex would notice and nudge him, and his lips would clamp shut. Then, after a few moments, the same thing again.

I stopped.

"*I'm fucking with you,*" Square Bash Willie said.

"I know you are," I said. I was beginning to wonder if Alex was such a great choice after all. There was no doubting that he had the necessary skill, but I was getting the feeling that his skill might be hard to contain. On the other hand, his had been the only response to our ad.

I pressed on.

"Max's parents ran a workingmen's club in the town. Whenever he was touring in the area, he'd come for a visit and stay with them. There was always publicity. He'd be asked to open some event, judge a beauty contest . . . one time he and Willie showed up at the football ground for a match and posed with the team. It always gave out the same message, that he never forgot where he came from. They value that around here."

Willie seemed attentive. It was rather unnerving. His eyes had inset irises of coloured glass, so they had depth without life. And every now and again, he'd blink.

I looked pointedly at Alex. "It was a clean act," I said, and Alex shrugged and glanced at Willie, as if to say, *Don't tell me, tell him.* "Respectable enough for the nuns at the TB sanatorium to ask for a visit as a treat for the children. He went, of course. He toured the wards and gave an hour-long show. About twenty minutes after the show, there was a fire in the basement. It started in the laundry room and got into the stairwell, and after that no one could reach the exit.

"Max went back in and tried to lead the children to safety. When he couldn't find a way out of the building he got them into a storeroom with a heavy door and closed it to keep out the fire. It held back the flames but not the smoke, so in the end it was for nothing and he died along with them. They found Square Bash Willie with the bodies.

"There was some controversy. No one wanted to blame the nuns but the fact is, doors that should have opened were kept locked. They didn't clear the building when they could have. But we're not going to get into that. It's not an occasion for opening old wounds."

Willie said, *"Speaking of nuns, do you know the difference between a nun in a choir and a slapper in the bath?"*

"Not now, Willie."

"One sings with a soul full of hope, while the other—"

"I said not now," Alex interrupted. "Is all your material like that?"

"I'll be honest with you. Some of it's not as good. How much is he paying us?"

"Who?"

Willie turned and leaned toward me and fluttered his eyelashes. There was a clattering as the paired lids went up and down. If there's any more disturbing sight than a cracked-up grinning moon-faced papier-mâché Cheeky Boy giving its most seductive leer, I don't ever want to see it.

Alex said, "We've already covered that. There's no money."

The doll's head snapped around to look at him.

"No money," Alex repeated.

"No money?"

"No."

"Excuse the anachronism," Willie said, speaking slowly. *"But W . . . T . . . F?"*

"It's to honour a fellow professional."

Willie put his face up close to Alex's, their foreheads almost touching. *"The point of a professional,"* Willie said slowly, with Alex flinching at every plosive sound, *"is that a professional gets paid. Compadre."* Alex's reaction made it look as if real spit were hitting him.

"We'll get a lot of publicity out of it," he said.

I was expecting some comeback with a joke, but Willie said nothing.

"And we might get something on YouTube."

Still nothing. Willie was staring, and Alex seemed increasingly uncomfortable.

"It'll look good on my CV," he added.

Willie's head turned slowly. Now he was looking at me. Then back to Alex.

"Remember when you were twelve?" he said. *"Eh, boy? Remember? It was never Disneyland with you. The one place you wanted to go was Vent*

Haven. Your parents saved up for three years to take you. That's love for you. Love for their strange little boy. To see all the figures from the acts who'd passed on."

Alex looked down. I remembered the picture in the cuttings book, the boy in front of row upon row of vintage dolls, each with a card bearing details too small to make out.

Willie said, "What's the unwritten rule in Vent Haven?"

Alex tried to look away, and he seemed to mutter something. But Willie wasn't letting him off the hook.

"I can't hear you."

"You never put a voice in a dead vent's figure," Alex said, clearly this time, and with some embarrassment.

I said, "But you're doing that now."

"That's because he's broke," Willie said. "He thought it was a paid job. And he's too polite to tell you to stick it."

"But you're not."

"That's the beauty of me," Willie said. "And while we're being honest, do you want to know what really happened in the fire?"

How do you answer that?

"Go on," he said. "You know you do."

I made a vague and helpless gesture.

He went on, "Picture the scene. There's Max. The show's over. Everyone's off to bed. He's given his time, but he's been promised expenses. Without his expenses he can't get home. When you're a name in the business, everyone thinks you're rich. And that's what you want them to think! They don't call it show business for nothing. I'm packed away in the dressing room, and he's arguing with the nuns while they bilk him out of his bus fare. Nuns, eh? Always quick to plead poverty."

Clack. He winked, and then continued.

"Then come the flames. A man on the street sees them first and bangs on the doors. The doors are locked. All the doors are always locked. Those young girls have to be protected. Or controlled. Little man-hungry minxes that they are. The fire brigade's on its way and the fire's down in the basement, so Mother Superior makes them stay in the building. Why? Because if they go outside, men will see them in their nightclothes.

"*Now the fire's in the stairwell, and the stairwell's roaring like a chimney. The girls downstairs can't get out, and the girls upstairs can't get down. Then a voice is heard. Far away. From the store cupboard they'd given us for a dressing room.*"

"You?" I said.

Willie took a little bow. Then he switched his voice to something tiny and far away. A doll with its own ventriloquist skills.

"*Don't leave me, Max. Come and get me.*" And back to normal: "*Max couldn't ignore it. He could never ignore me. He ran through the flames and up those stairs, and the girls on the landing saw him and followed. He was the man with the funny little friend who sat on his knee and made them laugh. He'd look after them, wouldn't he? He must know the way out. When the fire came up the stairs, they all crammed into the storeroom but by then it was too late. And all of them died.*"

"Except you."

"*Except me. How about that?*"

"Wait a minute," I said. "What am I saying? There was no one calling. None of that happened. Did it?"

"*Are you going to argue with a witness?*"

"You're not a witness." I looked at Alex. "You're not a witness."

Alex took a moment to react. As if he'd been caught up in the conversation and wasn't expecting to be included.

Willie said, "*You can tell it your way. I'll tell it mine.*" He rolled his head around to look at his handler.

"*Bad news, sunshine,*" he said. "*I don't think we're getting the gig. But you did a good job. Are you all right?*"

"Yes, Willie," Alex said. "I'll be fine."

"*Are you sure?*"

"Yeah."

"*I think we're done.*"

"I think we are."

"*You can put me back now.*"

The life went out of Square Bash Willie when Alex disengaged his hand from the controls.

As Alex was laying the figure back in its storage crate I said, "You can't give the people a story like that. It's nothing but tragedy. We're trying to find something to celebrate."

"Then perhaps," Alex said, "it's better if you don't ask the dead to speak."

After arranging the figure, he tied up the linen strips to secure it and put the tissue paper over it. Then with a brief and polite smile he picked up his book of cuttings and moved to the door.

I followed him down the stairs.

"You knew there were no other replies," I said. "Did you all get together and have a meeting? Are you the one they sent?"

He opened the main door and looked back at me. And I thought that if the dead ever could speak, then by today's example all of history would probably be fucked.

I said, "Money or no money. You never had any intention of taking the job, did you?"

He said nothing.

"Did you?" I said, and he still said nothing.

Then he went out, and closed the door behind him.

The Doll-Master

by Joyce Carol Oates

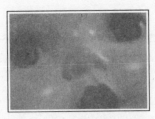

Y ou can hold her. But don't drop her."

Solemnly my little cousin Amy spoke. And solemnly Amy held
out to me her beloved doll.

It was a baby-doll, in baby-clothes, a little top adorned with pink baby
ducklings and on the tiny baby-doll-feet, little pink booties. And a baby-
diaper, white, with a silver safety pin.

A soft fleshy baby-doll with a placid baby-face, malleable baby-fingers
and fleshy little baby-arms and -legs that could be manipulated, to a
degree. The baby-hair was fine and blond and curly and the baby-eyes
were slate-blue marble that opened and closed as you tilted the doll backward or forward. There is a scary ticklish sensation you feel when you
see a baby close up because you think that the baby could be hurt and
this is how I felt about Baby Emily though she was *only a doll* . . .

My cousin Amy was three years old, which was younger than my age
by eleven months. This is what we were told. A birthday is an important event in our family, our parents said.

Amy was the daughter of my mother's younger sister, who was my
aunt Jill. So, Mommy explained, Amy was my *cousin*.

I was a little jealous sometimes. Amy could talk better than I could
and adults liked to talk to her, marveling at her "speech skills," which
made me feel bad, for nobody marveled at mine.

Amy was a little girl, shorter than me. Smaller all over than me.

It was strange—friends of our mothers thought it was "darling"—to
see such a small child as Amy clutching a baby-doll. Fussing and fret-
ting over Baby Emily as Amy's mother fussed and fretted over her. Even

pretending to "nurse" Baby Emily with a tiny baby bottle filled with milk. And "changing" Baby Emily's diaper.

Between her fleshy baby-legs, Baby Emily was smooth. There was no way for Baby Emily to soil her diaper.

I did not remember ever soiling my diaper. I do not remember now. I am inclined to think that, as a baby, I did not have to wear a diaper, but that is probably inaccurate and irrational. For I was a fully normal (boy) infant, I am sure. If there were "accidents" in the night especially, in my pj's, as my mother called them, I do not remember.

I do not remember "nursing," either. I think that I was "nursed" from a bottle.

All this was a very long time ago. It's natural not to remember.

You can hold her. But don't drop her—these were Amy's words, which I do remember. They were an echo of an adult mother's words that you often hear.

፠

It was a terrible surprise in the family, when Amy *passed away*.

At first they said that Amy was "going to the clinic for tests." Then they said that Amy would be "in the hospital for a few days." Then they said that Amy would "not be coming home from the hospital."

In all this time, I was not taken to the hospital to see Amy. I was told that my cousin would be home soon—"You can see her then, sweetie. That will be soon enough."

And, "Your cousin is very tired right now. Your cousin needs to sleep, and rest, and get strong again."

Afterward, I would learn that it was a rare blood sickness my cousin had. It was a kind of leukemia and very fast-acting in young children.

When they said that Amy would not be coming home, I did not say anything. I did not ask any questions. I did not cry. I was *stony faced*, I overheard my aunt saying to my mother. I wondered if to be *stony faced* was a bad thing or a good thing. For then, people let you alone.

If you cried, they tried to comfort you. But if you were *stony faced*, they let you alone.

It was around this time that I stole Baby Emily out of Amy's room.

We were often at my aunt's house, and while my mother and my aunt were crying together I went to Amy's room and lifted Baby Emily from my cousin's bed where the doll was lying with other, less interesting dolls and stuffed toys as if someone had flung them all down, and had not even made up the bed properly.

I did not think my parents knew I'd stolen Baby Emily inside my jacket and brought her home with me. But later, I would realize that probably they knew, as my aunt knew, and did not say anything to me; they did not discipline me.

Talk was all of Amy, for a long time. If you entered a room and adults were speaking in lowered voices, they would cease at once. Bright adult faces turned toward you: "Hello, Robbie!"

I was too young to consider whether such a rare blood sickness might be *genetic*—that is, carried in the blood from one generation to the next.

When I was older I would research *leukemia* on the Internet. But still, I would not know.

When I was alone with Baby Emily we cried because we missed Amy. I did not cry because Amy was *dead*, only because Amy was *gone*.

But I had Amy's baby-doll. I snuggled with Baby Emily in my bed, and that made me feel better, a little.

When I was five years old, and going to preschool, Baby Emily disappeared from my room.

I was so surprised! I looked under the bed and in the closet and in each of my bureau drawers and then I looked in all these places again as well as beneath the covers at the foot of the bed, but Baby Emily was gone.

I ran to my mother, crying. I asked my mother where Baby Emily was, for there was no secret about my cousin's doll-baby now. My mother told me that my father "didn't think it was a good idea" for me to be playing with a doll at my age. Dolls are for girls, she said. Not boys. "Daddy just thought it might be better to take the doll away before you got 'too attached'. . . ." Guiltily my mother spoke, and there was softness in her voice, but nothing I said could change her mind, no matter how I cried, or how angry I became, slapping and kicking at her and saying how I hated her, my mother did not change her mind, because my father would not allow it. "He said he'd 'indulged' you long enough. And he blames me."

In place of Baby Emily, who was so sweet and placid and smelled of foam rubber, my father had instructed my mother to buy me an "action toy"—one of the new-model expensive ones—a U.S. Marine Seal robot-soldier that came fully armed and could move forward across the room, powered by a battery.

I would never forgive either of them, I thought. But particularly, I would never forgive *him*.

※

The first of the *found dolls* was Mariska.

Take her. But don't drop her.

My Friend spoke quietly, urgently, glancing about to see if anyone was watching. Many times I'd walked to school, and home from school, avoiding the school bus, where there were older boys who taunted me. My family's house was at the top of Prospect Hill, above the city and looking toward the river, which was often wreathed in mist. The middle school was about a mile down the hill along a route I'd come to memorize. Often I took shortcuts through alleys and across backyards where I moved swiftly with the furtiveness of a wild creature. This street was Catamount, with a narrow lane that ran parallel behind it past six-foot wooden fences beginning to rot, trash cans, and piles of debris.

My Friend said, *Never make eye contact. That way they don't see you, either.*

No one ever saw me. For I moved quickly and furtively. And if they saw me at a distance they saw only a boy—a young boy with a blurred face.

My Friend was very tall. Taller than my father. I had never looked directly at my Friend (who forbade it), but I had a sense that my Friend had features sharp and cunning as a fox's and his natural way of moving was agile as a fox's, and so I had to half-run to keep up with my Friend, who was inclined to impatience.

Take her! No one is watching.

Mariska was a beautiful ceramic doll very different from Baby Emily. Mariska had creamy skin and on her cheeks two patches of rouge. She was dressed in the dirndl-costume of an Eastern European peasant— white blouse, full skirt and apron, white cotton stockings and boots. Her blond hair was braided into two plaits, and she had a rosebud mouth and blue eyes with thick blond lashes. It was strange to touch Mariska's skin, which had a hard and unyielding ceramic surface except where it had been cracked and broken.

Mariska's arms were outspread in surprise that such a prettily dressed blond girl with plaited hair and blue eyes could be allowed to topple from a porch railing into the mud, her hair soiled, her skirt soiled and torn, and her white stockings filthy. And her legs were at an odd angle to each other as if the left one had been twisted at the hip.

Walking with my Friend along the lane behind Catamount Street and between the rotted boards of a fence we saw Mariska. My Friend gripped my hand tight so that the bones hurt.

She is our prize. She is the one we've been waiting for. Hurry! Take her! No one will see.

It was a thundery dark afternoon. I was shivering with cold or with excitement. For my Friend had appeared walking beside me with no warning. Often I did not see my Friend for days, or a week. Then, my Friend would appear. But I was forbidden to look at his face.

When my Friend came into my life, I am not certain. Mariska came into my life when I was in eighth grade, and so it was earlier than that time.

Mariska's house was one of the ugly asphalt-sided houses down the hill. Not just one family lived in the house but several families, for it was a *rental*, as my mother said.

These were people who lived *down the hill*, as my mother said. They were not people who lived *on the hill*, as we did.

Yet, children played here. Played and shouted and laughed here at the foot of Prospect Hill, which was so very different from the crest of Prospect Hill, where my family had lived for decades.

Because of the steep hill, a flight of wooden steps led down from the crude porch at the rear of Mariska's house to the rutted ground ten or fifteen feet below. But no one walked here much—the ground was covered in debris, even raw garbage.

Mariska had fallen from the porch railing where someone had carelessly set her. I thought this must have happened.

Unless Mariska had been tossed from the porch by someone who had tired of her rouged cheeks, rosebud mouth, colorful peasant costume.

My Friend said eagerly, *She is our prize. No one else can claim her now.*

My Friend said, *Lift her! And put your hand over her mouth.*

My Friend said, *Inside your jacket. Walk quickly. Don't run! Take the back way.*

Mariska was heavier than you would think. A ceramic doll is a heavy doll.

Mariska's arms and legs were awkwardly spread. By force, I managed to subdue them.

I could not hide Mariska in my room, where she would be found by my mother or our housekeeper. I could not hide Mariska anywhere in the house, though it was a large house with three storeys and many of its rooms shut off. So I brought her to the "carriage house"—which was used as a garage for my parents' vehicles and as a place for storage and where I believed the beautiful ceramic doll would be safe, wrapped in canvas many times and placed in one of the horse stalls in the cobwebby shadows.

It had been proudly recounted to me: my father's grandfather had been mayor of the capitol city six miles to the south, which was now a *racially troubled city with a high crime rate.* After my father's grandfather was no longer mayor, he'd moved his family to Prospect Hill in this suburb of mostly white people beside the Delaware River. In those days there'd been horses in the carriage house, in four stalls at the rear, and still you could smell the animals, a faint odor of dried manure, horsesweat, hay. Here, I knew that Mariska would be safe. I would come to visit her when I wished. And Mariska would always, always be there, where I had left her, wrapped in canvas for safekeeping.

When my Friend did not come to me I was very lonely, but if there had been horses in the stable, as there had been in my great-grandfather's time, I would not have been so lonely.

My parents had warned me not to "play" in the carriage house. The roof leaked badly and was partly rotted. There was a second floor that sagged in the middle as if the boards had become rubbery. Only the front part of the carriage house was used now for my parents' vehicles, and the rest was filled with abandoned things—furniture, tires, an old broken tricycle of mine, a baby buggy, cardboard boxes. Nothing was of use any longer, but nothing was thrown away.

Hornets built their nests beneath the eaves. The buzzing was peaceful if the hornets were not disturbed.

No one had told me exactly, but I knew: my father's family had been well-to-do until the early 1960s; then, the family business had gone into decline. Bitterly my father spoke of *overseas competition.*

Still, the house on Prospect Hill was one of the old, large houses envied by others. There were real estate investments that continued to yield income, and my father was an accountant for a prosperous business of which he spoke with some pride. My father was not a distinguished man or in any way unusual except for living in one of the old, large houses on Prospect Hill, which he had inherited from his father. I thought that my father might have loved me more, if he had been more successful.

🐾

"What a terrible thing! Now it's coming *here.*"

The terrible thing was not a robbery or a burglary or an arson-set fire or a shooting-murder but a little girl missing here in our suburban town and not in the capitol city six miles to the south. The news was in all the papers and on TV and radio. Such excitement, it was like dropping a lighted match into dried hay—you could not guess what would erupt from such a small act.

At our school we were ushered into assembly and announcements were made by the principal and a police officer in a uniform. The little girl who was missing was in fourth grade and lived on Catamount Street, and we were warned not to speak with strangers or go anywhere with strangers and if any stranger approached us, to run away as quickly as possible and notify our parents or our teachers or Mrs. Rickett, who was our principal.

At the same time, it was suspected that the little girl who'd disappeared had been kidnapped by her own father, who lived in New Brunswick. The father was arrested and questioned but claimed to know nothing about his daughter.

For days there was news of the missing girl. Then, news of the missing girl faded. Then, ceased.

Once a child is *gone*, she will not return. That was a truth we would learn in middle school.

Mariska was safe in her hiding place, in the farthest horse stall in the old stable at the rear of the carriage house behind our house where no one would ever look.

⁂

It was not my fault that my cousin Amy *went away* and left me.

All your life, you yearn to return to what has been. You yearn to return to those you have lost. You will do terrible things to return, which no one else can understand.

⁂

The second *found doll* was not until I was in ninth grade.

Annie was a pretty-faced girl-doll with skin like real skin to touch except some of the dye had begun to wear off and you could see the gray rubber beneath, which was shivery and ugly.

Annie was a small doll, not so large and heavy as Mariska. She wore a cowgirl costume with a suede skirt, a shiny-buckled belt, a shirt with a little suede vest and a little black tie, and on her feet were cowboy boots. She had been partly broken; one of her arms was dislocated and turned too easily in its shoulder socket, and her red-orange curly hair had come out in patches to reveal the rubber scalp beneath.

What was pretty about Annie was her placid blue-violet marble eyes and the freckles on her face that made you want to smile. Her eyes, like Baby Emily's eyes, shut when you leaned her backward, and opened when you leaned her forward.

My Friend had seen Annie first, in the park near my house. Beyond the playground where children shouted and laughed swinging on the swings there was a little grove of picnic tables, and beneath one of the tables in which initials had been carved and gouged the cowgirl-doll lay on the ground, on her back.

Here! Hurry.

My Friend shoved me forward. My Friend's hard hand on my back.

What was this, beneath the picnic table? I was very excited—I stooped to see.

A doll! A cowgirl-doll! Abandoned.

Picnic debris had been dumped onto the ground. Soda bottles, food-packages, stubs of cigarettes. It was very cruel that the cowgirl-doll, with the freckled face and red-orange hair, should be abandoned here.

Her arms were outstretched. Her legs were at odd angles to her body and to each other. Because she had been dropped on her back her eyes were partly closed, but you could see the glassy-glisten beneath, of surprise and alarm.

Help me! Don't leave me.

Distinctly we heard this plea of Annie's, my Friend and me. Her voice was whispery and small, her chipped-scarlet lips scarcely moved.

Inside my hooded jacket, I bore Annie to safety.

My Friend guided me from the park by an obscure route.

My Friend preceded me, to see if the way was clear.

It was a quarter-mile to the carriage house and to the shadowy horse-stall at the rear.

In this way in a trance of wonderment Cowgirl Annie, the second *found doll*, was brought home.

By this time the little fourth-grade girl who'd lived on Catamount Street was rarely spoken of. For she had *gone away*, and would not be returning.

And this new girl who'd *gone missing*—from Prospect Heights

Park—when her older sister and brother who'd been supposed to be watching her at the swings had been distracted by friends—she too had *gone away*, and would not be returning.

Another time, much alarm was raised at our school, though the missing girl was a third-grader, at another school. We had heard the warnings about strangers many times by now, by ninth grade. The uniformed police officer who spoke to us from the auditorium stage reassured us that "whoever took this child will be found," but these too were familiar words, which some of us smiled to hear.

In the park that afternoon there'd been solitary men, always in a park near a playground there are solitary men, and some of these men have criminal records, and these were taken into custody by police, and questioned. But we knew the little girl would never be found.

Now I was no longer taunted by the older boys on the school bus, for I was not one of the younger children. In my eyes such hatred blazed for these boys, they had learned to avoid me.

I learned that to be respected you had to be steely-calm and still. Or you had to be reckless. You could not show weakness. You could not be "nice"—you would be ground beneath the boots of the strong like a beetle.

But now that the second of the *found dolls* had come into my life, I did not care what these boys, or anyone else except my Friend, thought of me.

The second of the *found dolls*. When I was fourteen.

🦋

Not soon, for my Friend cautioned me against recklessness.

Not soon, but within two years, the third of the *found dolls* entered my life.

Then, after eleven months, a fourth *found doll*.

These were not local dolls. These were dolls discovered miles from Prospect Hill, in other towns.

For now I had a driver's license. I had the use of my mother's station wagon.

At school I was a quiet student, but my teachers seemed to like me and my grades were usually high. At home, I was quiet in a way that maddened my father, for it seemed to him *sullen, rebellious.*

I had a habit of grunting instead of talking, or mumbling under my breath. I had a habit of not looking at any adult, including my parents, for it was easier that way. My Friend did not want me to look at *him*— my Friend understood the effort such looks require. You can look into a doll's eyes without fear of the doll seeing into your soul in a way hostile to you, but you can't be so careless looking at anyone else. And this too maddened my father, that I would not meet his gaze: I was *disrespectful.*

My father said, *I will send him into the army—not to college. They'll straighten him out there.*

My mother pleaded, *Robbie should see a therapist, I've told you. Please let me take him to a therapist.*

So it happened, on the day of my eighteenth birthday, I had an appointment with Dr. G., a (psycho)therapist whose specialty was *troubled adolescents.* I sat in a chair facing Dr. G. in a trance of fear and dislike, not raising my eyes to hers, but staring resolutely at the floor at her feet.

Dr. G.'s office was sparely furnished. Dr. G. did not sit behind a desk but in a comfortable chair, so that I could see her legs, which were the legs of a stout middle-aged woman, and I thought how much preferable it was at school, where our teachers sat behind desks so that you could see only the tops of their bodies, mostly, and not their legs. It was easy to think of them as big ungainly dolls that way, whose jaw-hinges were always moving.

Dr. G. asked me to sit in a chair facing her, about five feet from her, and this, too, was a comfortable chair, though I did not feel comfortable in it and knew that I must be vigilant.

"Robbie? Talk to me, please. Your mother has said that your grades are very good—you don't have trouble at school communicating, evidently—but at home . . ." The more kindly the woman was, the less I trusted her. The more insistently she looked at my face, the less inclined I was to raise my eyes to hers. My Friend had cautioned, *Don't trust! Not for an instant, or you'll be finished.*

It was then I noticed a doll in a chair on the farther side of the room. Her head was large for her body and her face seemed to glow, or glare, with an arrogant sort of beauty. And her thick-lashed eyes were fixed upon *me*.

Dr. G.'s clients included young children, I'd been told. Teenagers, children. *Troubled*.

Though the office was sparely furnished, there were a number of dolls of varying sizes and types, each distinctive and unusual, a collector's item: on shelves, on a windowsill, and in this child-size white wicker rocking chair. I could barely hear the therapist's voice, which was warm, friendly, and kindly, so powerful was the doll's hold upon me.

"You're admiring my antique Dresden doll? It's dated 1841 and is in quite good condition. It's made of wood with a painted face, the colors have scarcely faded. . . ." Dr. G. was clearly hoping that I would react to this information, but I sat silent, frowning. I would not smile as others had smiled in my place, nor would I ask some polite but silly question. As a boy, I could not be expected to care about dolls.

I stared at the doll, who stared at me with marble eyes that reminded me of Baby Emily's eyes; and in those eyes, a subtle sign of recognition.

It was exciting; the Dresden doll did seem to "know" me. Because of the therapist's presence, however, the Dresden doll was not in the least frightened of me.

She was a beautiful doll though made of wood, and unlike any of my *found dolls*. At first you thought she had dark wavy hair, and then you saw that the hair was just wood, painted dark brown.

"Some of my very young clients prefer to talk to a doll rather than to me," Dr. G. said. "But I don't suppose that's the case with you, Robbie?"

I shook my head no. It was not the case with Robbie.

Elsewhere in the therapist's office were smaller dolls. On a shelf was a gaily painted Russian doll, which I knew had another, smaller doll inside it, and another, smaller doll within that doll. (I did not like these Russian dolls, which made me feel slightly sick. I thought of how a woman carries a baby inside her and how terrifying it would be if that baby carried another baby inside it.) There were rag dolls arranged on a shelf like puppets. There were little music boxes covered in seashells and mother-of-pearl, and there were Japanese fans and animals carved of wood.

Though Dr. G. had furnished her office sparely, and the colors of the furniture and of the carpet on the floor were dull, dun colors that could not excite any emotion, as Dr. G. wore dull, dun-colored and shapeless clothing that could not excite any emotion, these collectors' items suggested another, more complex and secret side to Dr. G.

"Tell me why you find it so difficult to talk to your parents, Robbie. Your mother has said . . ." In her quiet, stubborn woman-voice Dr. G. spoke.

Because there is nothing to say. Because my real life is elsewhere, where no one can follow.

I did not like many people. Especially, I did not like adults who wanted to "help" me. But I think I liked Dr. G. I wanted to help Dr. G. establish a *diagnosis* of what was wrong with me so that my parents would be satisfied and leave me alone. Yet I could not think how to help her, for I could not tell her the secrets closest to my heart.

Badly I wanted to examine the Dresden doll with the painted face. Badly I wanted to take the Dresden doll home with me.

In all, I would see Dr. G. approximately twelve times over the course of five or six months. I was not a good client, I think—I never "opened up" to Dr. G. as "troubled" people do to their therapists in movies and on TV.

Never during these visits did I reveal anything significant to Dr. G. But I was riveted by the Dresden doll, who stared at me boldly through the full fifty-minute session.

The Dresden doll was not afraid of me because she was protected by Dr. G., who never left the office and never left us alone together.

You can't touch me—not me! I belong to her.

You didn't "find" me. I was always here. And I will be here when you are not.

Such a look came into my face, of longing, and anger, Dr. G. broke off whatever she was saying to exclaim, "Robbie! What are you thinking? Did something come into your mind just now?"

Something *coming into my mind* like a maddened hornet? A paper airplane sailing? A nudge in the ribs?

Quietly I shook my head no.

Lowering my gaze, to stare at a spot on the carpet.

As my Friend had warned, *Never make eye contact! You know better.*

This was so. I had made a mistake. But it was not a fatal mistake, for no one knew except the Dresden doll.

She was only a doll, I thought. Something made of wood.

She could not be a *found doll*—for I could never touch her.

Never bring her to the carriage house for safekeeping among her sister dolls.

"Is something distracting you, Robbie? Is it something in this room?"

Shook my head no.

"Would you be more comfortable if we moved to another room?"

Shook my head no.

Then at our next meeting (which would be our last meeting), I was shocked to see that the Dresden doll had been removed from the white wicker rocking chair. In her place was an embroidered pillow.

I said nothing, of course. My face locked into its frozen expression and would not betray me.

"I think you might be more comfortable now, Robbie?"

Dr. G. spoke gently, proddingly. I hated this homely, graceless female, now that she'd sensed the hold of the Dresden doll over me; she alone, of all the world, might guess of my fascination with *found dolls.*

I hated her and I feared her; feared that suddenly I might lose control, I might begin to shout at her, demanding to see the Dresden doll again; or, I might burst into tears, confessing to her that I had stolen the *found dolls,* hidden in the carriage house.

It is a terrible thing to feel that you might break down, you might utter a confession that could not then be retrieved. And so, I did not speak at all. My throat shut tight. Dr. G. asked her usual picky little friendly seeming questions, to which I could not reply, and after some minutes of awkward silence on my part Dr. G. handed me a notebook and a pen and suggested that I write out my thoughts, if I could not speak to her; I took the notebook from her and with the smile of a shy-but-determined boy I wrote GOODBYE and handed it back to her.

Already I was on my feet. Already I was *gone*.

After high school it was decided that I would "defer" college. My grades had been high, especially in physics and calculus, and at graduation my name had been asterisked in the commencement program to indicate that I graduated summa cum laude but had not gotten around to applying for any college or university. My teachers and the school guidance counselor were perplexed by this decision, but my mother understood, to a degree. For my father had departed from the house on Prospect Hill, and you might think that a concerned son would not leave his mother alone in such a large house, at such a time.

Only I knew I could not leave my *found dolls*.

I could not risk strangers finding them. The possibility of the *found dolls* being discovered was too terrible to consider.

Often when I couldn't sleep, I took a flashlight and went out into the carriage house. By moonlight the carriage house seemed to float like a ghost ship on a dark sea, and all was still except for the cries of nocturnal birds and, in summer, a raucous sound of nocturnal insects buzzing and humming like insidious thoughts.

The *found dolls* lay quiet in their makeshift cribs of plywood and hay. They had been placed side by side like sisters, though each doll was quite distinct from the others and might have made a claim for being the most beautiful.

Mariska. Annie. Valerie. Evangeline. Barbie.

Barbie was one of that notorious breed—*Barbie dolls*.

In this case, Bride Barbie. For the angelic blond girl-doll wore a white silk gown that shimmered and shook when you lifted her and on her flawless head a lace veil. Her figure was not a child's figure but that of a miniature but mature woman with pronounced breasts straining against the bodice of her wedding dress, a ridiculously narrow waist, and shapely hips.

My Friend had observed, *One of these will do. We should give Barbie a chance.*

Barbie had given me the most difficulty, in fact. You would not think that a doll so small and weighing so little could scream so loud, or that her fingernails, shaped and polished and very sharp, could inflict such damage on my bare forearms.

If she doesn't obey, you can chop her into pieces. Tell her she's on trial for her life.

In her makeshift crib of plywood and hay Barbie lay motionless as if in a trance of great surprise and great loathing. Not ever would Barbie cast a sidelong glance at her sister-doll beside her, a soft, boneless cloth doll with a startlingly pale, pretty face and a little tiara on her platinum blond curls that sparkled with tiny rhinestones.

Evangeline had come from Juniper Court, a trailer-village on the outskirts of our town. Hardly protesting, Evangeline had come with me at my Friend's suggestion, for she was a doll lacking a substantial body; her head was made of some synthetic material like plastic, or a combination of plastic and ceramic, but her body was boneless, like a sock puppet. She could not put up much of a struggle and seemed almost to fall before me in a swoon of abnegation, as a sock puppet might do for whom the only possible life is generated by another's antic hand.

No one had searched for Evangeline. It was believed that Evangeline was a *runaway* like other children in her family and in Juniper Court.

When I left the dolls I covered them with a khaki-colored canvas, neatly.

This khaki-colored canvas was the cleanest covering I could find in the carriage house.

Many items of furniture and other abandoned and forgotten things in the carriage house were covered with pieces of canvas that were soiled and discolored, but the covering for the *found dolls* was reasonably clean.

I would have drawn quilts over them, to keep them warm, but I worried that someone would notice and become suspicious.

No one ever came into this part of the carriage house. Not for years. But I had an irrational fear that someone might come into the carriage house and discover my *found dolls*.

My Friend said, *They're happy here. They're at peace here. This is the best they've been treated in their short tragic lives.*

One night not long after I'd stopped seeing Dr. G., I heard a sound at the entrance to the stable, like a footfall, and shone my light there thinking in dismay, *Mother! I will have to kill her. . . .*

But there was no one there, and when I returned to the house it was darkened as before.

I was relieved, I think. For it would not be an easy or pleasant matter to subdue, silence, and suffocate Mother, so much larger than any of the *found dolls*.

Most nights Mother slept deeply. I think Mother was heavily medicated. Sometimes I stood in the doorway of Mother's room seeing her motionless mannequin-figure by moonlight beneath the bedclothes of the large canopied bed and listening to her rhythmic breathing, which sometimes shaded into a soft snoring that was a comfort to me. For when Mother was awake and in my presence, always Mother was aware of me, and looking at me; always Mother was addressing me, or asking me a question, waiting then for me to reply when I had no reply for her.

Though I only murmured or grunted responses, and avoided looking Mother in the face, Mother was never discouraged and continued to chatter in my presence as if she were thinking aloud and yet at the same time addressing *me*.

My Friend laid a sympathetic hand on my shoulder. It was the first time that my Friend had appeared inside my house.

You know that it would be better, Robbie, if the woman were silenced. But this is not a task for the lily-livered.

❧

(How strange this was: *Lily-livered* was not a phrase my Friend had ever spoken before. But *lily-livered* was a phrase that my father had sometimes used in a voice of mockery.)

❧

There was a sixth *found doll*—as it turned out, a disappointing one. But I could not have guessed so beforehand.

Still, I kept Trixie with the others. Though sometimes I didn't remove the canvas from her crib, for her sour, curdled-milk pug-face and
reproachful green marble eyes were discomforting to me; and her cheap,
sleazy, silly costume, a low-cut sequined top that showed the cleavage
of her breasts, and a frilly-frothy ballerina skirt in matching turquoise,
and spike-heeled little shoes, were frankly embarrassing.

No more of Trixie!

I will draw the khaki-covered canvas over Trixie—*Voilà!* As my Friend
says.

And the seventh *found doll*—a boy doll.

His name was an exotic name: Bharata.

He had taffy-colored skin of the finest rubber that so resembled human flesh, you shivered as your fingertips caressed his face and felt a
semblance of warmth, as of capillaries close beneath the surface of the
skin. And his eyes were not glassy-brown but a warm chocolate-brown.

And thick-lashed. Beautiful as any girl's eyes.

Bharata wore chino shorts, a sky-blue T-shirt, blue sneakers on his
small feet, and no socks. His legs were well formed with a look of small,
sinewy muscle, more defined than his sister-dolls' legs.

The palms of his hand were lighter-colored than the rest of his body.
I was fascinated by this—did "people of color" normally have palms
lighter than the rest of their body? I had not ever known any "people
of color"—no one in our family did.

My Friend said, *You see, Robbie? You were prejudiced against boys but
now, you have a surprise in store.*

Bharata was one of the larger dolls, with a sweetly pretty boy-face
and very black curly hair; his black eyelashes swept against his cheeks,
which appeared to be lightly rouged. You could not have told if Bharata's mouth was a boy-mouth, or a girl's.

Bharata was the only doll who tried to speak in actual words, not
merely soft squeaking sounds. Bharata's mouth moved, and I leaned to
him, to listen, but heard only what sounded like *Where—where is—
who are you—I don't want to be—don't want to be h-here . . .*

The other *found dolls* might have exhibited some jealousy, or envy, of my taffy-skinned *found boy doll*. But they disguised their emotions well, for they knew their place and did not wish to offend me, who was their *Doll-Master*.

It was my Friend who had told me, one day, *Robbie, you are the Doll-Master. You must never surrender your authority.*

※

Mother said, "We have no choice, really. The house is so large, most of the rooms are shut off and unheated. A house of this size was meant for a large family, and now there is only us."

Only us was hurtful to me to hear. As if *only us* were an admission of such shameful defeat, it had to be murmured, near-inaudibly.

"So what do you mean, Mother? Do you want to . . . sell the house?"

A clanging in my ears had begun, as of a fire alarm. I could barely hear my mother's reasonable voice asking me if I would call a realtor, if I would oversee the selling of the house.

"It's a profound decision. It's a profound step in our lives. But I think we have no choice, the property taxes alone are . . ."

It was so: Property taxes were rising. Taxes of all sorts were rising in New Jersey.

"Now there's no one in our family going to public school, it seems a shame to pay for 'public education.' My sister was showing me brochures of condominiums on the river, two- and three-bedroom, very modern and stylish . . ."

Mother chattered nervously, excitedly. Mother would not expect me to react to her suggestion in any emphatic way, for that was not Robbie's nature.

Father had not only departed the sprawling old Victorian house on Prospect Hill but had dissociated himself from it entirely: in the divorce settlement he'd signed over the property to my mother. There were to be no alimony payments, for my mother had a small income from investments she'd inherited. Mother sometimes wept but more often expressed relief—*Your father has gone.*

Since the separation several years before, Father and I rarely saw each other. Father did not like to return to our suburban town—it was an effort for him, as he made clear, to attend my high school graduation and to resolutely avoid my mother and her relatives—and I did not like to leave our suburban town, so we exchanged emails occasionally and, less frequently, spoke on the phone. *It is the easiest tie to break,* my Friend consoled me, *the tie that was badly frayed to begin with.*

You could say that Mother and I were "close"—in the way of two actors on a TV show who had been together on the set for many seasons, reciting prepared scripts, uncertain of the direction in which their narrative was moving, what would be the fate of their "characters"— yet not anxious, not quite yet.

I was twenty years old. Soon, it seemed, I was twenty-two years old. No more than one *found doll* a year seemed necessary, or prudent. At the time Mother wanted me to sell our house, I was twenty-three years old. I had not attended college after all. In an alternative life, I would have majored in science and math at a good university—perhaps Princeton. In an alternative life I would be a graduate student now at Caltech, perhaps, or MIT. I might be engaged, or even married.

No, probably not: not engaged, and not married.

Time passes quickly if you don't keep up with your generation of high school graduates. Where time seemed to have virtually stopped for my mother, who continued to see a small circle of women friends, several of them widows, and older female relatives, over the years, time moved rapidly for me. I was not unhappy, though you would have to call me reclusive. I did not consider myself a dropout from society, or a failure, in the way that my father considered himself a failure, and that had poisoned his life. My relationships with the world were primarily through the Internet, where I'd established a website under the name *The Doll-Master,* through which I'd made many acquaintances; here I posted shadowy, oblique, and "poetic" photographs of the *found dolls,* images too dark and irresolute to be identified, though visitors to the site found them "haunting," "eerie," "makes me want to see more!" My website visitors have become faithful correspondents, and my emails take up a large part of my life for it is thrilling for me, as I believe it has to be for them, and some of them female (I think), that we skirt the edges of our essential subject, and seek metaphors and poetic turns of speech to express our (forbidden) desires. For it has been revealed to me as a fact that where the dull-essential nature of our lives is eliminated, such as age, identity, education, employment, place of residence, family ties, daily routine, etc., the thrilling-essential is revealed.

Mother believes that I have contacted a real estate agent in town and have met with her; Mother believes that the house is listed tastefully, with no ugly sign at the foot of our lawn, and only "serious home-seekers who can afford the property" considered; but Mother does not ply me with questions about the house sale, for Mother would rather not think of where we would live if the house were really sold, and what our circumstances would be. And I am comforting to Mother by saying, with a smile: "One step at a time, Mother. The real estate market is flat now—we might not have any serious interest until spring."

Yet, that domestic comfort has come to an abrupt end.

My Friend has abandoned me, I think. For my Friend has no advice to give me now.

It was the occasion of a new *found doll*. I had not brought a *found doll* back to the carriage house for thirteen months, which I believed was a sign of fortitude and character; for I could not be called impulsive, or reckless; rather, over-scrupulous, I think. For when I brought my new *found doll* to the carriage house, and lay her in her little crib beside the others, I lingered too long, in a state of infatuation; I lost track of the time, as dusk shaded into night, and I gazed at Little Farmer-Girl in the beam of my flashlight and marveled at her uniqueness. Of all my dolls, with the possible exception of the rag doll Evangeline, who lacked a substantial body, this doll was soft, will-less, hardly more than fabric with a hard doll-head, yet strangely appealing; not beautiful, not even pretty, but *winning*; for when I washed away the grime on Little Farmer-Girl's face, she was revealed as a sweet homely cousin-sort-of-girl, with stiff pigtails, a funny mouth, wide unblinking marble eyes of an amber hue; her body was made of cloth, from which some of the stuffing had leaked out; she wore denim bib overalls and a red plaid shirt beneath, and on her spindly legs, red tights, and on her tiny feet, boots. Her costume was dirty yet colorful—for she had not been discarded for long, it seemed.

I'd pulled Little Farmer-Girl out of the trash behind our suburban train station, where there is an old, unused railroad yard with a fence around it, long fallen into disrepair. No one comes there, though passengers awaiting the train are gathered on the platform only a quarter-mile away, except children, sometimes, or "runaways"—it was plausible to think that Little Farmer-Girl was a "runaway" whose difficult life had brought her to this place and to my discovery of her in the peaceful interregnum between trains when the depot is virtually deserted. It was a game of kidnap, I decided, since Little Farmer-Girl was so soft-bodied there was no effort involved in lifting her, folding her, and carrying her beneath my hooded jacket; when she struggled, I tied her wrists and ankles and stuffed a rag in her mouth so that her cries were muffled and could not be heard by anyone farther than six feet away.

No effort then to place Little Farmer-Girl in the trunk of the station wagon and to drive slowly back home to the top of Prospect Hill.

Why Little Farmer-Girl exerted such a spell over me is a mystery but I suppose, as my Friend would say, with a laugh, *Robbie, you're so funny! Each of your dolls was enthralling to you, initially.*

I thought, too, that I would begin taking pictures of Little Farmer-Girl that very night, to record more conscientiously than I had the others, before the inevitable incursions of time, decomposition, and decay intervened; my experience was that flash photos were particularly effective, in these circumstances, as more "poetic" and "artistic" than photographs taken by day, even in the shadowy interior of the stall.

"Robbie? Is that you? Why are you here, Robbie? What are you doing?"

So absorbed had I been squatting over Little Farmer-Girl, I hadn't heard Mother approach the rear of the carriage house; too late, I saw the groping beam of her flashlight, moving upon me, and upon the row of *found dolls* that occupied now most of the stall.

"Robbie! What is . . ."

In the crude light of Mother's flashlight the *found dolls* were revealed

as small skeletons with rags of clothing and wisps of hair on their battered skulls; their faces were skull faces, with mirthless grins and eye-
less sockets; their bone arms were spread, as for an embrace.

This was Mother's crude light, not the light of the *Doll-Master*.

Quickly I took the flashlight from Mother's shaking hand. Quickly
I comforted her, telling her that these were sculptures that I'd done, but
had not wanted to show anyone.

"S-sculptures? Here . . . ?"

I would explain to her, I said. But first, I would shut the outer door.

To Ellen

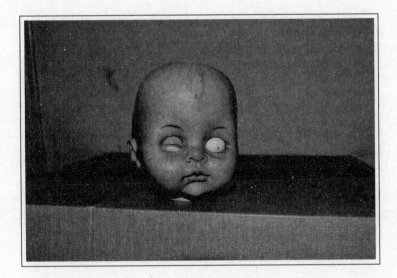

Gaze

by Gemma Files

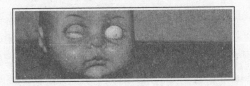

When full-dressed she wore around her neck the barrenest of lockets, representing a fishy old eye, with no approach to speculation in it.

—CHARLES DICKENS, *Dombey and Son*

It was almost exactly three weeks since George Neavins had posted the photo of the Hoxby eye miniature when she received her first email from the man who called himself Benedict Prowdham Proctor. Not that she had much cause to doubt that actually was his name, especially after she'd run him through Google and gotten the requisite twenty-plus hits she'd long since decided were enough to "prove" somebody existed, but . . . it was the Internet, you never knew, not really.

> *Dear sir,*
> *I am writing to you to see if the eye miniature you list on your site (formerly property of the Hoxby family, dated roughly 1786) might perhaps be part of a set . . .*

His inaccurate assumption about her gender was a problem inherent to having chosen to go with her nickname rather than "Georgina," but since doing so had been a frankly business oriented decision on her part, George didn't feel much obliged to correct it. She clicked along further, reading the rest piecemeal while simultaneously monitoring her latest eBay auction, and was surprised to find herself becoming interested.

. . . found in a safety-deposit box after my aunt's passing, along with several other oddities . . . apparently the work of an ancestor of hers, Gwilliam Prowdham, who was fairly well-known as a local miniature artist here in Boston from immediately after the Revolutionary War to the turn of the 19th century . . . a left eye, watercolour on ivory, framed in jet with a hair backing and pearls inset on the bottom of the frame, perhaps to symbolize tears . . . Please find photos attached, showing front and back views. If you could get back to me as quickly as is convenient, I would be very . . .

As the auction wrapped up, leaving George seven hundred to the good, she tapped forefinger against teeth and called up the item in question, sizing each view of it in turn next to Proctor's jpgs. On the one hand, the hair-work matched—same cross-braided stitching, same general tint (brown, with a reddish cast)—and so did the framing, though hers was missing its pearls, probably pawned or sold outright as the remaining Hoxbys sank into decay, long before the estate sale where she'd finally picked it up. Still, there was one very particular difference . . . two, really. And so distinctive she decided to lead with them, when drafting her reply.

Dear Mr. Proctor,

While I understand (and identify with) your enthusiasm at the prospect of such a find, I do feel constrained to point out first that there are almost no known historical instances of eye miniature sets being painted; such an instance would indeed be an amazing rarity, almost as much so as finding a mouth miniature, of which I'm sure you know very few exist. I also think it likely, given the striking resemblance of our items combined with the fact that mine is inscribed on its reverse face with a tiny maker's mark reading GP Bos., that Gwilliam Prowdham may indeed be responsible for both. However, since your miniature is of a pale green eye while mine is of a dark brown eye, it seems unlikely they belonged to the same person. Still, if you're interested in selling, I'd certainly love to help

match you up with a sampling of interested collectors, on either side
of the pond.

   All best,
George Neavins
http://georgiana-antiques.co.uk

She didn't think much about Proctor after that, aside from granting
his Friend request on Facebook. So she was surprised when, while checking her Facebook page, a chat pop-up with his name attached asked
her whether she was available to talk.

sure, she replied. Then added: *abt eye miniature?*

Yes.

kay, go head

Good point re the disparity, he began, *but it occurred to me that unless*
your photos are reversed, your miniature appears to be a left eye, while mine
is a right. So they might belong to someone with heterochromia. That's

2 dfrnt colourd eyes, kno th term. saw xmen 1st class 2

All right, great. So I took the liberty of doing some research on my end,
trying to figure out who Prowdham might have painted within the due time-
frame (1785-1790), particularly for a member of the Hoxby family. Made
up a little package. May I send?

George raised a brow, then realized he couldn't possibly see it. So:
sure, she repeated.

Seconds later, she was opening what seemed a disproportionately large
attachment, revealing a document made up of two parts scans to one
part notes. The former appeared to have been taken directly from yellowed Boston-area newspapers dated between May and December of
1787, while the latter she could only attribute to Proctor himself, though
he occasionally seemed to be jotting down quotes from materials not
included.

Much of the newspaper matter involved accounts—truncated and
metaphorical, by necessity—of a court case conducted behind closed
doors in late April 1796. The charge was child-murder through procurement of abortion, brought against a certain Mrs. Damaris Chadwent

of Boston, a young widow who supposedly made her living as a "dress-maker and fashiouner of dolls," but was rumoured to be "kept" by a member of "an olde and substantiall familie with Monarchial tyes." (*Hoxby?* Proctor's notes suggested, then added: *Hoxbys left Boston for Ontario by end of year, then back to England within next decade.*)

This all tallied with George's own research. At the time, the clan's leader would have been widowed matriarch Elephantina Hoxby (once the wife of Abishag Hoxby, successful spice merchant and importationist of other luxurious unnecessaries), who stepped into her husband's empty place only to find herself haphazardly shepherding the dregs of her once-prosperous brood from disaster to disaster, shedding properties as they went. First there was Abishag himself, dead of fever, in whose funeral's wake came warehouse fires and nautical scupperings, cutting their fortunes in half. Her oldest, Ephai—what sort of people named their son after a word which meant "gloomy," biblical or not?—had been slated to take over his father's concerns, but was struck down by a swirl of scandal (the mysterious Mrs. Chadwent's fault?), followed by a wasting disease with an archaic, faux-Latinate name, probably some undiagnosed form of lupus, quickly rendering him unsuitable for any position at all.

By the time the Hoxbys abandoned their Bostonian holdings entirely, their original complement had been reduced from a strongly tied familial consort to an ever-shrinking band of barely-survivors, denuded and near-destitute. So they'd married the last daughter off in what was now Toronto, booked passage for London with her bridal gift, and got as far as Liverpool, where they'd settled in to slowly decay from genteel poverty to outright penury. Much like every other treasure they'd once possessed, their eye miniature had already passed through so many different sets of hands by the time it made its way across George's desk that she'd never debated whether or not to make its provenance known; it wasn't as though she expected anybody named Hoxby to come asking after it, after all, given there was no longer anybody so named left to ask.

George clicked on, speed-reading. The trial itself, due to its secret nature, was referred to only elliptically; a lot of faff about "thatte most horrible crime against alle Sense & Propriety, contrary to ye lawes of

God & Man lykewise," as well as some implication that Mrs. Chadwent might have used "means un-Naturall" to attract the putative father of her unborn child in the first place, seeing that he was young, good-looking, and of "Stature," while she was none of the above. It did seem odd for a woman without means to have supposedly entrapped a rich heir into making her pregnant, only to then dispose of her bargaining/blackmail chip outright, however—didn't make much sense, strategically. What *could* she have been after?

Odder yet was the denouement, as described: Mrs. Chadwent had apparently been brought into chambers blindfolded, so that her accusers "might not be Forced to meet her eyes." Not to mention being later garrotted after sentencing, "according to the olde methods," with her head cut off postmortem and buried in an unmarked grave, the blindfold still on.

Oh, and here it was, at last—the most important detail. A description of Mrs. Chadwent, "taken from Life" shortly before her trial: *This notorious dame was oft observed walking about ye towne in ye smallest houres of ye night, without any great regard to her safety, yet never much disturbed in her perambulations. This being a great amazement to alle, seeing she was but of middle height, slender-made in ye hands and feet yet stout and womanly about ye body, with hair of a fox-like shade, and her fine eyes of two divers colours. . . .*

One brown, "dark and Fine, lyke unto an conker's shell." And one . . . pale green.

George got back on chat, pinging Proctor, who answered quickly enough that she had to wonder if he'd actually spent the last forty minutes sitting near his computer, screen up and occasionally refreshed, just waiting for her to reply. *what else in yr aunts box?* she asked, without preamble.

Documents, mostly. Correspondence, a few sketchbooks.

all prowdham?

That I've seen, yes. He signed everything, if only with that maker's mark.

She paused, thinking—without any particular inkling of why—*Oh, I'm going to regret this. Aren't I?*

Then she typed, a second later: *scan + send me? if dont mind.*

No problem at all. The screen went silent a moment, then pinged again. *May I,* then *take it,* followed by *you're interested?* Proctor's cursor wrote, slower than usual, almost as though shy.

y, she replied, finally.

※

"Sounds like they thought she was a witch," Antha said, stretching distractingly. "Which is weird, because witchcraft was a jailing offense at the most by then, in America—since 1706, I think. A charge no-body would've trotted out anymore, not in any court, even a secret one."

"Oh?" George asked. "Why'd you end up there, then?"

"Mmm, thing about the eyes, I guess. Blindfolding her; that's proof against the Evil Eye, or would've been, like . . . a hundred and fifty years earlier, maybe. She was a hairdresser, Mrs. Chadwent, right?"

"Dressmaker. Sold dolls, too."

Antha turned over, shrugging. "Well, then I could be wrong, but it's kind of six of one, half dozen of the other. I mean, in the Jacobean era, almost anybody involved in doing female-upkeep-related jobs might turn out to be a poisoner, like with Lady Frances Carr and Anne Turner; Lady Frances wanted to climb the social ladder, so she got her ruff-maker, Mrs. Turner, to poison anybody who got in her way, and when it all shook down she was fined and exiled, but Mrs. Turner ended up accused of witchcraft and hanged. 'Poisoner' used to be slang for abortionist, too. Did Mrs. Chadwent go to somebody to get rid of the baby, or did she do it herself?"

"Um . . ." George cast her mind back. "'Procurement' could mean either, I suppose. But they'd've brought the abortionist in as well, I'd think, if they knew who they were."

"Not necessarily. Easier to go with the person you already have in custody, right? A lot of women ended up being charged for simply hav-ing a miscarriage the authorities decided was a bit too convenient, just like today."

"Antha . . . this isn't what I'd call pillow talk, exactly."

Antha smiled lazily. "Yeah, well, I think it's fascinating. Love to see those miniatures laid side by side—the real things, not jpgs. It'd be as if you were looking in her eyes."

"Dangerous business, apparently. According to the file."

"Mmm-hmm. But danger can be *sexy*."

Apparently.

After, George lay there studying the ceiling as Antha dozed beside her, ruminating idly. Made perfect sense Antha'd know about such things, of course, having come to England to study them—a leggy blonde Canadian with a cheerful face and a sinful body, she often introduced herself as a "Regencyist," which George took to be some sort of shorthand, given she'd made Ph.D at barely thirty. Aside from the portion of it spent in bed, their time together mainly consisted of Antha nattering away on one subject or another, which George found cute and occasionally useful; George's own small store of historical knowledge tended to both the object-based and the ruthlessly practical, always gained with a mind toward profit, or (at the least) knowing how much she could get away with charging.

As she'd pointed out to Proctor earlier, eye miniatures constituted a sort of antiques dealer's daydream, given their rarity. The fad for such images had started in the late 1700s, peaking quickly and dying out sometime in the 1820s; either Richard Cosway or George Engleheart had painted the first one, though the idea didn't really come into fashion till 1785, when George-IV-to-be (then still prince of Wales) went through an entirely illegal form of marriage with pretty widow Maria Fitzherbert. In order to swap love tokens his disapproving father wouldn't recognize, the two exchanged "portraits" reduced to a single eye each, and George kept his pinned under his lapel, so he could take it out and gaze at it anytime he wanted.

Anonymity and decorum, that was the point of the exercise. Hoxby must have commissioned at least one of the eyes, obviously—Mrs. Chadwent wouldn't have had the largesse to make *him* one, unless the dress- and doll-making industry of old Boston paid out far better than George was inclined to think it possibly could. But where had the other come from? Who'd want *two* eyes, when one served perfectly well for everybody else?

Because without both, you wouldn't know either one was hers, she thought. *That might be it.*

She closed her own eyes, but sleep still eluded her. So, sighing, she got up—carefully, so as not to disturb Antha—and slipped into her office, closing the door quietly behind her.

An automatic email check revealed more scans from Proctor, plus a note: *Sent you the sketchbooks by courier, as they benefit from being read in person. Should arrive tomorrow afternoon, your time.* Over-egging it a bit, George thought, but shrugged, added, *thanx, GN,* at the bottom, and sent it back to him. Then, clicking on the first attachment, she fell headlong into what later proved to be two hours' worth of impromptu research, poring through tiny print on discoloured paper to peel back the layers on Prowdham's practice of minimized ocular portraiture.

Up top was what Prowdham called his "Fee-Book," more a memorandum or list of outstanding debts: *1789 Apr His Eye M. Jourdemayne £5. 5s.; 1789 Mar Mrs. F's Eye [probably Hesther Lomax, whose father owned Boston's third print shop, and married her into the Fitzwill family,* Proctor's comments pointed out] *£5. 5s.,* etc. There were maybe fifty entries for the period Proctor cited in his initial email, confirming Ephai Hoxby as having commissioned the first miniature ("with no Embellishment"), though it gave no hint George could see that a second had ever been painted, let alone paid for.

Underneath, meanwhile, was a letter from 1796—six years after Prowdham'd left off making them—in which he reminisced about the "Philosophy" behind the concept:

I first Began on acct. of viewing an eye worn by a Lady of my acquaintance, done at Paris & set in, a delightful Idea, which I admired more than I confess for its singular Beauty & ring. It seemd a true French idea to me, Originality knit w. craft, & when my Customers inquird as to whether I was capable of doing Such myself, I took it as challenge.

There is a strange Delight in translation of my Commissioners desires in this Manner, for the Eye is a symbol of great power—some believe it a window to the Soul, or to our Lord Himself, peering out

from this world unto an other: perhaps Heaven, perhaps elsewhere.
Tis why I believe people take such Efforts in their requests, twinning
Eyes with all manner of relevant Things; stones & flowers, pansies
for the French pensée (O Think of Me), turquoize for its Forget-Me-
Not colour, pearls for tears. One design I Undertook in or about 178—
did combine an altar workd in hair w. two hearts in Flame beneath
the wingéd Eye of Providence, on ivory, as Allegory of love both car-
nal & Divine.

But none of this elaboration had gone into Mrs. Chadwent's eye miniatures, aside from the pearls and the hair. Comparatively, they were
spare, almost dull, the eyes themselves the literal focal point: Mrs.
Chadwent's gaze, boiled down. Her polluted, blindfold-worthy gaze.

George had dated a witch once—someone who thought she was, anyhow. Vaguely, she recalled her talking about something called the Law
of Contagion, best illustrated by voodoo dolls and poppets: Make something look like something else, and whatever you do to it happens to
the thing it represents. So . . . *look at* something hard enough, and you
take a part of it inside you? Or vice versa?

Without thinking, she found herself pulling the jpg's up again,
brown on the left, green the right—just seemed correct, going by the
way they slanted, the tiny bit of flesh Prowdham'd allowed for context.
Very detailed indeed, when you allowed yourself to study them; just a
shade of smile-lines bracketing one, with what might be a beauty mark
stippling the other's corner. She remembered how nicely the hair
shone on hers, red-flashing in the light as George raised it, brushing
dust away with a few short flicks. There, in the green—was that a flaw?
A shadow?

She turned her head, slightly, to check the brown. And . . .

. . . found it *there*, as well, inexplicably. What seemed for all the world
like the same flaw, barely there, yet somehow unmistakable: unevenly
drawn, triangular-pulled, a fleck at the top. A keyhole or a person, de-
formed by distance. An absence, waiting to be filled.

Something twinged inside her temple, a plucked thread. A dim, shud-
dering echo that might, one day, bloom into pain.

She was so tired, suddenly. Far too tired to read any further. Too tired, almost, to see.

With a wracking yawn, she stabbed for the shutdown option, not even bothering to close out of anything—email, both documents, the jpg's. Simply flipped her laptop closed and felt her way along the wall, stumbling back to bed.

Behind her, the office lamp burned on. In front of her, Antha lay sprawled, snoring slightly; George barely avoided falling on top of her as she plunged straight down into sleep, and deeper.

❦

George's dream began in close, an oval mirror, just large enough to frame a face. A candle on either side of it provided light, of a sort, but it came and went, guttering; a wind blew from somewhere, cold and raw. In front of the mirror, a straight-backed chair. In the chair, a woman.

She had her fox-coloured hair down, loose to the small of her spine, combing it through with even, contemplative strokes. Her face George could not see, though its reflection shone, peeping intermittently over the woman's shoulder—white, featureless, mask-like; her body (likewise glimpsed only from behind) was ripe, hands and feet well made, and everything about her seemed trim, neat, compact. Yet at the woman's waist, still small by comparison to the rest of her generous curves, there seemed some slight suggestion of swelling.

Y'are caught short, madam, a disembodied voice remarked, suddenly, issuing almost from where George seemed to sit—so close, indeed, that George felt it resonate in her throat, as though it were her own. *Or so rumour has it. You will need a friend.*

The woman's clever hand stilled, midstroke, as she replied: *Do you think so, sir?*

Of a certainty.

Hmm. And are you not my friend already? Would that friendship cease, were I not so entrapped?

A harsh phrase. 'Tis Eve's own sin we speak of, after all—every woman's destiny, when all's said and done. You might rise, madam, were you to cleave to me entire. You need not work again.

And if I wish to? What then, supposing I considered my work the equal of yours, or any man's? Then added, raising that same hand: *Nay, do not answer; I know your thoughts a'ready, as I know every other young jack's: You would have me idle, stifled, made yours alone for only so long as you'd have it, to be coddled and then discarded, my brat along with me. But you will be disappointed, sir, for nothing happens to me but that I desire it.*

Watch now, and closely, as I disgorge myself of this burden. See how the curse you thought to lay 'pon me may be undone without time or trouble, by one better versed in cursing.

George heard a qualm enter the other speaker's voice, as if *he*, Ephai Hoxby, she could only assume, realized his mistake. Hastening to plead: *Nay, good, my Demaris, do you but wait a while—*

You wait, sir, an' you will. I am not so easily dissuaded.

Now things seemed to narrow, sharply. The darkness George floated in became a funnel, slanting inward, irising like a silent-film dissolve. Thus foregrounded, the woman (Mrs. Chadwent, just as obviously) put down her comb and sat enshrined in erratic candle flame, red-brown hair haloing her like a many-threaded Medusa corona, lit sidelong. In the mirror, though her face remained somehow blurred, her eyes came up sharply, clicking into relief: one green, one brown, equally lucent, two tiny windows.

I charge you, Mrs. Chadwent murmured, just beyond George's fading vision, *depart from me now, you mere sketch of a thing; absent yourself, however you see fit. Let no part of you touch what is mine. Die unborn, sad sacrifice to your own sire's folly—*

Something welling up in her lap now, freed with a gush as she shivered, though only briefly; shook herself off and shrugged at the feeling, first hot, then cold. Some spreading stain let loose from inside, by sheer force of will, to dye her white skirts red.

As I direct, then, let it be. For in my gaze are all things rendered but objects, to do my bidding or be cast down, on the very instant . . .

※

. . . and here was where George woke, alone, Antha having already gone about her business, leaving only a scribbled-on scrap of paper behind:

b good text later luv u m2m bb. George staggered up, barely making it to the bathroom, where she sat yawning, so wide her jaw cracked. A few minutes after, she stood in front of the mirror flossing, squinting at herself under the vanity bulbs' floodlight glare. Only to catch an ill-glimpsed hint that made her stop, peer even closer, searching the reflection for something she couldn't quite make out, though she felt (knew) it *must* be there—

(that flaw, skewed keyhole cracking her cornea, that)

(*absence*)

Oh my Christ, you need to stop thinking crazy, before someone notices.

Lingering on, though, nevertheless; frowning at herself, lips still foaming, a caricature of rabies. 'Til at last the doorbell rang—solid and normal, annoying as it ever had been—and freed her to turn her back, stride over, and pop the lock, braced to answer.

"Delivery for George Neavins? Sign here, love."

Proctor's package, right on time. The sketchbooks fell out when she ripped it open, one popping automatically to what George could only assume had been a series of studies Prowdham felt he'd invested far too much time in to just rip it out and start over, cramped and hastily executed though they might be: a bent head, napkin wound 'round the eyes Mary Hamilton–style, entirely failing to keep her ignorant of her fate. George would know the set of that jaw anywhere, those shoulders' jut, spine straight and neat little hands crossed in her lap, ripe bosom swelling above; impossibly recognizable, a clear-cut case of dreamsick *jamais vu.*

Mrs. Chadwent, 'tis, as I do live and breathe, a voice inside her head observed, wryly. *As I do, and she . . . doesn't.*

She turned the page, perhaps a bit too forcefully, and watched the motion shake a folded sheaf of papers free, mottled cream-brown as the Fee-Book scan. A letter, dated 1802, writ large and smearily. Here and there, parts had been struck through or forcibly erased, censored either before or after the fact. It was addressed "To my dear Sister," and George found herself speed-reading impatiently through the first few paragraphs—*if this Malady of mine prove fatal let it not be said I died Uncon-*

*fessd in absolute, though as I trust no Priest to shrive me, I am constraind
to Address my soul's black ills to you*—before things finally got under way,
half a page later:

> . . . *that I share equal Guilt for Mrs. Chadwent's downfall, see-
ing how after her break w. Young Master Hoxby she applyd to me for
Means enough to flee, only to be turnd over to the Law instead. For
given we were both his Creatures & subject to his patronage, she be-
lievd me trust-worthy—a foolish slip, from one who was no manner
of fool at all. More fool I, indeed, as things have since elapsed, that
(at the time) I feard more the earthly wrath of Mrs. Hoxby than that
more spiritual & Most Malign power I had already seen practicd by
Mrs. Chadwent upon me, him, even herself.*

Because of this "Judasry" on his part, Prowdham felt constrained to
attend Mrs. Chadwent's trial each day, recording her interactions with
the bench in a series of notes, which he had appended.

> *They askd if she was guilty & she said:* "Many foolish tales are told of
me, as with most solitary women."
> "In example?" *quoth one.*
> "Oh sir, 'tis said I may divide my gaze & thus look through my
dolls eyes as twere mine own, learning many secret things I later pass
to my compatriots, who rob my customers houses & split their goods
w. me after. But who can credit such imaginings?"
> "Like enough those dolls eyes do resemble yours," *one judge ap-
parently maintained,* "even to their disparity."
> *And in answer,* Prowdham wrote, *Mrs. Chadwent only gave
a low sort of laugh, brief and soft, yet most dread-full indeed to
hear.*
> "Do they so? Come, compare, & try." *At which the blindfold
slipped, disclosing her one eye—the green, not the brown—that when
it fell upon the judge his Honour he was struck down, as with Gods
own stroke. So she was seized once more, crying out:* "Thus be all

false accusers servd, when an innocent's gaze falls upon 'em. For doth the Bible not say, 'What you send unto me I will send back, an hundredfold'?"

Yet, Prowdham continued, the eye slid past me as well, in the confusion, just when the bandage was replaced—I felt my limbs lose their vigour, my face fix, as though I became a mere doll in her hands. And so has it remained, unto this very day.

That same night, being much enragd, Mrs. Hoxby bribd a Man of the watch to wrench Mrs. C's gaze apart, forcing her hold on Young Master Hoxby loose for good—taxd him to cut one Eye free & convey it away, burying it, that its former Possessor go to her doom halfblinded. But acting as I felt not on mine own accord, I bought up the Fruit of his labours w. what remained of my Fee, & once it was deliverd me (in a jar of spirit), applyd myself to one more Portrait. This last I send to you for safe-keeping, for I am loath to have it near enough to Watch me, as Ephai H.'s must surely Watch over him.

It stared at me, you see, all the time I painted, as though by staring it might scour me with hate. It cursed me, & I am to die from it, I know—if not now, then later. After as much pain as I can bear, if not more.

I do pray God Almighty not much later, sister, in my better moments. Though I doubt in my heart those prayers will be answered, except with laughter.

Keep it secret, please, therefore. Keep it safe.

She will come for it, one day.

Not copied from life, then; not exactly. Copied from death.

George's phone buzzed, a blessed momentary distraction. It was Antha, texting: *found quote u might find useful*, link appended. Clicking through, she found somebody's Tumblr, at the top of which was the following highlighted text banner:

"Gaze" is a psychoanalytical term brought into popular usage by Jacques Lacan to describe the anxious state that comes with the awareness that one can be viewed. The psychological effect, Lacan argues, is that the subject loses a degree of autonomy upon realizing that he or she is a visible object. This concept is bound up with his theory of the mirror stage, in which a child encountering a mirror realizes that he or she has an external appearance. Lacan suggests that this gaze effect can similarly be produced by any conceivable object such as a chair or a television screen. This is not to say that the object behaves optically as a mirror; instead it means that the awareness of any object can induce an awareness of also *being* an object.

(She made me into an object, an awful object.)

(She made a doll of me.)

Abruptly, George realised she had not just the beginnings of a migraine, but the very thing itself; it crystallised round her full-blown, without her ever having felt it forming, converting her limbs to wood and the air to treacle. Slowly, as if sleepwalking, she folded Prowdham's letter (*file that later, might be valuable,* she had the wherewithal to remind herself, at least) and went back into the office, opening first a little cabinet hidden beneath her desk, then the safe inside it. There, among everything else, her hand fell on a tiny cloth bag, from which she shook the Hoxby eye miniature. Raising it to the light, she angled it to catch and flare, hair turning foxy, keyhole flaw blazing up. The image blurred, doubled, making two eyes of one. Until, as her own eyes narrowed, as tears filled them, blurring the pair further still . . .

Don't look, don't. Put it down. Stop looking.

You have to stop looking, before she

(looks back)

. . . one of the two, formerly both brown, began to turn green.

That hole at the corner of the eye was back now, as George had somehow suspected it would be. Unable to stop herself from focusing on it, she watched as it seemed to move closer and closer, stretch up and out, become a figure: ripe in the middle and neat at both ends, wild reddish-brown mane hung down to frame a smeared white half-visage whose

sole open socket gaped empty. Mrs. Chadwent's ghost grasped the
Hoxby miniature, pried it from George's numbing fingers, and tipped it
toward her own phantom sketch of a face, then lowered it once more
as her previously empty eye socket resolved further, refilling: pupil, ring,
cilia. A shrewd brown eye, indistinguishable from Prowdham's image,
peered down at George, who whimpered and flinched from its attention, as if scalded.

Mrs. Chadwent, leaning down over George as she curled up on the
floor, whispered in her ear; at first she couldn't hear what was being said,
any more than she could interpret the reel of images beginning to un-
spool itself inside her head. Just lay there as the babble of her bruised mind
peaked and dimmed, nothing but one long squealing, begging plea—

*Make it stop, make it stop, make it stop. Not my fault. I'm sorry. I didn't
mean to.*

(Please.)

But: *Quiet, mistress,* the spectre told George, not without a species
of grim sympathy. *Calm yourself. Th'art in my grip now, firm as firm, with
no escape.*

George groaned. *What . . . what do you want?* she brought herself
to ask, hoarsely, at last.

What all want, in the end. An answer.

. . . about?

Mrs. Chadwent's form paused a moment, as though considering this.

It is hard for me, she said, eventually, *where I am now. A long way to
travel. One forgets one's self. But a likeness . . . a likeness is a mirror. A
mirror is a door. A door opens.*

Yes. Yes, I see . . . I think. I understand.

Aye, but do you? For I see, too—only one. Where is t'other?

Other . . . what?

Eye, mistress. Where is my other eye?

Not a weeping girl, George, not naturally—she never had been, even
under the worst of circumstances. Yet she could hear sobs, at that moment, and knew them for her own. Above her, what had once been
Mrs. Chadwent squatted down further, stare never shifting—so bright

and hot, her gaze, even halved. It would burn a hole clean through her, George thought.

Well, lay it by. The Hoxbys, then . . . they who divided me, Ephai and that bitch-faced dam of his, who buried me in pieces, like rubbish. Do they live still, and prosper?

George shook her head, grinding it painfully against the floor. Thinking, as she did: *No, they're dead, all dead. You won.*

Ah, 'tis good; I knew 'twould trap the Young Master, this one eye of mine, since he could not keep from study of it. And Gwilliam's seed, who first enshrined the same in paint for him? Who saw me swing and wept crocodile tears, knowing full well how he'd connived the same?

A tiny circle on George's cheek, pinpointing the bone, and God but it stung, almost sparked. She could all but hear the sizzle—smell her own flesh, cooking.

Proctor, she thought, desperate. *He did this to me. Made the introductions—put you in my head, the likeness, the image.*

Turning, painfully, to fix that place where the ghost should be: dark turned bright, full negative, hurting heart and eyes alike to contemplate. And thought again, in its direction:

One guy, that's all that's left. He's got it. Go after him, *why don't you?*

Oh, I will, madam, Mrs. Chadwent told her, softly. *Be very sure of it.*

Then—a blink. And nothing. Everything gone.

George included.

George left the hospital with Antha, hand in hand out of necessity as much as affection; led down the halls and out into the sun, free palm slapping up to shade herself, the flaw's fuzzy remains still emblazoned on her cornea. It *was* fading, but slowly—the doctors were baffled. But Antha, far more blithely accepting of the supernatural than George had ever suspected, trusted things would continue to resolve themselves.

"You're not going to look at it anymore," she said, "so that's *that* settled. Prowdham can look at the damn thing all he wants, from now on."

"Or not."

"Or not! His choice."

"You did cheat me out of my commission somewhat, though, by sending it to him while I was knocked out, and telling me about it after."

Antha shrugged. "Would you have let me, if I'd asked?" George shook her head. "Well, there you go; I was just being sensible. Besides, he kept on emailing, so I thought . . ." She hesitated, then allowed: ". . . to be frank, fuck him for getting you into this in the first place. Anyhow, I paid the postage."

"Very nice of you, that was."

"I'm a nice girl."

An instinctive decision, but probably the right one, considering what happened next. The friend who was with Proctor when he opened the package claimed he'd seemed compelled to lay the two miniatures side by side, then stared at them intently—refusing to respond to questions, shouts, or repeated shakings—until they burst into flame. The friend ended up leaping from a first-floor window, yelling at Proctor to do the same, but he must've not been able to hear; the house burnt to the ground, amazingly swiftly, with Proctor still inside.

George felt bad about it, at least slightly, for exactly as long as it took some anonymous third party to send her links to a blog Proctor'd kept under a pseudonym. Entries there implied he might have been having much the same problems as George, then had come across her initial listing and conceived a plan to pass *his* half of Mrs. Chadwent's gaze on, before things came to a head.

"Selling off all your portraiture?" Antha asked, a week later, looking over George's shoulder. "Very . . . Muslim of you."

"Makes me nervous," George answered shortly. "Documents and woodwork only, for me, from now on—anything nonrepresentational. Seems safer."

"Oh, she'll leave you alone from now on," Antha announced, with what George thought was rather easy confidence, given she'd experienced all this at one remove. "I mean, *you're* not a Hoxby or a Prowd-ham, just the chick who told her how to get what she wanted. She might even be grateful."

Mrs. Chadwent hadn't struck George as the grateful sort, really. But no point being difficult, not when Antha meant it kindly—it'd gotten her to finally move in, if nothing else. Best outcome possible.

"Wouldn't care to speculate," George said briskly. And went back to what she'd been doing.

In Case of Zebras

by Pat Cadigan

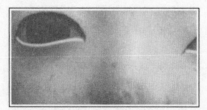

You know how your mother always told you to wear clean underwear in case you got hit by a car and had to go to the hospital? Well, don't. If they bring you into the emergency room unconscious, they cut your clothes off. *Snip, snip, snip*—in thirty seconds, everything you had on is rags. I wouldn't know this if I hadn't drawn Judge Mariah Mankiller.

Judge Mankiller took a creative approach to sentencing first offenders, particularly adolescents she thought would turn themselves around. At seventeen, I wasn't so much a first-time offender as I was a first-time court attender—I finally got caught. I was scared straight in the holding cell, before I even saw my lawyer. Sitting in court listening to the judge sentence everyone else who had been in the car with me scared me even straighter. We'd all been carrying some controlled substances, although I was honestly floored when I found out Andy and Lil had had needles; also that my boyfriend had a juvenile record. I'd only had some pot—and not very good pot at that—but as I'd been driving, I figured I was really in for it. Just the way she said my name—*Miss. Olivia. Claire. DiAngelo*—sounded like doom. I was visibly shaking when I stood up.

Judge Mankiller declared she wasn't impressed by the blizzard of statements my lawyer had produced attesting to my sterling character. However, the fact that I had tested stone cold sober made her think I might be worth all the effort my parents were making to keep me out of jail. She sentenced me to a thousand hours of community service in the Tri-County emergency room. The hours were not to be unreasonably long or disruptive to my family—i.e., I shouldn't be working seven days in a row or getting home at three a.m.—but I had to put in between twenty and forty hours a week doing whatever I was told, whether it was emptying bedpans, washing bedpans, or cleaning up whatever had missed the bedpans.

I almost blew it by smiling. Her Honor asked me what I was grinning about—did I think I'd gotten away with something? I assured her I didn't feel that way at all. No lie—it had been pure nerves; until then, I'd been close to breaking down in tears. But it was also because I knew she thought bedpans would gross me out. My paternal grandmother had lived the last year of her life with us when I was thirteen. Nonna and I had always been very close, and nothing in a bedpan had ever fazed me; it wasn't plutonium. And it was way better than twenty-four months of incarceration.

Okay, I'll admit to seriously underestimating the yuck factor of bedpans used by people I had no strong emotional bond with. But I got over it, and it's neither here nor there anyway. I'm just explaining how I happened to be in the ER when the guy with the doll came in.

Judge Mankiller said the ER staff would be glad to see me; her previous community-service appointee had finished a couple of weeks earlier and there would be plenty for me to do. She was almost half-right—i.e., almost half the ER staff were glad to see me, not including the nurse I reported to. Before I could even set foot in the place, I had to take a CPR course, six hours that didn't count as part of my community service; rather chintzy of them, I felt, and besides, I'd had CPR training every summer at camp. Or so I thought—this was a lot more extensive. Plus I'd never had a handsome fireman like Tyrone for a teacher, either.

I doubted I'd ever use my now-enhanced lifesaving skills in the ER, but Tyrone said just being able to identify symptoms of serious trouble might be crucial. Of course, if Tyrone had told me shaving my head might be crucial, I'd have kept a razor in my pocket. But I still think they were chintzy not to count those hours.

My first few days at Tri-County, I wasn't sure who was actually in charge of the place; the person in charge of me was Zelda Fiore, who said I couldn't go wrong by assuming the nurses were in charge. She was several firsts: the first Zelda I had ever met personally, the first person who ever called me Oly instead of Liv, and the first black person of my acquaintance with an Italian surname. And not by marriage—her middle name was Pasqualina, she said, after her grandmother. I thought maybe we'd bond over our grandparents, but I was wrong about that—she was Sicilian, I was Neapolitan ("Like the Sopranos," I said; she didn't crack a smile). She wasn't all that thrilled to have Judge Mankiller's latest project in her ER (unquote). I had a week to justify breathing her air, then she'd mail me back to the judge for a refund (also unquote).

For the first week, I didn't get near a bedpan—I made coffee, ordered lunches, fetched lunches, cleaned up after lunches, and refrigerated leftovers, making sure they were wrapped and clearly labeled. In fact, my very first chore was cleaning out the refrigerator—something had died in there (possibly before I was born; I don't want to talk about it). But I managed to impress Zelda at the end of the week by staying late to help clean up after a particularly nasty case of projectile vomiting (not as bad as the refrigerator).

After a month, I decided to take some initiative and went out to the waiting room, thinking I might spot someone having a stroke or a heart attack and be crucial to their survival. Instead, I became a lightning rod for complaints about how long everyone had been waiting; fortunately, the triage nurse intervened before things escalated into a riot.

"Believe me, little girl, I know if they're about to keel over or not," Hollis said. "If they are, they'll tell me, which is faster than them telling you first. If ya see what I mean." Hollis was built like a linebacker, which according to him was why he did triage more often than anyone else.

I'd been there just over two months when the guy with the doll came in.

By then, Zelda had stopped groaning *every* time she saw me, and even made an approving noise now and then, which was like an Olympic medal. Volunteering in an emergency room, even one like Tri-County's that isn't as overstretched and underfunded as a lot of other places, will change your perspective. Two months in, I had developed my first real case of existential angst and was reevaluating my entire life.

Not that I was thinking of becoming a doctor or a nurse. Human effluvia was gross, but you didn't have to be a pearl diver to hold your breath long enough to clean it up (usually). But pierce someone's living flesh with a needle? Not even with a gun to my head, and I said as much to my parents. (Actually, what I said was, they'd never have to worry about me becoming an intravenous drug user, and I felt damned by the faint praise of their disappointingly lukewarm reaction.)

Anyway, I'd just finished restocking bay number six with linens and waterproof pads when they wheeled the guy in, unconscious and wearing a collar to keep his head immobilized. Only the driver's air bag had deployed; he'd been in back and neither he nor the other two passengers had been belted in.

"Property bag," Zelda said to me as she began cutting his clothes off. I don't faint at the sight of blood (a totally physiological reaction, FYI), and there wasn't very much, which I'd learned wasn't necessarily a good sign. But I braced myself anyway, in case there was an injury the paramedics had missed, like something sticking in or, worse, out—rare, but when it does happen, you'll scare the patient if you gasp or even just look surprised. He didn't have much on him besides the usual—wallet, loose change, a few crumpled receipts, keys, cell phone—but Zelda missed the doll completely until it fell out of his pocket onto the floor.

I picked it up. It was a little man, a couple of inches longer than my middle finger, wearing a shirt, trousers, and sneakers. And I don't mean painted on, I mean tiny clothes and shoes. Actual hair, too—rooted, not pasted on.

The face was perfect. My close-up vision was nice and sharp, but I knew I'd need a magnifying glass to really appreciate the detail. Were those baby-doll eyes, the kind that could open and close? Nonna had had some very old dolls with eyes like that but none anywhere near as small, and this didn't look like an antique. I touched one tiny hand; the arm moved like there was a joint at the elbow.

"This is *amazing*," I breathed.

"Private property's what it is," Zelda said, still using her scissors. "In the sack."

I obeyed. "I'm not kidding, though. I've never seen anything like this."

"Child, you've led a sheltered life," she said with a small laugh. "You ain't seen nothin' yet."

"And not just what's in their pockets," added Jackie, who had come in to stick electrodes on his chest.

"Too much yakity-yak," Zelda admonished us. She put a hospital robe over the man and paused to write something on a piece of paper, which she taped on the wall next to him: THIS PATIENT CAN HEAR EVERYTHING YOU SAY.

"Is that true?" I whispered. The guy looked completely unconscious to me.

"Dunno," she said, "so we play it safe."

Normally, that would have been all and I'd have gone off to bag soiled linens or check the coffeepot in the lounge (Zelda had informed me that lives—*lives*—depended on it never burning dry, mine included). It was six p.m. and I knew things would only get busier. Zelda was working four to midnight, and I had volunteered to do the same. Midnight wasn't a disruptive hour for someone my age; I promised I wouldn't complain to the judge about it. Zelda only gave me the Eyebrow of Doom and said she'd wring my neck if I did (another disappointing reaction; lately, nothing I did pleased anyone).

But I couldn't stop thinking about the doll. Every chance I got, I'd peek around the drawn curtain, hoping he'd wake up so I could talk to him. I had no idea what I was going to say: *Ohai, cool doll, did you get it from Hammacher Schlemmer?* Or, *I've got some bad news about your clothes?*

Maybe I could comfort him. He was hooked up to a cardiac monitor with a blood pressure cuff on his arm and a pulse oximeter clipped to one finger. It can be pretty alarming to wake up to all the beeping and clicking and the cuff squeezing your arm and not know what happened.

Not that I could tell him—only a doctor or a nurse was supposed to talk to him about his condition. *I* wasn't even supposed to know what his condition was.

I was really after another look at that doll; I wanted to see if there was a brand name or some other mark identifying the manufacturer or maybe who sold it. But mostly I just wanted to *look* at it—examine it, scrutinize it, *stare* at it. All those details: Was the hair really rooted, did those itty-bitty eyes open and close, did the arms really bend? So much effort for such a little, tiny thing, as if it were a little, tiny work of art.

Maybe it was one of a kind, made to order, like you'd find on Etsy. None of that stuff was cheap, though. You wouldn't carry it in your pocket like loose change.

An hour later, we got our first drunk driving accident, what Zelda called the omen for the weekend. Fortunately, it was a single—i.e., one car, driver only. Trying to get away from the state trooper chasing him, he'd aimed for the exit ramp and missed. I knew the statie, and not just because she came in at least once a week. Trooper Woodbine had performed all the roadside sobriety tests on me twice, and Breathalyzed me three times, just to make sure the device wasn't broken. I got the impression that even now, she suspected I'd somehow pulled a fast one. But at least she'd stopped giving me the stink-eye when I said hello; now her response was a curt, wordless nod, as if state police regulations said she couldn't get too friendly with anyone she'd ever arrested (which, for all I know, is true).

After the paramedics transferred the driver from the gurney to the bed in bay five, she handcuffed him to the frame and started her "paperwork" for the arrest, but on an iPad now instead of a clipboard. That was new. I wanted to ask her about it, but she frowned and made a shooing motion at me. Not being an idiot (anymore), I obeyed and found myself standing outside the closed curtains of the bay next door, which happened to be the doll man's.

There was a laminated PRIVACY PLEASE sign on the curtains now, but that wasn't what gave me pause. The drunk driver was pretty banged up—not as bad as some, or even as bad as he could have been—he'd had his seatbelt on, but there'd been no air bag. Not to mention how fast he'd been going (thirty miles an hour only seems slow until you hit something).

In short, he looked a lot worse than a guy who'd been in a collision with no seatbelt at all.

I peeked in at the still-unconscious doll man. They'd removed the collar, and the head of the bed was at a forty-five- degree angle now. A cardiac monitor was beeping business as usual, his blood pressure and pulse were about the same as mine at rest, and his pulse-ox reading was 95 percent. There weren't any alarms going off, which had to mean everything was okay. Except it wasn't.

It was his color. He hadn't gone yellow or gray, his lips weren't blue or brown or too red, but something was off. I glanced up at the fluorescent lights overhead; they weren't flickering or dimming, and I knew that if I checked a mirror I'd look as normally crappy as I always did in any public restroom or department store changing room. It wasn't the lousy lighting.

Hell with it; I slipped into the bay.

I tried to picture how he'd looked when Zelda had been cutting off his clothing, what injuries he'd had, but all I could remember was a little blood on his shirt and trousers. Peeking under his gown was a line I'd never cross; I couldn't even bring myself to push up his sleeve a little. What I could see of him seemed to be unhurt. There was a scrape on the inside of his right forearm, but it looked old, from before the accident. No injuries to his face, either.

Well, car accidents are like that—one person walks away with barely a scratch while the person in the next seat is so mangled it has to be a closed-coffin service. This guy had barely a scratch, but he sure hadn't walked away. I wondered what would happen if he didn't wake up soon. (Well, I knew what would happen *around* him, depending on whether the unit secretary found his next-of-kin or whether they'd all been in the car with him.)

I took his hand and looked at his nail beds, although I couldn't remember what that was supposed to tell me, exactly. But his nails looked funny, too smooth and flat, like tabs glued onto his skin. His funny-colored skin. Which also *felt* funny—cool, waxy-oily, almost smooshy, like plastic on the verge of softening. Like one of those dolls that's supposed to feel like a real baby.

Or like a new kind of first-aid dummy?

The idea made the hair on the back of my neck prickle. A dummy with eyebrows and eyelashes, slight stubble on chin and upper lip, and pores on the nose. A perfectly human face . . . but, I realized finally, without any character lines or wrinkles. Greetings from Uncanny Valley.

Yeah, right. Even if some higher-up had signed off on bringing in a CPR doll as some kind of surprise test, Zelda wouldn't have let it go on taking up space and even if *she* had, Mrs. Beauchamp, the unit secretary, would have gone to Defcon 1. And for God's sake, since when did a cardiac monitor work on a CPR dummy? The only dummy here was me.

I bent down to look in his personal effects bag. There were two bags under the bed now—the second one held the rags that had once been his clothes. I took a look in the first one. Everything was there except the doll.

"What are you doing?" Zelda was peering in at me with a frown.

"I thought I heard him call out," I said.

She gave me the Eyebrow of Doom—one way up, one down.

"Or moan or something," I added unconvincingly. Court had turned me into the world's worst liar. Like "the truth, the whole truth, and nothing but the truth" was tattooed on my brain.

"The sign says, 'Privacy Please.' Should I cross out the 'please,' will that be easier to understand?"

"I thought I heard something. And then I saw his property bag—" I offered it to her. "Maybe someone was in here looking for something to steal."

Zelda looked weary. "Did you *see* someone in here looking for something to steal?"

"No, but maybe we should make sure everything's there." I pushed it at her again.

"Fine. You check." She started to leave.

"You should check with me," I said quickly. "Like a witness."

Now she groaned. "Damn, you community service kids *always* go all law-and-order on me." She grabbed the bag, rummaged through it for all of a second, and handed it back to me. "Everything's fine. Go check the coffee. *Lives—*"

"Everything *isn't* fine, the doll is missing."

"What doll?"

"The one that fell out of his pocket, remember? A perfect tiny little man."

Another Eyebrow of Doom. Two within minutes of each other; I was daring thin ice to get thinner. "Are you high?"

"No, I drove myself today and I never touch anything when I know I'm driving. At least one state trooper'll back me up on that." Also my parents, who were now locking the oregano in the liquor cabinet; it smelled like pot to them.

"Well, congratulations, but you still have a date with a court-ordered cup tomorrow. And don't give *me* a hard time," she added as I started to remind her I'd had a surprise spot-check on Tuesday. "When they say drop and squat, you say, 'You want fries with that?'"

I knew how my chilly probation officer would have reacted if I'd smarted off like that—i.e., not well—but I thought it was a hoot. Zelda was getting to like me, I thought, with what is probably the same kind of intense joy that makes a dog's tail wag. Today, Zelda, tomorrow, Trooper Woodbine. Then maybe I'd go for a real challenge: Judge Mankiller. If I were judged by the company I kept, then keeping company with a judge had to be instant win. I had no idea how to make friends with a state trooper, let alone a judge, but I'd think about that after I was sure I had Zelda in the bag.

Which was not the bag I was holding, I thought, as my gaze fell on the guy's belongings. Among the small jumble of items was a triple-A battery; just one. Weird.

Maybe the doll's head unscrewed so you could put it in and when you put the head back on, it completed the circuit—

Was this my brain now—fried sunny-side up with bacon and hash browns? Or had I always been this weird and I was only realizing it now because I was straight all the time?

I dropped the battery into the bag, shoved it back under his bed, and hurried off to the lounge just in time to catch Jackie putting the nearly empty pot back on the burner to fry. It was that old trick of trying to leave just enough coffee to avoid making a fresh pot.

They all kept doing that, and it made me nuts! These were people who knew science, who knew biology and chemistry and so, presumably, what would happen when you left a tiny amount of liquid in a large glass container on a hot burner. But it was like as soon as they touched the coffeepot, they forgot everything. I made a fresh pot and, not having mastered the Eyebrow of Doom, I had to settle for shaking my finger at her before I plumped down on the well-used plastic settee.

"Feet hurt?" Jackie asked, her brown features sympathetic.

"Actually, no," I said, perking up a bit as I showed her my new footwear. "Not since you tipped me off about these. I may never wear anything else for as long as I live."

"Wear what?" Zelda said from the doorway. "Never mind, I only care about coffee."

"Just made a fresh pot," I said.

"*Lives,*" she reminded me, and left.

That was my cue to find her cup, scrub it out, and fill. I was just getting to my feet when I remembered Jackie had been in bay six, too. "Hey, you haven't seen a doll around, have you?"

Jackie blinked at me. "A what?"

"A doll. A miniature man about this big—" I held my thumb and forefinger apart to show her.

Now she laughed. "There's a lot of those around. You'd be surprised how many."

"No," I said with exaggerated patience, "this was more like a figurine. It fell out of a guy's pocket while Zelda was cutting his clothes off. You were putting electrodes on him for the heart monitor at the time."

"Honey, you're gonna have to be a lot more specific or I can't help you." Jackie chuckled.

"It's okay, you did help," I told her, and went to find Zelda's coffee mug.

"Ask around," Jackie called after me. "Somebody might have picked it up."

Somebody had, right out of the guy's property bag, but they weren't about to admit it. On the other hand, I thought suddenly, someone else might have spotted them with it.

I told myself I was only being conscientious, not obsessing. On my first day, Zelda had said if anything went missing, no matter how small, I should report it, because it could mean a lot more had been stolen: thieves often grabbed up little things on their way in or out, she said, like impulse shoppers.

But this wasn't a case of someone swiping a picture frame off a desk, it was a patient theft. Patients always suspected the hospital staff of stealing. Janitors, orderlies, and nurses were usually first to be accused, but doctors weren't immune. The more valuable the missing item was, the higher up the food chain the accusations went, as if janitors only stole trinkets while doctors settled for nothing under three figures or twenty-four karats.

Volunteers, however, were prime suspects, especially any that happened to be doing community service. It wouldn't matter that I hadn't been sentenced for stealing—a criminal was a criminal.

With that in mind, I felt I had a responsibility to pursue the Case of The Missing Manikin.

"Why?" Maybe because I was handing her a fresh mug of coffee, Zelda didn't give me the full Eyebrow of Doom when I asked about the other people in the doll man's car, but one was already higher than the other. "You think you might know them?"

"No. Maybe. I don't know, I'm just cur—uh, wondering if they're okay."

"Uh-huh." She made a note on the patient chart she was holding. "Can you work while you're wondering? Dirty linen's piling up and bays need restocking. And then there's coffee. *Lives*, Oly."

"Got it," I said, and turned toward the nearest empty bay.

"And don't be snooping around; there're laws against violating patient privacy," she added. "*Oly*." I looked back at her; no Eyebrow of Doom, which was actually scarier. But all she said was, "And for God's sake, wear the gloves. That's what they're for."

She knew I hated the gloves. None of them fit right. My hands would get all sweaty and I'd end up with every finger stuck at a different level, and when I tried to push them into place, they'd tear. Everyone told me to use more powder; mixed with sweat and hand sanitizer, it made a weird sludge that gathered in the creases in my palms.

What bothered me the most, however, was not being able to feel things properly when I handled them; that actually creeped me out. But Zelda still had her eye on me, so I made a show of grabbing some out of a box on the nurses' station desk and pulling them on like a TV surgeon.

I went about gathering up used linen, wishing I'd paid more attention when the doll man had come in. The doll man—I hadn't even thought to look at his hospital bracelet for his name. What a genius I was, I thought, watching one of the doctors on duty follow Zelda into the doll man's bay.

The drunk driver in the bay next door was gone, bed and all, and so was Trooper Woodbine, probably to x-ray. It was the perfect spot for looking busy while I eavesdropped, or it would have been, except I couldn't hear much over the general noise. Then someone brought in a crying baby, and that was the only thing anyone could hear for quite a while.

Over the next hour, the baby finally stopped crying (uninsured ear infection), a possible coronary turned out to be an anxiety attack, and the drunk driver went for more x-rays, stolidly escorted by Trooper Woodbine, but the doll man remained unconscious in the bay with the curtains closed. I managed to sneak a quick peek at him from time to time. If he stirred even a little, it wasn't while I was looking. His color was still weird. More like a doll's than the doll. Which I still hadn't found.

"If you do find that contact lens," said Dr. Dreyfuss, catching me on my knees in the nurses' station, "I beg you, as a medical professional, do *not* lick it and put it back in your eye."

I felt myself blushing as I got to my feet and brushed off my trousers. "I'm looking for something a patient lost. A little figurine." I showed him how small.

"Like a plastic Jesus?" He smiled wryly.

"No, more like a little action figure."

He closed the file he was holding, put it in a tray, and picked up another. "Some kid stick it up his nose?"

"No, it belongs to an MVA who came in earlier."

"Probably still in the wreckage."

"No, it disappeared out of his property bag."

His interest switch had already flicked off. "Well, good luck," he murmured absently and walked away. I decided to check the coffeepot.

To my surprise, the unit secretary was in the lounge with her shoes off and her feet up. Mrs. Beauchamp was in that age group I found hardest to gauge: definitely older than my parents but not quite old enough to be *their* parents. Her curly salt-and-pepper hair hugged her perfectly shaped head. She was never rude or mean to anyone, but she wasn't what you'd call sociable, either—all business, no nonsense. We didn't interact much but when we did, she treated me like another adult, which made me a little nervous.

"If you tell anyone where I am," she said casually, "I'll kill you."

You couldn't make a martini that dry in the Sahara, as my mother would have put it. "Your secret's safe with me," I assured her. The carafe had about a cup left, but I washed it out and made a fresh pot anyway, before anyone had a chance to drink most of it and fry the residue.

"The coffee's never been so good," Mrs. Beauchamp said, watching me load the filter. "How long are you here for?"

"Another four months. Then I have to get a paying job till I start college. I delayed my enrollment a semester." I didn't explain, figuring she knew.

"Avoid Starbucks. They'll just ruin you." She sat up and put her shoes back on. "I'd better go back before it occurs to someone to look here."

I blurted the question out without thinking. "Mrs. Beauchamp, you haven't seen a doll lying around, have you?"

She paused with one fist on the settee cushion, about to push herself to her feet. "Some kid lose it?"

"No, it's not a toy. It looks made to scale." I described it to her.

"Really." She sat back, looking surprised. "How about *that.*"

I was even more astonished. "You've seen it?"

"Not the one you're talking about," she said, her brown face thoughtful. "But I've seen this sort of thing before. It's very old. And *very* private."

I tried but I couldn't figure out a polite way to say, *WTF?* "I put it in a property bag with the rest of his stuff," I said, "but when I went back and looked later, it was gone. I don't know if it fell out or someone took it or . . ." I shrugged, feeling stupid.

Mrs. Beauchamp seemed not to notice my brain fail. "Show me."

We went out to the ER and I started to take her over to bay number six, where the curtains were still closed.

"Thank you, I'll handle it." She looked through a stack of folders on the nurses' station desk, found what she wanted, and tucked the others under her arm while she scanned the contents, her glasses so far down her nose I thought they'd fall off. Then she looked up, saw me, and blinked, as if she were surprised I was still there. "Thank you," she said again, a bit more emphatically. "You may resume your duties."

I walked off like I was going somewhere specific. After a few steps, I patted my pockets pretending I'd forgotten something, and turned around just as she slipped behind the drawn curtains.

I hurried toward number five but just before I got there, a porter brought the drunk driver back with Trooper Woodbine in tow. I changed course, noticing the man had definitely gone downhill since his arrival. Jackie hooked him up to a cardiac monitor while another doctor on duty closed the curtains. I heard the click of handcuffs being removed before Trooper Woodbine parked herself on a chair just outside, her expression composed and neutral.

I thought number seven was empty and barged in on a nurse-practitioner talking with two men, one sitting on the bed in his street clothes with his shirt open and the other holding his hand and looking very worried. The conversation cut off as they looked at me in surprise.

"Is there something you need?" Cherie, the nurse-practitioner, asked, giving me a subtler but no less serious Eyebrow of Doom.

"I'm sorry, I thought I heard someone call me," I lied, turned to flee, and nearly knocked Mrs. Beauchamp over as she emerged from the doll man's bay.

"Do you mind? I'm walking here, thank you," she said. I knew that she meant it to be funny, but it only made me feel more conspicuously weird. Trooper Woodbine was gazing at me the way I imagined she watched the road from her hunting blind. I looked around guiltily, half-expecting Zelda to suddenly pounce on me for taking up space.

But it was Dr. Dreyfuss who materialized behind me. "Haven't found your doll yet?"

"It's not *my* doll," I said. He chuckled sympathetically and patted my shoulder, possibly because he thought I'd said *Midol*.

Mrs. Beauchamp gave me a Look over the top of her glasses. "Have you got the whole ER hunting for dolls?"

"Just the one," I said, wincing.

"Are you still going on about that doll? Or did you lose another one?" Jackie said. "Never mind. Tell me after you get back from the canteen. The sandwich order should be ready by now." She pushed a list wrapped around some bills into my hand and aimed me at the elevators.

The canteen wasn't that far away, but I had to wait because they hadn't finished making all the sandwiches. Tri-County didn't use a catering service so you could specify things like no mayo or extra tomatoes, and everybody did. Normally I wouldn't have minded—they usually had a volunteer on the cash register and another to help out behind the counter; we'd compare notes about our respective days or share some gossip.

But the volunteers had left and the place was on reduced nighttime service, so diversions were hard to come by. Someone had left a newspaper on a table but only the sports section; to add insult to injury, someone had already done the Sudoku, in *ink*. I checked out what flavors of yogurt were left in the cooler—raspberry, boysenberry, and mango, the usual unholy three—before I resorted to browsing limp pages of jargony headlines, grainy photos, and undecipherable tables. It being baseball season, both my parents stared at this stuff like it was holy writ. They had failed to pass the gene on, however; to me, it was opaque and not the least bit intriguing.

When I finally got back to the ER, I was surprised to find I hadn't even been gone twenty minutes. The drunk driver was still in number five and not looking any better. Trooper Woodbine had moved to a row of seats on the other side of the nurses' station, where she was sitting in a more relaxed posture with her right ankle on her left knee and gazing at something on her iPad. The privacy sign was still on the doll man's drawn curtains; number seven was vacant.

Better make sure it was fully stocked, I thought, pausing on my way to peek through a gap in the doll man's curtains to see how he was doing.

The bed was empty and his gown was on the floor.

I stared, unsure what to do. Zelda had told me that sometimes frightened patients (bad trips or psychiatric cases) would try to "escape" or start to wander off if they were disoriented (head injuries or old people) but they'd never actually lost anyone.

Which would make this an instance of the fabled first time, I thought. Should I run around alerting everyone, including the other patients, or find Zelda and whisper in her ear?

Instead I slipped behind the curtain without a word to anyone.

I looked around, but the doll man wasn't braced ninja-style in a corner up near the ceiling or perched on the crash cart while he jerry-rigged a weapon out of gauze pads, intubation equipment, and hand sanitizer. After reflecting briefly on the shortage of action sequences in my life, I tiptoed over to the gown on the floor and surprised the hell out of myself by daring to pick it up. I held it between thumb and forefinger and tried to avoid breathing on it while I looked for—well, I didn't know what, but I found nothing. No rips, no marks, and no blood, nor sweat nor tears. As I dropped it on the bed, I saw the bags with his personal effects were still underneath.

Could the doll man really have left unclothed, unfettered, and unnoticed?

He must have been sent for tests, maybe in a wheelchair if he'd woken up, and someone decided he needed a change of gown before he left; that was all. I hadn't been around to whisk away used linens with my usual efficiency, and the gown had fallen on the floor. I remembered something Dr. Dreyfuss had said, about reminding one of the new residents that when you heard hoofbeats, you should expect horses, not zebras. Maybe I should do that one in needlepoint, I thought as I crouched down to check the property bags under the bed.

The doll was still missing. Then it occurred to me that I'd never checked the other bag with the remains of his clothes. I turned to reach for it and froze.

Dr. Dreyfuss hadn't mentioned what to do in case of zebras.

❦

I was looking side-on and he had his back to me, so it took me a few seconds to realize he was in the fetal position in the corner behind the bed. And he was curled up *really* tightly—his upper back and shoulders were stretched so wide, it made me think of bats.

Had he crawled back there to die? I watched carefully for almost a minute and still couldn't tell if he was breathing. Then I saw something move under the skin near his right shoulder blade, like a tiny muscle flexing.

"Excuse me, sir," I whispered. "Are you all right? Do you need any help?"

He gave no sign he'd heard me. I got to my feet and raised the head of the bed higher so I could look behind it more easily.

"Excuse me, sir," I whispered again. "Should I get—" My voice died in my throat.

I saw him quite clearly, but my brain tried to send it back for a refund. The images were contradictory: something melting, something growing, something congealing, something tightening. Utterly natural, but not my nature.

Very old, and *very* private.

As soon as I looked away, I felt relieved, as if the sight of him had been a physical strain. I waited a bit before taking another look—or trying to. My eyes didn't want to focus.

I was supposed to leave my cell in my locker, but most of the time I forgot and just kept it on "silent." It wasn't a smartphone, but it did have a camera.

Very private.

The camera wasn't that good anyhow, I thought, putting the cell back in my pocket without using it.

I was barely out of the bay when someone walked into me.

"Where've you been?" Zelda demanded. "I've been looking all over."

"P-picking up sandwiches." As relieved as I was that she hadn't caught me, I was also a little unnerved.

"Took you long enough. Did you have to make them yourself?" She turned me around, and for a moment I thought she was going to push me back into the doll man's bay. Instead she pointed at an empty bay farther down. "And don't forget to put on gloves,"

I had to tell her about the doll man, I thought, glancing at the closed curtains. She followed my gaze and gave me the Eyebrow of Doom.

Things got busier as they always did—two more DWIs, several un-insureds, three elderly people in various states of befuddlement, and a non-driving drunk in the waiting room who became Meltdown of the Week by stealing a woman's crutches and trying to kill one of the vending machines with them. Plus it seemed like everybody had to puke at least once, regardless of what was wrong with them, like they'd all gotten a memo saying it was Vomit Day. It wasn't as bad as norovirus, but it did keep me too busy to get another look at number six. By the time it occurred to me to talk to Mrs. Beauchamp again, she'd already left.

I grabbed the first nurse I found at the desk, which happened to be Hollis. "I think there's something very wrong with the patient in number six," I said.

"He wouldn't be here if there weren't." The big man chuckled.

"No, this is different. He's all . . ." I fumbled for a moment. "Weird."

"Uh-huh." Hollis waited for me to elaborate.

"I went in there and . . ." My voice died and I couldn't bring it back. Hollis looked less patient and started to move away.

I caught his arm. "He was . . ." My voice started to fail again, and I cleared my throat forcefully. "You should look," I croaked.

"That's what I'm gonna do," he plucked my hand gently out of the crook of his arm, "if you let me."

He went into number six and I waited to see what would happen, whether Hollis would call for someone to help him or push the alarm or come out again and ask me why I hadn't said something sooner. He'd probably ask me that anyway, and I dreaded it because I had no justification.

Unbidden, Mrs. Beauchamp's voice came to me: *Very old, and very private.* And then Zelda's: *There're laws against violating patient privacy.*

Sure were; all kinds of laws for all kinds of patients. Your garden-variety horses were covered by legal statutes. Zebras, on the other hand, had something else, like a muffler to keep things quiet. So as not to scare the horses.

Part of me was thinking I should probably never get high again so my brain could straighten out, but a larger part was thinking that for once, I actually had a clue.

Hollis came out of the bay and looked over at me with an expression that said I was out of my mind. *What did you see?* I thought at him as he stopped to talk to Zelda. For a moment I was afraid he was telling her I was out of my mind, but she didn't turn to give me the Eyebrow of Doom. She found a folder on the desk, and they were looking at it together when the elderly woman with the broken hip and the loudly upset daughter came in. It was the perfect distraction.

The doll man was back on the bed with the sheet pulled up. Someone had put another gown on him but though his arms were in the sleeves, it wasn't tied. He still wasn't awake, but he looked a lot better; his color had gone back to a human shade.

"Excuse me, sir?" I whispered.

He didn't stir, but I could see his chest rising and falling. My gaze fell on the bracelet around his right wrist. I figured I might as well find out what his name was so I didn't have to keep calling him "the doll man."

His skin felt like normal human skin, too. As I turned his arm over, his hand opened and the doll rolled out onto the sheet.

It wasn't the same doll.

For a long moment I could only stare. The clothes were identical but they didn't fit as well on the stiff little plastic body. The face did have a lot of detail to it, and the eyes looked almost three-dimensional but didn't open and close. The paper the hair was pasted on had curled away from the head a little.

It was always like this, wasn't it? said a sneaky little voice in my mind. *You've just been having a weird little fantasy because you're bored. And because you're a teenager all hopped up on hormones, and your brain is fried sunny-side up with bacon and a side of brown hash.*

I wished I'd taken the photo. Except it probably would have looked like an out-of-focus blob because my cell phone camera really did suck.

Just to be sure, though, I looked through the property bags; no other doll. Then Zelda came in.

"I thought I told you—" She did a double take. "Damn, I was starting to think you were imagining things. Where'd you find it?"

"In his hand."

Zelda gave a small laugh. "The one place I guess you didn't think to look."

"He was unconscious—"

"Or not." She nodded at the wall: THIS PATIENT CAN HEAR EVERY-THING YOU SAY.

She picked up the doll, looked it over, and tucked it into his hand before ushering me out. "*Now* will you leave the poor man alone?"

"I didn't do anything—" I cut off. There was no arguing with the Eyebrow. "Lives, right?"

"Thank God, you don't have amnesia."

"Zelda, do you remember what Dr. Dreyfuss said about horses and zebras?"

She gave a short, surprised laugh. "What about it?"

"What if zebras actually do show up?"

"Then they're uninsured zebras, and if we don't treat 'em, nobody else will. Anything else I can help you with?"

"I guess not. I know, I know, lives," I added, heading for the lounge.

I was on my way home when I realized that I'd forgotten to check the doll man's bracelet for his name. Of course, he was long gone by the next day, and nobody remembered whether he'd been admitted or discharged, and it wasn't any of my business anyway. I didn't think I'd have the nerve to ask Mrs. Beauchamp how she knew about this very old, *very* private whatever-it-was—some people have the Eyebrow of Doom, some people *are* the Eyebrow of Doom—but after a while, it bothered me so much, I had to or go nuts. Fortunately, I found her in the lounge again and when she threatened to kill me, I made a joke about making a deal for some information; I didn't even have to specify what.

"I didn't think you'd have the nerve," she said, looking at me sidelong through half-closed eyes. "Are you familiar with poppets?"

I hesitated. "I guess you don't mean puppets?"

"How about voodoo dolls?"

"That was a voodoo doll?" I said, surprised.

"Don't be ridiculous. A voodoo doll is a crude effigy made with someone's hair or nail clippings. Believers think they can use it to cast spells."

"Yeah, by sticking pins in it," I added.

"No, that's acupuncture."

I wasn't sure if she was joking or not. "So, what then—that was some kind of reverse voodoo doll?" I sat forward a little and lowered my voice. "I saw him. On the floor."

"Some forms of life can regrow limbs, some have protective shells, some can change color for camouflage, some shed their skins. And some hibernate to wait out unfavorable conditions."

I shook my head, not understanding.

"Everything and everyone has particular resources for healing or regenerating, a way of protecting or preserving the undamaged part of themselves."

"Are you saying the doll was—"

"I'm not saying a thing. I told you before: very old, very private."

"How do you get a . . . one of those? Do *you* have one?" I asked.

Mrs. Beauchamp sighed noisily. "You're a *very* nosy girl. I'm going back to work." She sat up and put her shoes on.

"You do, don't you?" I said. "Who else knows—Zelda? Dr. Dreyfuss? Or is the whole ER in on it?"

She shook her head, laughing a little like I was talking nonsense. "You could ask them," she said, standing up and straightening her skirt. "But they'll probably start testing your urine a lot more often, and maybe your blood, too." She smiled at my expression. "Never mess with the unit secretary. And don't go poking your nose into things that aren't your business, especially when it has to do with hospital patients. There are laws about that, and they won't just give you *more* community service."

                                   ❧

The next week, they started loaning me out to other areas of Tri-County. Judge Mankiller had signed off on it and even sent me a personal note congratulating me on being such a helpful and trustworthy volunteer that the hospital felt I could be "promoted" to a position with more responsibilities. I still reported to Zelda, but some weeks I spent half my time escorting visitors or helping with meals in the geriatric ward, where I'm pretty certain no one had a doll.

I thought about continuing to volunteer afterward, maybe some nights or weekends, but working full-time really took it out of me. Plus I was sure Mrs. Beauchamp would only have to take one look at me to know I was working at Starbucks (they were hiring).

I also didn't want her or anyone else in the ER to see the doll. I found the basic figure in a hobby/crafts shop and painted it myself, which was really hard. It's no work of art, but it'll pass; the hair hides a lot. The clothes were easier; I cut down an outfit from one of Barbie's little friends, and while I'm not Dior for dolls, I didn't do too badly.

No, I'm not so far gone that I think I can become a zebra just by painting stripes on myself, so to speak. I just keep it in my pocket and every so often, I let people get a glimpse of it: I "drop" it and pick it up quickly, or I let it poke out of my pocket for a few moments. I figure sooner or later one of them will notice and give me the secret handshake or something. Then I can get the true story.

And, I hope, a lot more. If only Zelda hadn't walked in on me when I found the doll in the guy's hand—I don't know how long it'll take to find the real thing, but I'd rather it was before I get too much older. I mean, if I really could get restored, it might as well be to the best possible form, right?

There Is No Place for Sorrow in the Kingdom of the Cold

by Seanan McGuire

The air in the shop smelled of talcum, resin, and tissue, with a faint, almost indefinable undertone of pine and acid-free paper. I walked down the rows of collectible Barbies and pre-assembled ball-jointed dolls to the back wall, where the supplies for the serious hobbyists were kept. Pale, naked bodies hung on hooks, while unpainted face plates stared with empty sockets from behind their plastic prisons. Clothing, wigs, and eyes were kept in another part of the shop, presumably so it would be harder to keep track of how much you were spending. As if anyone took up ball-jointed dolls thinking it would be a cheap way to pass the time. We all knew that we were making a commitment that would eat our bank accounts from the inside out.

I looked from empty face to empty face, searching for the one that called to me, that whispered, *I could be the vessel of your sorrows.* It would have been easier if I'd been in a position to cast my own; resin isn't easy to work with compared to vinyl or wax, but it's possible, if you have the tools, and the talent, and the time. I had the tools and the talent. Only time was in short supply.

Father would have hated that. He'd always said time was the one resource we could never acquire more of—unlike inspiration, or hope, or even misery, it couldn't be bottled or preserved, and so we had to spend it carefully, measuring it out where it would do the most good. I could have been making beautiful dolls, both for my own needs and to enrich the world. Instead, I spent my days in a sterile office, doing only as much as I needed to survive and stay connected to the Kingdom of the Cold.

My head ached as I looked at the empty, waiting faces. I had waited too long again. Father did an excellent job when he made me, but my heart was never intended to hold as much emotion as a human's could. "Perfection is for God," he used to say. "We will settle for the subtly flawed, and the knowledge that when we break, we return home." Because we were flawed—all of us—we had to bleed off the things we couldn't contain: sorrow and anger and joy and loneliness, packing them carefully in shells of porcelain, resin, and bone. I needed the bleed. It would keep me from cracking, and each vessel I filled would be another piece of my eventual passage home.

Times have changed. People live longer, but that hasn't translated into longer childhoods. Once I could have paid my passage to the Kingdom just by walking through town and seeing people embracing my creations, offering up their own small, unknowing tithes of delight and desolation. Those days are over. Father was the last of us to walk in Pandora's grace, and I do what I must to survive.

A round-cheeked face with eyes that dipped down at the corners and lips that formed a classic cupid's-bow pout peeked from behind the other boxes. I plucked it from the shelf, hoisting it in my hand, feeling the weight and the heart of it. Yes: This was my girl, or would be, once I had gathered the rest of her. The hard part was ahead of me, but the essential foundation was in my hand.

It didn't take long to find the other pieces I needed: the body, female, pale and thin but distinctly adult, from the curve of the hips to the slight swell of the breasts. The wig, white as strawberry flowers, and the eyes, red as strawberries. I had clothing that would fit her. There was already a picture forming in my mind of a white and red girl, lips painted just so, cheeks blushed in the faintest shades of cream.

Willow appeared as I approached the counter, her eyes assessing the contents of my basket before she asked, "New project, dear?"

"There's always a new project." I put the basket down next to the register. "It's been a long couple of weeks at work. I figured I deserved a treat."

Willow nodded in understanding. The women who co-owned my favorite doll shop were in it as much for the wholesale prices on their own doll supplies as to make a profit: I, and customers like me, were the only reason the place could keep its doors open. I prayed that would last as long as Father did. I couldn't shop via mail order—there was no way of knowing whether I was getting the right things, and I couldn't work with materials that wouldn't work with me. I'd tried a few times while I was at college, repainting Barbie dolls with shaking hands and a head that felt like it was full of bees. I could force inferior materials to serve as keys to the Kingdom, but the results were never pretty, and the vessels I made via brute force were never good enough. They couldn't hold as much as I needed them to.

My total came to under two hundred dollars, which wasn't bad for everything I was buying. I grabbed a few small jars of paint from the impulse rack to the left of the register. Willow, who had argued Joanna into putting the rack there, grinned. "Will there be anything else today?"

"No, that's about it." I signed my credit card slip and dropped the receipt into the bag. "I'll see you next week."

"About that . . ."

I froze. "What about it?"

"Well, you know this weekend is our big get-together, right?" Willow smiled ingratiatingly. "A bunch of our regulars are bringing in their kids to share with each other, and I know you must have some absolutely gorgeous children at home, with all the things you buy."

I managed not to shudder as I pasted a smile across my face. The tendency of some doll people to refer to their creations as "children" has always horrified me, especially given my situation. Children live. Children breathe. Their dolls . . . didn't. "I can't," I said, fighting to sound sincere. "I'm supposed to visit my father at the nursing home. Maybe next time, okay?"

"That would be nice." Willow barely hid her disappointment. I grabbed my bag and fled, and this time the bell above the door sounded like victory. I had made my escape. Now all I had to do was keep on running.

※

The cat met me at the apartment door, meowing and twining aggressively around my ankles, like tripping me would magically cause her food dish to refill. Maybe she thought it would; it's hard to say, with cats.

"Wait your turn, Trinket." I shut and locked the door before walking across the room—dodging the cat all the way—and putting my bag down on the cluttered mahogany table that served as my workspace. Trinket stopped when I approached the table, sitting down and eyeing it mistrustfully. The tabletop had been the one forbidden place in the apartment since she was a kitten. She badly wanted to be up there—all cats desire forbidden things—but she was too smart to risk it.

The half-painted faces of my current projects stared at me from their stands. Some—Christina, Talia, Jonathan—had bodies, and Christina was partially blushed, giving her a beautifully human skin tone. Others, like Charity the bat-girl, were nothing more than disembodied heads.

"I'm sorry, guys," I said to the table in general. "You're going to need to wait a little longer. I have a rush job." The dolls stared at me with blank eyes and didn't say anything. That was a relief.

Trinket followed me to the kitchen, where I fed her a can of wet cat food, stroked her twice, and discarded my shoes. I left my jacket on the bookshelf by the door, hanging abandoned off a convenient wooden outcropping. I was halfway into my trance when I sat down at the table, reaching for the bag, ready at last. The tools I needed were in place, waiting for me. All I needed to do was begin.

So I began.

⚶

The doll maker's art is as ancient and revered as any other craft, for all that it's been relegated to the status of "toymaker" in this modern age. A maker of dolls is so much more than a simple toymaker. We craft dreams. We craft vessels. We open doorways into the Kingdom of the Cold, where frozen faces look eternally on the world, and do not yearn, and do not cry.

I learned my craft at my father's knee, just as he'd learned from his father, and his father from his mother. When the time comes, when my father dies, I'll be expected to teach my own child. Someone has to be the gatekeeper; someone has to be the maker of the keys. That was the agreement Carlo Collodi made with Pandora, who began our family line when she needed help recapturing the excess of emotion she had loosed into the world. We will do what must be done, and we will each train our replacement, and the doll maker's art will endure, keeping the doors to the Kingdom open.

I fixed the face I'd purchased from Willow to the stand and began mixing my colors. I wanted to preserve its wintry whiteness, but I needed it to be a living pallor, the sort of thing that looked eerie but not impossible. So I brushed the thinnest of pinks onto her cheeks and around the edges of her hairline, using an equally thin wash of blue and gray around the holes that would become her eyes, until they seemed to be sunken sockets, more skeletal in color than they'd ever been in their pristine state. I painted her lips pale at the edges and darkening as I moved inward, leaving the center of her mouth gleaming red as a fresh-picked strawberry. I added a spray of freckles to the bridge of her nose, using the same shade of pink as the edges of her lips.

She was lovely. She'd be lovelier when she was done, and so I reached for her body and kept going.

Somewhere around midnight, between the third coat of paint and the first careful restyling of the wig that would be her hair, I blacked out, falling into the dreaming doze that sometimes took me when I worked too long on the borders between this world and the Kingdom of the Cold. My hands kept moving, and time kept passing, and when I woke to the sound of my cell phone's alarm ringing from my jacket pocket, the sun had risen, and a completed doll sat in front of me, her hands folded demurely in her lap, as if she was awaiting my approval.

Her face was just as I'd envisioned it in the store: pale and wan, but believably so, with eyes that almost matched her lips gazing out from beneath her downcast lashes. I must have glued them in just before I woke up; the smell of fixative still hung in the air. Her hair was a cascade of snow, and her dress was the palest of possible pinks. She was barefoot, and her only ornamentation was a silver strawberry charm on a chain around her neck. She was finished, and she was perfect, and she was just in time.

"Your name is Strawberry," I said, reaching out to take her hands between my thumbs and forefingers. "I have called you into being to be a vessel for my sadness, for there is no place for sorrow in the Kingdom of the Cold. Do you accept this burden, little girl, so newly made? Will you serve this role for me?"

Everything froze. Even the clocks stopped ticking. This was where I would learn whether I'd chosen my materials correctly; this was where I would learn if they would serve me true. Then, with a feeling of rightness that was akin to finding a key that fits a lock that has been closed for a hundred years, something clicked inside my soul, and the sorrows of the past few weeks flowed out of me, finding their new home in the resin body of my latest creation.

It's no small thing, pouring human-size sorrow into a toy-size vessel. Sorrow is surprisingly malleable, capable of adjusting its shape to fit the box that holds it, but it fights moving from one place to another, and it has thorns. Sorrow is a bramble of the heart and a weed of the mind, and this sorrow was deeply rooted. It held a hundred small slights, workdays where things refused to go according to plan, cups of coffee that were too cold and buses that came late. It also held bigger, wider things, like my meeting with Father's case supervisor, who had shown me terrible charts and uttered terrible words like "state budget cuts" and "better served by another placement." Father couldn't handle being moved again, not when he was just starting to remember his surroundings from day to day, and I couldn't handle the stress or expense of moving him. Not now, not when I was already out of vacation time and patience. Lose my job, lose the nursing homes. Lose the nursing homes, and face the choice so many of my ancestors had faced: whether to share my space with a broken vessel who no longer knew how to reach the Kingdom, or whether to break the last dolls binding him to this world, freeing their share of his sorrow and opening his doorway to the Kingdom one final, fatal time.

I could send him home. No one would call it murder, but I would always know what I had done.

It was a hard, brutal concept, one that had no place in the modern world, but I had to consider it, because Father had always told me that one day it would be my choice to make. Life or death, parent or duty—me or him. And I wasn't ready to decide. So I poured it all into the doll I had crafted with my own two hands, and Strawberry, darling Strawberry, drank it to the very last drop. I couldn't have asked for anything more than what she offered, and when I felt the click again, the key turning and the doorway closing, I had become an empty vessel. My sorrows were gone, bled out into the doll with the strawberry eyes.

"Thank you," I murmured, and stood. I carried her across the room to a shelf of girl dolls who looked nothing like her, yet all seemed somehow to be family to one another: There was some intangible similarity in their expressions and posture. They all contained a measure of sadness, decanted from me through the Kingdom and into them over the course of these past three years. I set Strawberry among her sisters, adjusting her skirt and the position of her hands until she was just so and exactly right, as if she had always been there.

Then, light of heart and step, I turned and walked toward my bedroom. It was time to get ready for work.

❧

The day passed in a stream of tiny annoyances and demands, as days at the company where I worked as an office manager so often did.

"Marian, do you have that report ready?"

"Marian, is the copy machine fixed yet?"

"Marian, we're out of coffee."

I weathered them all with a smile on my face. I felt like I could handle any challenge. I always felt that way right after I opened a channel to the Kingdom. People like my father and I used to be revered as surgeons, the doll makers who came to town and helped people remove the parts of themselves that they couldn't handle anymore. The bad memories, the pain, the sorrow. Now he was a senile old man fading away by inches and I was a woman with a strange, expensive hobby, but that didn't change what we'd been designed to do. It didn't close the doorway.

"Hi, Marian."

The sound of Clark's voice wrenched me out of the payroll system and sent me into a state of chilly panic, my entire body going tense and cold with the sudden stress of living. *No, no, no,* I thought, and raised my eyes. *Yes, yes, yes,* said reality, because there was Clark, useless ex-boyfriend and even more useless coworker, standing with his arms draped across the edge of my half-cubicle like I'd invited him to be there, like he was some sort of strange workplace beautification project gone horribly wrong.

"Hello, Clark," I said, as coolly as I could. "Is there something I can help you with?"

"You can tell me why you're not answering my calls," he said. "Did I do something wrong? I know you said you didn't want to be serious. I didn't think that meant cutting me out entirely."

"Please don't make me call HR," I said, glancing around to be sure no one was listening. "I said I didn't want to see you socially anymore. I meant it."

"Is this because I said your doll collection was childish and weird? Because it is, but I can adjust, you know? Lots of people have weirder hobbies. My little sister used to collect Beanie Babies. She was, like, twelve at the time, but it's the same concept, right?"

I ground my teeth involuntarily, feeling a stab of pain from the crown on my left rear molar. I had sliced half of that tooth off with a hot knife when I opened my first doorway to the Kingdom. Early sacrifices had to hurt more than later ones to be effective. "No, it's not," I said stiffly. "I told you I didn't want to talk about this. I definitely don't want to talk about it at work."

"You won't take my calls, you won't meet me for coffee, so where else are we supposed to talk about it? You haven't left me anywhere else."

He looked so confident in his answer, like he had found the perfect way to get me to go out with him again. I wanted to slap him across his smug, handsome face. I knew better. I flexed my hands, forcing them to stay on my desk, and asked, "What do you want me to say, Clark? That I'll meet you for coffee so we can have a talk about why we're never going to date again, and why I'll report you to HR for harassment if you don't stop bothering me?"

"Sounds great." He flashed the toothy smile that had initially convinced me it would be a good idea to go out with him. I should have known better, but he was so handsome, and I'd been so lonely. I'd just wanted someone to spend a little time with. Was that so wrong?

No. Everything human wants to be loved, and wants the chance to love someone else. The only thing I did wrong was choosing Clark.

I swallowed a sigh and asked, "Does tonight work for you?" Better to do it while I was still an empty vessel. If I waited for the end of the week, I'd have to pull another all-nighter and add another girl to my shelf before I could endure his company. That would be bad. Not only would the cost of materials eat a hole in my bank account that I couldn't afford right now, but the strain of opening a second doorway so soon after the first would be . . . inadvisable. I could do it, and had done it in the past. That didn't make it a good idea.

"So what, first you play hard to get and now you're trying to rush me? I thought you said you didn't like games." His smile didn't waver. "Tonight's just fine. Pick you up at seven?"

"I'd rather meet you there," I said.

"Ah, but you don't know where we're going." Clark winked, pushing himself away from the wall of my cubicle. "Wear something nice." He turned and walked down the hall before I could frame a reply, the set of his shoulders and the cant of his chin implying that he really thought he'd won.

I groaned, dropping my head into my hands. He thought he'd won because he *had*. I was going out with him again. "What the hell is wrong with me?" I muttered.

My computer didn't answer.

❀

The bell rang at 7:20 p.m.—Clark, making me wait the way he always had, like twenty minutes would leave me panting for his arms. I put down the wig cap I'd been rerooting and walked to the door, wiping stray rayon fibers off my hands before opening it and glaring at the man outside.

Clark took in my paint-stained jeans and plain gray top, his jovial expression fading into a look that almost matched mine. He was wearing a suit, nicer than anything he ever put on for work, and enough pomade in his hair to make him smell like a Yankee Candle franchise. "I thought I told you to put on something nice," he said.

"I thought I told you I was willing to meet you for coffee," I shot back. "Last time I checked, the dress code at Starbucks was 'no shirt, no shoes, no service.' I have a shirt and shoes. I think I'll be fine."

Clark continued to glower for a moment before shouldering his way past me into the apartment.

"Hey!" I yelped, making a futile grab for his arm. It was already too late: He was in my living room, turning slowly as he took in all the dolls that had joined my collection since the last time he'd been here, some three months previous. I tried not to open a doorway to the Kingdom more than once a week, but sometimes it was hard to resist the temptation, especially when I had more than one trouble to decant. Dolls like Strawberry held sorrow, while others held different emotions—anger, loneliness, even hope, and love, and joy. Positive emotions took longer to grow back and had to be decanted less frequently, but they were represented all the same.

Clark's examination took about two minutes before he focused back on me, disdain replaced by pity. "This is why you broke up with me?" he asked. "I mean, you said it was because of the dolls, but I thought that was just a crappy excuse, you know? The weird-chick equivalent of 'I have to wash my hair on Saturday night.' But you meant it. You like plastic people better than you like real ones. There's something wrong with you."

"My dolls aren't plastic," I said automatically, before I realized I was falling back into the same destructively defensive patterns that had defined our brief relationship. I glared at him, shutting the door before Trinket could get any funny ideas about making a run for the outside world. "You want to have this talk? Fine. Yes, I chose my dolls over you. Unlike you, they never tell me I'd be pretty if I learned how to do something with my hair. Unlike you, they don't criticize me in public and then say they were just kidding. And unlike you, they shut up when I tell them to."

"You really are a crazy bitch." He strode across the living room, grabbing the first thing that caught his eye—pretty little Strawberry in her mourning gown. His hand all but engulfed her body. "You need to learn how to focus on real things, Marian, or you're going to be alone forever."

"You put her down!" I launched myself at him as if he weren't a foot taller and fifty pounds heavier than I was. I was reaching for Strawberry, trying to snatch her out of his hand, when his fist caught me in the jaw and sent me sprawling.

I'd never been punched in the face before. Everything went black and fuzzy. I didn't actually pass out, but the next few minutes seemed like a slideshow or a Power Point presentation, and not like something that was really happening. Static picture followed static picture as I watched Clark stalk around my apartment, grabbing dolls off the shelves. When he couldn't hold any more he walked over to me, looking down, and said, "This is what you get."

He kicked me in the stomach, and then he was gone, taking my dolls with him, and I was alone. At some point, I came back to myself enough to start crying.

It didn't help.

❧

Trinket stuck her nose through the curtain of my hair and mewled, eyes wide and worried. I sniffled, wiping my eyes with the back of my hand, and sat up to pat her gently on the head. "He didn't hurt me that bad, Trinket. I'm okay. I'm okay."

I was lying to myself as much as I was lying to the cat: I might be many things, but I was distinctly *not* okay. I picked myself up from the floor inch by excruciating inch, finally turning to take stock of the damage.

It was greater than I'd feared. Fifteen dolls were missing—at least one from every shelf, as well as one of the unfinished dolls from my table. Relief washed over me when I saw that. At least not everything he'd taken was a weapon. Shame followed on relief's heels. He'd stolen fourteen full vessels, fourteen doorways into the Kingdom of the Cold, and I was relieved that it wasn't one more? What was the difference between fourteen and fifteen when you were talking about knives to the heart? Fourteen would be more than enough to kill. The only question was who.

If I was lucky, he'd accidentally kill himself, and all my troubles would end . . . but that might leave full vessels floating around the world outside, ready to be found by someone who didn't know what they were holding. Open a vessel improperly, and everything it contained would come flooding out. And there were many, many improper ways to open something that had been closed.

I wanted to go after him. I wanted to demand the return of my property, and I wanted to make him pay. I glanced to the remaining unfinished dolls, assessing the materials I had, automatically counting off the materials I'd need. Forcibly, I pulled myself away from that line of thinking. Revenge was satisfying, but it would be hard to explain if he had some sort of bizarre accident, and I'd already been reminded that I couldn't take him in a fair fight.

Hands shaking, I pulled out my cell phone and dialed the number for the police. When the dispatcher came on the line, voice calm and professional, I began to tell her what had happened.

I made it almost all the way through the explanation before I started to cry.

That night was one of the worst I'd had since Father started getting bad. We'd both known what his lapses in memory meant, but we'd denied it for as long as possible, he because he wasn't ready to go, me because I wasn't ready to be alone. Every keeper of the Kingdom eventually develops cracks. It's a natural consequence of being a vessel that's been emptied too many times. There's a reason we don't use the same doll more than once for anything other than the most basic and malleable emotions. That was the reason I couldn't make myself a new doll, one big enough to hold my shame and grief and feelings of violation. I'd emptied out my sorrow too recently. I was too fresh, scraped too raw, to do it again.

The officers who came in answer to my call were perfectly polite.

They took pictures of the empty spaces on my shelves and of the bruises on my face and stomach, and if they thought the number of dolls still in my apartment was funny, they had the grace not to laugh in front of me. Eventually, they left me with a card and a number to call if Clark came back, and the empty promise that they'd see what they could do about getting my stolen property back. One of them asked me, twice, about filing a restraining order. I refused both times.

I didn't sleep. All I could do was lie awake, staring at the ceiling and thinking about the dolls who had been entrusted to my care, now lost in the world with their deadly burdens of emotion. They were so fragile. They had to be if they were going to properly mirror the fragility of the human heart, and do the jobs that they were made for.

When morning came I rolled out of bed and dressed without paying attention to whether my clothes matched. My face hurt too much for me to bother with makeup, so I left it as it was, bruises like smeared paint on the side of my jaw and around the socket of my left eye, and exited the apartment with my head up and my thoughts full of nothing but vengeance.

A shocked hush fell over the office when I arrived. I ignored the people staring at me as I walked to my desk. Something white was trapped under the keyboard. I pulled it loose, only to gasp and drop it like it had scalded my fingers.

Strawberry's whisper of a dress fluttered to the floor, where it lay like an accusation. *You failed us*, it seemed to say. *You didn't protect. You didn't keep. You are no guardian.*

I clapped my hand over my mouth, ignoring the pain it awoke in my jaw, and fought the urge to vomit. Bit by bit, my stomach unclenched. I bent, picked up the dress, and walked calmly down the hall to the door with Clark's name on it. He had an office; I had a cubicle. He had a door with a nameplate; I had a piece of paper held up with thumbtacks. I should have known better than to let him buy me that first cup of coffee. Even if I didn't have that much sense, I should have known better than to let him take me out for dinner even once. I was a fool.

Foolishly, I raised my hand and knocked. Clark's voice, smooth as butter, called, "Come in."

I went in.

Clark was behind his desk, a broad piece of modern office furniture that was almost as large as my worktable at home, if not half as old or attractive. He looked . . . perfect. Every hair was in place, and his tailored suit hung exactly right on his broad, all-American shoulders. His eyes darted to the scrap of fabric in my hand, and he smiled. "I see you found my present."

"Where are my dolls, Clark?" I'd meant to be more subtle than that, to approach the question with a little more decorum. Father always tried to tell me you got more flies with honey than you did with vinegar, but he'd never been able to make the lesson stick, and the words burst out, hot with venom and betrayal. "You had no right to take them."

"And you had no right to call the police over a little lover's spat, but you did, didn't you?" The jovial façade dropped away, leaving the snake he'd always been staring out of his eyes. "I was going to give them back. As an apology, for losing my temper. I shouldn't have hit you, and I know that. But then the cops showed up at my apartment saying you'd filed a domestic violence complaint against me. I'm sure you can see why I didn't like that very much."

I stared at him. "I didn't file a domestic violence complaint against you, *Clark,* because you're not any part of my domestic life. I filed an assault charge. You didn't just hit me. You beat me down. Where are my dolls?"

His smile was a terrible thing. "I'm not a part of your domestic life. How would I know where your silly little toys ended up? As for your trumped-up charges, my lawyer will enjoy seeing yours in court. Now you might want to get out of my office before I tell HR that you're harassing me."

Wordlessly, I held up Strawberry's gown, daring him to say something that would deny that he was the one who'd left it on my desk.

"What, that? I found it in my car and thought you might want it back. You know how it is with grown women who play with dolls. They're just like children. Leaving their toys everywhere."

He sounded so smug, so sure of himself, that it was all I could do not to walk around the desk and snatch his eyes from his head. I kept my nails long and sharp, to make it easier to position delicate doll eyelashes and reach miniscule screws. I could have had his eye sockets bare and bleeding in a matter of seconds.

I balled my hands into fists. I was my father's daughter. I was the keeper of the Kingdom and the maker of the keys, and I would not debase myself with this man's blood.

"This isn't over," I said.

Clark smiled at me. "Actually, I'm pretty sure it is," he said. "Bye, now."

There was nothing else that I could do, and so I turned, Strawberry's dress still clutched in my hand like a talisman against the darkness that was rushing in on me, and I walked away.

The rest of the day crept by like it wanted me to suffer. My eyes drifted to Strawberry's dress every few seconds until I finally picked it up and shoved it into my purse, hoping that out of sight would equal out of mind. It didn't work as well as I'd hoped, but it made enough of a difference that I was able to complete my assigned work and sneak out the door fifteen minutes early. Thanks to Clark, I had lost track of fourteen filled vessels. I needed to find them, and that meant I needed help. There was only one place to go for that.

My father.

The Shady Pines Nursing Home was as nice a place to die as money could buy, with all the amenities a man who barely remembered himself from hour to hour could want. I had made sure of that. Even though I was keeping him alive past the point when he was ready to go, I wasn't going to make him suffer.

Part of what that money paid for was an understanding staff. When I presented myself at the front desk an hour after visiting hours, a long white box in my hands and a light layer of foundation over the bruises on my face, they didn't ask any questions; they looked at me and saw a dutiful daughter who had experienced something bad, and needed her father.

"He's having one of his good days, Miss Collodi," said the aide who walked me through the well-lit, pleasantly decorated halls toward my father's room. "You picked an excellent time to visit."

I could tell he meant well from the look on his face—curious about my bruises but eager not to offend. So I just smiled, and nodded, and said, "I'm glad to hear that."

We stopped when we reached the door of Father's room. The aide rapped his knuckles gently against the doorframe, calling, "Mr. Collodi? May we come in?"

"I told you, the dollhouse won't be ready for another three days," shouted my father, sounding exactly like he had throughout my childhood: aggravated by the stupidity of the world around him, but trying to improve it however he could. "Go away, and come back when it's done."

I put a hand on the aide's shoulder. "I can handle it from here," I said. The aide looked uncertain, but he nodded and walked away, leaving me alone with the open doorway. I hefted the box in my hands, checking the weight of its precious burden—so few left, and no way to make more—before taking a deep breath and stepping into my father's room.

Antonio Collodi had been a large man in his youth, and that size was still with him: broad shoulders and a back that hadn't started to stoop, despite the deep lines that seamed his face and the undeniable white of his hair. The muscle that used to make him look like a cross between a man and a bear was gone, withered to skeleton thinness; his clothes hung on him like a shroud. He was standing near the window, hands curled like he was working on an invisible dollhouse. I stopped to admire the workmanship that had gone into him. I must have made some small sound, because he turned and froze, eyes fixing on my face.

"I'm your daughter," I said, before he could start flinging accusations. He usually mistook me for Pandora—a natural misunderstanding, since I looked exactly like she did in the painting that we had been passing down, generation to generation, since the beginning. He didn't like being visited by dead people. He said it was an abomination, and a violation of our compact with the Kingdom of the Cold, which some called

"Hades," where the dead were meant to stay forever. "Daddy, I need your help. Can you help me?"

"My daughter?" He kept staring at me, dawning anger melting into amazement. "You're beautiful. What did I make you from?"

"Bone and skin and pine and ice," I said, walking to his bed and putting down the long white box. I rested a hand on its lid. "Pain and sorrow and promises and joy. You pried me open and called me a princess among doors, and then you poured everything you had into me, and kept pouring until my eyes were open." I remembered that day: waking on my father's workbench, naked and surrounded by bone shavings, my teeth tender and too large in my little girl's mouth, my face stiff from the smile it had been painted wearing.

My family has guarded the trick to calling life out of the Kingdom for centuries, since Pandora brought it to us and said she was too tired to keep the compact any longer. No one you didn't make with your own two hands can be trusted. That's the true lesson of the Kingdom, and what I should have remembered when Clark smiled his perfect smile and offered me his perfect hands. But my father made me too well, and when he bid me to become a woman, a woman I became. If I'd stayed a doll of bone and pine, Clark would have had no power over me.

"Yes, that's how you make a daughter," said my father, following me across the room. "Is that why I'm so empty?"

"Yes," I said. "I'm sorry."

"I should be in pieces by the road by now."

"I still need you." I took my hand off the box and opened the lid, revealing a blue-eyed boy doll. He was dressed in trousers and a vest a hundred years out of date, and his face was painted in a way that subtly implied he had a secret. I undid the ribbons holding him in place and gingerly picked him up. He weighed more than he should have for his size, and my hands shook as I held him out toward my father. "There are five of these in the world. That's why you can't go. If you break this one, there will only be four, and you'll be one step closer to entering the Kingdom."

We doll makers were supposed to be at peace there, finally home among our own kind. We were supposed to be rewarded for the things that we had done while we pretended to be human. I didn't know if that was true . . . but I knew that the humans lived for the promise of Heaven with much less proof of its existence than we had of the Kingdom.

Pandora and Carlo Collodi had been real people, flesh-and-blood people. Pandora had carried a vase like a broken heart, meant to contain all the dangers of the world, both sweet and bitter. She had been tired from her wandering, from years on years of struggling to recapture the evils she had accidentally released. Carlo Collodi . . .

He had wanted a daughter. Of such necessity are many strange bargains born.

Father took the doll. I didn't look away. This was on me; this was my fault, because I was doing this to him. I could have crafted my child as soon as it became clear that the vessel of Father's thoughts had cracked. I could have set him free. I was the one who wasn't willing to let him go.

"Oh, my brave boy," he murmured, cradling the doll in his hands. "Your name was Marcus, wasn't it? Yes, Marcus, and you were a vessel for my anger. The world was so infuriating back then. . . ." He raised the doll, pressing his lips against the cold porcelain forehead.

It felt like the temperature in the room dropped ten degrees, the doorway to the Kingdom of the Cold swinging open and locking in place as all that Father had poured into that blue-eyed boy came surging out again, filling him. He stayed that way for almost a minute, lips pressed to porcelain, drinking himself back in one sip at a time. The chill remained in the air as Father lowered the doll, and the eyes he turned in my direction were sharp and clever, filled with the wisdom of two hundred years of making dolls to hold every imaginable emotion.

"Marian, why am I still here?" he asked. All traces of confusion were gone. The sad, broken vessel was no longer with me, and I rejoiced, even as I fought not to weep.

The dolls he had filled before he had broken grew fewer with every visit, and his lucidity faded faster. I was running out of chances to call my father back to me. "Four dolls remain, Father," I said, rising and sketching a quick curtsey, even though I was wearing trousers. "Until they're used up, you can't finish breaking."

"Then use them. Stop wasting them on me. I command you."

"I can't." I straightened. "I would if I could. I love you, and I know my duty. But the world has changed since you were its doll maker, and I can't do this without you. I need to be able to ask my questions, and have someone to answer them."

He frowned. "Have you made a child yet?"

"Not yet. I can't." Once I made myself a child—made it from bone and skin and pine and ice, like my father had made me, like his father had made him—my own cracks would begin to show, and my essence would begin leaking free. A vessel can only be emptied so many times. The creation of a child was the greatest emptying of all. "I'm not ready. But Father, that isn't why I came. I need your help."

"Help? Help with what?"

I took a deep breath. This was going to be the difficult part. "There was a man at my office. . . ."

I spilled out the whole sordid story, drop by terrible drop. The smiles, the flirtation, the dates for coffee that turned into dates for dinner that turned, finally, into Clark deciding he had the right to start dictating my life. From there, it was a short progression to him knocking me to the floor and stealing my dolls.

Father listened without a word, letting his precious moments of lucidity trickle away like sand. When I was done, he inclined his head and said, "You have been foolish, my Marian. But you're young as long as I'm in this world—children are always young when set against their parents—and I can't fault you for being a young fool. I was foolish, too, when I had a father to look after me." He held out his empty doll. I took it. What else could I have done? He was my father, and he wanted me to have it. "You know what you need to do."

"I don't want to," I said weakly—and wasn't that why I'd come to him? To find another way, a better way, a *human* way, one that didn't end with someone broken and bleeding in the street?

But sometimes there isn't any other way. Sometimes all there can be is vengeance. "You have to," he said gently.

I sighed. "I know." The empty doll was light as a feather, nothing but a harmless husk. I could sell it to a dealer I knew for a few hundred dollars, and watch him turn around and sell it to someone else for a few thousand. It didn't matter who profited, or how much. All that mattered was that this shattered little piece of my father's soul would no longer be in my keeping. One more doorway, permanently closed.

"Now come, sit with me." My father sat down on the edge of his bed, gesturing for me to return to my previous place. "I don't have long before the cracks begin to show again, and I would know what you've been doing with your life."

"All right," I said, and sat, settling the empty doll back into his box. Father reached for my hands. I let him take them. We sat together, both smiling, and I spoke until the understanding faded from his eyes, and he was gone again.

There are always consequences when you spend your life standing on the border of the Kingdom of the Cold.

I spent the night at my worktable, a rainbow of paints in front of me and Charity the bat-girl's delicate face looking blindly up at the ceiling as I applied the intricate details of her makeup, one stroke at a time. She'd been waiting for the chance to be complete for months, but I'd passed her by time and again to focus on newer projects. I'd always wondered why. It's not like me to leave a doll languishing for so long. Now I knew: Charity had a purpose, and until the time for that purpose arrived, I would never have been able to finish her.

Charity was meant to be my revenge.

Morning found me still sitting there, now drawing careful swirls on the resin body that would soon play host to her head. Her wings would get the same treatment before they were strung into place. She was less a bat-girl than a demon-girl, but "Charity the bat-girl" had been her name for so long that I couldn't stop thinking of her that way. I reached for my silver paint, and cursed as my hand found an empty jar.

"Shit."

I'd been working without pause and hadn't stopped to assess my supplies. Charity needed the silver to be properly finished. I glanced at the clock. The doll shop would be open in ten minutes. This was their big gather-day, but I could be in and out before anyone had a chance to notice that I was even there. I wiped down my brushes, capped my paints, and stood. Just a few more supplies and I could finish my work.

The drive to the doll store took about fifteen minutes, minutes I spent reviewing what I was going to buy and how I'd explain why I couldn't stay if Willow or Joanna asked me. I was deep in thought when I got out of the car, walked to the door, and stepped inside, only to be hit by a wave of laughter and the smell of peppermint tea. I stopped dead, blinking at the swarm of people—mostly women, with a few men peppered through the crowd—who moved, chattering constantly, around a series of tables that had been set up where the racks of pre-made doll clothes were usually kept. A second wave hit me a moment later, this one redolent with sadness, and with the smell of cold.

My stolen dolls were here.

I shoved my way through the crowd, ignoring the startled protests, until I reached the table. There they were, all my missing vessels, even Strawberry, although someone had re-dressed her in a garish red and white checked dress. All fifteen were set up as a centerpiece, surrounded by a red velvet rope, as if that would ensure that people looked but didn't touch.

"Marian?" Willow's voice came from right behind me. She sounded surprised.

I couldn't blame her for that. I had other things to blame her for. I whirled, pointing back at the table as I declared, "Those are *my* dolls! How did you get my dolls?"

Willow's expression changed from open and genial to closed and hard. "I'm afraid I don't know what you're talking about, dear. Those dolls were sold to us by a private collector, and you've always been so adamant about not showing or selling your work that I can't believe you'd have sold this many to him. They're a fine collection, but they're not yours."

I ground my teeth together, pain lancing from my damaged molar, before I said, "Yes, they are. They were stolen from my apartment two nights ago by my ex-boyfriend. I filed a police report. We can call the station and get them down here; I'm sure we'll find your 'private collector' matches Clark's description."

Her eyes widened slightly at his name. I resisted the urge to smack her.

"He didn't even lie about his name, did he? Clark Hauser. You probably wrote him a check. You'll have a record." I shook my head. "You had to know those weren't his. I bought most of these materials *here*, and they're not common combinations. You knew. But you took them anyway." The crowd around me was silent, watching. I turned to them. "Think they'd buy your dolls, too, if you got robbed?"

"We didn't know they were stolen," said Willow. "We bought them legally. We—"

"Give the lady back her dolls," said a weary voice. Willow turned, and we both looked at the dark-haired woman in the workroom door, leaning on her cane. Joanna focused only on me. She walked slowly forward. It felt like she was studying me, taking my measure. She stopped about a foot away and said, "Doll maker. That's what you are, isn't it? You're the doll maker."

I nodded mutely.

"I always wanted to meet one of you." She waved a hand at the table. "They're yours. Take them. I knew we couldn't keep the collection as soon as I put my hands on it. They're dangerous, aren't they?"

I nodded again.

"Then get them out of my store. Was that all you came for?"

I found my voice and managed, "I needed some silver paint."

"Take that, too. Call it our apology." She smiled thinly. "When you take your revenge, doll maker, don't take it on us. Willow, get the lady her paint." Willow hurried to obey.

I looked at the crowd, and then back to Joanna, and said, "Thank you."

Joanna smiled. "You're welcome."

⁂

Restoring the vessels to their proper places made me feel infinitely better, like a hole in the world had been closed. I apologized to each of them, and twice to Strawberry: once as I was stripping off that horrible checkered dress, and again as I placed her back on her proper shelf. I felt their approval, and the approval of the Kingdom beyond. Silver paint in hand, I sat down and got back to work.

Crafting a vessel for the self is easy, once you know how. It requires understanding your own heart—a painful process, to be sure, but your own heart is always close to hand. Crafting a vessel for someone else is an uphill struggle, and I felt it with every stroke of the brush. I mixed the last of the silver paint with blood taken from the small vein inside my wrist, and it made glittering brown lines on Charity's skin. There was a moment right before the designs drew together when I could have stopped; I could have put down the brush and walked away. But Clark had struck me, had stolen from the Kingdom, and he had to pay for what he'd done.

I dressed Charity in a black mourning gown and placed her in a long white box, covering her with drifts of tissue paper. Then I fed Trinket, left the apartment, and drove to Clark's house. I left the box on his doorstep. I didn't look back as I drove away.

⁂

Clark didn't come to work on Monday. That wasn't unusual. Clark didn't come to work on Tuesday either. People were talking about it in the break room when I came to get my coffee.

Wednesday morning, I called in sick.

The key Clark had given me still fit his lock. I let myself in. There was Charity on the floor, full to the point of bursting, and there was Clark next to her, eyes open and staring into nothingness. He was still alive, but when I waved my hand in front of his face, he didn't blink. There was nothing left in him.

"You shouldn't open doors you don't know how to close," I said, bending to slide my arms under Clark and hoist him to his feet. He would have been surprised to realize how strong I was. "It's dangerous. You never know what might happen."

Clark didn't respond.

"I never told you where my family was from, did I? We're doll makers, you know. We go all the way back to a man named Carlo Collodi. He wanted a daughter, and he used a trick he learned from a woman named Pandora to open a door to a place called the Kingdom of the Cold. It's a good name, don't you think? There's no room for sorrow there. The people who live there don't even understand its name. He called forth a little girl, and as that girl grew, she learned so many things the people of the Kingdom didn't know." I carried Clark to his room as I spoke.

"Sometimes that little girl sent things home to them. Presents. But more often, she used the things her father had learned from Pandora. There's too much feeling in the world, you see. That's what Pandora really released. Not evil: emotion. So the little girl collected feeling like a cistern collects the rain, and when she held too much, she pulled it out and sealed it in beautiful vessels. Sorrow and anger and joy and loneliness, all held until her death. We can't contain as much as you can. We're not made that way. But we need something to pay our passage home." Home, to a place I'd never seen, with halls of porcelain and nobility of carved mahogany. We were revered as craftsmen there, and all we had to do to earn our place was keep repaying Pandora's debt, catching the excess of emotion that she had released into the world, one doll at a time.

I unpacked my father's last four remaining dolls before I unrolled the bundle that held my tools, pulling out the first small, clever knife. "Every vessel holds a piece of the maker's soul. We pack it away, piece by piece, to keep us alive after we cut out our hearts and use them to make a child. Our parents' dolls give us the scraps of soul we'll need to create a new one for the baby. They're not the only thing we need, of course."

The scalpel gleamed as I held it up to show him. "Puppets come from blocks of wood. Rag dolls come from bolts of cloth. What do you think it takes to construct a child?"

Clark never even whimpered.

҈

There was a message from Father's nursing home in my voicemail when I got back to the apartment. I didn't play it. I already knew what it would say: the apologies, the regrets, the silence where my father used to be. That didn't matter anymore. My chest ached where I had sliced it open, and I rubbed unconsciously at the wound, looking around the room at the rows upon rows of dolls filled with my living. They would sustain me now that I had no heart, until the day my daughter was ready to be the doll maker, and I was ready to stop patching the cracks left by her creation.

She snuffled and yawned in my arms, wrapped in a baby blanket the color of tissue paper. She'd have Clark's perfect smile and perfect hair, but she wouldn't have his temper. I'd given her my heart, after all, just like my father had given his to me.

The police would eventually notice Clark's disappearance. I'd left no traces for them to follow. A good artist cleans up when the work is done, and I had left neither shards of shattered porcelain nor pieces of dried, bloodless bone for them to track me by.

I walked to the couch and sat, jiggling my daughter in my arms. She yawned again. "Once upon a time," I said, "there was a man who wanted a son. He lived on the border of a place called the Kingdom of the Cold, and he knew that if he could just find a way to open a door, everything he dreamed of could be his. One day a beautiful woman came to his workshop. Her name was Pandora, and she was very tired. . . ."

The dolls listened in silent approval. Trinket curled up at my feet, and the world went on.

Goodness and Kindness

by Carrie Vaughn

Where are you going?"

"Just hang on a minute." Harry left Annie behind as he went to see what all the commotion was about. Smoke hung above a row of booths a ways up the midway. There looked to be firemen dragging hoses.

"Harry, I thought we were supposed to be on a date." She marched after him, hands on her hips, skirt swishing around her knees, shoes slapping on the pavement.

"I have to see, it'll just take a minute." This looked like a story, and he hadn't had a solid story in a week. Annie could wait. It wasn't like a Sunday afternoon at Coney Island was a serious date, anyway.

"Harry!" She was sounding shriller.

"I'm a stringer, I only get paid if I get stories, and this is a story."

She crossed her arms and pouted, a bad sign. "We're supposed to be having a good time here. I've been waiting all week for this. Can't the story wait?"

"No, it can't. You want me to make money so I can keep taking you out like this? Then I'm going after the story."

"Taking me out like *this*? No thanks." She turned and marched away, hands in fists, arms swinging at her sides.

"Annie!" She didn't turn around, and he didn't call to her again.

Too bad. She was a nice girl, mostly.

The smoke smelled acrid, more rubber burning than wood. A cloud of it drifted up and was scattered by a breeze coming in off the bay. A crowd had gathered, but Harry pushed past, mumbling a halfhearted "excuse me," and started taking pictures as soon as he could see the first sign of blackened plywood and a soot-covered fireman. He'd brought along his cheap camera—he always brought it along, because you just never knew.

Three or four gaming booths had caught fire, it looked like. Roofs had caved in, signs blackened and illegible, contents scorched and scattered. At the first burned-out booth, what must have been hundreds of Kewpie dolls had melted and exploded into a thousand broken pieces and plastic blobs. They still managed to keep looking up with those big baby eyes, smiling with rosy cheeks through the scorch marks. *Win a Kewpie doll for your sweetheart, yeah, right.* He grinned at the thought of what Annie would do if he gave her one of these monsters.

The rest of the midway went on as usual: Ferris wheel turning, calliope plinking out circus music, kids shouting. The fire was small, contained. Maybe not a story after all, but he was committed, so he kept going. He needed to talk to someone, get a good quote or two. Find some scandal or angle. Maybe someone had gotten hurt.

A small crew still worked, wetting down hot spots and breaking down walls before they collapsed. Their truck was blocking the back alley, so he couldn't get through there easily. Outside a roped-off cordon, Harry found a guy in a blue uniform, official looking. Some kind of security guard or cop, someone who looked like he was in charge.

"Hey, Officer, you got a minute? I'm Harry Baker, with the *Post*." Not exactly the truth, but he had to have some kind of credential or no one would talk to him.

The cop frowned but didn't tell Harry to scram, which he took as a good sign.

"So what happened here?" Harry asked. He took out his notebook and pencil stub. Made him look more serious, he thought.

The guy gave the notebook a suspicious frown. "I can't make a statement at this time, I'm sorry."

"You think it's arson, maybe? Did somebody maybe set it on fire?" *That* would make this a story.

Smirking, the cop said, "Usually fires like this are an accident. Something in the wiring breaks and causes a spark. You see all those Kewpie dolls? They're made out of celluloid. Stuff burns like tinder. Once the flames start, there's no stopping them."

"And an arsonist would have known that?" Harry pressed.

"And why would someone want to burn down a couple of Coney Island game booths? Those Kewpie dolls never hurt anyone." He turned away, a clear dismissal.

There was no story.

Harry talked to a few more people. Some of the bystanders, normal folks out for an afternoon at the midway, were happy to talk to him. Man-on-the-street quotes were all right—*wasn't it shocking, oh, it was terrible*—but nobody knew anything.

He just had to dig a little deeper was all. He went to light a cigarette, thought better of it after taking another look at the scorched debris, and took a sip from his flask instead.

Harry snapped a few more pictures. Surely one of them would turn out and make a good quarter-page spread, unless some bigger news story bumped it. That seemed to happen a lot. Bad luck, wrong place, wrong time. That wasn't what his editor said, of course. "You gotta have a better nose for this kind of thing, Harry. You end up in the wrong place, it's your instincts need work. You gotta have the instincts for news, to chase the stories down. Come back with something good next time, something people can really sink their teeth into, something that'll sell papers."

Harry thought about the newsboys on the corners yelling, "Coney Island Burns, Arson Likely!" Sounded good, sounded like a hook. His instincts were good, dammit.

⁂

A good newspaperman had to dig for a good story. Maybe it was arson, maybe it wasn't, but if it *was*, Harry would get the scoop before the cops, even. Who'd benefit from having the booths burn down? The owners, if they had insurance. Wasn't that how these arson cases always went? If nothing else, he could still get a juicy quote from the owner. Maybe it was a guy with ten kids to feed who'd now lost his income.

Maybe that was the story. A good newspaperman knew the story was all in the angle.

The ownership of the stretch of gaming booths turned out to be a more tangled puzzle than he expected—a real estate firm managed the buildings and leased them out to various tenants. Too many people to try to track down. He'd be better off sitting back and waiting to see what the official investigation turned up. But he needed a story and didn't have time to wait.

At a phone booth, he made a few calls. He pretended to be a cop when he talked to a secretary at the real estate firm and got her to reveal the name of the building's owner. Even better than a guy with ten kids, the owner was a spinster living alone who'd been persuaded to invest in various real estate schemes. Turned out she also owned a share in a company that imported the cheap prizes for the games, the Kewpie dolls and plush puppy dogs and all. She had money coming in from both sides. Figured. She'd give him some kind of choice quote, all maudlin and tear-jerking about her income gone up in smoke. He got her address, in Greenwich Village. If he hurried, he could talk to her before nightfall.

He had his strategy all worked out. She was a spinster, lonely to start with and shocked by the fire and such. He'd charm her, commiserate with her. She might be an heiress—the family lost money in the Crash, that was why she invested—used to being flattered and getting her way. He could flatter her. A little sympathy and she'd pour out her heart. The story would suddenly turn into a tragedy for readers to sigh over, and be glad it wasn't them.

Her place was pretty swank. She probably walked her poodle along the river every day. Harry rang the bell and waited a full minute for a flustered young housemaid to answer. A demanding heiress, then.

Harry donned a charming smile. "I'm here to see Miss O'Neill, is she in?" He should have had a mint before he stepped up to the brownstone's door.

He expected at least a question about who he was and what he needed—he had his story all worked out, about being from the insurance company, here to help, etcetera. But the maid only gave him a long-suffering eye roll and stepped aside to let him in. "They're in the parlor," she said.

She closed the door and walked off, leaving him to wonder where the parlor was. The brownstone's foyer was nondescript, no decoration to speak of, plain wood paneling and a tiled floor. Stairs led up, and a hallway led to what must have been a kitchen. He heard voices behind a set of double wooden doors. Maybe this was it. He donned his smile again, knocked, and opened the door.

"What? Yes?" a bright female voice said, and Harry stepped in.

The stately interior he expected was a bohemian mess, silk scarves in place of curtains, Persian rugs layered over each other, velvet chaises, overstuffed armchairs, enough knickknacks to cover every surface, crammed on the mantelpiece of the fireplace and in china cabinets placed against every wall and in every corner. And art—at least he supposed it might be art—from marble busts to gilt framed paintings to half-formed shapes worked out in clay and startling lamps done in winding wrought iron.

And Kewpie dolls, everywhere. All sizes and materials, figurines dressed up as gardeners and fishermen and doctors, as anything he could think of. Pictures, too, of Kewpies flying, dancing with babies and puppies, all of them round-cheeked and pink-faced, cowlicks of colorless hair sticking straight up. They were overwhelming, disconcerting. He almost preferred them burned and melted.

The woman holding court over it all was also not what he expected. She wore a flowing, paisley kaftan that seemed to billow, even indoors without a lick of a breeze. He couldn't tell if her dark hair was supposed to be like that, all curled and pinned up in a haphazard mess, a pouf gone wrong, or if she simply hadn't noticed how disheveled it looked. Tall, she still wore heeled sandals that raised her another two inches.

She had other visitors: a young woman in a short dress lying prone on a velvet chaise, wineglass dangling from lazy fingers; and a young man sitting at an easel, painting the young woman, Harry assumed. The canvas was turned away from him. Something classical was playing on a phonograph in the corner, and the tall woman—Miss O'Neill?—was standing behind the man . . . giving instruction? He looked around again—some of the art was unframed canvases, set against walls, and some of it was unfinished, charcoal sketches and amorphous scenes done in pastels. Was she an artist? Had he gotten this all wrong?

Harry worked to gather up his scattered charm.

"Hello, ma'am, yes, I, ah . . . I guess you heard about the fire? The buildings you own, out at Coney Island?"

"Ah, yes. My lawyer called with the news an hour ago." She *tsked* like a schoolmarm. "Very sad. Ah well. And who are you?"

"My name's Harry Baker. . . ." Being from the *Post* would not impress this woman. "I'm part of the investigation." *Marginally.* "I just wanted to express my condolences."

"That's very nice of you. Watch your perspective there, Arnold. You want the sensuality of it, right through there." She waved a hand at the painting, and the young man nodded.

Harry blinked. "I know you had a lot of money tied up there, not just with the booths but with the prizes, the dolls." He gestured to a shelf full of Kewpies. What the ones at the midway would have looked like before the fire.

"Oh, not *a lot* of money. Money isn't everything. It's about the dolls, Mr. Baker. It's always been about the Kewpies, and getting them to where they're most needed."

She swept over to a set of shelves—a different set of shelves—and picked up one of the figurines, sitting under a framed copy of an old Whiting's ad, hanging next to a set of suffragette postcards, all featuring Kewpies. The woman was a collector.

O'Neill cupped the doll to her cheek and puckered a fake kiss at it. "These need to go into the world, where they can do the most good. They bring happiness wherever they go! That's why they're so important." She set it back in just the same spot, giving it an affectionate brush with her finger.

She didn't have children—Harry was sure about that. A spinster with her bohemian hideaway, surrounding herself with these substitute babies. It was sad. Sick, really. But what a great story. He had to get this down; he pulled his notebook out of his pocket. He wondered if she'd let him take pictures. "Greenwich brownstone, decorated entirely in Kewpies!" had to be worth something.

"Oh, you're a writer, Mr. Baker?" She noticed the notebook and seemed pleased.

He froze, tried to remember his cover story. Part of the investigation. "Um, sort of. Just making a report, really." What he really wanted right now was his flask.

"Oh, I see." She seemed disappointed, looking him up and down, studying him.

"If you don't mind me asking, ma'am—what is it about the dolls?"

"Well, if you were a real writer you'd understand."

He bristled at that—he was a reporter, dammit, a journalist, a real writer. Like Hemingway. "Understand what?"

She floated around the room, her epic sleeves poofing like sails. She'd moved on to a cabinet by the wall, where she took a cut glass decanter and poured a tiny bit into a delicate liqueur glass. She didn't offer him any.

"I've got you pegged, Mr. Baker. You always see the worst in people, don't you? You're here asking questions, investigating like you're some kind of detective, like you're serving some kind of public good by solving this puzzle. But that's not you, not really. You look like you're watching a train wreck. You have to see the worst in people, or there'd be no story. Not like the Kewpies—they always see the best in people. They spread joy, that's their whole reason for being. They teach goodness, kindness." She went to a sketch on pasteboard on an easel by the fireplace. Large, a foot across and a couple feet high, the space was filled with Kewpies, a finer version of those cheap carnival dolls. They were even chubbier, shading making their cheeks and bellies round, their smiles even bigger and their eyes even brighter. A dozen of them tumbled around one another, hanging off a ribbon, the tiny blue wings on their backs somehow keeping them aloft. "They're here to make the world a better place, despite everything."

She kept on. "The Kewpies protect the innocent, children and animals. They carry babies out of harm's way. They're good, pure good. So it's no wonder you don't understand them. Isn't that so, Mr. Baker? What have you done to make the world a better place?"

Harry shivered—a motion hidden inside his suit jacket. "I'm a reporter, ma'am. I get the news out, I inform people—"

The two young protégés giggled quietly. At him, he knew.

She'd picked up another doll—he hadn't noticed when. Maybe she pulled it out of a pocket. The way O'Neill held the Kewpie, it seemed to be looking right at him, out of the corner of its eye. Smiling, potbelly stuck out, arms straight as if to prove its harmlessness. This one was one of the cheap carnival prize dolls. The kind of thing you threw away when you got home.

"Mr. Baker," she asked, "are you kind?"

"Sure, I like to think—"

"If you saw a man on a window ledge about to jump and had a chance to save him, would you? Or would you let him jump and take a picture of it?" She nodded at the camera hanging on its strap over his shoulder.

He wasn't going to pick up a story here. Not even about a crazy lady with a room filled with dolls.

"I'm sorry to bother you, ma'am. I'll show myself out."

"Here, Mr. Baker. I think you should have this. Don't worry, I won't miss it, I have plenty more." She smiled sweetly—a lot like one of the happy Kewpies—and came over to hand him the doll. "You can take it home to your sweetheart, and you didn't even have to throw any rings over bottles for it."

He imagined handing the doll to Annie—and remembered Annie had walked out on him. "I don't have a sweetheart," he said absently.

O'Neill shrugged like she wasn't surprised at this. She returned to her giggling protégés without a backward glance.

The doll was lying in his hand before he could do anything about it, and he was too numb to just drop it. It felt strangely weightless, as if made of air, and yet warm to the touch. The plastic skin seemed to hold heat. He shoved the thing in his jacket pocket and left.

On the stoop of the brownstone he gasped for air, like he'd been hold-ing his breath for the last fifteen minutes. He took a long drink from his flask and finished off the last of the bourbon.

Next he headed to the *Post* offices to drop off film and turn the day's work into some kind of story.

Not that he had a story. At least, not a front-page story. Page three, maybe. There was a fire, here are the facts, moving on. As much as he wanted some sensationalist exposé about insurance fraud or flaming re-venge, or even a profile of some pathetic spinster made destitute by the tragedy, the story wasn't there. He'd followed his instincts, followed the lead, and had nothing to show for it. He couldn't afford this. He had to hope the news editor, Freeman, would buy some of the pictures he'd taken.

The newsroom was busy, snapping with the sound of typewriters, humming with the promise of Things Happening. He moved through it like an unmoored barge, out of place.

If Freeman didn't seem particularly happy to see him, he didn't seem unhappy, either.

"What have you got, Baker?"

He put the story and film on the desk and waited. Freeman sighed, and Baker knew he was screwed.

"If the whole midway burned down it'd be one thing," Freeman said. "But just a couple of buildings? It's not news, it's gawking. Sure, it was worth checking out, but please tell me you didn't spend all day on this?"

The whole day, and Annie. Of course he was right, but Harry ar-gued anyway. "Sir, a lot of people love the Coney Island midway; it may only be a couple of booths, but they'll want to know—"

"It's not news." He set the pages aside, just like that. "But here, I've got an assignment for you. It's not glamorous but I need someone on it—you feel like covering city politics?" He offered a note; Harry read it: a city utilities board meeting tomorrow morning, deciding where to build new sewer lines uptown. Three hours of boredom, with nothing to print at the end of it but a list. Maybe the fire wasn't news, but neither was this. It was housekeeping.

Harry frowned at Freeman. "This is scutwork, a nothing story. I can do better—"

"Then do better. Meantime, I need that meeting covered because what they decide there is going to affect a lot of people. You want the job, or you want me to give it to someone else?"

A dozen other reporters in the newsroom looked through the glass at him, hungry.

Harry grabbed the page with the assignment and walked out.

⁂

He overslept, which gave him half an hour to get to the board meeting. He had just enough time to comb his hair and put on yesterday's clothes.

If he really wanted to impress Freeman he'd have gotten there early to interview the board members, get quotes, maybe find some of the residents of the neighborhood the utilities department was planning to tear up. Too late for that, so he'd have to do interviews after. Plenty of people would be talking during, so he'd get good quotes then, all on the record. He stopped off for a fifth of bourbon to refill his flask.

On the last couple of blocks to the meeting, he witnessed an accident. The whole thing. The sequence of events happened before him like a play on a stage: the automobile swerving, the woman at the curb freezing in panic, a bystander screaming. Time really did slow down, and Harry really could see how it was all going to play out. The car hit her. Tires screeched as other vehicles skidded to a stop. Bystanders turned to statues with their mouths round and eyes wide. Out of control, the car kept going, scooping the victim along with it, pinning her to a corner lamppost. The vehicle's motor was smoking, obviously not working right; the driver flailed, unable to move the car. The woman's head was thrown back, her face wrenched with pain. A couple of people ran forward, crying for help, grabbing the car by the windshield, the rear bumper, the smooth metal of the door, but they couldn't move the car off the woman.

Harry had his camera in hand, and he snapped the shutter and took a picture.

The victim screamed, spitting blood from her mouth. Moans of despair came from the would-be rescuers. He took another photo.

A siren rang down the street—someone had called the police, an ambulance maybe. The gathering crowd separated, a path cleared for the white van coming around the corner.

People were still trying to get the car off the woman, but she was too far gone. Nothing could have saved her. Still pinned to the post, she now slumped over the car's hood. Her shapeless knit hat had fallen partly down her cheek.

Bystanders continued shouting for help. But they weren't shouting at *him*. He took more pictures. Then he looked down at his camera as if he didn't know where it came from.

He'd done exactly what that O'Neill woman said he'd do. He was exactly the failure she said he was. He suddenly felt the weight of the doll in his pocket. Like the Kewpie was poking him through the fabric. He pulled it out, looked into those big, ridiculous eyes. The doll pressed its terrible warmth against his hand.

He threw the thing in the gutter and walked away.

⁂

The board meeting was half over by the time he got there. He took a long drink from his flask to calm his nerves and settled in the back, as unobtrusively as he could. The talk was all about zoning issues and neighborhood complaints and engineering difficulties and contract bidding. He couldn't make heads or tails of it. Just like he thought, this wasn't news, this was housekeeping. He jotted a few notes.

The pictures he'd taken—that was a story. Freeman would see that and forgive him.

⁂

When Freeman wouldn't look him in the eye, Harry knew he was done. Well, really, he'd known that for a long time.

Freeman put a hand to his temple, like he had a headache. "I can't use these. I can maybe run a couple of inches on the accident, but I'm not putting this in the paper. I . . . I just won't." He scooped the prints together and shoved them in an envelope, out of sight. He thrust the envelope back at Harry, who clung to it.

Harry tried to argue. "It's public interest, people want to see this—"

"There's what people want, then there's good taste. I'm not running these."

"But the story—"

"Doesn't need pictures." He took a deep breath and let it out, as if he had decided something difficult and momentous. When Freeman's gaze met Harry's, it seemed weighted. "Baker. Harry. I'm sorry, but I don't want to see you here again."

And that was that, the bottom of the cliff Harry had been crashing toward for such a long time now. "But—"

"Go home, get some rest. Pull yourself together."

He had nothing left to pull together. Ducking Freeman's gaze, he nodded quickly and fled, patting his pockets all the way down the stairs for a pack of cigarettes and a book of matches, but he couldn't seem to find them. So his hands flailed, until they found the flask. Standing on the street outside, leaning against the brick wall of the building, he drank, but the liquor seemed to set him on fire rather than calm him down.

Plenty of other papers in this town. Plenty of other rags to write for. Some would even print those pictures he'd taken. He'd shop them around until he sold them.

⚈

No one wanted to buy the pictures. More than that, everyone he asked gave him this look, half pity and half revulsion. So he kept walking, block after block.

Passing by a five-and-dime, he stopped and looked in the window. The place sold Kewpie dolls, not just the celluloid ones, but the fancy ones made out of bisque. They were lined up in the display, along with wooden spoons and paper pirate hats for kids.

Those big baby eyes didn't blink, didn't look away from him. Didn't pity.

Try again, you'll do better next time. He imagined a swarm of them, tiny wings fluttering, dancing airborne with looping ribbons, surrounding him with love. Goodness and kindness.

He went in, picked one off the shelf, took it to the cash register.

"Is that for your sweetheart?" the girl at the counter asked.

"I don't . . ." The question stopped him. He reconsidered. "Sure. Sure it is."

Harry stuffed the doll in his jacket pocket and walked out.

❧

He went back to the scene of the accident. The wrecked car was gone, but shattered glass and twisted scraps of metal lay strewn along the curb. Maybe a few smears of blood, or it might have been oil. Didn't matter.

No chance the doll he'd thrown in the gutter, the one the O'Neill woman had given him, would still be there, but it was, a bright pale figure against the muck, and that felt like a miracle. He retrieved the doll and put it in his pocket.

He got to Coney Island after dark, the best time to be there. Walking the midway, surrounded by kids and families, couples holding hands, all of them smiling, he was painfully out of place. Everyone must have noticed him here by himself, no sweetheart, nothing, as if a spotlight shone on him, all those eyes looking at him.

He reached the row of gaming booths, different than the ones that had burned, and the eyes gazing on him changed. They became round, happy. Kind.

He knew the trick, or he thought he did, so he set his quarter down at a milk can toss, and the carnie put three baseballs in front of him. A hundred Kewpies lined up on the walls watched him. Cheering him on, laughing with him, not at him. Winking at him out of the corners of their eyes.

His hand was shaking so he took extra-careful aim. Missed one, and it felt like a punch in the gut. Almost walked away, because clearly he couldn't do anything right. But the round eyes and pink smiles looked down on him.

The next ball landed in the mouth of the can. So did the next. Harry's heart lifted, and the world turned beautiful.

The carnie smiled his huckster's smile. "I know what prize you want—I see you looking at them Kewpies."

"Yes," Harry said, dazedly. "Yes, that's it."

"Here you go, big guy! Take it home to your sweetheart!" He made a show of presenting a doll from the shelf, placing it in Harry's hand with a flourish. And for the first time in recent memory, Harry was happy.

He put the Kewpie in his pocket and another quarter on the ledge. "Again."

"You want to try for the big one?" the carnie said, pointing to the shelf of premium prizes, the wristwatches and toy trucks.

"No, I want another one of those, another doll." He said it the same way he might have ordered bourbon at his local dive after a long night in the newsroom.

The carnie took the quarter and gave him three baseballs. He won again. Another doll went into his pocket.

"Again."

A third doll.

He had some magic in his hands, winning like this.

"Your girl must really like them Kewpies," the carnie said, baffled now.

After twenty minutes, the carnie cut him off and made him leave, but that was okay, because Harry was out of quarters. He was out of just about everything, but his pockets were stuffed with Kewpie dolls.

He'd used all his change on the game, so he walked home. That was okay, too. Midnight, he pushed into his room at the boardinghouse, exhausted, but tired was good.

Above the counter with the sink and hot plate, shelves were filled with cans of food, coffee and sugar and the like. He cleared it all off, dumped it on the floor, and pulled all the dolls out of his pocket to line them up there. Somehow, his pockets had become filled with Kewpies. He'd lost his flask somewhere, and his cigarettes. He hardly minded.

He filled the shelves and still found more dolls. So he moved to the next wall, stood them on door frames, on windowsills, on the back of the armchair and over the cabinet with the Murphy bed. They had propagated in his pockets—that seemed like something they would do.

Hundreds of them, all around him. Everywhere he turned, they watched him. He sat on the floor in the middle of the room and pulled his knees to his chest. The dolls multiplied, and their eyes grew large, their smiles even more knowing. They would keep watch. They would be kind.

It was just, it was right. It was exactly what he deserved.

Daniel's Theory About Dolls

by Stephen Graham Jones

I'm twelve when this all starts, and Daniel's about to be five. And I thought he was like the rest of us, then. I thought he was like I had been, at his age. But he wasn't. It could be he had been born different, of course. Or maybe one day, walking down the hall on his short legs, there had been a click in his head, a deep, wet shift in his chest that made him roll his right shoulder, look at all of us in a colder way. Not just me and Mom and Dad. After that click, he looked at *people* in a colder way. I should have been watching him the whole time. I should have never slept. Then I could have seen him in his twin bed across from mine one night, when he coughed up a shiny black accretion, studied it in the moonlight sifting through our bedroom window, then wrapped it in a tissue, leaving it on the nightstand for Mom to throw away.

It was his soul.

None of us would know for years.

For our whole childhood he was just Daniel, always the full name. My little brother seven years younger, the accident that almost killed my mom, being born, like he'd been picking at the walls of her womb, latching his mouth onto places not made for feeding. He didn't talk until he was four. The doctors said not to worry, that some kids just took their time.

This isn't about him getting all the attention, either. This isn't about me growing up off to the side, taping and gluing my action figures and trucks back together and starting them on another adventure I was going to have to make up alone.

I'm good with the alone part. Really.

Those first four years when Daniel wasn't talking, the house was always buzzing anyway. New wallpaper, the trim painted over and over, slightly different shades each time, like a bird's egg fading in the sun, its inside baked rotten.

Our mom and dad were preparing for our little sister. Trying to make her room at the end of the hall so perfect that she couldn't help being born. Perfect enough that she wouldn't listen to the doctors, who told Mom there was no way, that Daniel had messed her up too bad, too forever.

Dad wanted a little princess, see. And our mom would kill herself to give him that princess, if she had to.

So, when the baseboards finally matched the color of the new knobs on the cabinets, when the corners had been sanded off all the tables and footboards, when Dad had parked all the tractors in a line by the barn, then reparked them again, it finally happened: Janine.

Our mom and dad named her early so they could coo to her through the tight wall of skin my mom's stomach became. They named her so they could lure her out, so they could talk her through.

To explain it to us, what was happening, my dad got a black marker with a sharp point and drew the outline of a sideways baby onto Mom, like a curled-over bean with fingers and toes and an open eye watching us. If we'd been a family that already had a daughter, we might have had a leftover doll to use to explain this process, but what we had instead was Dad's strong bold lines on our mom's belly.

Years later, at a movie theater, I would see the outline of a person taped off on the street, where they'd died their dramatic movie death, and I would lean forward, away from my date. I would lean forward and turn my head sideways, to see if I could hear that person under the asphalt, whispering.

Daniel told us it's how he learned to talk: hours on the couch with Mom in her seventh month, his head pressed flat to her bared stomach, Janine whispering to him.

When she died just like the doctors had said she would, Dad had to break down the bathroom door to keep Mom from eating all the soap from the towel cabinet. I remember him carrying her down the hall, bellowing at us to get out of the way. How her mouth was foaming, how her eyes were so blank.

I don't know if she was trying to choke herself to death or if she thought she was dirty on the inside.

After she was sedated on the couch and Dad was pouring me cereal at the formal dining room table we never used, I heard Daniel speaking words for the first time.

I stood from my chair, peered over the back of the couch.

Daniel had rolled Mom's shirt up, had the side of his head pressed to her stomach.

He was talking to Janine.

It was the only time I ever hit him.

⁂

Mom's theory, when she checked back into the world, it was that some people are born for a reason. That they're born to do a specific thing. And, in teaching Daniel to talk, Janine had done that specific thing. It released her from having to be born at all.

We held a private service for her in the woods behind our house. I got dressed up and combed my hair flat and everything.

We walked single file out to where we used to have picnics, under the big tree. It was maybe five minutes past the edge of the pasture. Our dad was trying not to cry. Our mom was squeezing his hand. Daniel was standing on the other side of the hole from me. I guess our dad had dug the hole the night before, or early that morning.

"Will the ants get her?" Daniel asked.

Because they always found our watermelon as soon as we cut it.

My mom shook her head no, not to worry.

The box they had for her was cardboard and waxy and as long as Dad's arm. It smelled like flowers, and because Mom's stomach was still big, that box made less sense than anything else in the history of the world, ever.

They didn't explain it to us.

We raised our voices, sang one of the children's songs Mom had been humming down to Janine since the first month.

It was nice, it was pretty, it was good.

Except for that box.

It fit into the hole perfectly, and all four of us used our hands to clump the dirt back in over it. Then my dad pulled a little sharpshooter shovel from behind some tree and scooped a little more on and tamped it all down into a proper mound.

"No marker," our mom said, her hand over her own heart, like cupping it. "*We'll* be the marker, okay?"

This is how families survive.

"Okay," Daniel said, trying the sounds out.

Dad rustled Daniel's mop of hair. It was like a hug, I guess.

"I think he's had the words in there the whole time," Dad said.

"My big boys," Mom said, and lowered herself to her knees, pulled Daniel and me to her and held on, her belly between us, a hard, dead lump.

"Okay," Daniel said again, quieter.

He wasn't talking to us.

Three nights later I woke softly, my eyes open for moments before I could see through them, I think.

They were fixed on Daniel's bed.

It was empty.

I trailed my fingers on the walls, felt my way through the darkened house. Living room, kitchen, utility room. Dad's study, Mom's sewing room. Their bedroom, the two of them breathing evenly in their musty covers.

Then Janine's room at the dead end of the hall.

I would get in trouble if the sound woke my parents—Janine's room was already in the process of becoming a shrine—but I clicked the light on.

It was like stepping into a cupcake. Everything was lace and pink and white-edged, like a thousand doilies had exploded and fallen into an arrangement that before had only existed in our dad's head.

Daniel wasn't there, either.

I turned the light off, trying to muffle the sound in the warmth of my palm, and in that new darkness I saw a firefly bobbing outside the window.

Except it was a yellowy flashlight, moving through the trees.

Daniel.

I pulled my shoes on without tying the laces and crept out the front door, left it open a crack behind me.

Five minutes later I caught up with him.

He'd seen where Dad put that little sharpshooter shovel. It was just his size.

By the time I got to Janine's grave, he'd already dug down to the waxy-cardboard-box center.

I reached out to stop him—he didn't know I was there—but it was too late.

He'd already stepped down into the open grave, the box not supporting his weight, the sound of a jumbo staple popping loud in the night.

And then I didn't say anything.

What he pulled up from that box, holding it under the armpits like a real baby, was the doll Dad had bought for Janine, the doll he hadn't had to demonstrate the baby in Mom's stomach.

She'd been stripped naked, of course.

If her eyes rolled open, it was too far for me to see, and too dark.

❦

Because I'd left the door open, when I got back to the house there was something turning in slow, deliberate circles on the couch.

A possum. It was following its rat tail around and around, like it had lost something, or was patting down a bed for itself.

It hissed at me, showed its rows of teeth, sharp all the way back to the hinge of its jaw.

I fell back, clutching for the coatrack, to pull it down in front of me maybe, to hide what was going to be my screaming escape, but what my fingers dug into, it was the shirt of Daniel's pajamas.

He didn't even look over at me as he crossed the living room, the shovel held over his shoulder like a barbarian axe.

The possum screamed when he swung the blade into it, and by the time our mom and dad had clambered into the living room, my dad with his pistol held high like a torch, my mom's silk sleep mask pushed up on her forehead like a visor, the possum was biting at its own opened side, and rasping.

Daniel looked up to Dad, then to Mom.

"*Daniel,*" our dad said, his voice trying to be stern, I think.

It didn't work.

"Oh," Mom said then, and stepped back from the bloody couch. From the dying possum.

The possum's babies were calving off. They'd been hidden under the dark fur on her back. They looked like malformed mice.

I clapped my hand to my mouth, threw up between my fingers.

Daniel brought the flat of the shovel down on the fastest of the babies; he was, as our dad said later, too young to know better, too young to understand.

Dad wasn't standing where I was, though. He wasn't close enough to hear Daniel.

Daniel was whispering to someone.

❈

I'm thirty-eight now, and that night under the tree, the Night of the Possum as we came to call it, it's still as clear in my mind as if it just happened.

Daniel would be thirty-one, I guess.

I wish I could trace a line from the year Janine died to now, and put hash marks on it. This is Daniel's first date. This is the neighbor's new colt. This is when he figured out the bus lines—when he figured out he could go into the city by himself. This is him in the guidance counselor's office, the counselor not finding an explanation for him in any of the college textbooks she'd saved.

This is Mom and Dad, watching him return again and again into the trees.

This is me, growing up to the side.

My first date is with Chrissy Walmacher. The neighbor's new colt is hers. I sat with her while it was dying, for horse reasons I never really understood. This is me and Chrissy, riding the bus to a concert in the city. This is the guidance counselor, veering her to this school, for that life, and veering me to a different school, for a different life.

This is me at thirty-four, standing at my dad's funeral, my mom there, Daniel pulling up at the last moment, his suit perfect, his face set to "mourning," his eyes drinking the scene in for cues.

We had had the same grades, played the same sports.

Without me providing the model of what to do, I think Daniel would have had to reveal himself. As it was, he could just step into my shoes, follow my lead, fit in, attract zero attention.

What Dad died of, it wasn't anything. Just cigarettes. Just too many years.

Standing there, I was only on my second job of the year. I'd tried normal jobs, offices, even manual labor, but indexing books in the privacy of my apartment on the second floor was finally the only thing that fit. It was work that made sense.

Contracts were getting fewer and farther between, though. There's software that can do what I do, more or less. With a little fine-tuning afterward, even I have a hard time telling any substantial difference.

Dad dying, it wasn't a windfall for me, or for Mom or Daniel, either, but it was going to help. My grief was a little bit of a mask as well.

After the funeral, to escape the house, I drove Daniel down to the bar my dad had been loyal to in the years after Janine—before he cut drinking off altogether, at my mom's request.

This was the real funeral. Walking through a space Dad had walked through, at our age. Moving as he moved, our reflections in the smoky mirror perhaps vague enough to fall into step with his. We were trying his life on, and before we'd even sat down, we were finding his life not that interesting.

Saying goodbye, it's complicated.

Daniel ordered the same beer I did. He'd never cared about beer, probably wasn't even going to drink this one to the bottom.

"So what's what these days?" I asked.

I'd seen actors on TV open conversations exactly like that, in places like this.

"You know," he said.

He'd bloomed into an electrical engineer. In his senior year, when I was first getting on the job market, I remember him building model intersections on Dad's shop table, and wiring stoplights, giving them this or that trigger, this or that safety. The traffic was imaginary, but the lights always clicked through their cycles perfectly.

Mom and Dad would stand in the doorway, Mom's hands balled at her throat with pride.

Everything they'd been saving for Janine, they heaped it onto Daniel.

My one-time girlfriend Chrissy Walmacher's second wedding had been two weeks ago. She'd invited me, and it had put a picture in my head of me standing at a white fence, looking over. Just another sad postcard I sent to myself in a weak moment. One of many.

"Any girls to speak of?" I asked.

Daniel leaned back, shrugged his right shoulder in that way he had, like he was about to shove his right hand deep into his pocket for the perfect amount of change. He wasn't looking at me anymore, but at a college girl with hair so metallic red it had to have just been dyed, or colored, however that happens. She was sliding darts from the dartboard, one booted foot pulled up behind her like she was kissing someone in a movie.

"Stay single," I told him, raising my glass. "These are your good years."

He came back to me, his fingers circling his own beer.

What he didn't say, what he didn't ask, was, How would I know this gospel I was preaching?

Big brothers are required to say certain things, though. To give advice, whether it's from experience or from a book of celebrity interviews that now has a comprehensive index.

"You going to miss him?" Daniel said then, watching my eyes for the lie.

"He's Dad," I said, taking another long drink.

"But still."

Behind me a dart struck home, and the redhead tittered.

"I miss him for Mom," I said.

"Yeah," Daniel said, nodding like this was true. Like this was something he hadn't thought of.

"I saw you that night," I said then, trying to spring it on him. "Did you ever know?"

I'd been saving it for more than half my life.

Daniel looked to me, his head turned sideways like for clarification.

"Night of the Possum," I said, in our family way.

"Oh, yeah," Daniel said. "The possum. Man. I'd nearly forgot her."

Until just that moment, I'd never once thought of that possum as having a sex. But of course it had been a mom. It had had babies. Of course.

Her.

The way he said it was so personal, though. So intimate.

"*What* did you see?" he said, setting his glass down after touching the beer to his lips again. He wasn't drinking it, I didn't think. He was just doing what I did. He was fitting in. He was looking like one of us.

He wasn't, though.

Not even close.

According to Daniel, he'd been out to Janine's grave in private in the weeks since her funeral—a behavior learned from Mom and Dad, he claimed, from following them on the sly, making their little pilgrimage of grief before dinner two or three times a week, if it was just a casserole cooking. He'd been there, sure, but never with a shovel. Never to dig that little cardboard coffin up. What did I think he was, a ghoul? Can a preschooler even *be* a ghoul?

"That's what I'm saying," I told him, a beer deeper into this night of nights. "You were just, like, curious, I think. As to what we'd actually buried."

"Janine," he said.

I stared at him, waiting for him to see it.

I'm an indexer, Daniel an electrical engineer, but still, we'd both figured out long ago that what happens with Mom's kind of miscarriage is that the body either reabsorbs the fetus or the body chunks it up, delivers it bit by bit, to be assembled never.

Not pleasant to think about, but the human body's crawly and gross when you look too close.

Each of us figuring that out about Janine, it was probably why we'd gone into comparatively sterile work settings: desks, drafting tables.

Nothing with blood.

"It would have messed me up, though, right?" Daniel said, touching that warm beer to his lips again. "Given me a unique perspective on . . . on *life*."

I took a real drink, waited for him to say the rest.

I didn't want to disturb this moment.

He was watching the redhead behind me again, talking to the two girls she was with. It was like he was taking a series of still shots with his mind. With his heart.

The reason he dismissed my question about girls was because girls were all there was for him. I could tell by the way he watched her. But it would be cruel for him to flaunt it in front of his big brother. In front of his practically celibate big brother.

"If I'd dug her up like you say, I mean," Daniel said, coming back to me for a moment. Holding my eyes with his, probably so he could gauge how I was taking this: as hypothetical or as confession.

"You did dig her up," I said. "That's why you had that little shovel. For the possum."

"It was right there on the porch," Daniel said, his voice falling into that little-brother whine I hated. "I was on my way back from the bathroom and I heard you, came to see. The door was open behind you, man. The shovel was right there where Dad left it. It's where he always left it, for snakes. Remember?"

I studied the grain of the tabletop, trying to track this version.

Mom *had* had an encounter with a king snake. That little sharp-shooter shovel *did* have a handle at the top, perfect for holding the shovel blade steady over a snake's head.

But I'd seen.

"So, *if* you'd dug her up," I finally said. Because there had to be *some* ground he would cede.

Daniel pushed air out his nose in a sort of one-blow laugh, a version of the way Dad used to dismiss our pleas for money or keys or permission, and said, "Then . . . she would have been dug up?"

"We should go out there," I told him.

He wiped his mouth with the back of his hand. "There wouldn't be anything," he said. "Not after all these years. Maybe an eyeball. Those are hard plastic, right?"

"You're talking about Janine," I said.

"We're talking about a doll," Daniel said. Obviously. "And, say we go out there, and that doll's still there," Daniel said, leaning over his beer. "Would that somehow prove that I dug up the . . . the surrogate of Janine, and then put her back exactly as she'd been?"

He was right.

"Or it would prove that nobody'd ever dug her up at all," he said, lifting his beer and setting it down, for emphasis.

"I thought—" I said then, looking behind to the group of college girls as well. "I guess I just thought that . . . you were a kid, man. I thought that, that you might really think that stupid doll *was* Janine. Whether you dug her up or not."

"It. Whether I dug *it* up or not."

"I thought you'd think that was what Mom had had inside her all along. That, I don't know, she would have grown up into a mannequin or something. That everybody was always walking around with these dolls lodged in them, waiting to get out."

"The women at least," Daniel added, in his playing-along voice.

"It's your theory," I said. "Or, I mean, it would have been."

Daniel wasn't watching the college girls anymore. Just me.

"I was four," he said finally. "Not stupid. But thanks, big brother."

I nodded like I deserved that, and kept nodding, drank another beer, talked about nothing, and left him there with the college girls, didn't talk to him for two years, I think it was. And that was just for Mom's funeral.

Her granite headstone came in two months later.

Carved into it was that she'd been mother to three beautiful children.

I ran my fingers over the jagged valleys of those letters, and watched cars pass on Route 2.

"Guess you can die of being alone," Daniel had said to me earlier that day, about Mom.

Or, not about Mom, but *because* of Mom.

He was talking about me, though.

I was becoming the male version of a spinster.

It can happen when you grow up without enough light.

Ask anybody.

⁂

For the next year and a half or two years, Daniel was a ghost. He lived in the city, I even knew where, but the life he led—it wasn't even a mystery to me, really. I assumed it would be a follow-through of who he'd been before. And I was happy for him. One of us deserved that.

I was out at the farm, sleeping in the same bedroom I'd slept in as a boy.

Someday I'd move into Mom and Dad's room, I told myself. Someday.

The lacy drapes in Janine's room were so fragile now that touching them made them crumble. Nearly three decades of sunsets can do that.

At night, crossing to my desk for another round of pages, I would find myself watching the window over the kitchen sink. For fireflies. For Janine. She never came, though. She'd never even been born. Finally, as I'd known all along was going to happen, I walked out into the trees with a new shovel, to settle this argument.

Our big tree was the same as it had always been. In tree-years, the intervening decades hadn't even been a blink.

The grave mound was long gone, of course. Now there were beer bottles and old magazines scattered around, meaning teenagers had discovered our idyllic spot. The models in the magazines were wearing clothes from years ago, staring up at me from the past.

I pushed the blade of the shovel into the ground, leaned over it, gave it my meager weight and dug deeper than my dad had, just to be sure.

Nothing.

That night I dug two holes.

The next night, three.

On the fourth night, angry, I raised the shovel before me formally, like a cross I was about to plant once and for all, and sliced down through a long slender root. I closed my eyes, sure this had been the taproot. That this tree had lived two hundred years just to have me kill it by accident. Kill it to settle a debate that was only happening in my head.

If it had been the taproot, and if my dim recollection that this was a good way to kill a tree was accurate, it would be a week or more before the leaves wilted at the edges, anyway.

I didn't know if I could force myself to watch. Meaning, this tree was either going to be alive or dead to me for the next few decades. When I'd think about it, the picture of it in my mind would shudder between possibilities, and that clutch in my gut would be either guilt or relief. Either absolution or condemnation.

And Daniel was right: The waxy cardboard box, it had long since been reclaimed. I kept hoping for at least a rusted staple to prove the burial, the coffin, the funeral, we'd all been complicit in staging, but even staples would have turned back to earth, this long after.

It was about this time that something started going wrong with my stomach. With my digestion. The doctor my plan allowed told me it was nerves, it was stress, that I would push through, get better. Not to worry. Then he clapped my shoulder, guided me back out into the daylight of the city.

I stood in the parking lot by my car for longer than the attendant understood. He watched me the whole way past his little guard booth, perhaps trying to gauge for himself the news I'd just received. It would be a game you would come up with just to stay sane, sitting in that booth day after day.

I was dying, I didn't tell him.

It was that house. Living there, it was killing me the same way it had

Dad, the same way it had Mom. Because I had no real connections to the world, no fibers or tendrils reaching out from me, connecting me to people, the world was letting me go. Letting me slip through. Maybe it was even a mercy.

And the house was the mechanism. My stomach had been fine before, my digestion nothing I'd ever had to think about.

Radon, lead paint, asbestos, contaminated water, treated lumber sighing its treatment back out: It could be anything poisoning me.

I had to warn Daniel. Sell the house after my funeral, I would tell him. After I'm gone, get rid of it. Don't keep it because of Janine. She was never even real, man. And she's not there anymore, either. I looked. I looked and I looked. She's gone. And it's for the best.

Driving to the address I had lodged in my head like a tumor, the townhouse listed under Daniel's name for years in our shared legal documents and invoices, I indexed in my head the talk I was going to give him. It made it more real, having an index. Being able to turn to this page for that part, another page for a different part.

It calmed me, kept me between the lines the whole way over.

I parked behind his garage, blocking him in if he was there—the visitor slots were all taken—knocked on his door. No answer. I didn't knock again, just sat on his patio and studied the sides of my hands, my stomach groaning in its new way. After twenty or thirty minutes, the super or maintenance man came by, greeted me by Daniel's name.

"Brother," I corrected, stopping him, waving off the apology already coming together on his face.

"Oh, yeah," the super or maintenance man said, close enough now to see. "Mr. Robbins not home yet?"

"Guess not," I said. "I can wait. He didn't know I was coming by. Kind of a surprise reunion."

"Here," the maintenance man said, and stepped past, and, just on the authority of family resemblance, opened the door with the master key, pushed it open before me as if to prove this was really happening.

It was an indication of how little of a threat I looked to be. An indication of how frail I must appear, that sitting on patio furniture in the sunlight could be considered cruel, could be something he would want to save me from.

"You can die of being alone," I said to myself, once I had Daniel's door pulled shut behind me.

Daniel's place was much as I guess I'd imagined it: black-and-white prints bought as a set—some national park, and the sky above it—a sectional leather couch, a large television set rimed with dust. An immaculate kitchen. Ice-cold refrigerated air.

I called Daniel's name just to be sure.

Nothing.

I settled into the couch, couldn't figure out his remote control.

I felt like an intruder. Like one of those people who break into vacation homes and move through them like ghosts, running their palms over the statuettes, over the worn arms of the dining room chairs.

I almost left, to do this right, to call him, arrange a proper visit.

For all I knew, when he came home there would a girl under his arm fresh from happy hour, him having to guide her shoulders so she could find the couch. So she could find the couch occupied by her date's pale reflection.

I stood, breathing harder than made sense for somebody alone in a room, and told myself just the bathroom, and that I was to leave it exactly as it was, no splashes, no drops, no towels hung obviously crooked, no smudges on the mirror. And then I would leave.

Except on the back of the toilet was a mason jar, one of those kinds with the lids that have wire cages on them, to trap all the air. Behind the thick glass was what I assumed to be potpourri, or some sort of collection of dried moss strands. I picked it up gingerly, turned it to the side.

It was hair. Long winds of dry hair.

I rolled the jar in my hand, studying it. The hair was in sedimentary layers. Like a curio from a gift shop.

I shook the jar timidly. All the hair stayed the same. And it really was hair. I set it down, zipped up, and was going to leave it there, had told myself it was the only sensible thing to do. It wasn't sensible to interrogate strangers' decorations. And that's what my brother was, by now, a stranger.

Still. I came back to the jar, tried to twist the top off to smell—this *had* to be something decorative, something all other single men knew about as a matter of course—but the lever had rusted shut, from the steam of a thousand showers.

"Good," I said out loud. This wasn't my business anyway. This wasn't my life.

When I saw the metallic red hair a few layers up from the bottom, though, my fingers opened of their own accord.

The jar shattered on the side of the toilet, the hair unwinding on the tile floor, taking up the space of a human head, and still writhing, looking for its eventual shape.

I could still hear that redhead's dart sucking into the dartboard. Could still see her standing at the line painted onto the floor of that bar. But I couldn't see the rest of her life.

She hadn't been the first, and she hadn't been the last.

The way I made it make sense was that Daniel had become a hairstylist instead of an electrical engineer. That, when he'd hit thirty, he'd changed professions, gone with his heart instead of a paycheck. He got more interested in the people in the crosswalk than in the traffic queue-up at the lights.

Daniel, who was just as indifferent with his wardrobe and appearance as I'd always been. He'd be no better a hairstylist than I would.

Still, this couldn't be what it seemed.

I felt my way out of the bathroom, made myself walk not into his bedroom—smelling where he slept would be too intimate—and not back down the stairs like I'd promised myself, but to the only other door on this floor I hadn't been through. The only door that was closed.

I told myself I was just going to reach in, turn the light on in there long enough to catalog it as storage or living space—*I might need to stay here one night someday, brother*—but then, the door open just enough for my forearm, my hand patting the wall for a light switch, something scurried behind me.

I turned, didn't catch it.

The sense the sound left in my head, though, it was an armadillo, somehow.

No: a possum.

I clutched the door frame, my heart slapping the inside walls of my chest, a sweet, grainy smell assaulting the inside of my head, and looked into what was neither living space nor storage, exactly.

This was an operating room.

On the table, tied down at all four corners, was the latest woman.

All Daniel's attention had been focused on her stomach.

He'd been looking for something, I could tell.

Above the table, on the ceiling, was a large mirror. Meaning the girl had been alive when this started.

I shivered, hugged my arms to my sides, and felt my chin about to tremble.

On one of the flaps of skin that had been folded back from her middle, there was still a black line.

Daniel was drawing that baby shape on the body before he cut in. And he was cutting in to free the doll, the doll he knew had to be there, the doll Mom and Dad had practically promised was going to be there.

Janine was still whispering to him.

I shook my head *no, no, please,* and when I turned to leave, there they were on the wall. All the dolls he'd . . . not *found,* that was impossible, that was wrong.

The dolls he'd bought and salvaged and sneaked home. The dolls that completed the ritual he'd learned before his fifth birthday.

They were all wired to a pegboard, their smooth plastic bodies covering nearly every hole, and the pegboard was the whole wall, by now. This was the work of years. This was a lifetime.

To honor them, the blood and meat the dolls had been wrapped in to simulate the birth for Daniel, it had all been left to dry on them.

I threw up, had to fall onto my hands to do it, it was so violent.

And then the scurrying again. In the hall.

I looked up just after *something* had crossed from one side of the doorway to the other. And where my ears told my eyes to look, it wasn't up at head-level, at person-level, but at knee-level.

Instead of a possum now, what I saw in my head was the doll my dad had bought for Janine. The one we'd buried. Only, it was crawling around on all fours, its elbows cocked higher than its back, its face turned up to keep its eyes opened.

And when she talked, it was going to be that same language she'd taught Daniel. That same dead tongue.

I stood, fell back, dizzy, not used to this kind of exertion, and my hand splashed into the insides of the girl on the table, and I felt two things in the same instant. The first was the warmth of this girl's viscera, when I'd assumed she'd been dead for hours, long enough to have cooled down. The second thing I felt was what Daniel was always looking for: a hard plastic doll foot. From the doll inside each of us, if you know where to look. If you cut at the exact right instant, and reach in with confidence, with faith.

My hand closed on the smooth foot and the moment dilated, threatened to swallow me whole.

I brought my hand back gently, so as not to disturb. So as to pretend this hadn't just happened.

Whatever was in the hall had seen, though. Or heard the girl's insides, trying to suction my hand in place.

Save her, a hoarse voice whispered, from just past the doorway. *Don't let her drown.*

I stared at the wall of dolls, none of their lips able to move. I stared into the black abyss of the doorway. I studied the front and back sides of my gore-smeared hand.

"Daniel?" I said. Because I'd recognized the voice. Because who else could it be?

Save her, the voice whispered again, from lower in the hallway than a person's head would be.

Unless that person was crawling. Unless, in the privacy of his own home, that person flashed around from room to room like that. Because that was who he was. That was *what* he was.

"Please," I said.

No answer.

I backed to the wall, shaking my head no, shaking my head *please,* and, from this new angle, could see into the supply closet, the one Daniel had taken the door off of. Probably because his hands, in this room, didn't want to be touching doorknobs.

The doll our father had buried in our childhood, she was standing between two stacks of foggy plastic containers.

She'd been dressed, was just staring, her eyelashes black and perfect, her expression innocent, waiting.

Janine.

I wanted to fall to my knees—to give up or in thanks, I wasn't really sure. I put my hand to my face and didn't just smear my cheek and open eyes with the black insides of this dead girl, but my lips as well. My tongue darted out like for a crumb, just instinct, and the breathing in the hall got raspier. Less patient. Like this was building to something for him.

It made me cough that kind of cough that comes right before throwing up.

Out in the hall, Daniel sighed from deep in his mania, and then there was a sound like he'd fallen over. From my wall, I could see one of his bare feet through the doorway, toes up.

It was trembling. Like something was feeding on his face. Like the possum had come for him after all these years.

I crashed to the doorway to protect him, my little brother, to kick away whatever had him by the face.

It was just Daniel, though. He was spasming, his whole body, his eyes closed. It was a seizure. It was ecstasy.

"Daniel, Daniel," I said, on my knees now, taking his head in my lap.

He trembled and drew his arms in tight, his mouth frothing.

After a whole life of being alone with his task, with his compulsion, with his crusade, I'd finally joined him, I knew.

This wasn't a seizure, it was an orgasm. A culmination of all his dreams. I was the only one who could possibly understand what he'd become. What he was doing. And I was here.

His breath, it smelled like soap, and I had to picture him flaking a bar into a pile then lining his gums with it.

I sat down farther, to better cradle his head, and when I had to angle him up to an almost sitting position, his eyes rolled open and he looked over to me, then down to my stomach as well, for the gift he'd been denied. The miracle he'd trained himself to sense.

My stomach. My digestion.

It wasn't nerves. What I was experiencing, what I was feeling, it was smoother than nerves. More plastic.

I unsnapped my shirt, looked down where Daniel was, and the vague outline of a tiny hand pressed against the back side of my skin when I breathed in, like it was stable, it was steady. It was me doing the moving.

I pushed away, into the hall wall, let Daniel's head fall to the carpet and bounce, his eyes closing mechanically, his right foot still trembling.

I was breathing too fast and I was breathing not at all.

And I could hear it now, too, the whispering.

From the shop.

A whispering, but a gurgling, too.

The doll in the dead girl's still-warm entrails. The doll Daniel had wanted me to save.

The whole wall watched me cross the room on ghost feet. I looked to Janine for confirmation, and when she didn't say this was wrong, I plunged my hand back into the remains on the table, found the foot I'd felt earlier, and birthed this smooth plastic body up into the light, the woman's corruption stringing off it.

When I turned the doll right side up, its eyes rolled open to greet me, its lashes caked with blood.

I carried the doll by the leg to Daniel and brought it up between us like a real fresh-born baby, but it only made him shake his head no, like I wasn't getting it. Like I didn't see.

"Over, over, over again," he said, turning sideways to reach down the hall. He tried to stand but wasn't recovered from his fit yet. He fell into the wall, slid down.

I looked where he'd meant to go, though.

The only light that way was the bathroom.

I drifted there, the doll upside down by my leg again, its hard plastic fingers brushing my calf through my slacks.

The hair. The sedimentary tufts of hair.

That had to be what he meant. Over, over: *start* over. The traffic light goes red, then it cycles back to green again, and hovers on yellow, spilling back to red.

I carried the tufts of hair back, jewels of glass glittering on those dried strands.

When I knelt down by Daniel again, he opened his mouth like a baby bird and I knew I was right: this was part of his process. You save one doll from inside a woman, and you start over with hair from one of the other women. Like paying. Like trading. Like closing a thing you'd opened.

"Here, here," I said, fingering the hair from the jar, packing his mouth with it. His eyes watered, spilled over with what I took to be joy. "It'll be all right," I whispered. "We're saving her, Daniel. We're saving her."

He coughed once, hearing his name, then again, and, using two fingers, I shoved the wad of hair in deeper, so it could bathe in his stomach juice like a pearl. So it could become a soul for him again.

I kissed him once on the forehead when his body started jerking again, this time for air, and when he bit the two fingers I was using to make him human again, I inserted the new doll's hand instead.

It held the hair in place until Daniel calmed. Until he went to sleep. Until there was no more breath.

I moved his right foot, to get his tremble going again, but there was nothing left.

My little brother was dead. His mission was over.

I kissed Daniel's closed eyes, my lips pressing into each thin eyelid for too long, like I could keep him here, at least until I removed my lips.

Behind those eyelids, though, the balls of his eyes were already turning hard like the yolks of boiled eggs.

This is how you say goodbye.

I stood, wiped that new doll's ankle clean—plastic holds prints—and stepped back into the shop, used a scalpel to remove the patch of carpet I'd thrown up onto. I rolled the carpet up like a burrito.

Without looking up to them, I nodded to the open-eyed dolls then turned the light off with my wrist, stepped over what was left of Daniel, and made my way through the living room, out the front door.

"He ever show up?" the super or maintenance man asked, suddenly pruning something in the flower bed that didn't need pruning. Meaning he'd had second thoughts about letting me in. He was standing guard now. He was on alert.

In one hand I was clutching a small patch of rolled carpet I'd never be able to explain.

On my other hip, her cool face in my neck, was Janine.

I looked back to the door I'd just locked.

"No, never did," I said, "but there's water on the floor in his kitchen."

The super or maintenance man stood, his brow furrowed.

"Sink?" he said.

"Refrigerator," I said, and followed him back in, pulled the door shut behind us, twisting the dead bolt.

Ten minutes later I stepped out again, my breathing back to normal, almost.

"Well, that was different," I said to Janine, and hitched her higher.

Walking along the side of the house back to the garage, to my car, I had to turn my head away from her to cough, and then place my hand on the wall to steady myself.

What is it? she asked

Her voice was perfect.

I spit a shiny conglomerate of segmented blackness up into my palm, and studied it.

"Nothing," I told her, and somewhere between there and the car, I left my soul behind me on the ground.

After and Back Before

by Miranda Siemienowicz

Kayna pulls herself to the top of the woven metal structure that is the uprooted base of a great, fallen spire. The bars that make up the monument are almost too hot to hold, and even her feet feel the heat through their rough wrappings of cloth. She shades her eyes with a grin. Across a deep, dry riverbed are the tallest standing ruins on the rubble plain. They are two brick shells on the far bank, one high and sharp, one low, long, and dome-topped: the church and the station building.

She climbs down and waits for Bel. When they were younger, before either had any responsibility in the commune, he would have been the one in front. He used to drag her up the sheer gully walls to lie in the dirt and look out across the endless, undulating rubble. This is the first time they have been more than a half day from the gully, and she hasn't seen his back ahead of her since they left. Now she squats, watching the hot plains wind stir dust off the heaped debris until he finally reaches her side.

Bel kneels and unwraps the small cloth bundle at his hip. He offers her a strip of dry possum meat from their dwindling supply—all they could take unnoticed.

Kayna shakes her head. "I don't want to get thirsty."

He tucks the bundle away and runs a dusty hand through his short, ragged hair. "I thought we would have found water by now," he says.

"I know." She sees her own wry smile echoed on Bel's face. Mrs. Mary had always told them they might as well have been identical. That as soon they could walk she would leave them naked just so she could tell them apart.

"You take her for this," Bel says. He hands Kayna their small leather Smiling Face, just bigger than his fist. She cups the little doll's head, runs her thumb over the twisted hair stitched through its curved lips.

"She won't talk to me here," says Kayna. "It's full of dead things."

He shifts his feet. "And she'll talk to me? It's been—"

"Months," Kayna finishes. "I know." She hooks the twine that is wound around its upswept hair through her belt. They stand.

Back before, there had been a bridge between the riverbanks. This has fallen in as a concave stretch of broken asphalt slabs. The brick bases of two sets of supports still rise from the silt. They cross the river-bed upstream from the bridge and scramble up a hillock of broken brick and pavers. Tall wooden and steel poles spear the ground here and there.

The face of the church is a gargantuan brick sheet, laced with nar-row windows, each capped with a tightly curved arch. At one side of the facade, the needle-sharp spike of a spire rises. Its mate is fallen in, the base jutting up like a hollow stump. Between and beyond them, at the rear of the building, the third and largest spire still holds court over the rubble.

"Blinding light," Bel curses. "I never thought it would be so—"

"Enormous. I know. The elders would burn to know we're here."

Bel reaches for her hand.

"We'll find something. I know it," says Kayna.

All of a sudden, Bel drops to the ground. He pulls Kayna with him, hissing: "Get down! Get down!" and drags her in a crouching, clumsy run toward the yellow expanse of the station building.

"Go!" he says. "There's someone there."

Kayna cranes over her shoulder as she staggers. Then she sees it. Be-yond the debris-covered junction of roads that separate the two build-ings, the church steps are clear and clean. Someone is living here.

The station building looks looted and abandoned. Great hunks of concrete fill the open mouth of the ancient entrance like rotten teeth. They scramble down and run across the buried street, striding between the biggest boulders, slipping as the smaller rocks and chunks of debris shift under their feet. The Smiling Face bounces against Kayna's hip and she catches it in her free hand. They are halfway to the building's stained steps as the first projectile lands, cracking against the rubble an armspan in front of Bel. He veers as a second rock slams to the ground near the first. This one Kayna has managed to see coming, falling in the end of an arc that must have begun from the heights of the church. A spray of grit from the impact showers her leg as she turns after Bel and they run, now frantic, toward cover. More rocks strike the rubble behind them, and then they are outside the range. The shadow of the station building falls cool over Kayna's head.

They clamber between the mounds of fallen concrete until the church is out of sight and fold, gasping, to the cold floor. Kayna wraps her arms around Bel. His eyes are wet.

"I'm sorry," she says. "I'm sorry. This wasn't supposed to happen. They're supposed to be dead. Everyone else is supposed to be dead."

"I know, Kay," he says. "It's okay. It's not your fault. I wanted to know, too."

Kayna closes her fist around the Smiling Face and pulls Bel's hand down over her own. She tries to listen over the sound of her racing heart. She does want to know. She has wanted to know for as long as she can remember.

"Clean born! Clean born!" screamed the little girl keeping Kayna and Bel cowering against the gully wall. Though they were only a handful of years her junior, she was far taller than either and, in any case, she had their Smiling Face dangling aloft from one hand.

Kayna leapt for the swinging totem.

"Can't jump high enough, clean born?" One twitch, and the Smiling Face flew in a long arc through the air, trailing hair and twine, toward the hands of two older boys standing ten paces behind. The younger of the pair caught it with a snatch and clambered up the gumtree beside them, to be quickly masked by the pale green leaves. The older boy leaned against the slick trunk. His skin was whiter than the ghostly bark, paleness broken only by three thick bands of shallow scar across his chest. Fabric burns. Many elders and some children had these permanent emblems of the clothes they were wearing when the light came. He spat a thick gob of blood into the dust at his feet and grinned, his teeth pink.

Kayna planted her feet apart. "Give that back."

"Why should we?"

"You're no better than us," said Bel.

"Do you think so?" said the girl. "Want to make a bet? Simon—ask them something. About back before."

"No blinding way!" said Bel. "Simon's old. He remembers things. You . . . you could barely walk. You don't know any more than we do."

The girl bristled. "I know, all right. I remember it. Trees in the park when the light came. Real trees, a forest. Millions. My mother took me and we ran as far as we could. There was fire everywhere. She was burned all down her face and her arms. We tried to get to my father, but we never made it. I remember."

"Do you remember what your mother looked like? Without the burns?" asked Kayna.

The girl froze, her eyes wide. Kayna took a ragged breath, her heart pounding, and then she was on her. They fell. Sharp fingernails raked Kayna's face as she tried to curl up to protect herself. Then she felt Bel's weight land on the two of them.

"You don't even remember anything about your mother," came the girl's voice, muffled by Kayna's defensive hands. "She makes it through when the light comes, then dies when you're born! You don't have any memories at all. Just a little luck totem!"

"I bet you wish you had even that!" screamed Bel on top of her. There were fingers in Kayna's hair now, tearing at the roots. The two thrashing bodies held her pinned so tight to the ground she couldn't fill her lungs.

"Okay, Rebecca," came Simon's voice from the base of the tree.

"Get lost!" she screamed. "Little stupid clean borns don't know a thing!"

"Yeah, but that's enough. Mrs. Mary is really going to burn if she sees you hurt them." Simon's voice neared and then Rebecca was dragged away. Bel staggered up and Kayna was left blinking at the midday sky. She crawled backward until her back hit the secure wall of the gully cliff. She shot a glance up the gum. The boy crouched in the branches, waiting for his next cue.

"Give it," said Simon, walking back to the tree. The boy dropped the Smiling Face into his waiting hands.

"Thanks." Simon grinned. He spat another gob of blood into the dirt and threaded the twine into his belt, the little head jostling another just like it hanging at his hip. "I've always wanted another one. Wait 'til I get these two Faces talking."

"Ha!" Rebecca shouted. "Stupid clean borns."

Kayna lunged for Simon. He grabbed her wrists and, with a foot in her belly, forced her back into the dirt. Turning back to the commune buildings, he walked lazily, like his fatigue was all arrogance. Rebecca ran to keep up and the boy in the tree slid down and trotted after.

"They took it," said Bel. He knelt beside her.

"What do you think they remember that we don't?" she asked.

"What? What do you mean?"

"There's something. Something they all know," she said. "That's why they're like this."

"Don't be stupid," said Bel. "You can't listen to what they say. We know everything there is to know. You've heard your lessons." He punched her softly in the ribs and she leaned away, mouth pursed.

"Sure, I have. But don't you wonder if there's—"

"Something else? Like what?"

"I don't know. But they're right. We don't know how it happened."

Bel shoved her harder. "Stop it! Rebecca's making that stuff up. You know she is. She doesn't remember the forest. She just says that. Most of the other kids were younger than we are now. None of them really remember. Maybe Simon. And probably Lauren before she died. That's it."

She looked at Bel. "You really think so?"

He nodded.

They waited for the others to be lost behind the trees before making their way back to the buildings. That was the first night Mr. John took Bel to work on the generator. Kayna didn't want to eat without him. She went to their room as the motor started rumbling in the distance, pouring light into the only building they were allowed, intermittently, to power. The elders were talking as food was prepared. Rebecca ran past outside, grabbing at the heavy linen that hung in the window frame.

"Stop it," hissed Kayna, tugging the fabric straight. She crawled onto the mattress to wait for Bel. And there it was, their Smiling Face under the rags beneath the window. The smug curve of the matted, stitch-crossed mouth smiled up. Yet another all-knowing face. She took it anyway, hung it around her neck. Then she pushed the window hanging aside and slid over the sill to the ground. The night air was still brisk, and the hairs on her arms rose.

The moon cast an orange glow on the walls around her. She padded to the next building. The heavy wooden panels that would cover the doorways in the coldest months were propped against the walls. Kayna slipped inside and felt her way in the gloom.

"Simon?" she called. "You gave it back. Bel hasn't seen it yet. He went to see Mr. John." She raised her voice. "Simon?"

Simon lay curled and still on his mattress, his face on a bundle of bloodstained rags, eyes half open. His skin was already cool under Kayna's fingers. She jerked her hand back with a gasp, then swore under her breath. She should have been used to this already. She crouched.

"Thank you, Simon," she whispered. His own Smiling Face still hung around his neck, its soot-black hair a little pool of night in the dim room. She touched the twisted hair crossing its lips. "Thank you."

⁂

Huddled with Bel in the ruined entrance of the station building, Kayna can hear nothing. She shifts in her crouch, her ears straining. Shards of light pierce in angles through the broken concrete around them, cast down through the yawning space. High above—as high, it seems, as clouds should hang—the ancient ceiling is partly fallen in. A great room is visible above through jagged holes, and more light spears down from that incredible height.

"We can't stay here," she says. "They've seen us go in."

"You want to go back out?"

She shakes her head. "Inside. There may be another way out."

A high, alien cry pierces the air. It is a pained, enraged sound that sings off the vast, pillared walls around them. That first peal is distant. Their hands are locked, fingers clutching. There are faint sounds of movement. The second cry is clear and near.

They scramble upright, stumble away from the sound and the light and through an ancient charred doorway behind them. In the sudden, enclosing gloom there is a small room, another doorway, a narrow passage, and then stairs. They could go down and out to the street, try to outrun the survivors. Their eyes meet. Another shriek comes from immediately outside and they charge the last dusty stretch to the stairs and climb up into the ruin of the station building.

The stairs wind around three great turns until they come to the final floor. Out into a passageway and Kayna is now higher than she has ever been. She flattens her back against the wall as the wind pours through the gaping window frames and whips her hair. The rubble plain is spread far below, a roughened flat with mounds of ruins scattered, insignificant below this giant. Back past the broad scar of the dry riverbed, the fallen metal spire stretches toward them. It was softened in a great heat as it fell, and the woven poles of the shaft look tossed down like a bundle of rope.

They pass room after filthy room. Every commune building could be laid end to end along this passage and still not stretch its length. Finally the passage expands into a long, broad space under a curved ceiling, the walls two series of rolling arched window frames, partly boarded with plywood and sheet metal. Vague in the new gloom is a mass of scavenged junk. Kayna recognizes chairs and tables, but there is a heap of other, stranger objects strewn between. The hot wind whistles off the edges of the boarding and stirs the high, acrid stink of urine and shit. She freezes.

"Bel—"

He is pressed close beside her. The tremor she feels could be either of them. The howl of the wind drops for a moment and another wail sounds from below. It's inside.

Something shuffles in the murky depths of the room.

"Young people," a voice drawls. It is older than anything she has ever heard. The crackle and waver of it is terrifying.

"Did our son bring you?" The speaker stands in the darkness and moves toward them.

Another voice: "Who is it? Who's there?" Deeper, more tremulous than the first.

Kayna and Bel take two steps back, turn, and run. On their right, the empty windows over the plain. On their left, the doorways onto small, dusty rooms. Fallen sheets of patterned metal lie on the floor. Pipes cling unsteadily to the walls. But through the next doorway, stairs heading up to . . . where? Something had caved in from above the day the light came, or after, and there is more debris than there is clear space. They climb over and may even be halfway to the next landing when everything slides out from under them, collapsing down toward the passageway below. Kayna's face slams into the concrete as she slides. She throws herself over onto her back.

"Bel!" she screams, looking down. He is moving, near the base of the stairs, but slowly. She slithers over the rubbish to reach him. "Bel?"

"Kay. I'm . . . I'm not sure. I . . ." He looks up. His hands are covered in blood. He is kneeling beside a ragged sheet of knife-like tin, one leg of his trousers a shock of vivid red.

"It doesn't hurt," he says. He stands and falls, looks down at his leg.

There is movement in the passage. The wind hums in gusts, and over that there is the sound of someone walking with slow, painstaking steps.

"Young ones?" That first voice again, like footsteps in the rubble. This one is probably a woman.

"Who?" The other one calls in the distance. A man?

"He's brought us—did you see?—two of them."

"Bel," whispers Kayna. "She can barely walk. Come on. All we have to do is run. Blinding light, we should have just gone out."

"Kay?" Bel's face is soft. "Sure." He looks at his leg again.

She pushes past him. The ancient woman is shuffling toward them, still two or three doors down and hidden in the half-dark. Kayna seizes Bel's wrist and drags him behind. He falls again and her grip breaks, sending her to her knees.

"Come on!" she shrieks, scrambling up and taking his hand. He looks up, for a moment angry and confused, then his face falls and he pushes himself up on his good leg. He begins to lumber down the passage, Kayna taking some of his weight.

It takes an eternity to get back as far as the first stairwell. Kayna looks back. "Bel? Down? Or not?" But he is staring past her, down the stairs. She turns.

Her heart stalls. On the landing is a man, the height and age of Mr. John. He is half the weight, his hips sitting sharp above a rough cloth skirt. His chest is laddered with ribs, and across it are emblazoned the regular, stamped outlines of a fabric burn. It must be lettering. Kayna can't slow her head enough to try to read it.

He opens his arms wide. Deep hollows sink above his collarbones. He wails. The sound is a celebration now, and it trails into high, frantic words.

"Welcome, welcome, welcome—well, well! Welcome! Here you are! I could see you since yesterday, you know. See you, seeing you out on the desert dry desert dump out there walking. Well! What to do, what to do, now that you're here?"

They back across the passage. Cold brick hits Kayna's knees but she is up against a window frame, not solid wall. Another flinch and she would be over the low ledge and into that unreal, miniature landscape outside.

"What to do?" He begins to climb the last flight of stairs. "What do I do? Doing, seeing that, now that you are here?" Kayna glances back along the passage. The old woman continues her patient trail. She is halfway to them, now shuffling through a spill of light. She too wears a ragged skirt. An old shirt hangs torn from a shoulder, a thick, gnarled skin burn extending up across her face. One breast is free, pale and thin as if pouring down her chest.

"You know, I don't know. I don't know if I should keep you. I don't know."

Farther up the passage, long enough for two, maybe three more rooms, there is a dark doorway. More stairs? She can't see.

"I don't know if I should kill you." He's at the top of the stairs. He could touch them now. "I don't know if I should fuck you." He pauses, one hand on the wall. "I don't know if I should eat you. Hey!" He laughs, a sharp peal that makes Kayna grip the dusty windowsill. "Hey! Eat you drink you shit you piss you. Back into the dirt. Into the goddamn dirt!"

Kayna shoves Bel ahead and they stagger toward the darkened doorway. It isn't far. If they can make it. If there are stairs.

"Dirt!" the man yells, making no move to follow them. "Dirt and dark and dung and damn goddamn hey! Hey!"

Past more fallen rubble, they reach the doorway and beyond is not darkness after all. Through an anteroom into another and there is light, falling through four square, pillared window frames. The wind is hot and clear. There are no stairs, just the ragged holes in the floor they had seen from below as they cowered on the entranceway floor. It is so far beneath them now she can't even imagine having stood there. They stop in the doorway and Bel falls heavily against the frame. Kayna tests the concrete with a foot. A crack resounds through the building and a massive hunk of floor splits off and plummets to the ground below. There is half a heartbeat then the flat thud of its landing. Kayna staggers back. Bel falls, winded, his legs and feet over the edge. She seizes his arms.

"The pack," he says. Their little bundle of rags has slid below his hips, trapped by the edge of the broken masonry.

"I can't get it," says Kayna, dropping to her belly, still holding Bel's outstretched arms. He kicks his legs and she pulls and somehow he is back, safe and panting, on the floor. The pack is gone.

※

Mrs. Mary was bent over the low fire. The coals were a mound of red as hot as the sun just cresting above the gully walls. She wore a ragged skirt and a broad scarf to bind her breasts. The palm-size flowers of fabric burns cascaded down her broad back. Thick skin burns, like a whorled armour, spread across her right arm and shoulder.

"Is Aybel with Mr. John?" Mrs. Mary asked. Her rippled, scarred arm moved stiffly as she assembled a frame over the embers.

"Yes," said Kayna. "He goes there every day now." She smoothed the fabric wrapping the bundle beside her in the dirt. "Every day." The coals crackled.

Mrs. Mary looked at her for a long moment. "Okay, Kayna," she said finally. "It's low enough now. Bring him here."

Kayna lifted the limp thing from its shroud. The little feet were turned in to each other, the hands a splash of too many tiny fingers. The eyes were open to nothing, a pair of filmy orbs at the crest of a stunted face. This one had not moved, had not even taken a breath.

"Why did Mrs. Karen have another baby? We knew this was going to happen," she said.

Mrs. Mary's calloused hands laid the little body across the struts. "We didn't know for sure, Kayna. Mrs. Karen is the only one of us who has carried since the light came. We don't know if it's her or the men—why this happens. If she is strong enough, it's important that we keep trying."

"It's not going to work."

"You don't know that, Kayna." Her voice was low. Kayna settled back on her heels to watch the fire, took a blackened poker in one hand and nudged the coals.

"Poor pretty thing," Mrs. Mary whispered. She shifted the limbs, folding them across the tiny, bell-shaped chest.

"How long is this going to take?" asked Kayna.

"Tomorrow's dawn. It needs to be slow. Everything must be completely dry or he won't keep."

"Am I just supposed to sit here?"

"Be watchful. Turn him when he needs. Don't let the frame rest on his face."

Kayna pushed at the coals again. They spread out beneath the frame.

"Don't leave them too thin, or the heat will be too low. Here. We'll shore them up better," said Mrs. Mary.

"Do you want more of those rocks?" Kayna pointed.

"Concrete, Kayna," said Mrs. Mary, hefting a fist-size hunk. "What's this? A piece of concrete. Show me a rock."

Kayna fussed in the debris near the fire, reciting. "Concrete, we made. Rocks, the earth made. I know, I know. Here." She held out a smooth, yellow-brown rock.

"Good," said Mrs. Mary. "Be careful. Don't mix those up. You know better."

⁂

Bel crawls to the dim anteroom, slumps against the wall. Kayna sinks down beside him. Shouts come from far down the passageway. He lets her pull the torn fabric of his trousers aside, expose the long, clean wound below his groin. Blood oozes slowly from its dark lips.

"Push on it, Bel. You've got to push on it." She pulls a strip of fabric from her trousers, bundles it into a hard ball and holds it against the wound. She takes Bel's hands and presses them down. "Can you? Push." He nods. She feels his arms stiffen weakly. "Hard, Bel."

She lets go of his hands and presses her forehead against his. "So what if we can't run," she whispers. Her fingers find the Smiling Face and she holds it against his chest. "We'll be okay. She may not be talking now, but she's still listening."

Kayna hears the words coming from her mouth, sees Bel nodding yes. She doesn't believe them. And she knows he doesn't either. She keeps talking.

"I love you, Bel. You know that. Just you and me. Clean borns. And maybe that's what they're missing. Not able to see all this how it is, because they're crying inside for back before. But we don't get that. We can see and know everything how it is now." She looks down, turns the little head over in the gloom. The pale stitching across the mouth is barely brighter than the rest. She feels Bel's shallow breath on her face.

"Let's get home, okay?" she says.

She kisses him. They are trapped. The survivor is shouting back down the passageway and, just then, she doesn't want to miss the chance of something. So she kisses him. Not on the head or the cheek, not like she would to wake him or thank him, but on the mouth. Bel's mouth, so like hers, a sweet thing she has watched and heard since she can remember, is altogether new and incredible when she feels it pressed like this on her own. She can smell his skin. And for now it doesn't smell like generator grease or diesel. It smells like her. A shock of heat goes through her gut and, in the dirty gloom, her eyes flash open. She sees his filthy hair, his own closed eyes. She pushes at him with her body, runs a hand up his back and closes her fingers around the hair at the back of his neck. For one blissful moment, his back arches and his chest presses against hers. This is it. Then he pushes her away and scrambles back into the corner.

"Don't!" His voice is tight and angry. "Why did you do that?"

"Bel? What do you mean? I . . ." Kayna's belly is a cold pit. The words and wailing down the passage sound so distant she can hardly hear them.

"I love you," she says again. This time she realizes he doesn't say it back. "I'm sorry. I didn't mean . . . I just—"

"You've ruined it," he spits at her. "Look at you. You've ruined everything. You're just like him."

"Bel, I—" She makes to crawl toward him.

"Don't touch me!" He backs farther into the corner. He starts crying.

"Oh, blinding light, Bel. What have I done?" She is sitting on the cool floor of the anteroom. Two or three strides from Bel, but it might as well be a day's walk between them. She stretches an arm out to him, fingers extended in the empty air. He is wiping his face and mouth, running his hands frantically through his hair.

"What did he do, Bel?" The passageway has fallen silent. "What's Mr. John been doing?" He won't answer. He drops his head between his knees. Kayna crawls to the doorway. The passage stretches into dusty darkness. The survivors are small shapes moving near the far end.

She turns back. "Bel?" He is wiping his face, but his hands are slow.

They tremble as the fingers ball again around the bundle of rag and push down on his thigh.

"Bel," she says. "They're up the other end. We need to try now." He doesn't answer.

"I'm sorry, Bel, I'm so sorry. Please. We need to get out of here."

"Go then," he whispers.

She waits. His hands grip the rag, now dark with blood. Kayna realizes she has been holding her breath and exhales in a rush of air. She stands and walks out into the middle of the passage. With her back to the cavernous room over the entranceway, the light glows across the rubble in the next doorway. So there were stairs after all.

This flight is less cluttered. She picks her way through quickly and quietly, testing each fallen block to be sure it will take her weight. Still no sound in the building. There is clear air ahead.

One full turn and there is open light. Sky. Kayna ducks, a defensive reflex in the sudden expanse.

The rubble filling the stairs is the fallen roof. Around her are the ruins of a room that led onto the rooftop itself. A great, green dome is intact over the corner of the building: the roof above the entranceway. She straightens slowly to the sighs of the wind. Past the dome she can see the church. Only the rear, tallest spire rises higher than her line of sight, the others level with where she stands. In the other direction, away from the dome and the church, the station building stretches along the riverbank. Smaller domes hump up off the rooftop and, at the end, a short, square tower squats, its crumbled summit lost. They won't get down from here, this tableland of concrete and domes suspended above the rolling expanse of rubble and ruins. They'll have to get past the others and out down the stairs they came up. She turns back inside and picks her way down.

The survivor is waiting at the foot of the stairs, sitting against the far wall of the passage. His legs are crossed beneath his skirt.

"So you're not dead," he says. "Just him, then, eh? Dead! Hey, didn't take you long, walking walking walk in the hot hacked-up desert then you get here and, you know what, you're just dead like the others."

It takes Kayna a moment to realize what he means. Then she sees the blood on his hands and the smears he has wiped onto his skirt. She leaps across the last of the concrete and dust and runs to the anteroom.

Bel is slumped on the floor. She crouches beside him and lifts his head. It lolls in her hands, his face warm on her skin.

"Bel, I'm sorry," she whispers. Her gut knots, a wave of nausea so strong it hurts. She turns Bel's face toward her and for a moment his eyes flutter open, looking through and past her. In the half-dark only the faintest light glints from them. A moment later and even that is gone, sinking suddenly under a film of tarnish. Kayna cries out. She holds him tighter. Then her feet are wet and she sees she is crouching in a sticky pool of blood.

"You think I don't know why you're here?" asks the survivor, behind her. "I know it, you know, you know I know you want it."

Kayna sinks to the floor, crawling around to cradle Bel's head and shoulders on her lap. "I don't want anything," she says. She holds him close, her arms between them and the survivor.

"You think I'm going to let you have it?" he asks. "Ha! Little animal! Scurry in and try and squirrel away my things? Creep in and crawl in and carry it all away? No. I can't let you."

"Please, just leave me alone," she whispers.

The survivor steps closer. Now she can't make out his face, his angular frame silhouetted against the brightness from the doorway. He seizes her wrist, pulling her arm away from Bel.

"You can't have it," he says.

"I'm not going to take anything," she whimpers. His clutch tightens and he drags her to her feet.

"Give it back!" he says.

"I didn't take anything!" Kayna's arm is wrenched above her head. She can smell the survivor's rancid breath. "I didn't take it!"

"But it's gone!"

Kayna stops her struggle. She gazes past him, to the doorway and the corridor beyond. A slow breath. She tries to still her wavering voice. "She took it."

The survivor straightens. "Who?" He loosens his grip and she slowly pulls her arm back, taking a step toward the wall.

"The old woman," she says.

"Mother?"

Kayna nods, her heart beating against her ribs.

He twitches his head, clenches both fists. "Mother," he snarls, turning and stalking back into the passage. "Mother!" His voice rings through the building. "I need it I want it I need it! Give it back! Mother! Fathers! The little animal is dead!"

Kayna pads to the door. The survivor is marching down the corridor, one hand punching the air, toward the room with the old people. She goes to Bel, takes his ankles in her hands and pulls him toward the door. He is so much heavier than she thought. She can just slide him if she walks backward.

She shuffles out of the anteroom, struggling to get purchase on the floor against Bel's weight. She steps down the threshold and his back and chest slide after, his head following with a loud crack. Kayna gasps.

"Bel!" She drops his feet, takes his wrists instead and swings him around. His head lolls back, hair scraping the floor. She jerks him higher, takes his elbows and somehow manages to half-lift, half-drag him to the stairs in the centre of the passage. Kayna can hear the survivor hollering. The old woman is nowhere to be seen.

As she goes down the stairs, Bel's weight leans into Kayna, urging her faster than she wants. She can't see where she's going. After half the first turn, she takes his arms behind her back and goes down forward, but even so her thighs are burning before they are halfway down. She stops on a landing, lets him slide to the ground and curls up beside him, pressing the curve of her back against his belly. She takes his arm and pulls it over her shoulder. She can see the stairs above them, a smear of blood stepping down each tread to mark their path. With her other hand she presses the Smiling Face into her chest.

"Bel," she whispers. "Don't be angry with me." She takes a deep, dusty breath, her nostrils filling with grit. "I'm so sorry. How are you ever going to forgive me now? I can't even get you home."

"Where's your brother?" asked Rebecca.

"With Mr. John."

"Again? What does he do there—hood the diesel with him? Is Bel just a sniffer, too?"

"I don't care what Mr. John does with the diesel. He's teaching Bel how to repair the generator and look after us. More than you know how to do."

Kayna was perched on the crumbling brick wall of one of the commune's ruins, her knees under her chin. Rebecca pulled herself up alongside, leaned her elbows in her lap, and swung her Smiling Face, a scruffy head with short, cropped hair, back and forth in front of her.

"Yeah. I guess I don't know much," she said. "Probably doesn't matter, though, right?" The grinning pendulum carved another arc. "I can't have too much longer to live."

"You didn't tell me you were sick already."

Rebecca shrugged. "Not that I can tell. But, you know. Why should I learn about the generator? You two clean borns . . ."

Kayna narrowed her eyes. The plains wind barely reached the gully that housed the commune buildings. Already the early sun was dragging droplets of sweat down her chest.

"We don't know if Bel and I are going to get sick, too. Just because we were born a few months after the light came. That may not make a difference."

"Sure. But it might, too."

Kayna didn't answer.

"Mrs. Karen is pregnant again," said Rebecca.

"Okay," said Kayna. "Mr. Keith?"

"Probably Mr. Chris."

Kayna shrugged. "What's this, eighth?"

"Ninth."

The gums shimmered in the gentle breeze. Through the trunks, Mrs. Mary was making up a mound of firewood. Farther out, the generator turned over in the silence.

"You still planning to sneak out? To the Epicentre?"

Kayna looked at Rebecca. The older girl had her eyes fixed, her Smiling Face loose on one palm.

"Maybe."

"You think you'll find some kind of answer?"

Another shrug.

"You think the elders aren't telling us something," said Rebecca, not taking her eyes from Kayna. "Well, I think you're wrong. There'll be nothing there but death. It's just the same as it is everywhere."

Kayna slid down from the ruined wall. "I've got to go and help." She nodded toward Mrs. Mary, now hanging a shallow pan above the fire. "That's a ritual fire." She turned her back.

"Hang on," Rebecca called.

Kayna turned.

"I do think you're wrong," said Rebecca. "But I'll go with you anyway. If I don't get sick." She grinned. "You never know."

Bel didn't come back from Mr. John until after dark. When he came into their room, Kayna was already curled on the mattress, watching the glow of the red moon through the hangings. One of the ever more scarce possums scratched softly on the roof. Bel sat with his back to her and bent to unwrap the cloth binding his feet. The stink of grease hung on his clothes.

"How's the generator going?"

"Fine."

"You were there forever tonight."

"So?" His back was curved, shoulders hunched, as he pulled at the fabric.

"Nothing, I guess," said Kayna. "Let's go to sleep, okay?" She shuffled back against the wall, clearing his side of the mattress.

Bel tossed the cloth aside. "I don't want—" He broke off. "It's really hot, Kayna. Give me a sheet. I'm going to sleep on the floor."

⁂

Kayna lies in Bel's arms until her hectic heartbeat slows to a softer pound. Then she staggers to her feet and hefts her burden into position. She can't look at his face. Her throat stings and she pulls on, but when they reach the landing where they had first found the stairs she stops. She lets Bel slip to the ground again and stumbles down the steps to the street. These have been swept as clean as those of the church, and a track has been cleared in the centre of the road passing back to the bridge, past the entranceway they had fled into for shelter. Where does she think she could get him? Away from the station building? To the riverbank? The commune? She can hear muffled clangs from movement on the third floor.

Back inside, Bel is a bloodied heap against the wall, face to the ground. Kayna's chest aches at the thought of the hours' walk between here and the commune; the hours between them and Mrs. Mary, who would take Bel and make him safe. And Kayna is going to leave him.

"Can you come just a little further, Bel?" she asks. "Then I'll let you rest. I will. I'm sorry."

Her forearms cramp from the grip she has on Bel's wrists. It is only a handful or two of panting breaths farther, deeper into the building, into a small, quiet, dirty room on this empty ground floor.

"This is far enough, isn't it? I'm sorry, Bel, that I can't get you home. But this is okay, right? We'll be okay. I just need the pack." She leaves him and walks back to the entranceway, to where their bundle of rags has fallen among the concrete boulders. There, she looks up, half-expecting the survivor's gaunt face to be grinning down through the broken ceiling. But there are just the same spears of light that fell through on them when they had cowered there before. She shakes her head, goes back.

"I've got it, Bel. I found it. I'm going to try and do this right, okay? You know I helped Mrs. Mary before. I'm a little slow, but she said I was good."

She unties the pack. A few strips of meat are still tucked in the folds. The knife is the cleanest thing in the room, its blade a wide sweep of shining sky.

"You'll like the way I do it. I was going to show you, when I helped with Simon, but you were . . ." With Mr. John? "You were busy. You'll like it."

The first cut is the line along the back of the skull, down the bones of the spine. The second is a necklace, round the front and to the back again. Where they meet they make corners, and this is where the blade works in and lifts skin from muscle. It separates from the pink beneath, the filmy white that held them together spreading like a web between the two layers. The blade clears the threads, weightless and without resistance, one hand lifting the freeing skin, the other guiding the sweep of the knife. It peels back slow and pretty, both undersurfaces glistening with secret moisture.

"She said I was good, Bel. Just wait."

Both sides of the neck skin roll up to the head like a high collar. Then the hair helps, and Kayna fills her fingers with it, pulling and lifting the skin free in the path of the blade. Her neck aches and partway through she has to drop the knife and stretch her fingers against the floor. She clenches her fists, then spreads her fingers wide. Clenched, spread, clenched, spread.

"Mrs. Mary is going to help me make you round and small, Bel. I only watched with Simon but she said she'll let me do it next time. You know it's not concrete? It's rocks. We heat sand in the shallow pan, and rocks."

Kayna takes another handful of hair and sweeps the blade again. The pink over the skull is duller, less garish than the neck. The skin rolls further and further up until she has come over and around to the backs of the ears. These are firm to cut and she pulls first one, then the other, to tauten the base as she slices beneath. Then the cheeks and forehead are smooth and soft again and the work is quick.

"I wish I could bring your eyes home, Bel. I know you'll hear me, like Mother does, but I wish you could see me, too."

Eyelids soft and careful, nose tough again like the ears, lips soft and oh so very careful. Then the full skin lifts away and slides into Kayna's lap, a soft, formless mound. "Here you go, Bel. You're not angry with me anymore, are you? Look, you're free. Mrs. Mary's going to make you warm and small and round and listening to it all. I love you."

Bel's body gazes back from the floor, his face and neck a red flush, teeth grinning, eyes wide.

"I'm glad you like it, Bel. I really am."

She wraps the knife and the bundle of precious skin and binds them to her belt. One last rag she drapes over Bel's smiling face before she goes out into the rising heat to walk home across the rubble plain.

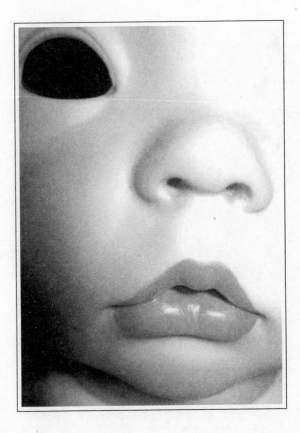

Doctor Faustus

by Mary Robinette Kowal

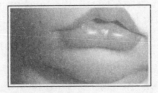

Julia stretched her back until it popped. *God*. It felt like she'd been on the marionette bridge for days. But a chance to do a remount of Orson Fucking Welles's *The Tragical History of Doctor Faustus?* Off-Broadway? Not a chance a girl turned down, even if the theater was just a blackbox crammed in the basement of an old Masonic lodge. It was still off-Broadway and still Orson Welles. And puppets for adults. Give her blood and guts over fake fur and feathers any day, thank you very much.

She leaned farther out against the rail and looked down to the stage where Kurt was doing some of the detail painting on the floor beneath the marionette bridge. "Want to take a break soon? Maybe grab a slice?"

He was scowling at the stage floor, one paint-smudged hand holding a book open near him. As per usual at this point in his process, he totally hadn't heard her.

She ran Gluttony over to him, hopping the puppet over the wet paint of the circle. "Kurt. Pizza."

"Hmm?" Blinking, he looked at the puppet, and rubbed a splash of phosphorescent paint on his forehead. Sitting back on his haunches, he tilted his head back to find her in the rafters. "What?"

"Piiiiiiiizzza." If they weren't in the basement, she'd totally call for delivery, but there was crap reception down here. She hauled the wooden control of the puppet up, catching the study lines across her left arm, to swing it over the bridge. Setting its hook carefully on the upstage side of the rail, she rolled her shoulders. Strong back muscles or no, after tech week, she always felt the full weight of the puppets. "Come on.

I'm at the point of diminishing returns and have to have a modicum of intelligence for rehearsal tomorrow."

"Sorry, I—can I just finish this?" He held up the book he'd brought in. It was a giant, battered leather-bound thing he'd found in the stacks at the New York Public Library. "I realized that I put the dot on the wrong side. It'll bug me."

She leaned back over the rail and studied his work. Parts of it still shone wetly, but once they did the final umber wash, Faust's protective circle would have a distinct, dried-blood look. From above, the sigil he was pointing at was utterly symmetrical, except for one dot on the right side. "Sweetie. No one will know."

"It's not that archaic. Someone will know the difference between a summoning and a banishing sigil. The dot has to be on the left."

She grabbed the sides of the ladder and half-slid, half- climbed down. "Seriously. I'll buy you pizza for the rest of the run if we get called on a misplaced dot."

"Remember the Civil War uniform?" He dipped his brush in the stage base paint and blotted out the offending dot. "Half the column was taken up with having a single stripe inverted. You know some re-viewer will totally lose their shit about it. Half of them are demons already."

She snorted. "Fine. I'll wash up. But as soon as you fix that, you are buying me pizza."

"Deal." He was staring at the floor again, already reaching for the red he was using for the sigils.

Julia shook her head, turning toward the washroom. The lights flared. She blinked the trails of purple from her gaze. Ozone burned her nose. A light must have blown. "Gotta love old buildings . . ."

The stage curtains billowed, rippling in dark waves up to the grid. Against her skin, the air felt tight and clammy, without a trace of a breeze, but the marionettes hanging by the bridge swayed on the ends of their long strings, creaking a little.

Wetting her lips, Julia forced herself to turn around. Kurt stood by the edge of the circle, still staring at his book. In his right hand, he held the red brush and a bright dot of red lay at his feet. The sigils . . . It was probably just an after-effect from the light that blew. They didn't have the UV on, so there was no reason the sigils should look like they were glowing.

The creaking of the wood controls on their hooks sent a shiver across Julia's back. She crossed her arms over her chest. "Hey . . . let's get out of here."

He glanced around and then did a double-take. "Jesus. Are you okay?"

"Just . . ." She looked back at the puppets that twisted in the wind. They were in a basement. Where was the wind coming from? "I just want to go."

He grinned at her. "You aren't scared, are you?"

"It's late. I'm hungry." She took a step back from the circle, feeling more nauseous than hungry. "Can we go?"

He winked at her. "Sure. Just let me summon some pizza for you." Kurt stepped into the circle.

Light flared from the center of the circle, like a stupidly big pyro effect. Except they weren't using fire in the show. She took a stumbling step backward and her legs went out from under her as if someone had dropped her control.

A thing . . . a sack of pus and gristle and teeth slid sideways out of the air. An ozone stench rippled out from it. It turned, dripping blood on the floor, until it saw Kurt. How it saw him, she didn't know, because the thing had no eyes, but all of the teeth focused on him.

Kurt dropped the book.

The thing sprang forward, wrapping itself around Kurt's thighs. He screamed as the teeth in its sides pinned his arms down. The sack twined around his neck and shoved into his open mouth. Kurt gagged, bucking in its grasp.

Then it began forcing its way down his throat. His neck distended with its bulk. Kurt's eyes bulged, face purpling, as he choked on the mass. With a wet crack, his jaw dislocated.

Julia staggered to her feet and grabbed a gallon of paint, flinging the container at the creature. It bounced off. The thing ignored the blow, crawling down Kurt's throat. The paint bucket landed on the stage, top flying off in a spray of vermillion. Kurt's stomach bulged, pushing his

T-shirt up to reveal his skin bloated and straining around the bulk of the thing.

His eyes had rolled back in his head.

All that remained visible of the thing was a twisting beard of teeth dangling from Kurt's mouth. The teeth raised up, like the snout of some terrible questing beast, and focused on Julia. Then on the floor.

The red paint had run downstage, crossing the circle and covering one of the sigils.

Kurt's body turned toward her. He took a staggering step, leg dipping under the weight it carried, before straightening. The next step was steadier. The teeth clattered against each other as it took another step.

Julia did not wait to see if it could leave the circle. She ran. The exit was at the back of house right. A flight of stairs would have her on the street and away from whatever the hell that was.

The footfalls were faster now, teeth rattling.

It would reach her before she got to the door. Julia veered toward her workbench. Something to slow it. Anything. She grabbed a chisel and flung it behind her. It spun end over end and bounced off the thing's shoulder.

God. It was so close. She snatched her Japanese handsaw and swung it wildly. The flat of the long, narrow blade slapped against the bloated mass of Kurt's stomach. Maybe if it wasn't inside him anymore . . . She swung again, backing away as it kept coming, and missed. Again . . . The saw teeth snagged in the flesh of his belly, scoring a bright red line across the straining skin.

It pushed toward her, teeth stretching out from the sac of pus in Kurt's mouth. Shrieking, Julia swung the saw again, dragging the teeth down his stomach. Blood oozed from the ragged scrape.

She swung again.

The thing caught the blade, twisting it out of her hand.

She ran for the marionette bridge. Scrambling sixteen feet up with the speed of years in puppetry, she hauled herself onto the narrow platform. The metal structure shuddered as the thing started up after her. Julia waited until it was nearly at the top, then kicked the ladder free.

The thing fell sixteen feet to the stage floor. The ladder landed on top of it with a heavy crack. The thing lay still.

Gasping, she clung to the edge of the bridge.

God. God. What was that thing? What had just happened? Her hands were shaking so badly it took three tries to get her cell phone out of her pocket on the off chance that it had a signal. Nothing. She would have to climb the scaffolding to get off the bridge. Or stay there until the morning.

No. That was clearly not going to happen.

She crawled to the far end—she couldn't climb down next to it. It was just . . . she couldn't see Kurt's face. She leaned over the edge, feeling for one of the support beams. Below, metal clattered against wood. Julia tightened her grip on the support beam. *No. Please, please, no.*

She let go and staggered to her feet. With a hand on each of the leaning rails, she walked back down the length of the bridge. It shuddered under her grip.

Again, the vibration transmitted up the metal. "No."

She ran to the end and looked down. The thing was on the lowest level of the scaffolding, reaching up for a handhold. Julia spun. There had to be something she could use.

Leaning on the rail, she grabbed the control of Gluttony, and swung the wooden marionette at the thing. At the end of the long strings, it slapped against the side of the thing. For a moment, the thing's hand was knocked away from the scaffolding. She swung the marionette again, cursing the delayed pendulum action.

In a long graceful arc, the puppet swung out and back, clattering against the monster. Again. So slow. Too slow.

The teeth turned, watching as Gluttony swung in, and closed on the puppet's legs. It yanked down, hauling the puppet out of her grasp. The control fell in a tangle of strings, clattering to the stage before the thing dropped the puppet.

Julia grabbed another puppet, Pride, more focused this time. If she could just think of it like a show . . . —She pulled Pride's leg bar off the control, holding her arms wide in a way she would never, ever do in performance. The puppet looked as if it were on a giant invisible swing, legs bent up in the air in front of it. Julia brought it in, hitting the thing on the back of its head. Kurt's head. It knocked forward, slapping the sack of teeth against a metal support.

Out and back again. *Smack.* She kept the rhythm, letting the thing see it. It turned, to watch the puppet arc through the air. As it reached, Julia straightened her back, letting the arc fly higher than it expected. The puppet slid over its arm, and the wooden body fetched up against the horrible teeth. Bringing her hands together, lifting and twisting, Julia wrapped the strings of the puppet around Kurt's neck.

She leaned her full weight back, drawing the strings tight. Without being able to see it, she could feel the vibrations up the strings as the thing bucked below. It hauled her forward, but Julia grabbed the rail. Wrapping an arm around one of the uprights, she clung to the marionette and pulled sideways on the strings, trying to jerk the thing loose from the scaffolding.

The strings hummed with tension.

The entire bridge shook. The control twisted in her hands and a hard yank pulled her off balance. All of her training told her not to let go of the control. The rest of her screamed to *drop it, drop it, drop—*

Julia lost her balance and fell over the side of the bridge.

The scream was knocked out of her. Black and gray spots danced in front of her eyes as she struggled to draw in air. Something was terribly, terribly wrong with her leg.

She still had the marionette control in her left hand. Blood coated the right and mixed with the still-wet vermillion of the sigils on the floor.

The thing was still clinging to the bridge, no more than sixteen feet away, still tangled in her marionette's strings. It lowered itself from the bridge as she dragged the first, groaning breath into her lungs.

One knee bent backward, giving it a jerking, uneven gait. When it turned, strings draped down from livid red cuts in its neck.

The skin of its stomach . . . Where she had scored it with the saw, the skin had stretched and torn to reveal a glistening red-gray bulge. It pulsed with movement.

If she could knock it down, maybe the tear would widen, maybe—

she had nothing else to try. She wrapped her hands around the control and yanked as hard as she could on the strings, falling backward to add her mass to the pull.

The thing staggered forward. Its leg gave, and it fell forward, landing on the edge of the circle.

It shrieked with Kurt's throat—a wet, muffled cry.

A miasma of burning ozone filled the room and red light flared, as if her blood were on fire. Julia rolled away, choking on the stench. And then, with a wet pop, the thing's howls cut off. The lines to the marionette control went slack.

She raised her head, blinking.

Kurt's form lay twisted and crumpled across the sigils, rolled slightly onto his back. The distension in his stomach was gone, but the tear was still there. The bloated sack of teeth no longer hung from his broken jaw.

Plastered across his chest was a livid vermillion sigil. She pushed herself up on her elbows, trying to see better. The last thing Kurt had painted must have still been wet. It had to have been. The whole struggle couldn't have taken more than ten minutes.

Kurt's body had fallen on the summoning sigil, and now that symbol was printed on his chest. For a long moment, she could only stare at the vermillion sigil, not understanding what had happened, before she realized that the symbol on his shirt was the mirror opposite of the image on the floor. The dot was on the wrong side.

No. No, it was on exactly the right side.

Doll Court

by Richard Bowes

1

He bought and sold me!" said the figure in the witness stand. "He stuck me in a box without looking at me or addressing me by name and handed me over to an even more horrible man!" And I heard the murmur of an audience.

Anger made her voice tight and her eyes glisten as she stared right at me. The face, though, was that of a smiling child while the body was adult. I knew this even though both were obscured by black veils and a gown of exquisite Spanish lace. Her look was a trademark of Maison Calixte Huret, classic nineteenth-century Parisian doll makers.

Years back, I'd dealt in all manner of antique toys and dolls. I remembered acquiring this item at an auction with a bribable auctioneer for much less than she was worth. Early in life I'd learned that better than being honest, I *looked* honest. So this scam passed without notice.

A third party had set up this deal. I passed the doll on to him and received a nice fee. He then sold her to the wealthy collector he worked for.

The courtroom was all dolls. The jury box contained everything from a Chatty Cathy to classic Asian porcelains. Dolls and I had a history going way back. I'd bought and sold many like these. All stared at me. When I tried to explain my relative innocence I was booed and hissed. The judge doll on the high bench looked on with icy disapproval. She seemed familiar, though I wasn't sure why. I was gaveled and shouted down.

Then I realized I was dreaming and woke up. Outside, Greenwich Village was still dark. I'd recently had a couple of bad doll dreams but none as intense as this. A comfortably retired old queen, I listened to music, did a little yoga, and tried to forget the nightmare.

Dozing for a moment, I caught what looked like a photo of me from sixty years back. I sat on a curb wearing a striped jersey, jeans, and sneakers. My year-older sister, Patricia, and her girlfriends played hopscotch on the sidewalk behind me. It was the summer of 1953. I was nine and bored. I wanted to play with Pat and the girls but knew guys my age wouldn't let me live it down.

This evoked other memories of that summer and the confused kid I was. It made me recall *The Secret of the Widow's Walk*, a book I'd read back then.

The next day I found an old copy at the Strand. Allison Keyes Staunton was the author. Above the title in red letters was *A Debbie the Doll Detective Mystery*.

My sister, Pat, read dozens in this series when I was a kid. And so, semi-secretly, did I. We had the early 1950s reprints with kids dressed like us on the covers. What I held was the original 1931 edition with everyone in pinafores or knickers. Then I read the first lines and suddenly was nine years old.

> It was high summer in Odenville. Susan sat on the curb in front of her house. "It's too hot to walk to the beach. And Freddy's bike has a flat tire so he can't ride there with us," Susan told Debbie, her doll.
>
> "Don't look now," said Debbie. "But the man driving the red car has stopped at Mrs. Cochran's house like he did last week."
>
> As Debbie had taught her, Susan pretended to look at a cardinal in a tree. She heard the car door slam, waited a moment before turning slowly. The man's suit was loud green stripes. His hat brim was worn so far forward it was like a mask. He turned on Mrs. Cochran's porch and looked around. Susan was staring in another direction, but Debbie was not.

The gimmick of the books was that Debbie could speak, but only did so when no one but Susan was around. These two solved crimes, unraveling at least one mystery per book. Susan got described as Debbie's "human friend." But Debbie was the brains of the act.

2

Like Fate, the same day I bought the book, my old pal Eva Harrigan called and wanted me to attend an auction. The Isabella Delgard Stepney Doll Collection was going under the hammer at Dillons on the Upper East Side.

Eva still had her interior decorating business and needed my advice. She was interested in a dollhouse as an accessory for a lesbian couple's triplex overlooking the Highline. I owed Eva and couldn't refuse.

Mrs. Stepney was the owner of the doll who testified against me in the dream. The coincidence made me curious.

When I went to an auction or two every week, people found the idea fascinating and wanted to come along. Once there they'd sit stupefied as the twelfth lot of antique linoleum samples got bid on. To prevent my becoming that bored onlooker, I brought *The Secret of the Widow's Walk* with me.

Dillons Auctions is a comfortable place where old-line New Yorkers dispose of dead relatives' belongings. We arrived early for the pre-auction viewing. These always reminded me of old-fashioned Irish wakes. But instead of a casket, a corpse, and every relative you've ever avoided, we saw dolls in their thousands and the wealthy who worshipped them.

The collection was valued at just under eight million. Mrs. Stepney had everything, including a two-thousand-year-old Roman doll—a skeleton constructed out of real bones and minus a few parts. Hers was the world's largest collection of porcelain Paris fashion dolls. Over the years whenever war prevented customers from going to Paris, couturiers dressed these models in miniature gowns of silk and lace, then sent them to England, Russia, and all points in between.

Magnificence and quiet money were on view. Standing under glass was a superb example of a French Second Empire peddler doll. Several feet tall, dressed in a peasant bonnet and beautifully embroidered top, she held her floor-length skirts wide. On them were pinned lockets and hair ribbons, silk scarves and hand-painted wooden angels—trinkets and whimsies galore. Once this had been a sales display. Now, immaculately preserved, it was appraised for something not far south of a half million dollars.

A priceless eighteenth-century automaton, a child in a satin jacket and britches, played Mozart's "Turkish March" for us, but only once. Bidding started in the six figures.

"I thought of you, and here you are," murmured a familiar voice. I'd expected to encounter the Minx. Lesley Minx was my age but somehow still had black plastered-down hair and a tiny black mustache that looked like a clip-on bow tie.

The Minx was the one I'd helped get the Calixte Huret doll that he then sold to Mrs. Stepney. He was thanked in the auction catalog for curating the collection. I assumed he'd skimmed something off the top. My opposite: He always looked guilty.

"I had a dream that reminded me of you."

His eyes narrowed. He stared at the book in my hand, forced a horrible smile, and said, "We have things we need to talk about!" I caught tension in his voice.

"Who *was* that creepy little man?" Eva asked as we walked away.

Kind of avoiding the subject, I said, "Dolls were buried with the pharaohs; Barbie changed the way people thought they should look. Dark magic and money draw people like Lesley Minx."

Eva looked quizzical. But I distracted her by finding the dollhouse she'd heard about. Not some extravagant miniature palace, but a 1950s wooden split-level job handmade by Andrew Dorchet in Philadelphia.

"One of a kind," she said. "Nineteen fifties nostalgia is *the* hot fetish of the moment, especially among those who didn't, like us, have to live through it."

An old skill kicked in. I found an Eames-style dollhouse furniture lot in perfect scale with the house. Eva marked her catalog as the auctioneer stepped to the podium and introduced herself.

The room was full of live bidders. Behind the podium, assistants on phones and laptops took care of off-site clients. We seated ourselves as the auction began, and I opened *The Secret of the Widow's Walk*.

> The man with the loud suit and the hat like a mask went inside Mrs. Cochran's house. Debbie gave the signal, and Susan strolled down the street with her doll under her arm. At that moment, Freddy, the boy next door, appeared and yelled in a voice easily heard a block away, "Look at that car! Who owns it?"

Reading these books long ago, I tried, as kids do, to fit myself into the plot and imagine myself as Freddy. But he was too big an asshole. A couple of times Susan got him to disguise himself as a girl for purposes of Debbie's investigations. Once he got caught, which was bad. The other time he passed unnoticed, which I thought was worse. Mostly he was around to say the wrong thing and make fun of Susan for having a doll. He didn't even know Debbie could talk.

> But when Susan described the man with his hat pulled down just above his eyes, like he wore a mask, Freddy got interested and the three cut through a backyard and climbed up the side of Mrs. Cochran's rickety porch. Hanging onto the railing, they listened through an open living room window.
>
> Mrs. Cochran, the widow of an admiral, told the man in the hat, "This house was in my husband's family for decades, Roscoe. He never mentioned maps or treasure."
>
> Just then Freddy stepped on a loose board and fell onto the grass with a thud. But the man with the hat was so busy whining, "I have a sentimental interest in my uncle, Aunt Phyllis," that neither he nor Mrs. Cochran paid any attention.

At Dillons, Eva's furniture lot came up. She waited until the hammer was about to fall and the high bidder relaxed. I nodded, and she sank her bid in like a knife at the last moment, and he folded. Thirty pieces of wood and plastic went for about what it cost to furnish an actual house in 1953.

Then the book had me again and, skimming, I got to the place where Debbie, Susan, and Freddy paid a visit to Mrs. Cochran. By then Debbie knew that the nephew, Roscoe, wanted his aunt to move out of the house so he could make "repairs."

Debbie had a secret plan, which Freddy almost blew. As he and Susan were leaving, he was about to say, "You forgot your doll!" But Mrs. Cochran's back was turned and Susan put her hand over his mouth.

The doll detective was left behind the sofa on purpose. The author assured the reader that dolls miss nothing. Debbie saw Roscoe and Jasper, a big man in work clothes, arrive. She saw Roscoe put something in Mrs. Cochran's tea. A bit later when Mrs. C. was passed out on the couch, Debbie saw Roscoe go to her writing desk and find a very old scrap of paper from a drawer. He started reading it: "P35 L5, W2 . . ."

Debbie, with what the author called "Infallible Doll Memory," caught every single detail. She watched and listened as Roscoe and his pal ransacked the house, dug up the cellar, looking for treasure they were sure was there. Eventually they came back upstairs with Roscoe really pissed about not being able to figure out the code, and stomped out.

The next day Susan knocked on the door and apologized to Mrs. Cochran for having accidently left her doll behind. Mrs. C., still a bit dizzy, invited her in, and Debbie was found behind the couch.

Just then at Dillons I felt someone staring at me, and I glanced up and into wide blue eyes painted on the faces of a pair of Russian dolls at the front of the room. Cossack figures, carved with peasants' knives out of blocks of wood 150 years ago, they looked at me as blank-faced and unsmiling as cops.

At that moment Eva's dollhouse came up. A bidder with a gray beard was in competition with a phone bidder. The price was north of 6K when the caller dropped out. The beard took a deep breath and made what felt to me like a final bid of 7K, and I nodded. Eva's winning bid of 7.5K was about what a human-size version of the place would have cost sixty years ago.

With thoughts of a very late lunch, I accompanied Eva to the cashier's desk and arranged shipping for her items.

Lesley Minx appeared and said, "We'll talk. You have the same number?" I caught desperation in his voice. He whispered, "It's about Doll Court." A well-dressed woman overheard this and was wide-eyed.

3

Eva and I ate and joked and kissed each other goodbye. Then I went home to Greenwich Village and read more of *The Secret of the Widow's Walk*, looking for answers to questions I had trouble forming. The plot whizzed by.

To summarize: Debbie, proving that a doll detective never forgets, had memorized the numbers Roscoe rattled off. She explained them to Susan: "It's a book code with a message: "P35, L5, W2. 35 is page 35. L5 is the fifth line on that page. W2 is the second word on that line. But we don't know what book it is, and there's no clue."

The Debbie adventures were full of secret passwords and exotic codes. While Mrs. Cochran took a nap upstairs, Debbie, brilliant as always, studied her library and saw a book of memoirs by the Admiral, a famous explorer, way up on a top shelf.

Freddy almost got killed climbing up there and back. But once Debbie got her little bisque hands on it, she traced the long list of letter/number combos. She figured out that the Admiral had a treasury of jewels he'd found in his explorations, hidden under the boards of the widow's walk on the roof.

Then Roscoe and Jasper showed up, locked Mrs. Cochran, Susan, and Freddy into a closet, and started to ransack the place. But the silly criminals left Debbie in the living room, and she got the receiver off the phone cradle and called the police, pretending to be Susan. The book ended with the widow celebrating by buying new bikes for Susan and Freddy.

Around then I must have fallen asleep, because the next thing I remembered was waking up in a courtroom. This time the doll in the witness stand had a bald vinyl head and an angry face, and stared at me through blue glass eyes. The face, the pink and white flowered dress, the black leather shoes, were all familiar. I recognized Genevieve, my sister's doll from our childhood, and my guts tightened.

"He tore off my hair," Genevieve said in a high, tiny voice. "He and his pals dressed as wild Indians, chased our human friends away, and then scalped us."

In the jury box Chatty Cathy sat next to a classic Ideal Toys Betsy Wetsy. Several Kewpie dolls in sailors' hats and grass skirts were just in front of them. They stared at me with murder in their eyes. Genevieve was telling the truth. But she and the rest of the crowd didn't understand my side of the story.

The judge glared down. This time I looked closely and saw the nameplate: *The Honorable Deborah*. I'd known her as Debbie the Doll Detective.

I realized I was dreaming, but before I could wake up, Judge Deborah told me, "Doll Court is where you get tried for crimes against dolls. In Doll Court there's no such thing as inadmissible evidence. Your dreams and even email posts are treated as signed confessions."

Then I was awake, chilled. I hadn't seen a psychiatrist in forty years. But I thought about it now. I'd turned off my phone. There was a message on it from Leslie Minx. "I can tell you know about Doll Court. It's insane. They're in our minds! We need to get our stories straight before they convict us!"

I called him and didn't get an answer. We were deep in the night, and maybe he was asleep. I don't drink or take drugs anymore. But in the medicine cabinet was a bottle of night cold syrup, and I hated myself as I took a double swig.

In my next dream, I stared at an image of me from that fateful summer. My crew cut was so high and tight it could have been a Mohawk. Two kids my age were with me: Alex and Billy. We were nine or thereabouts, and the guys older than we were didn't want us around. That day we were shirtless, our chests smeared with iodine subbing as war paint. Scalps hung on our belts. We demanded respect.

Then I realized I was in Doll Court and this memory had just been shown to the jury. On the witness stand was a doll smaller than Genevieve. She had belonged to my sister's friend Kathy O'Neil. Her bright smile contrasted with her chopped hair and her tears. ". . . hacked away with penknives," she was saying. "My human friend, Kathy, tried to stop them. But she couldn't."

She dipped her head, displaying patches of bare scalp. Gasps came from the audience and the jury. Judge Deborah gaveled them into silence. Again I was awake and not able to get back to sleep.

This time I carefully considered going to a hospital emergency room but rejected the idea. It was dawn of a lovely fall day.

Then the phone chimed and Lesley Minx said, "There's got to be a lawyer to take our cases to!" He sounded hysterical. From the background noise I knew he was outside and moving fast. He wasn't making any sense. "How did you know about the Doll Detective books?"

"What is Doll Court? Where is it?" I asked.

"In our heads: like parasites. Customers used to trust you because they didn't know what you were really like. The dolls will. You've got to go beg them and . . ."

There was a pause, and all I heard was traffic noises. "Lesley?" I said.

Exhaustion and the medicine must have taken me. Instead of a response I got Doll Court and Lesley Minx being dragged away by the wooden Cossack dolls, now standing six feet tall, as everyone cheered. Judge Deborah banged her gavel and Minx screamed, "You goddamn lumps of papier-mâché have no right to do this!"

The next thing I saw was yet another victim, this one a bit worn and also with butchered hair, in the witness box staring at me. "Passed down in the Daly family from mother to older sister and finally to Beth. After what he did to us that awful day, she never wanted to look at me again." The audience gasped. Beth Daly was another of my sister's friends.

Debbie called for order. "What have you to say?" she asked.

I knew I was dreaming but realized this was the moment to plead my case. I told her, "What I wanted was to hang around with my sister and her friends. But they were older by a year and more, which is a big thing when you're a kid, and anyway, they didn't want a boy playing with them.

"Guys could sense I was different and hated that. So I had to be tougher and wilder than them. It was stupid, but I was nine years old. I regret what I did, but I was punished."

Judge Deborah indicated that I should continue. I started to tell them about my old man whacking my ass with a hairbrush and yelling, "You're interested in dolls? You want to wear a dress from now on, maybe you'll like that?"

I realized the dolls could somehow envision this. They saw me crying, tripping over the pants bunched around my ankles, proclaiming my profound sorrow and lack of any desire to wear a dress.

The audience, even the jury, was clapping—a muffled sound of plastic, cloth, and bisque hands slapping together while more delicate china hands snapped fans and waved warning fingers at me.

Judge Deborah gaveled them down. "Doll Court," she said, "takes it into consideration when a defendant displays evidence of true repentance. I will grant you probation in place of a lifetime sentence and advise you to apologize and beg for forgiveness from the owners of the dolls and the dolls themselves. You must also do service to our community. You will be contacted and instructed. Failure to do any of this will end your probation and begin a life sentence."

This time I awoke around noon. I showered and dressed, drank a pot of hot tea, went down the street to the Café Reggio, and drank three cups of espresso. I brought *The Secret of the Widow's Walk* with me. Within a day the little book by Allison Keyes Staunton had gone from being a piece of nostalgia to being a slice of a nightmare.

I noticed letters and numbers written on the inside back cover—a book code. Like Debbie, I had no idea what book the code referred to. But with nothing else at hand I tried it out on *Widow's Walk* itself.

The first clump of pages/lines/words gave me "justice," which might have been a coincidence. But a little more work gave me, "Justice for the Silent Companions," which was no coincidence. The next slogan was "Let our human friends revenge us!" I recovered an address, 5 Covington Street, and an old-fashioned telephone number: CA7-1680.

While I was still deciphering, my phone rang. It was the same number but with an area code and digits instead of letters. A woman, quite businesslike and a bit formal, said, "We will be supervising your probation and would like to see you this afternoon." I made an appointment for three p.m. at 5 Covington Street.

4

In almost fifty years in the city I'd never heard that street name. It showed on Google Maps and wasn't that far away—a dozen blocks south of me in that forgotten land between low-lying Greenwich Village and tall Tribeca. I killed a little more time, then decided to walk downtown in the bracing fall afternoon.

South of the Village new glass office buildings dominated the avenues, while old commercial structures and warehouses lined the side streets. Scattered among them were short rows of brownstones and an occasional five-story apartment building. Sometimes these were clustered like a hamlet around a restaurant or an old bar with a vaguely familiar name.

Covington was a single, short north-south block just above Canal Street and the Holland Tunnel. The constant traffic rolling to and from New Jersey gave the neighborhood a background sound like a mighty river.

Covington Street itself was deserted. The old brick warehouses looked like Hopper paintings you've never seen before. But number 5, near the southern end, was a nicely preserved four-story brownstone that possibly dated from before the Civil War. Below the doorbell was a name: *Silent Companions Society.* I'd never heard of the organization but was unsurprised. Doll collectors are tighter than the Mafia.

I pressed the buzzer, said who I was when asked, and got buzzed in. A businesslike young lady identified herself as Anna, apologized for "Ms. Keyes," who would be my probation supervisor, being late, ushered me upstairs to a second-floor study, waved me into a comfortable chair, and disappeared.

Late afternoon sun shone through the curved windows. The only sounds were the tidal traffic and Anna's distant voice. It felt like I was being watched even before I saw the wood Cossack figures. Each stood on a pillar behind the large desk in the middle of the room. Their eyes followed my every move.

The walls were covered with art—paintings of dolls, of children with dolls, of old Europeans of another time making more dolls. To the left of the desk on shelves behind glass doors was every illustrated tome on the art of the doll that I'd ever heard of.

To the right of the desk was what looked like a small lighted window set into the wall. It was impossible not to get up and peer inside. It felt like I was looking at a room through the eyes of a little girl. I saw the arms of the miniature chair in which she sat and her white lace dress with pink velvet embroidery. On her lap was a china-headed Parisian doll from, I would guess, the 1880s in a pink lace dress with white velvet embroidery. On the child's bed across the room were satin pillows with the faces of the sun and the moon.

On a shelf above the bed were marionettes: Punch looking like he was ready to jump down to the floor, Judy with a twinkly smile, Saint George and the Dragon leaning against each other. At the end of the shelf was Lesley Minx dressed in prison stripes. He seemed to stare at me, desperate and motionless.

And I was certain it was intended that I see this and understand I could end up on that shelf.

Stepping away, I saw a bunch of old Debbie the Doll Detective books. I'd read lots of them. But a title I'd never heard of, *Order in Doll Court*, got my attention. The book had been published in 1939 and apparently was never reprinted.

I sat down and sped through it. The plot involved Susan's parents taking a trip to New York and bringing her, and of course Debbie, and, for comic relief, Freddy, along. Susan's clothes in the illustrations were considerably upgraded compared with those in other books, but Debbie now looked amazing with a new outfit in every picture. She was running things, even directing the parents via Susan. Debbie explained to her human friend, "Someone must defend dolls, puppets, even manikins."

That was okay, maybe. But other aspects of the book were off-putting. The villains had Jewish names. African Americans were regularly caricatured. And about sixty pages in, when Debbie began entering Susan and Freddy's dreams, I stopped reading.

Then a woman said, "Your expression was mine the first time I read that. Much different than Staunton's Odenville books. We try to keep this one off the market."

"Alycia Keyes," the woman said as I arose and we shook hands. Ms. Keyes was, I guessed, in her late fifties and white blond. Her dress was like money—light green with flashes of gold.

"A granddaughter?" I asked.

"Allison Keyes Staunton was a grandaunt. She was the first to discover the power of dolls. I'm an attorney and manage the foundation she established. This was her house."

"Did the dolls get into Allison's mind? Do they get into yours like they do mine?"

"Not our minds, our dreams. I welcome them."

I found that chilling. "How do they do it?" I asked. She just shook her head and shrugged, though I felt she had some idea.

"I guess I have to go along with this. I see how poor Lesley ended up."

"That really is just a puppet. Mr. Minx is in excellent health—just a trifle . . . confused."

"And I don't want to end up confused."

"No indeed. With Mr. Minx, Judge Deborah and I worked on the principle 'Set a thief to catch a thief' and hoped with his knowledge of the illegal doll trade, he would be an asset. He was even more dishonest than he looked. Mr. Minx stole money intended to help dollkind."

"Whereas I . . ."

"At least look honest." She smiled, and I found it scary. "I think you understand that dolls need human friends to assist them, just as in the books."

"What are my duties?"

"What Lesley was doing badly—safeguarding dolls and doll collectors' interests. All will be explained soon."

"I'm retired."

"And bored, perhaps?"

"You'll call off the hounds? Let me sleep?"

"As long as you obey the rules. But you must begin making amends for your crimes. Your immediate assignment is to beg forgiveness of the dolls you hurt and their owners."

She rose and walked me to the door. "We'll soon be in touch again. You know better than to speak about any of this."

I nodded. "People would think I was confused."

Walking up Covington Street I looked back once or twice, expecting number 5 to have disappeared.

5

My next appearance in Doll Court was a couple of weeks later. Prepared and repentant, I faced the cold glass eyes of judge, jury, and injured parties.

First I showed how I called my sister, Patty, and how she forgave me easily enough. "It was when you were trying to be 'all boy,'" she said, amused. Doubtless she thought I was crazy, but by now that doesn't bother her.

"I need Kathy and Beth's numbers," I told her. Patty had Kathy's number, and she was no trouble. We'd been at a family wedding the summer before last. All was nostalgia and forgiveness in our conversation.

Beth was a problem. My sister said, "She and I fell out of touch, and I haven't heard from her in years." This was bad. If anyone knew of her, it would be her doll. But Beth's doll glared at me.

However, at an online auction I had won a superb lot of doll wigs. There was an audible sigh in court when all saw the variety, the sheen, the richness of texture. I begged my victims' forgiveness and implored Beth's doll to tell me where her human friend was.

Spectators, jury, Cossacks, and judge awaited her reply. She stared first at a shoulder-length blond wig, then at me. And I hoped my honest face would do its work.

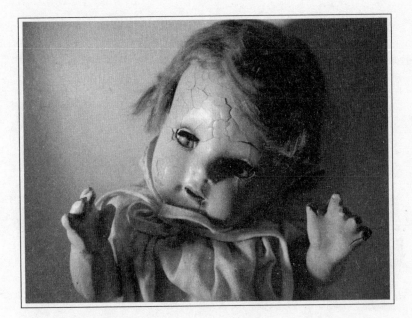

Visit Lovely Cornwall on the
Western Railway Line

by Genevieve Valentine

1

The girl in the train car is all alone, except for the doll. She looks tended to—hair neatly pulled back at the crown of her head, a few shiny ringlets at the ends left largely undisturbed from where her mother must have pinched them into the iron.

It could have been a maid who did her hair, but the wife who sits down opposite her thinks not; the girl's dress is navy cotton, the sort of thing chosen for practicality in washing, and the wife's first thought—not unkindly—is that the girl must have wandered up alone from the third-class carriage as the train pulled away from Paddington.

She has second thoughts when she sees the doll. It's wearing a dress of rust silk (a colour out of fashion, just at the moment), and in the early morning light its hair is icy blond, leached of any vibrance under the tiny velvet hat, two twists of pink ribbon and a green sequin on the brim standing in for roses. It's an elegant doll—the dress is in an odd style (it feels much too old, though she couldn't say why), but there are petticoats peeking out from under the skirt, which just brushes the boots fastened with tiny pearl buttons; this is a doll that's been dressed with care.

The train rackets across empty countryside, startling birds out of the nearest trees and, once or twice, a deer far off. The wife thinks deer are odd. She knew sheep from back home, but they were solid and stupid and stubborn in a way that felt like they were part of the land. The dainty deer and their long, nervous necks always seem like visitors from someplace else.

Though they've come from a holiday at her mother-in-law's, whose neck is markedly similar, so that's probably not fair to the deer. Her mother-in-law definitely thinks the wife's too close for comfort to the sheep. Their country house is merely a complement to the house in London, where they make their home; she doesn't want to be reminded how her son married someone whose country house was a bit too fixedly in the country.

"Poor" is a word they never said, or "common." But the wife has worked so hard to make her vowels shallower and to lift her *r*'s and to bring back her *h*'s that she hardly speaks anymore; every time she opens her mouth, the farmhouse falls out all over again. She might as well point them to the dirt road down to the village and the fields pockmarked with stands of trees anywhere you looked.

But the wife doesn't want to think about it—either her husband's family or her old home—and she looks at the girl across from her (solemn, not looking at much of anything) and casts about for something to say.

"I had a doll very much like that," she says to her husband—to his collar, stiff and white as enamel. He's so much taller, and it already seems like too much trouble to look up the extra few inches to his face when he's never looking back at her no matter what she says.

He glances up from his paper, back down. "I doubt it," he says to the international report.

He's right—she'd never had anything so fine; her cloth doll had worn a dress made out of a scrap of something the last of her brothers outgrew— but still, the grit in her stomach is churning like to make a pearl. She rubs her fingers against the seams of her gloves; practical, plain cotton gloves, fitting for the wife of a professor teaching his first year at Exeter. So his mother had said, at any rate.

Exeter is a fine town, his mother had said, finer than any the wife had been likely to see before she married. (The Jewel of the West, a poster in Paddington had assured her, the spire pointing up into a watercolour sky like the blade of a knife waiting for you to impale yourself.)

The girl across the seat is looking from one of them to the other.

"It's a lovely doll," the wife says to the girl, remembering too late that you should never speak about a person before you've spoken to them. She learned that, too, from someone—her husband or his sister or his mother, they all enjoyed giving advice—and though she doesn't understand half of what they tell her, she doesn't ever really mean to be rude.

The girl's looking from one of them to the other, lingering on her husband, her face unmoving but somehow venomous in that way children sometimes manage.

The wife has the urge to reach for her husband, to say, *This is Roger*, like it's a spell that will protect him—from what, she doesn't know. But she watches the girl's fingers curl until they disappear into the skirts of her doll, and she watches the girl's eyes slide to her, and she realizes it's not her husband she cares much about protecting.

He was beautiful, she wants to say; *his kind don't often ask to marry mine, and the way he kissed me I didn't think it might have been for spite of someone else; I didn't think.*

She wants to say, My *daughters will have dolls like yours, not dolls like mine*, but that thought sifts into sand and blows away before it can even take hold in her throat. It's been a long holiday, and she knows more than she did about how her children will be looked upon by her husband's kin (*family*; they don't say "kin," they don't know what kin is).

When the train pulls into Ide Halt station, which rises up out of the trees and the bushes beside the tracks like the skeleton of a thing that a thousand springs have grown over, she's still looking at the little girl, skin white as the porcelain doll's. The girl hasn't spoken in all this time. The girl's not even looking at her anymore; she's looking through her, or beyond her, as children do.

Her husband's folded his paper under his arm and looks carefully at the pocketwatch he makes a point of checking often, which she thinks is showy but that he explained once was an heirloom, and therefore looking at it in public was only a demonstration of respect for punctuality, in a tone that suggested how amusing it was that she should think to correct him about manners.

He stands and moves almost as soon as the train's stopped; she takes her bag from beside her and moves to stand up. The girl watches. In her hands the doll pivots, too, following them, and the hair on the wife's neck stands up to see it.

"I have a dress just like that," she says, and doesn't know what possessed her to say such a foolish thing to a stranger when it couldn't matter less (there are lies and there are lies).

Outside the window, her husband's on the platform looking for her, watch still in hand and glinting under the high sun. Though she can't see from here, she can feel the spires from the church and the university rising up ahead of her like a devouring mouth.

Before she steps down she straightens her shoulders, tugs the hem of her jacket, pinches her cheeks to bring up the color. Her husband married her kind for only one reason besides spite: she's handsome, and has married one of her betters, and she can guess he wants her to make a good showing.

She's guessed right; as he takes her hand to help her onto the platform, his thumb runs hot across her knuckles, right through her gloves. (The wife of a professor should be beautiful enough to raise interest, and demure enough to deflect gossip. No one's told her that, but some lessons no one need bother to explain.)

※

On her way to the high street for shopping, she passes a building so sharp and square it reminds her always of a tomb. Her husband told her it was a morbid thing to say, but she avoids the corner where she'll have to turn and see it looming, hated.

Still, to turn the other way and avoid it means passing by the toy shop that lines up dolls in the window on a shelf above the train sets. Their porcelain faces crack a little more every month they sit in the window under full sun, everything about them leaching brightness, so a dress the colour of a robin's egg slowly gives in to the watery blue of a spring sky, and the doll with the darkest hair is going gray at the temples faster even than the wife. One of the dolls had violet eyes that have turned unnervingly pale. She can't remember the colour of the doll's eyes in the train car, long ago, no matter how hard she tries.

She takes the street that passes the tomb.

That's where she finds the little dress shop that has the rayon frock in the window: high necked and plain, with the skirt long enough and the bloused top with its fluttering suggestion of sleeves being stylish and respectable at the same time. It's the colour of rust. She tries not to think about it as a victory; what a strange thing it would be to think.

Her husband makes a little face when he sees her in it, as if it worries him. But after a moment of study he must not know where to explain the fault, because he only says, "I hope it wasn't expensive, you know how I feel about profligacy," and kisses her on the cheek.

"Profligacy" means wasteful extravagance. She's been educating herself; he asked her to, as the wife of a professor.

⁂

She wants to go out walking—they're so close to Dartmoor she can smell it when it rains—but it doesn't suit the wife of a professor, he says, to be tromping around in the mud and getting brown as a nut.

She goes anyway, when he has his long teaching days; she can't stand being still, as if the air in the house is too thick to breathe. So she puts on her rain boots and her mackintosh and walks as far as she can, like Exeter's pushing her out, the moor pulling her in.

When she's passed the farmsteads and the neat fields and the copses of trees, she strikes out into the moor, brambles catching on her coat and muck slapping at her boots across the wide swathes of open space, the sky rolling out in every direction, the scrub in the far distance laid out in red and purple and threaded through with rocks. It feels barren of life, and she breathes as deep as she can. (Sometimes she hears the train whistle, far to the south, and shivers like it's an animal calling out for her.)

Almost too far to see, there's a dark ridge along the horizon that might be trees, but she can never walk far enough to tell before she has to turn around.

She always knows when. She has no pocketwatch, but some people are born able to tell the time.

⁂

At the end of their third winter in Exeter, the husband finds her standing in front of the toy store, staring at the line of dolls.

One of them seems to be dressed as Marie Antoinette, which he finds a little morbid, but most of them are meant for simpler children: a blonde girl in a navy dress, a lady with roses in her hat.

She has a few flakes of snow caught on the brim of her cloche, and her lapel's turned up against the cold, her hands tucked into her pockets. She looks as unhappy as she did the night he told her he was leaving, just before he asked her to marry him.

He rests his hand on her back, wonders how he's missed how badly she must want children.

⚜

She disappears in spring.

Her valise is still at the bottom of the wardrobe, and there's a roast wrapped in twine still sitting in the cold oven when the husband comes home, and so he thinks at first she's gone walking, and then that she's gone shopping. Nothing else occurs to him until everything has closed for the night, and he wonders if he should have gone down to the train station to ask about her rather than expecting her to come home.

The professor's wife had not gone to the train station. She hadn't hired a cab, or sought a bus. The police search obligingly after he realizes her rain boots are gone, but there are only so many miles of wilderness one can bear to look through, and though they send someone as far south as the Haldon tower to look out for her, the answer to every question is always, unspoken, the moor.

Someone could walk the moor if they dared to, someone hardy and determined to head southwest and catch up with the railway line. (Ivybridge would have been safe enough for someone hoping not to be noticed.)

But someone determined to cross all the way to Cornwall could still slip off a tor and crack their skull, or fall into Aune Mire a few days after rainfall; that bog was an open mouth and never had its fill. A body could lie dead amid the scrub in a dress the colour of rust, and never again be found.

2

The girl in the train car is all alone, except for the doll. She looks distracted, starved-out shadows around her eyes, not quite focused on anything and her fingers plucking absently at the waist sash of the doll teetering in her lap.

The man who sits opposite her looks over one shoulder and then the other, deliberately, to catch the eye of whoever should be coming to claim her. No doubt some tantrum got her over here alone, and he doesn't care for it. A pliant child has her charms, but he doesn't find willfulness amusing. Still, beggars can't be choosers.

"And to whom do you belong?" he asks, only half-intending for her to hear.

But her fingers twitch, the doll's head tilting another inch into his periphery, its hat tipping over its face, so she hears him. She should answer him, then, he thinks—he's technically addressing her, and she's old enough to know her manners.

She looks at him with her mouth pressed into a thin, unfriendly line. It offends him, somehow; he's been nothing but pleasant—isn't he helping her look for her parents, who should know better than to leave a young girl alone in days like these?

But no one seems to be looking for her, and finally he gives up, sits back, rests a hand on the valise he never lets the porter carry. (This is the war effort, and he's made a promise to look after it; he's its rightful steward.) It occurs to him to move seats, but for all she looks as if she's gritting her tiny teeth, her skin is white as her doll's, and her eyes are two deep blue saucers, and it wouldn't be the first petulant little girl he's come across in his line of work.

"Is your trip very long?" he asks, more softly. "Have you brought only your lovely doll with you? She seems very sweet. Such a pretty face; do you think she looks like you?"

It's not really a lovely doll. It looks old, like it's been handed down from her grandmother; its dress is the colour of a bloodstain, and the roses on the brim of its hat are beginning to fade.

She fixes her eyes on him, but her mouth never moves, never even looks as if she wants to answer, as it does with the shy little girls he much prefers, who blush when you speak to them and stammer thankfully if you press a piece of Brighton rock into their clammy hands. Ungrateful girl, he thinks, looking at the fold of her socks above her black buckled shoes pointed at him like accusations; isn't he keeping her company, when she could be here all alone?

"I said you have a lovely doll," he says, feels the sharp edges of his words but does nothing about it. "Let me see her."

The girl's face shifts, her eyes narrowing, but she tilts the doll slightly upward to his gaze.

The doll's eyes aren't lost under her hat as he'd suspected, the man realizes; the doll's eyes have been blacked out with something dull that reflects no light, and when the train passes under a stand of trees he has the sudden crawling sense that the doll is soaking up those shadows, too. Its mouth is lipless, just a thin, poisonous line on the verge of speech, on the verge of saying something terrible.

"Taunton station," the conductor calls, and the man startles (*It can't be; has the train grown wings?*), but when he looks out the window they're sliding along the banks of the Tone, and any minute the station itself will pop sidelong into frame like a spool gone astray at the cinema.

He stands up before it's strictly necessary, brushes at the front of his jacket, wraps his hand around the handle of his valise until a knuckle pops.

"Mind the platform," he mutters as he moves for the door. "A girl your size might fall in, and if they knew your temper they wouldn't exactly run to your aid."

On the platform a poster blazes in colours, gold sand and bright blue water and a handful of people in candy-coloured bathing suits under the block-letter shout of CORNWALL, promising MILES OF BEAUTIFUL SHORE ALONG THE WESTERN RAILWAY LINE.

He can just see the top of the girl's blonde head, a flash of a white satin bow, but the rest of the window is murky, as if no light at all is getting out.

✼

By 1940, he's the third most successful door-to-door man in the company, which is just enough to get him a raise and a slightly larger circuit. He only sees the inside of the London office when he's dropping off papers. The war effort needs him on the Great Western Railway.

Last fall it had been chaos in town, children everywhere until it felt like he was being punished for every sweet face he'd ever lingered on too long, a sea of solemn expressions and little smears of jam from some homemade sandwich their mothers had pressed into their sticky hands as they boarded a train for countryside destinations unknown. They were all polite, so there was no reason it should have made him uneasy—they were so terrified they would have been grateful for any sort of kindness—but there were so many of them, and some looked out from under the brims of their caps like their eyes soaked up the shadows, and his Brighton rock sat in his suitcase untouched.

There are no more posters for tourism—sometimes you see a sliver of one underneath a poster of handsome young soldiers running for glory, or beatific families standing amid the garden of English pride. The daughters are almost always golden-haired, and he never really looks at them for long; his eyes sting, or something passes by behind him and he glances over, and by the time he's settled his mind about whatever the matter is, the train's moved on and there's nothing outside the window but open hills and the thickets of green.

✼

He has a flat in London, but it's never looked like much besides a hotel room without the service, and the bombs have hardly made it more appealing, so there's little reason for him to take the holidays when the office suggests it. There's nothing much to stay in London for—he doesn't care for theatre, even the ones that are still standing—and the idea of getting on a train for pleasure makes him slightly ill by now.

But eventually the office begins to insist, and so he agrees to take a long weekend and leave on his next circuit two days later than planned. The city's as awful as he remembers, but at least he gets to walk the path to his mother's house mostly free of rubble, which fills him with some small amount of personal satisfaction he chooses not to examine; the war bonds pay for street cleaning as much as they pay for bombers, he's certain. Every little bit helps.

It startles him to read the news about the accident near Taunton. Out that way, the best way to get a housewife to listen to you is to let your vowels drop a little longer and lower than they do in London, to offer up a little Brighton rock to the little girls that crowd the doorway, and doff your cap respectfully to older boys. He knows just what it looks like there, when the train pulls away from Taunton station and starts the curve toward Western Somerset, where he's never seen the beaches for the spreads and spreads of green.

But he's always been a man of circumspection, and it doesn't escape him, when he opens his eyes in the pitch black to the wail of the air raid siren, that a man from the War Bonds Office being bombed to death on one of the three days a month he spends at home is something that the papers will talk about.

Still, he doesn't have long to worry about it.

3

The girl in the train car is all alone, except for the doll. She looks tired—shadows under the eyes—but it seems as if she's fighting it, sitting back against the seat as tall as she can. Her doll's standing, too, though when her hands slip lower on its waist, it bows forward like it's sinking to sleep.

The train pushes out past Plymouth, clacking west through far-off villages into places where the greenery can barely hide the rock underneath, a layer of glossy enamel brushed just over the stone, ridged and rolling toward the water, and you hope that sooner or later you'll be able to mark the sea.

It's a terribly old-fashioned train car, with the seats so worn they're more springs than padding. It didn't look quite so shabby from the outside, but that's Great Western Rail for you.

Why you sit across from the girl who's alone instead of looking for another car, you can't say. You aren't fond of children. The seat across from her looks wider, though, more open. And it's the only one left that's facing front—you can't sit backward in trains. You say it makes you sick. Really, it's something about only seeing things once they've slipped past you that gives you the shivers, but that wouldn't get you anything but strange looks. No point explaining. Better to admit to a weak stomach than sound like the sentimental sort.

It's raining out, leaching everything of colour, and as the train rolls in and out from under dark clouds it casts everyone into melancholy grays.

You smile at the girl to reassure her, say, "I don't like the rain either," just in case she's frightened more than she is tired. Why she'd be frightened of a light rain you don't know, but the oddest things used to frighten you, so it can't hurt.

As the train picks up momentum, it rocks back and forth at that magic speed that always used to put you right to sleep all the way to Newbury—and sometimes past it, if you weren't careful. The conductors were always very sweet about it, but three felt like the ceiling for times you could trudge across to the return-journey platform with a ticket and bleary eyes and trust the conductor to let you back on with nothing but a warning. You've been more careful since, and if you're too tired to stay awake under your own power (which is almost always), you try to do something that will make you too uneasy to go to sleep. Sitting across from a child, for example.

Still, it's exciting to be on board the train, farther west than you've ever tried before. Not that you expect to be happy—this train car's not changing your circumstances, just the geography—but maybe a change in geography is enough.

The girl's watching you. She looks uncertain, still weighing something, but you've probably been found wanting; that's how it usually goes.

"Are you all right? Can I help?"

She shakes her head, barely, not even enough to disrupt her fresh-curled hair. The doll in her lap shifts backward an inch or two, and for a moment it startles you into thinking something that gives you the shivers, but it's just the girl reaching out to cage the doll's arms in her fingers and pull it back tight to her chest.

You weren't going to take it. You're sorry that's what she thinks of you. Still, she wouldn't be the first person to assume the worst of you; you must just have one of those faces.

The land here shouldn't be as different as it is, only a handful of miles to the west, but somehow it is, like the nearness of the sea has settled over everything and made it seem nearer, better.

"Where are you going?" asks the little girl, with a voice that sounds long disused. You wonder if she's been on this train all the way from London, with no food or drink. Oh God, maybe she's run away, and you'll look like a kidnapper.

"My ticket's for Penzance," you say, glancing down the aisle for a conductor, but even as you say it you get the feeling she already knows exactly where you're going, and that she'll be going all that way with you.

It feels too far west, suddenly. Horribly far west, for no gain—there are other places close to the sea, without being quite so far beyond the reach of home. (Strange thought; you haven't considered that factory-choked Northeast town home in a long time. Must be the rain.)

When the conductor calls for Truro, the girl shifts in her seat. Under her hands, the doll looks as if it's trying to get footing. The girl grips it tighter.

You reach for your traveling case.

"Safe journey," you say as you stand, and she glances at you sidelong, unsurprised you're getting off early. That's all right; you're not surprised she looks like she expected to have the seat to herself the rest of the way.

The clasp on your suitcase breaks just as you head for the station exit, and by the time you've packed it again and wrapped it shut in your nicest scarf (the only one long enough to hold the damn thing together), a train's arriving from the Falmouth line. A little girl steps off the train between her parents. Her dress is the blue of a robin's egg; the bow at the end of her braid is white.

You get on the train.

Penryn isn't a bad place to live. You spend the next forty years making sure. The seasons are fine, even if your knee aches a little with the damp, and work is all right so long as you don't mind the blisters and the skimping pay.

The only thing that really grates—besides your landlady, who occasionally bangs on your door before dawn and accuses you of making noise when it's just the owls that live in the kitchen eaves—is the toy store. It has a pile of dolls in the window, a halfhearted jumble set out next to the trains. It looks disrespectful, somehow, but that's the sort of thing you know better than to say. You're not the shopkeeper, and you're not about to buy one of them, and what other reason would you have?

You never go a step farther west; the thought of getting on the Western Rail makes you uneasy, though you try not to think about why. No point in sounding like the sentimental sort.

4

The girl in the train car is all alone, except for the doll.

The train stops at Penzance, only a handful of steps from the shore. At high tide, it looks as though the water's trying to suck at the wheels of the train and drag it under. If there were ever a storm strong enough, a whole train might disappear under the waves some night with no one the wiser.

There's service here, for anyone who wants to make it all the way to Land's End. The Great Western Railway has left no track unturned; it wants to see the whole thing through, right to the end of the line.

When the conductor walks through the train to make sure all passengers have disembarked, he leaves her be; he glances up at the luggage rack and down at the floor and never lingers on her.

The girl with the doll doesn't move for a long while. She doesn't turn to look at the afternoon sun scattered in pieces over the waves, doesn't glance out the window where the shoreline curves toward the entrance to the quay. They put flowers out in summer, if you were lucky enough to see it, flowers tumbling everywhere. ("Only six and a half hours express to the most beautiful coast in the world!" the advertisements promise, under a watercolour of a village always empty of people, or a beach spotted with a handful of the fashionable sort.)

Eventually, the train will sigh and squeal and lurch forward again, heading slowly back for London, past the sea and the cities and the moors.

The little girl won't be there. She'll be walking down the quay in a school dress of serviceable blue the colour of the sea just after the sun goes down, before it's really night. A secondhand doll of the old-fashioned kind will be tucked in the curve of her arm, her elbow gently squashing the rosettes. She's already scratched its eyes off with her charcoal, because green eyes looked too much like the eyes of a headmistress she'd quarreled with.

The quay is dotted with couples walking arm in arm, and one or two families, and one old man with a dog that looks like the old man, somehow.

The girl sits on a bench facing the bay, where the water level sinks inch by inch as you watch it, until some of the ships hit bottom and tilt over. It always makes her grandfather smile and tell a joke about the old drunk sailor, a joke she's promised never to tell her mother and father.

He'll be here soon. She sets the doll in her lap, and smooths the deep red skirt, and settles in to wait.

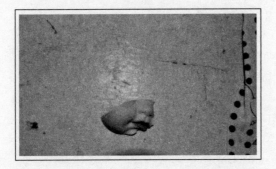

Ambitious Boys Like You

by Richard Kadrey

Witt pulled his father's '71 Malibu to a stop down the block from the derelict house. The car coughed a couple of times. It wasn't vintage. It was just old.

Sonny was riding shotgun. He said, "There it is."

"I've been driving by this place my whole life," said Witt. "Didn't ever think I'd have a reason to go inside. Didn't ever want to."

"Why's that?"

"When we was young, we figured it was haunted."

"Haunted? How come?" asked Sonny.

"Well, look."

"At what?"

"The bodies."

"Jesus fucking Christ."

Sonny, his cousin, was from Houston, but being from the city wasn't why Witt found him interesting. It was that while Witt believed in everything—God, the Devil, spooks, not spilling salt without throwing some over your shoulder—Sonny believed in absolutely nothing. Not 9/11 or the Kennedy assassination, not heaven or hell. The way he talked, Witt sometimes wondered if Sonny believed in him.

"Those are dolls, you psycho hillbilly."

"They don't look it at night," said Witt. "At night it looks like a whole cemetery in those trees."

Sonny had to give him that. There were at least a hundred small dolls nailed to the apple trees around the old man's yard. There were even a few on the porch and the low picket fence that surrounded the property.

"It's called hoarding," said Sonny. "These old assholes, their dog or their wife dies and their brains turn to Swiss cheese. They can't let go of anything. That's why we're here, right?"

Witt nodded.

"I know. I'm just all of a sudden amused that after all these years, I'll finally see inside the place for real. You know, we wouldn't ride our bikes by here at night. We'd go clear around the block to avoid it."

"What a great story. Promise me you'll write a memoir. You ready to go?"

"Hell yeah," said Witt, trying to sound more ready than he was.

It was just after two a.m. Witt had set the interior light on the Malibu to not come on when they opened the doors. Sonny carried the bag with their tools. They wore sneakers and latex gloves from the Walmart by the freeway. Sonny pulled on his ski mask. Witt kept his in his windbreaker's pocket. The night was hot and humid, and the mask had itched like a son of a bitch when he tried it on in the store. He'd put it on once they got inside.

Sonny was the first through the picket fence. He held the gate open for Witt, not because he was polite, but because he didn't want it to slam shut. That's the other thing Witt liked about Sonny. He was a thinker.

It was only about thirty feet from the fence to the porch, and even though it was night and he was wearing a mask, Sonny kept his head down. Witt followed him, covering the side of his face with his hand. Witt stepped onto the front porch gently. He didn't want the old boards to squeak. Sonny turned and looked at him.

"Where's your fucking mask?"

"In my pocket."

"Put it on."

"There's no one here."

"What if he has automatic lights or security cameras?"

"Cameras? You think this old son of a bitch is James Bond?"

Sonny sighed.

"Just put the damned mask on."

While Sonny got out his lock pick tools, Witt took the mask from his pocket and pulled it down over his face. He was sweating and itch-ing in seconds. *There better be something inside worth stealing*, he thought. Gold coins or silver candlesticks or a goddamn treasure map from back when the hovel had been the nicest house in town, eighty some odd years ago. The old man had lived there by himself for as long as Witt could remember. No one had ever seen him take anything but the trash out, and even that was a rare thing. Witt hoped it was cash inside. He wasn't a pirate. He wouldn't know what the hell to do with a bunch of gold. When it was over, maybe he could buy his dad's Malibu and get it fixed up. That would be sweet. He was about to ask Sonny what he thought about the idea when Sonny said, "Well, damn."

"What?"

"You were right. The old man isn't exactly security-minded."

Sonny put the picks back in the bag and turned the knob on the door. It opened.

"The hayseed doesn't even lock the place."

"I told you," said Witt. "Folks don't like it here. There's no reason they'd want to go inside."

"But we're not just folks, are we?"

Witt smiled. Sonny reached up and pulled down a doll held with wire over the doorframe. He handed it to Witt. The doll was about eight inches long. Its body was straw, and the head was made of rough, un-tanned leather, with button eyes.

"Toss it," said Sonny. "Time to grow up. This is no cemetery. It's a flop-house."

Witt threw the doll into the yard, and it felt like a hundred pounds of bullshit lifted off his back. He'd been afraid of the house for so long, he took it for granted that he'd be spooked forever. And now he wasn't. The old wreck, with its rotten gables and broken windows covered with cardboard, wasn't Dr. Terror's House of Horrors. It was just a prison for a pathetic old man. Witt all of a sudden sort of felt kind of sorry for him, but sorry didn't mean that he and Sonny weren't down for busi-ness.

Sonny pushed the front door open and Witt followed him inside.

The stink hit Witt hard, an overpowering combination of mildew, spoiled meat, and something like copper, with a sour sting that brought tears to his eyes.

"Jesus. Does this old fuck ever flush his toilet?" said Sonny.

"Sometimes in these old places, rats or raccoons will get in the walls and die there."

"Smells like it was Noah's whole goddamn ark."

Sonny flicked on a small LED flashlight and Witt did the same as they went deeper into the place.

They were in a wide foyer. The floor was covered with a carpet turned black with grime and mold. To the left was a parlor. Wallpaper peeled from the walls like burned skin. To the right was a dining room. A hallway led off from the foyer. A door to the kitchen in the distance. A closet. Another door under the stairs that Witt thought led to a basement. The place was even worse than he imagined.

"You sure there's anything left in here worth taking?" he said. "I mean, it smells like the damned dump."

"Spend a lot of time out there, do you?" said Sonny. "You said the family were bankers. People like that, they know what to squirrel away for a rainy day."

"I suppose."

"Damn right you do. Now, let's get to work. Don't forget what I told you. Slow and steady wins the race. Take your time, but don't get lazy. Don't make noise, but don't go so fast you're going to miss valuables."

Witt nodded. He wanted to breathe through his mouth, but he didn't want to look like a pussy in front of Sonny. He swung his light into the parlor.

"As good a place to start as any," Sonny said, and they went inside.

They went to opposite ends of the room. The plan was to work their way in and meet in the middle. It sounded good when they'd talked it over, but now Witt wasn't so sure. What the hell was he looking for, exactly? He was sure they weren't going to find a pile of hundreds just lying around the place.

He looked at the dusty paintings. Generations of the old man's family, each more mean and joyless than the last. It eased Witt's conscience a little.

Witt checked the bookcase and drawers on rickety old end tables. Picking up some old books, he wondered if they were worth something. Or one of the lamps. His grandma had an old gilt lamp from France that she swore was worth more than his granddad's soul. Witt shook his head. No. They weren't there for lamps or shit like that. He checked around the cushions on a sofa that kicked up enough dust that it looked like a west Texas sandstorm.

"What are you doing?" said Sonny.

"Searching. What do you think?"

"What are you looking for, bus fare? Leave the sofa alone."

Sonny played his light over the room. Witt checked his watch. They'd been in the room for fifteen minutes, but it felt like an hour. *I might not be cut out for this life,* he thought, but he kept his mouth shut.

Sonny pursed his lips like he was going to spit.

"There's nothing in here. Let's check the dining room."

They went across the hall and inspected the room the same way they'd done the other. The dining room was even less interesting than the parlor. Just a big table, some chairs, and a sideboard. There was a crystal chandelier in the center of the room, covered in cobwebs. That was probably worth something, thought Witt, but how would they get it out of there?

"Nice."

It was Sonny's voice. Witt went and looked over his shoulder. He had one of the sideboard drawers open and was holding up a shiny butter knife. Sonny handed it to Witt.

"You know what that is?"

Witt shook his head.

"Gold-plated silver. Old, too."

Witt turned the knife over. It was pretty, and it reflected a buttery light onto his jacket where the flashlight caught it. It was nice, but it didn't seem like a fortune.

"Is this what we came for?" he asked.

Sonny took the knife back and shook his head.

"It's a start. We've got a few thousand dollars here easy. I know people who love this kind of shit. They sell it to antique dealers and designer fags for a fortune."

Sonny put the knife back in the drawer.

"Aren't we going to take it?" said Witt.

"It's heavy. We'll get it on the way out. But this is exactly what we're looking for right now. Smalls. The old man will know where the big ticket stuff is, but for now remember to keep your eyes out for cash or watches or rings. We'll finish down here and go upstairs to roust Grand-dad."

A few thousand dollars already, thought Witt. *Maybe I am cut out for this after all.*

Sonny went ahead down the hall, and Witt followed him inside an office. There was a heavy wooden desk with an old-fashioned type-writer on top. To the side, an office chair with bad springs. It sat low and leaned back at a funny angle. There was a hat rack with a moldy fedora and ancient lacquered file cabinets so swollen with moisture that some of the drawers were twisted and wedged tight. Sonny started to work on them while Witt looked through the desk.

It was one of those old kind you see in movies, with lots of cubby-holes on top. He shone his light in each one and stuck a finger in the holes where he saw something. All he found were a few dead roaches, some rusted paper clips, and mouse turds. The drawers weren't any better. Letterhead stationery, old pens, and a rusty letter opener. In one of the bottom drawers he found a dusty bottle of bourbon. He was tempted to take it until he saw that the seal had been broken. Did whiskey go bad like beer? He didn't want to take a chance, so he put the bottle back and opened the top middle drawer.

There was a doll inside, like the ones in the trees. A goddamn funny place for one, Witt thought. He reached in the drawer and picked it up. It hung for a second, like it was caught on a nail, but it came free with a little tug.

Something black boiled out from the drawer and spread across the desktop, up the walls, and down onto the floor. Witt almost shouted, but kept himself under control. Some of what writhed on the desk hopped off and landed on the legs of his jeans. He pointed his light down.

There were spiders, pouring out of the desk and trying to crawl up his legs.

"Fuck!" he yelled, and shook his legs like he was barefoot dancing on coals. Someone grabbed his jacket collar and pulled him into the hall.

Sonny turned him around and looked him over.

"Spiders," whispered Witt.

Without missing a beat, Sonny bent and brushed the spiders away with his sleeve. When they hit the floor, he stepped on them like it wasn't anything at all.

"Thanks," said Witt. "I'm scared shitless of those things."

Sonny slapped him across the face.

"Don't you make another goddamn noise, you hear me?" he said.

Witt was still trying to catch his breath. His cheek stung, but he nodded. Sonny walked over and closed the office door. Seeing the spiders locked inside, Witt relaxed a little.

"You got a thing about those bugs?" asked Sonny.

Witt nodded.

"So did my old man. Turned to jelly at the sight of 'em. That's okay. You just better hope the old man didn't hear you and call the cops."

"Maybe we should leave?" asked Witt.

Sonny shook his head. Stood quiet for a minute, listening for footsteps or a phone.

"No. We're just getting started," Sonny said.

Witt looked around.

"This place is huge," he said. "It could take all night."

"No. When you've got a big place like this, what you do is hurt somebody. In this case, the old man."

"Why?"

"Because he's obviously crazy, and we're going to want him back on planet Earth for a while. Don't sweat it. I'll handle things. You just watch and learn."

Witt waited while Sonny walked down the hall. He wasn't sure how he felt about what Sonny wanted to do. Witt had been in plenty of fights over the years, but they were always stand-up, man-to-man things, not slapping an old cuss around. Still, the gold up front was awfully pretty, and he didn't think Sonny was the kind of man who was going to be talked out of a plan once he'd set his mind to it. Witt knuckled his cheek where Sonny slapped him. Better the old man getting hurt than him.

He realized that he was still holding the doll. It was like the others. A few inches long and with a leather head. There was a piece of string around its waist, trailing off to a frayed end. Witt remembered the feeling of the doll getting snagged on something in the drawer. Then he thought of something else.

Sonny was halfway down the hall, headed for the kitchen. Witt came up behind him and grabbed his shoulder.

"I think it was a trick," he said.

"What?"

"The spiders. Look." He held up the doll so Sonny could see the string. "They could have been in a bag or a net or something, and when I picked up the doll it let 'em loose."

Sonny looked at him and a smile crept across his face.

"Be cool, man. You're just spooked. We're about done down here. We've got the kitchen and if there's a basement, maybe give the downstairs a quick once-over. Then we go upstairs and we're out. Okay?"

Witt wanted to agree. He didn't want Sonny mad at him, but he didn't want spiders even more.

"I still think it was a trick," he said. "Something the old man set up."

Sonny glanced upstairs.

"I doubt this old guy can find his way down to the shitter. Stay focused and do the job."

Sonny started away and Witt wanted to say something, but he knew it wouldn't do any good. He played his flashlight over the walls and floor.

"Stop," he said.

Up ahead, Sonny did. He dropped his head a little. His shoulders were tense like he was about to hit something.

"What?" he said.

Witt didn't get any closer to him. He kept his light pointed at the floor a few feet in front of Sonny.

"Look down there."

Sonny took a couple of steps forward and stood for a moment, then went down on one knee.

"I'll be goddamned," he said.

Witt came to where Sonny knelt. Their lights illuminated a length of monofilament fishing line across the hall about six inches off the ground. Sonny grinned up at Witt.

"What do you think? More spiders? Maybe ninjas'll fall from the ceiling?"

"Don't touch it," said Witt as Sonny hooked a finger around the wire and pulled. It snapped. Witt froze. Nothing happened. Sonny looked up at him, then stood.

"I've got to give you points, man. You were right. Grandpa has been up to some funny games. But he's still an addled old man. This one didn't work."

Witt looked around the hall, expecting more spiders to come raining down. But nothing happened. He pointed at something shiny near the ceiling.

"What's that?" he said.

Sonny saw it, too. He moved closer, pulling a pistol from his jeans. He used the barrel to brush the tiny specks of light above his head. They made a small sound swinging against each other, like tiny wind chimes. It was fishhooks. Dozens of them hanging at eye level on more monofilament.

Sonny swept the gun barrel through the hooks, sending them swinging.

"This is good news. Know why?"

Witt shook his head.

"Because it means there's something in this house worth protecting. We're going to make ourselves some money tonight."

Sonny ducked under the hooks and stood when he reached the other side. He turned all the way around, checking the floor and walls for wires. When he was done, he motioned for Witt to follow him.

Witt hated creeping under the hooks almost as much as the spiders. He darted through and didn't stand again until he was past Sonny.

"We do the job just like we planned," he said. "Just keep your eyes open for any more pranks."

"Yeah. Okay," said Witt.

"And get rid of that fucking doll. You look like an idiot."

Witt looked down. He was still holding the doll with the string. He tossed it back down the hall the way they'd come and flinched, afraid it might set off another trap. But nothing happened.

"There's another wire up ahead," said Sonny. "I'll go that way. You check the closet."

As Sonny moved off, Witt checked the ceiling for hooks, and moved his light slowly over, around, and below the closet door frame. Ran his fingers around the doorknob feeling for a trip wire. He didn't find one. He looked down at Sonny, wondering if he could just *say* he'd checked the closet. But Witt knew he wasn't a good liar. There was nothing he could do.

He put his hand on the closet doorknob and turned. It opened. Nothing happened. He swung the door open the rest of the way and shone his flashlight inside.

The closet was full of rotting coats and rain boots, some umbrellas and a couple of canes with silver tops. *Those could be worth something,* he thought. There were boxes on the floor and more on a shelf above the coats. He checked around for more lines but didn't see any signs of them. *The canes first,* he thought, and reached for one.

A board under his foot sank a couple of inches. Witt froze. There was a metal-on-metal squeak. He pointed his flashlight at the floor. A board with long butcher knives pushed through it hung a foot away from his legs. It was supposed to swing out when he stepped on the board and hit him in the knees, but the house had betrayed the old man. The hinge the board hung from was caked with rust. Witt was so happy he wanted to laugh, but he didn't want to piss Sonny off by making noise. He grabbed one of the canes and stepped back. The board under his foot rose back up into place.

And another board swung out, this one chest-high. Witt jumped back, slamming his head into the wall opposite the closet. He went blind for a second as light exploded behind his eyes. When it cleared, he saw the second knife board, embedded in the closet door. It had missed him by a few inches. The doll he'd thrown away earlier lay by his side. He kicked it into the closet.

Footsteps pounded down the hall.

Sonny pushed him out of the way. He looked over the scene and then at Witt.

"You okay?"

Witt nodded, but he was still a little light-headed from his collision with the wall. Sonny grabbed his shoulders and pulled him to his feet.

"Fuck this," said Sonny. "Let's find him."

He was already on the stairs when Witt saw it.

"Stop!" he yelled.

Too late.

He ducked as Sonny's foot broke the fishing line.

A shotgun blast ripped across the hall, right by Sonny's head. It looked like an old sawed-off was inside the wall, hidden behind a flap of wallpaper, now scorched and torn by the blast. Sonny stumbled down the stairs, holding a hand over one ear. He pulled his hand away and checked it. There was blood on the palm.

Witt came over.

"You okay?" he said.

Sonny looked at him for a second, then snapped out of it.

"I think I'm fucking deaf in this ear. I think that fucker blew out my eardrum."

"Maybe we should get the knives and forks and just go," said Witt.

Sonny took out his pistol.

"We're not going anywhere. I'm going to find out what that old fuck has and kill him."

Under normal circumstances, Witt would argue about something like killing a person, but these circumstances were damned far from normal and the old bastard was kind of asking for it, Witt thought. He followed Sonny up the stairs. They weren't quiet as they went. The old man had to have heard the shotgun. There wasn't any point in being quiet anymore.

"Careful," Witt said.

A few steps up, Sonny said, "There's another doll and another wire. Duck."

Sonny bent over and when he was through, Witt followed him. As Sonny stood Witt saw the other line, the one strung so if you missed the first, you'd hit the second. Witt closed his eyes and what felt like a thousand pounds crashed down on them.

They were pinned to the steps. Sonny cursed and thrashed. Witt tried to push the weight off, but every time he moved, the net ripped into his skin. He managed to get his flashlight turned around and finally understood what had happened. The net they were trapped in was made of barbed wire. And they weren't alone. There was a body with them. A bag of bones and rags. Some other poor asshole who'd wandered into the old man's house and never left. Behind him, Sonny cursed and growled about all the ways he was going to murder the old man.

"Hold it," said Witt. "Stop moving a minute."

Sonny thrashed for a few seconds more and stopped.

"Barbed wire don't weigh much, but this net has got big weights on the ends," Witt said. "We keep thrashing, we're going to wrap ourselves up and die here like Mr. Bones."

"Who the fuck?" said Sonny.

"Turn your head."

Sonny did. The net dug into Witt's skin again as Sonny jerked back from the body.

"Fuck me," said Sonny.

"What are we going to do?"

"One of us has got to get out. Then he can hold the net up for the other to get out."

"So who does what?" said Witt.

"I hate to admit it, and if you repeat it I'll deny it, but I think you're stronger. I can't lift for shit flat on my back here. You get me out and I can help you."

"Okay," said Witt. "Can you help push a little?"

"I'll do what I can. Just keep those goddamn bones away from me."

"How am I supposed to do that?"

"I don't know. Forget it. Just push."

Witt got hold of one of the weights holding the net in place. The problem was that it was wrapped in barbed wire. Each time he grabbed it, the metal barbs tore into his fingers and palms. On his first try, he moved the weight up about six inches before the pain got to be too much. The good news was that it allowed Sonny to turn and wriggle up next to him. They both got ahold of the weight and lifted it just high enough for Sonny to crawl out. Witt dropped the net back where it was. Sonny lay on the stairs, panting.

"Sonny?"

"Yeah."

"Think you can start helping me out of here? I don't want to spend the night with this dead boy."

Sonny got to his knees and came up a step to where the weight lay. He put his hands on it and yanked them away.

"What's wrong?" said Witt.

"That dead fucker touched me."

"Use your jacket," said Witt. "It'll help with the barbs, and you won't feel the bones."

Sonny looked at him like Witt was speaking Chinese. Then he took his jacket off and wrapped it around his hands. Taking hold of the weight, he pulled up, leaning back against the staircase railing for support.

There was a spark and a thump. The weight came down, almost smashing into Witt's hand. Sonny flopped on the stairs next to it.

"Sonny," said Witt. "You all right?"

Sonny opened his eyes and looked at the banister.

"The railing is electrified. Zapped me good," he said.

"Can you lift the weight without touching it?"

Sonny reached up and pulled off his ski mask. His face was slick with sweat. He wiped it out of his eyes with his jacket sleeve.

"No, I can't," he said. He looked over. Witt knew Sonny was staring at the bones more than looking at him. Sonny frowned.

"I think I'm about done here, hoss," he said.

"What do you mean?"

Sonny put his jacket back on.

"I'm done. I'm over. The old fucker won."

Sonny stood and pulled his ski mask back on. He jerked back when he almost touched the railing and shook his head.

"I'm sorry, man. I can't help you."

He turned and started down the stairs.

"Sonny," yelled Witt. "Please!"

Sonny kept walking. Witt yelled after him. "You can keep my share of the forks and stuff. Just don't leave me."

Sonny stopped at the bottom of the stairs. Witt waited for him to come back up. Sonny said, "Sorry, man." He turned and headed for the door.

"Sonny!"

Down in the dark, Sonny cursed.

"What is it?" said Witt.

"The goddamned door. It's locked."

Witt listened to Sonny walk around downstairs, cursing and punching things.

He came back into the hall.

"The windows are barred from the inside. What the hell kind of house did you bring me to? This is your fault, you hayseed prick. I hope you fucking rot up there with your dead pal."

Witt watched as the circle of Sonny's flashlight disappeared down the hall.

"Sonny?"

Silence.

"Sonny?"

Nothing.

Witt lay on the stairs sweating. He pulled his ski mask off, too. He tried wrapping it around his hand to keep the wire from tearing into his palms, but when he lifted the net, the barbs cut into him and he couldn't hold on. His hands were ragged and bleeding. He lay there, breathing hard and trying not to completely lose his mind. Sonny was a thinker, but he lost it. *Be a better thinker. What would a better thinker do?*

Witt's elbow brushed against the skeleton. He reached over and twisted one of the bone hands and, with some sweating and swearing, snapped it off at the wrist. He'd torn up his shoulders doing it, but it was worth it. He found the dead man's other arm and snapped off the second hand. That's when he noticed a doll duct-taped into the dead man's mouth. Witt elbowed him away and turned back to the weight.

Balancing the skeleton hands over his palms, he grabbed the weight. When he pulled, the barbs dug into the bones, but didn't touch his hands. It took three tries, but he finally got the weight high enough to set it on the step above him. Slowly, he crawled forward, using the skeleton's hands to hold up as much of the net as possible.

He cut his legs up wiggling, but finally, he was out. Witt lay on the stairs facing the dead man. Another thief, he wondered? It couldn't be the old man. Maybe his family were embezzlers and it was someone from the bank come to confront him. That meant Sonny was right all along. There was a treasure somewhere in the house, and now neither one of them was going to get it.

Witt stood and started down, careful not to touch the railing. A gunshot boomed through the house. He went down the stairs as fast as he could and crouched by the wall, keeping low. The place was quiet now.

"Sonny?" whispered Witt. "Sonny?"

He looked down the hall and saw an open door. Warm light, like dawn over a river, lit up the walls and floor. Yeah, he thought, Sonny was a yellow dog piece of coward shit, but if he left now, that would make him just as bad. Witt started down the hall. He'd lost his flashlight on the stairs, so he went slowly, looking for any trip wires he might have missed earlier.

The basement door was open. A doll was perched on the top step, nailed in place through the stomach. Witt looked at it for a good long while, searching for monofilament, funny floorboards, or electric wires. He didn't find any, but he couldn't make himself step past the doll. Maybe Sonny wasn't close enough family to go searching this crazy-ass dump after all.

A voice echoed up the stairwell. Witt looked downstairs.

"Sonny?"

Something hit him in the back of the head and the building seemed to tilt, swing around, and hit him in the face. His vision collapsed to a tunnel and went out.

※

Witt awoke handcuffed to a rough stone wall. His hands tingled with pins and needles, and his face hurt like fire. He tried to say something, but it hurt so much he screamed, only there wasn't any sound. His lips were sewn shut.

The basement stank. The moist reek of decay down here was why the rest of the house smelled like Death shitting in a Dumpster. The blow on his head made it hard for Witt to see clearly. The glare from the bare bulbs strung along the ceiling hurt his eyes. He heard a splash, like someone was dragging wet laundry across the floor. Witt blinked, shook his head, and tried to focus.

Sonny hung on the wall like Jesus on the cross, held there with nails through his hands. A scrawny old man in overalls and a barbecue apron that read I LIKE MY PORK PULLED was gutting him with a long, curved butcher knife. The old man sawed his way up Sonny's stomach, stopping when he hit the breastbone. Then he made a cut across Sonny's belly, set down the knife, and reached inside, yanking out a long tangle of intestines. The old man let them flop into a plastic trashcan pushed up against the body. Sonny's head moved from side to side as the old man worked. His eyes opened, showing the whites. Witt's breath caught for a minute. Sonny was still alive. He wanted to scream, but remembered the pain.

The old man glanced at him, then turned back to his work.

"I'm not ignoring you, son," the old man said. "It's just that I'm a little busy right this second." His voice startled Witt. He expected an old coot, but the voice was strong and cultured, like someone in one of those ancient-aliens documentaries on cable.

The old man pulled Sonny's stomach wide, pinning the folds of skin to the wall with hooks and monofilament line. Sonny's abdomen was splayed open like a wet red flower. The old man took the knife and cut a couple of more things from Sonny's gut and dropped them into the trash. When he looked at Witt again, the old man's gaze lingered on him.

"I suppose you're wondering what's going on," he said, and smiled. "Since you're in no position to ask questions, I'll do my best to guess what you'd like to know."

The old man tossed the knife onto a worktable and pulled off bloody dishwashing gloves, dropping them next to Sonny's gun.

The man's face was creased and yellow, like a kid Witt remembered from grade school. The one with hepatitis, and they'd all had to get shots because of him. The man's knuckles were swollen and bent like he had rheumatism. His teeth were gray. Still, as beat-up as he was, the closer the old man got, the more Witt saw something hard and ferocious in his eyes.

"First of all, nothing you see here tonight is about torture or cruelty, though Lord knows you boys deserve a little of both, showing up here with a gun," said the old man.

He turned and pointed to a couple of little dolls lying on his worktable.

"My eyes and ears," he said. "I saw you two coming a mile away." He looked at Witt. "Made all these dolls myself. A trick my *grand-mère* taught me long ago and far away. Made them out of ambitious boys like you and your friend."

The old man wiped sweat out of his eyes and pushed back wisps of thin white hair.

"On the other hand, I'm grateful you're here. If it wasn't for boys, and a few girls, like you two, I wouldn't be where I am today." He held out his arms like the filthy basement was Hollywood Boulevard. "That was a joke," he said. "Don't try to laugh. It'll hurt."

When he got close, the old man held open each of Witt's eyes and looked at them, like a doctor examining a patient. His breath smelled like a swamp and he wheezed a little. Witt tried to squirm from his hands.

The old man looked away for a moment, as if he was lost in thought.

"Did you ever think about living forever?" he said. "I don't mean like fluttering off on angel wings and sipping tea with Jesus on a cloud, but living forever right here. Like a man. Well, I'm here to tell you, it can be done." He smiled wide, showing his rotten teeth. "Now, I know what you're thinking. If living forever looks like me, you're not interested. But you see me, this body, it's only a part of the story."

Sonny moaned, and the old man walked back to him. He put on his gloves, picked up his knife, and got back to work, cutting into Sonny's stomach. He talked as he worked.

"Immortality isn't what you think it is. It's not like in movies where you stay young and pretty forever. It's harder than that, and in a way it's more poetic. You live your life and grow old and when the time is right, you're reborn in new flesh. A bit like a phoenix." He turned to Witt. "You know what a phoenix is, don't you? Surely even a crude lad like you must know that."

Things from inside Sonny fell into the can.

"Your young friend here is my phoenix. When I shrug off this old meat, I'll be reborn in his. But first," he said, "I have to clear away the clutter."

He winked at Witt and pulled out more of Sonny's insides, until Witt could see his cousin's spine.

"The heart and the brain. That's all I need. They're the only things I don't take out."

The old man stood, kicked off his work boots, and started to undress. He moved slowly, like each joint was stiff and painful.

When he struggled to get the apron up over his head, Witt pulled at the cuffs holding him to the wall. The ring that held the cuffs in place felt loose. He put slow, steady pressure on it, not wanting the old man to notice what he was doing.

Finally, the old man was naked. His skin sagged like it was melting off his bones. Patches of white, stiff tumbleweed hair bristled on his crotch and under his arms. He picked up the knife and looked over. Witt stopped moving.

"I know you think what I did to your friend hurt him, but consider this: At least he didn't have to do it to himself. Watch this."

The old man took the butcher knife and reached behind his head.

He made a deep cut at the base of his skull, dragging the blade up and over his head to just above his eyebrows. This time, Witt screamed, and the pain brought tears to his eyes.

The old man's hands were shaking when he set down the knife. He reached behind his head with both hands and pulled. The skin slid away from his skull like he was skinning a dead deer. He kept pulling, and the flesh came down over his face, his neck, his chest, and down his legs. He moaned the whole time, but the old man's pain didn't give Witt any satisfaction. He pulled on the ring that held his handcuffs to the wall. It turned a little. He kept twisting, wondering how long it would take the old man to snake all the way out of his skin, and if it was enough time to get free.

It wasn't. Witt was still pinned tight when the last of the old man's skin hit the floor. He stepped out of it like he was kicking off dirty socks and fell against his worktable, panting. A glistening wet mass of sagging muscle and bone, the old man reached over and picked up Sonny's pistol. He pointed it at Witt.

"Stop that wiggling or I'll do double worse to you what I did to your friend," he said. "Besides, you'll like this next part. Slithering out of my old skin isn't fun, but I'm used to it. This next part is what really hurts."

He pushed a stool under Sonny's ass, then used a hammer to pull out the nails that held his hands to the wall. Sonny's body dropped onto the stool like someone cutting the strings of a marionette. The old man eyed the opening in Sonny's stomach like a Peeping Tom looking through a window, thought Witt.

The flayed man bent over, stiff and arthritic. When he was down as low as he could go, he grabbed his head and yanked it forward. Witt heard his neck snap. The old man screamed, and his head hung like it was held in place by spaghetti. Then he reached his arms around in front, like he was trying to hug himself. He jerked hard, dislocating both of his arms at the shoulder. Another scream. Witt closed his eyes, afraid he might throw up and drown inside his sealed lips.

The old man continued with whatever it was he was doing, the ritual coming to Witt as a series of horrible sounds. A wet tearing of muscles and snapping of bones. The old man's screams. When the noise stopped, Witt opened his eyes a fraction of an inch. He couldn't be-lieve what he saw.

The old man lay on the filthy floor. He'd folded himself up like a god-damned origami bird. His legs were up around his shoulders, and his head was buried beneath his ankles. The only thing that still sort of worked were his arms, and even they were kind of loose and dangling. Groping blindly, the old man's skinless hands went up Sonny's body, finally stopping when they found the opening in his stomach. They got a good grip on the edges and hauled the rest of the old man's body up and into the hole.

Witt knew that what he was doing would never work. There was no way he could get his whole body into Sonny's stomach. And yet, as Witt watched, the old man did it. By whatever magic or skill or madness he'd learned over the years, the old man kept squeezing and squeezing his body tighter and tighter until he'd worked his way completely inside Sonny. Then he reached out and pulled the loose stomach flaps closed. The slits he'd cut into them healed as Witt watched.

Sonny twitched. His body went stiff. His eyes fluttered. He relaxed and his head fell forward. He pissed himself. Then he laughed.

"That always cracks me up," Sonny said. "I start off each new life by pissing myself like an infant. It's all right. It's how I know all the plumb-ing is working."

Sonny stood, holding himself with his hand against the wall. He took a stiff step. Then another, his balance coming back to him. He breathed deeply, as if relishing this new, younger flesh.

"*Que penses-tu de ma nouvelle poupée?*" he said, then, "What do you think of my new doll?"

As Sonny came over to him, Witt braced himself against the wall like maybe if he pushed hard enough he could pass through solid stone.

When Sonny reached him, he held Witt's head in his hands.

"The worst part is over. Don't worry about me gutting you like your friend. All I need from you is your head. I just pull out the skull, scrape the fat from the inside of the skin, and shrink the rest of it down for one of my dolls."

He looked around the basement.

"These dolls are old. I'll be moving on soon, and I'll need new ones. You'll be the first in my new life. Try to relax. It'll hurt less if you're calm. Be extra good and I'll kill you quick with the gun."

The thing that used to be Sonny went and picked up the old man's skin from the floor. He dumped it into the garbage can with Sonny's insides. It took him a while to drag the can over to an ancient gas furnace. He didn't quite have the hang of the new body yet.

While Sonny had his back to him, Witt pulled as hard as he could on the ring holding the handcuffs. He picked his feet off the floor, using his body weight to pull down. The cuffs felt like hot metal digging into his wrists. He gritted his teeth and swallowed so he wouldn't make any noise. He felt the ring move an inch. Then another. But the pain was too much. His vision started fogging again, and he was afraid he might pass out. He put his feet on the floor and looked over. The old man had the body parts in the furnace and was fiddling around with the controls. He touched handles and gauges randomly, like he was having trouble remembering how they worked. *Good*, thought Witt. He still had some time. If he could get to the table, he could get the gun. *That's all I need.*

Witt took a breath, getting ready for the pain when he pulled his feet off the floor. Hanging there, his hands turning dark with trapped blood and feeling like they were going to pop off, he raised his head.

He stopped what he was doing when he saw the doll nailed to a beam a few feet above. That's why the old man was taking his time. He knew everything Witt was doing. He wasn't going anywhere. And probably, he thought, he wasn't going to get that quick death after all.

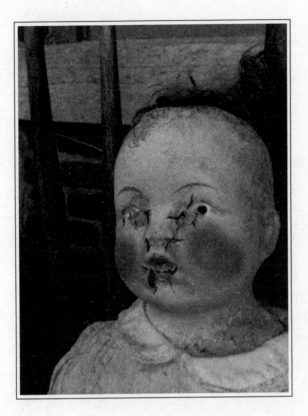

Miss Sibyl-Cassandra

by Lucy Sussex

EddKnight@sothebys.com
Attached is the draft listing for our little addendum to Mon's auction. Correct as you see fit. The antique toy mafia sent through their opinion, though turning up their noses at the condition of Miss S-C. True, not exactly mint, but provenance, as I pointed out, is everything. I have instructed Althea not to put through any more calls from biographers, let alone the Society—that's another mafia entirely. Edd

ZLefroy@sothebys.com
Typos (2) corrected. The rest is fine. Zara

EddKnight@sothebys.com
Thanx. Photography did their best, but Miss Sibyl-C is really a most unprepossessing little object. Did you hear the vendors nearly listed her on eBay? Lucky someone thought to read the letters in time. E

ZLefroy@sothebys.com
Lucky them! Care to pluck a leaf from dolly's skirt and predict her fortune?

EddKnight@sothebys.com
If I am to put my hand up a petticoat, I prefer the wearer not be 200 years old. And in any case the doll is hexed. Or as these Georgians put it, hex'd.

ZLefroy@sothebys.com
I'll tell her fortune: she will travel to a distant land and live in a safe.

EddKnight@sothebys.com
Over the Society's dead body

ZLefroy@sothebys.com
You wish. Ha ha, gotta go!

෯

Item 41: Doll, late eighteenth century. Wood and colored paper, coral, 5" in height. Painted head, some damage from fire (as noted in accompanying letter, item 43). Orange paper bodice and sleeves, wig of human hair, gray. Styled as Roma, with shawl and turban cut from red and yellow patterned paisley muslin. Coral necklace, strung on embroidery thread. An early example of the fortune-telling doll, with voluminous coloured paper skirts, largely intact. Handwriting on some of the leaves is the same as in letter, item 43. A rare and unique item.

෯

My dear Goddaughter Nancy,

Since I received your last letter, which I am glad to say arrived in time for my birthday, along with the conserves and ivory fan (for the which, my delighted thanks!), I have been giving some thought to your forthcoming New Year's party. I fully understand your concerns with holding such an entertainment, given that you are but new to the village. What a maze of protocol and ancient history (which you have no way of knowing) you will have to negotiate, my dear! I do have perfect faith in Cook and the servants, but as you say, a certain *je ne sais quoi* is needed, for entertainment purposes.

Here is my suggestion, which I enclose, along with a length of Indian muslin, whose colours I think you will find becoming. Our peddlar-woman came later than usual this season, with her tray of goods. Amidst the pins and ribbon cards I saw the little peg face, peering out at me. "Oh what is that?" I cried, and she replied that it was the latest thing in Bristol-town, a Madame Fortuna. "And it spares ye the gypsies," she added, with a toss of her bonnet.

It struck me as eminently sensible. At this time of year people's thoughts naturally turn to the year to come, what God has will'd for them. You are to add the fortunes yourself to the paper skirts. Do make sure that they are suitable for the company. The sheer novelty is certain to amuse your guests, and to win you acclamation as a hostess.

> With all good wishes,
> Your loving Godmother,
> Anne Pendlebury

My dear Godmother,

My warmest thanks for the muslin, which I immediately began to cut up for a summer gown, though that season seems very far in the future, with the weather we have suffered of late. And also for the doll, which Sophronia and Harriette would have squabbl'd over, had I not proclaimed that you specifically intended it for the New Year party.

While we were thus engaged (with tears!) Georgiana came down, carrying Baby, whom the quiz of a girl had dress'd as a Negro slave, his face blackened with charcoal. I therefore had to turn from remonstrating with two daughters to reproaching their elder sister, which gave Baby the chance to seize hold of the doll. Sophronia tried to wrest it from him, but Baby most wantonly threw it into the fire. Tears again, from my tenderhearted girls, but Georgiana most enterprizingly seized the tongs and rescued dolly from the fiery furnace. True, her poor head was singed, and her skirts entirely consum'd. But enough remained for me to see the pattern, and know I could repair her loss.

Come the afternoon of the party, I had a small casement of time between my preparations and the receiving of the guests. I rang the bell for young Hannah, the acutest of the servant girls you so obligingly recommended to me. I also summoned Miss Fairfaxe, the new governess. I had a box of coloured pages, from when I thought to play Mrs. Bailey, and ape nature with cut paper flowers.

Once I had explain'd, the two proved apt pupils. Miss Fairfaxe cut paper skirts, and Hannah and I constructed the top half of dolly's dress. We were in the midst of a discussion about whether we should construct a paper bonnet also, and in which fashion, when who should arrive but Mr. Harley, who had quite mistaken the time, and was hours early, with none of us properly dress'd yet!

"As I encountered your New Year's Prophetess on the road, and it is snowing yet again, I thought to give her carriage in my gig. . . ."

Vexing man! Peering over his shoulder I beheld an old Gypsy woman, plainly expecting to have her palm crossed with silver. I would have no recourse but to pay her good riddance, and hope she had not observed our henhouse too closely.

So I stumbled out that we already had a Prophetess, and were in the process of finalising her costume.

"Then my passenger can be your model," said Mr. Harley. Vexing man again! but the Gypsy obligingly stood still by the fireside, warming herself. Oh, she was so dark, lean, and tall, with a gaze as sharp as broken glass! I had scraps from your Indian muslin, so I copied her shawl and turban. Georgiana, who had joined us, scamper'd upstairs and returned with gleanings from Grandmamma's comb, a white crowning glory, and some beads left over from restringing her coral necklace.

It was strange, but under our ministrations, and the Gypsy's gaze, the doll became less of a bedizen'd peg, singed with flame, but something . . . else, I cannot say what. Nothing else can explain the events of that evening.

"Let me finish her!" That was the Gypsy, speaking for the first time, her voice deep and with such command that I handed the doll to her, quite involuntarily. She took it and passed her hands over the wooden head, muttering all the while.

"What have you done?" That was Mr. Harley.

"Why nothing, kind sir, but making her prophecies honest and true. And I have added a little charm, to preserve her from fire, as I see she has suffered already."

"You have made her a Sibyl then, a foreseer, or a Cassandra, whom nobody will believe?"

"What ye do with her words is as ye wilt," she said, ominously.

I had had quite enough by then, so I rang for Jenkins and instructed him to show our visitor the door. She actually bit my good coins, in front of me! but left readily enough, though with a parting leer. Time was getting short, and so I set the company around the table to writing fortunes, which Hannah gathered up as they came, and sewed together with stout thread. I even wrote some myself, oh, the usual stuff: You shall go on a long journey, you shall marry a rich husband, you will gain your true love's heart. So I left them to it, for I had to supervise the rest of the party.

And thus, my careful plan went awry. Oh to be sure, everything else seem'd perfection, after all our bustle and worry. I wore my claret-coloured velvet with the fur trim, and Georgiana my old silver-grey merino, cut down to fit. The dinner was a veritable feast, and the dancing to the pianoforte decorous, if vigorous. But when Hannah, in her best pinny, brought in the doll, for whom Jenkins had improvised a stand, the fortunes were not quite what I had intended. I blame Mr. Harley, who had already prov'd vexatious—but as Georgiana was present, I had thought they might get the better acquainted while writing fortunes. He will inherit, it is rumoured, 10,000 pounds. In my retrospection I realise Georgiana was clearly not to be relied upon as a scribe-seer, and Miss Fairfaxe was entirely of an unknown quantity.

Vous aurez une belle dot et un vieux mari méchant et jaloux.

You will have a nice dowry and an old, nasty, and jealous husband.

Now I wrote the first half, in my best French, but somebody else had added the second. And who should get it but Miss Mereweather, who is to be sent out to the East Indies to marry Lieutenant-Governor Fettiplace—a man twice widowed, with thirteen children? It was a match that had only been contracted over Christmas and not noised outside the family. The poor girl burst into rivers of tears.

Less misappropriate was:

La vertu est souvent méconnue sur la terre, elle ne le sera pas dans le ciel.

Virtue is often underestimated on the earth, but it will not be in the sky.

A pretty phrase, for which I took credit, though I have no recollection of writing it—though when tasked I had to admit the hand was mine. That went to widowed Mrs. Anstey, who smiled even more sanctimoniously than is her wont, though she had protested the doll at its advent, saying: "Is it Godly to be tearing petticoats in public?" Our Vicar, who is rather more worldly than Mrs. A, got: "You will lay on your final pillow in a fashionable watering place," which caused him to laugh immoderately and declare that he might as well do something fashionable for once in his life.

I got: "You will welcome a new soul to this earth"—true enough, as anyone who looks at my silhouette currently will know. My dear husband got: "A horse is a good servant but a poor master"—as if somebody had merely copied down a motto. Mr. Harley's fortune was: "Do not stay in solitude too long, you will find nothing there." Good advice, I thought, for when Georgiana has grown up a little, and has less sensibility and more sense. She got: "You will earn great renown"—really most unsuitable, though it sent her capering down the hall to fetch the children, who had been throwing snowballs in the coachyard, with Jenkins and Hannah supervising. Of course they had to have their fortunes, too, though I was beginning to tremble at what they might receive. At least Baby was abed, and could not grab at the doll again.

And so they all came in, red-faced and snow-bedraggled, to scry their futures, the two Anstey boys, my three girls, and the Vicarage children, with their forward young cousin Eliza. She picked two by mistake, and got: "You shall be a Countess" and "True love is found in cousinage." It caused her to declaim that she would shake the family tree forthwith, to dislodge a Count-Cousin! I daresay she will find one, as the gossip is that she is the natural child of someone quite grand. The Vicar's littlest sons got near-identical missives, about going to sea to find their fortunes. The Ansteys got pious messages about being Godly and traveling far, or being Godly fare. Since the boys are intended as missionaries, it pleased their Mamma if not them. My dear Sophronia got: "Beware of men wearing red," and Harriette: "Your bridal robe will be woven from snow."

For the most part the children laughed off their dooms, and merely wanted an extra pull on the doll's skirts, which I absolutely forbade. But oddest of all were the reactions of the Vicarage's little misses, two girls unobtrusive in matching frocks, quite overshadowed by all those rowdy boys in the family. The elder got: "You shall have but one true love, and will love him all your life." She held it to her heart and cried: "Oh I will, oh I will!" like a heroine from a sentimental novel.

The younger had the misfortune to get quite the most cross-grained fortune of the night: "You shall have six children and die with another half-made."

The child read it out aloud, and then looked up. Such a bright, clear, unsettling gaze, from one so young: "What does it mean?"

Somebody at the back of the room (I never established who) murmured a riposte. It carried, as the roomful of guests had unexpectedly fallen silent, except for the crackle of the fireplace logs: "Means the chit'll die in accouchement, I suppose."

What a thing to say! But the child merely said, calmly: "Well, then I shall never marry." Something which her brothers will surely teaze her about, when she grows to woman's estate and sets to husband-hunting.

Before I entirely run out of paper and have to cross my letter, I will merely add that Hannah got: "You shall travel to the other side of the world, and find a rich husband"—how ridiculous, for a servant girl! And Miss Fairfaxe got: "Your one true love you met tonight," which is equally ridiculous, for a governess.

Your loving goddaughter, Nancy

On another sheet of paper, inserted into the letter:

My dear godmother, I quite forgot to send this letter, and as well I did not, for I have a postscript. On the first Sunday of the New Year, I went up to Miss Fairfaxe's room, to ask why she had not risen yet, and found the fortune, neatly laid out on her bed, and the lady gone—chattels and all. It has transpired that she and Mr. Harley eloped, doing as they wilt with the fortunes prophesied for them, which is sorely trying. Now I must find another governess! Could Mr. Harley possibly vex me more? I did say as much to Georgiana, in my passion, and she did declare she wouldn't marry him anyway, as she was going to be an actress. What on earth am I going to do with the girl?

On the reverse, in a different hand:

My poor mother never did send this letter, for it fell behind a crack in her dresser, and was only discovered this month, when I was having said item of furniture repaired. Such memories it brings back, and what a strange story it tells! Whatever charms that witch of a Gypsy laid on the doll, she spoke honest and true. Mamma did have a son that year, my brother Edward, and then four more. My poor father did not die from his favourite pastime of hunting, as was Mamma's terrible fear, but when his favourite painting, a Stubbs, fell on his head, in his eightieth year. Miss Mereweather did marry her Governor, who proved horrible indeed, but he was dead within a year. She then married his aide-de camp, a dashing gentleman, I am told. Mrs. Anstey died that summer, sanctimonious to her deathbed. I am told her two sons were eaten by cannibals in the South Seas. My poor sister Harriette died at the age of twelve, during the bitterest winter of our sojourn in Northumberland. Georgiana did not become an actress, as she threatened, but Quakeress. Her renown is in good causes, and she is of late reforming the penitentiaries. Next she plans to visit the Americas and abolish slavery.

As for myself, I did fall several times in love with soldiers, in my madcap days, but always bore the prophecy in mind. And to be sure, the red-coated gentlemen proved to be rakes indeed. When I married, I was thirty, and sensible enough to see the virtue in a sober country lawyer. My dear Alfred is, as it happens, distantly related to

the Harleys. As he had business at one of their estates, I took the
liberty of bringing the letter, to show them. What a pair of lovebirds,
at seventy! And Mrs. Harley, my governess as was, she shed a smiling
tear at such sentimental memories.

"What became of the doll?" I asked, for I did not recall seeing it
after the party.

"Why," said she, "I took it with me, as an omen of good luck."

She rang a bell for a footman, and within a short while Miss
Sibyl-Cassandra, as Harriette and I had christened her, was produced,
in a satin-lined box.

"How strange the fortunes were," said old Mr. Harley. "And yet so
uncannily true. What became of Hannah, who so deftly sewed that
skirt of fate?"

"Our serving wench? Oh she got transported for theft:
Grandmamma's pearls. We all thought it far too severe to hang her,
and Mamma pleaded her youth. Jenkins had a letter from Hannah,
much later, to say 'twas the best deed she ever did in her life, for she
had married the second wealthiest merchant in the colony of New
South Wales."

"But the most surprising fate in store was for the Vicarage
children," said his wife.

I must own I had not thought of them in years, since Papa's
regiment moved to Northumberland. "Pray tell."

"The youngest boys became Navy captains, and one is even an
admiral, I forget which."

"And the eldest daughter, Cassandra like the doll, I remember that,
she found a lifelong true love?"

"She did, but he did not live, and she would never court again."
She sighed.

Mr. Harley took up the tale once more.

"And their cousin Eliza, such a pretty little minx. She did marry a
French count, though his title was dubious, and they lost all in the
Revolution. Her second husband was, as foretold, her cousin Harry."

"And then, the youngest miss, what became of her?" I asked.
"Surely she could not avoid dying in childbed, sad fate though it is?"

"You do not know?"

"I cannot even recall her name. I only remember that it was commonplace."

"Why," he cried, "little miss Jane, of the Steventon Austens. She who declared she would never marry, to 'scape bearing six children, then dying with an unfinished child? And so she did, the seventh and last of her novels."

They have insisted on giving me the doll, as I had desired it so much as a child, and poor Harriette will not dispute the ownership now. It has brought them good luck, they claim, and as they are at the end of their lives, they say they are not in need of a charm against fire anymore. With that in mind, I will stow this letter and the doll in a trunk in the attic, both to be securely locked. I merely add this missive as a warning, lest anyone else take what they wilt from a Gypsy-doll's skirts.

Sophronia Smith-Harley

The Permanent Collection

by Veronica Schanoes

Here is what you would have seen if you had visited the last doll hospital in Manhattan:

You would have spotted the upper-story sign after walking up and down the street peering at address numbers more than once, and with a feeling of rising doubt, you would pry open the dirty tenement door, now so out of place in midtown, and step into a foyer whose walls and ceiling were hidden under years of the grime that accumulates on any city surface. In some eras it is soot and in others oil and in still others exhaust, but in all eras it is neither more nor less than the lost souls of the city made visible, and ground to greasy dust.

Forgive me for waxing philosophic.

It happens to so many of us; there is very little for us to do but think, after all. We watch years pass, unable to blink or lie with our eyes shut instead. Thinking.

Back to the foyer, where the door slamming behind you shuts out even the memory of light, and you stumble toward the narrow staircase. It is steep, with only a few stray wisps of lost and lonely lamplight drifting down to guide your feet.

You would never before have seen a place so Gothic. Almost gloomy enough to be comical, and perhaps you would have tried to find the whole thing funny, but the laughter would have died in your throat. Perhaps you would have tried to turn the gurgle into a cough, to save face in front of the cockroaches and rats that are never more than a few feet away in this city.

The stairs would have creaked as you climbed them, and more than once you would slip on the warped and worn treads. After three or four flights (you would have lost count), you would have seen a door propped open, and light streaming out from it, and perhaps you would even hear some shrill laughter. You couldn't be sure you'd found the right place, but you would no longer care too much. By this time you'd just be grateful for an exit from the hopeless staircase. You might trip, or stagger, or even walk perfectly calmly through the door.

And you would have arrived at the Midtown Doll Hospital.

That is what *you* would have seen.

What I saw was the inside of a knapsack.

My girls had been dead for years by the time I was brought to the Doll Hospital. I'd had only the life of the mind for a long, long time.

My first girl led a charmed life in the beginning. I was clear evidence of her good fortune: In 1935 Clara Hoffmann's father, a big man in the rag trade who knew how to make the most of a Depression, put down $6.95 in exchange for an eighteen-inch Shirley Temple doll. Those dolls—myself included—had been sent out to stores for the release of Shirley's—should I say "my"?—new movie.

What is my relationship to Shirley Temple?

I am not entirely sure. Once it seemed so clear. She was a celebrity, and I was a copy. But she is no longer who she was, no longer the bright-eyed, plump-cheeked child with a head full of carefully set curls. So I think that I am now closer to being the original celebrity, the child who was never anything more than a trick of projected light or flickering pixels. The original, which had been a carefully constructed and maintained persona, a doll, to begin with.

In many ways I believe that of the two of us I may be the luckier.

Can you imagine growing up as Shirley Temple?

Six dollars and ninety-five cents in 1935 was the equivalent of almost $120 today.

I would now be worth almost ten times that.

Clara Hoffmann's father paid $6.95 for me, and Clara carried me to the theater to see *Curly Top* on her lap. Do you know it?

In *Curly Top*, Shirley—I—Shirley . . . let us say "I," then, and make things easier. In *Curly Top*, I and my teenage sister are being mistreated in a rundown orphanage, when a wealthy gentleman takes a shine to me and after mooning around a bit adopts us both. He and my older sister then fall in love and marry.

While the gentleman in question is supposedly in love with my sister, he is really in love with me, singing me love songs and seeing my face wherever he looks (the film, which opens with a steady close-up of my adorable face, is quite overtly in love with me).

In retrospect, it is not a little disturbing.

But in 1935, it was one of the biggest box office draws of the year.

I have my original clothing and my original shoes and a Shirley Temple button that alone is worth over $150, and, though it is battered, I still have my original box. Needless to say, I have my original wig. My curls are a little mussed, but at my age, one cannot expect perfection.

⁂

I was worth a lot more than $6.95—or even $1,200—to Clara Hoffmann. I became her constant companion. It is indeed a miracle, given how fervently she played with me and held me, that I am still in one piece, let alone that I still have all my clothing down to my oilcloth shoes. It is a point of pride for me that despite my wholeness, my good condition, I was played with. I was well and truly played with. I have been loved.

Any minor signs of wear and tear were long since taken care of by Nathan Coppelius.

Perhaps I should be grateful, but I am not. The man is a master craftsman, but he is also a monster.

Clara, as I said, led a charmed life until she reached adulthood. Her marriage, to Sigmund Apfelbaum, was a happy and loving one. And in time, she gave me to her firstborn, her daughter Dora. Poor Dora, though, Dora lived on the knife edge of despair, buffeted by ill winds that never blew any good at all.

Clara would have given all her luck to bring joy and good health into her daughter's life. But luck does not work that way; it is not fungible, and it is not transferable.

What Clara could give to Dora was me.

I know that Clara felt this way, for she had been my girl, so despite her adulthood, I still knew every feeling that passed in her heart, and I felt every twinge of love, fear, and happiness within her.

I stayed whole in Dora's hands thanks not to luck but to Dora's meticulous care. The child took every precaution lest her ill health somehow affect me as well; she knew she could not trust my preservation to an unkind fate. Every morning and every evening she inspected me, and refused to begin or end her day unless I was safe and complete.

I have been much loved.

But Dora did not have Clara's energy. She was often tired and slept frequently during the day. My time with her was significantly less bumptious. Three years after I passed into Dora's hands, Dora was taken to the hospital. She was so frightened, and eventually Mr. Apfelbaum brought me to her. She could barely play any longer, and mostly just held me in her arms while she slept.

Eventually Mr. Apfelbaum brought me home, but Dora did not come with me.

She did not suffer, not like Clara did. I know that for a fact.

What I also know is that at some point over the following year, Mr. Apfelbaum came in while Clara was visiting her parents and carefully packed up every toy, every scrap of clothing, every document, and every photograph that could remind Clara of their lost daughter. They could not bear to dispose of these relics of their first child, but neither could they have them in the apartment on Sutton Place.

Eventually, Mr. Apfelbaum rented a storage unit in Danbury, Connecticut, locked the boxes inside it, and never returned.

Clara had many moments of joy in her life, and I, though I was far away from her, felt them all. It was not until Clara's death some forty-five years later that their younger daughter's son opened the door to the storage unit and brought the boxes back to his own apartment in Queens, where he unpacked them in growing confusion. Neither he nor his mother had ever been told about Dora's existence, apparently. It was not until he unpacked her birth and death certificates in a folder from the boxes that he understood what he was looking at.

And that was when he found me, as well.

It was my first glimpse of light in forty-five years.

❧

As I said, my girls have been dead for years.

It becomes very lonely in the private enclosure of my thoughts.

And so it was that I was brought along with Dora's other dolls and stuffed animals to the last doll hospital in Manhattan.

As I said, I saw only the inside of a knapsack as I was brought upstairs, and that only because the lid of my box slipped off. But I smelled the grime and penny-ante Gothicism, and I heard the stairs creak and groan. I was again in the long-familiar dark, waiting patiently, for what, I did not know.

❧

Here is what you would see as you stumbled into the doll hospital, after your eyes adjusted to the bright, unforgiving, white lights:

A shabby counter.

A narrow pathway winding through various piles, heaps like grotesque haystacks.

The piles themselves.

A pile of heads, most with staring eyes, and some, only a few, the sleepyheads, with lashes resting serenely on cheeks, lips curved sweetly up, seemingly as oblivious to the absence of their bodies as they were helpless to do anything about it.

A pile of left arms of various sizes, in a variety of different attitudes, some jointed, most not. And nearby, a similar pile of right arms.

Piles of left legs and right legs, and a pile of limbless, headless torsos.

They were made of plastic, vinyl, composition, even wood and bisque porcelain. And they were almost all a pale, slightly pink peach color.

And sitting on a squat chair, sometimes with his brother and sister on nearby stools, but usually alone and giggling softly to himself, was Nathan Coppelius.

❧

A doll specialist should be kind to children, and tenderhearted. He should see himself as a healer of beloved, forlorn creatures, just as a doctor should be a healer and a comfort. But surgeons see the body as meat to be cut, and Coppelius? Coppelius was quite mad, and a sadist to boot.

Perhaps he would have been mad no matter what, and perhaps we made him mad, for he could hear us, and very few people can do that. And yes, of those who can, many do go mad.

Once I saw a mother come in with her seven-year-old daughter and a doll precious to them both. She had been well and vigorously played with, and her hair was in mats and tatters. Coppelius grunted briefly at the mother, and then, in full view of the child, he slowly and deliberately tore off the doll's wig, exposing the patchy, blotchy decay of her scalp.

Coppelius and I and the other dolls of the permanent collection heard her scream. It was clear from the child's face, all round staring eyes and pinched lips, that she didn't need to. It was clear from Coppelius's face that he took as much pleasure in the sight as he did in the sound.

He glued a classic wig to the doll's head—Jane, her name was as classic as the wig—all long golden ringlets, and reluctantly handed her back to the mother, who passed her to the child. The child stroked Jane's new curls and whispered comforts to her, but continued to stare at Coppelius.

Children and dolls have this in common: We are both so vulnerable to the whims of those bigger than us.

෯

Fifteen years later, Jane's child returned. Once again, she was with her mother, and this time she had with her a Paddington Bear, one from London. He looked worn and threadbare, but contented. He trusted the girl, I think.

I noticed that she carried him in a shoulder bag just low enough for his head to peer out into the world. Low enough for him to feel the air on his snout.

I couldn't quite hear all that she said. Unlike her Paddington, she seemed apprehensive. Well, the Doll Hospital had only become more grotesque over the years, as Coppelius had performed ever more unpleasant experiments on the permanent collection. By then I numbered among my companions a doll in whose head Coppelius had carved out space for a third eye, a doll whose mouth had been erased, and a doll whose arms and legs had been swapped.

And I remained, pristine and unharmed.

I am not sure why. At first I thought it was because he intended to sell me, but he never did, and I saw him take a hammer to the head of a Baby Peggy doll once, far more valuable than I. Perhaps he simply liked *Curly Top*.

I was the only doll in the permanent collection who had not been . . . altered.

There was a Chatty Cathy whose voice box had been changed.

Oh, I know some of you find that sort of thing amusing, the cherubic child's toy bellowing obscenities:

Suck my cunt.

See? I can do it, too.

But we were loved, once. We were. With love no less real than what you feel or what is felt for you. Most of us were loved tenderly, passionately, by children, whose feelings are the rawest, the least refined, the least contained. And some of us were worshipped, doted on by collectors, and that, too, is a kind of love.

So if you find our humiliation funny?

Suck my cunt.

⁂

So. The hospital had only grown more grotesque with age, and Jane's child, standing with the bear in a carefully chosen bag, was clearly growing unhappier by the minute. I did not hear what she said, something about the worn, disintegrating patches on the bear's skin. She showed them to Coppelius, but I noticed that she did not relinquish her hold.

I heard Coppelius quite clearly and with relish explain how he would have to skin the bear, pull his pelt off inside out and upside down, and then glue it to a linen under-skin, and then restitch the entire construction back to the bear's carcass.

The girl looked down at her bear. He looked back at her, though of course they did not see that. The girl asked, with the look of somebody determined to do the right thing no matter the cost, how much this . . . repair would be.

Coppelius quoted her a figure of several hundred dollars, adding that he took cash only. Then he said, somewhat contemptuously, that after all, such bears had never really been made to last.

This, I think, was a mistake on his part, for the girl exchanged another look with her bear, and they took their leave quite decisively.

I have not seen them since.

※

Ultimately, Coppelius miscalculated. He thought that as the proprietor of the last doll hospital in the city, he could charge what he wanted as well as indulge his contempt and sadism openly.

But he could not.

Business slowed, and then fell off.

And doll dealership was no longer such a rarified enterprise, not with the Internet. Nowadays, I suppose that Dora's nephew could have just sold me on eBay, or Etsy, or Ruby Lane, and perhaps I would have ended up as part of some collector's horde, a nice retirement for me. Instead of being the only untouched piece in the permanent collection of the doll hospital, my pristine smiling face and perfect body an abomination among so many obscene alterations.

※

A midtown storefront, even on an upper story, is not cheap. Coppelius was not making money any longer. But, then, he had insurance. Oh yes, he had insurance.

※

If I could, at this point in the narrative, I would quote Coppelius's insurance policy, paying special attention to the portion having to do with fire. But of course, I have never seen his insurance policy. I am not even sure I could have read it if I had. The only schooling I have had was in Clara's and Dora's pretend classrooms. After all, I was only a doll.

Even without having read the policy, I wonder how Coppelius imagined his scheme. Surely deliberate fire-setting on the part of the owner would be the first thing investigated, and he was no master arsonist. But he had never been right in the head, and by this time he was an old man. And of course, he was desperate.

There were not many of us left by then. Business had been off for some time, and we in the permanent collection had never been many, just a handful of monstrosities and me. Even the heaps of disarticulated parts were somewhat diminished, no longer higher than a full-grown adult, though still taller than the few children who managed to find their way into the store, and who invariably edged out as quickly as they could. Of course, they dwarfed me.

We had a walking doll in the shop once. I remember her in particular, in part because she was one of the rare times we saw a black doll. She was tall, for one of us, and jointed, which made it easier for her to move. We *can* move, but it's hard for us to move *around*. Most of us can't even stand on our own, after all. And our arms and legs are locked at the elbows and knees.

Monica was tall, and she could walk.

It would have been helpful to have had her around when Coppelius began dousing us all with gasoline.

Still, I'm glad she wasn't. Coppelius did his work well with her, and she walked out the door in the arms of somebody's mother.

Coppelius thought about preserving me, I know he did. Before he uncapped the gasoline, he picked me up and stared at me intently. For a moment, he turned and started toward the duffel bag he had brought in with him. But then his shoulders slumped and he put me back. He doused us all, but he lingered over me.

Maybe he'd had a Shirley Temple doll he'd loved as a kid. Maybe he'd always envied a younger sister hers. Maybe he'd seen something terrible happen to that doll, and that was the root of the whole problem. I don't know, and I suppose it doesn't matter anymore.

᷒᷒

We tried to get away when he began pouring the gasoline, straining legs never meant to carry us, arms that could not balance us. All we succeeded in doing was toppling over in a heap.

No, it was not us, not the permanent collection at all that was able to take any action, not even after he lit the match, dropped it, and turned toward the door.

It was the heads.

All those nameless severed heads, some with eyes wide open, some appearing to sleep, all slick with gasoline, slipping, rolling, tumbling forward. All choosing their moment carefully, all moving together. All smiling as they fell on him, smiling through the flames.

He screamed out in pain and shock, stumbling for a few moments while we, the collection, in a heap on the floor, held our breath.

Metaphorically speaking, of course.

We were already aflame, but I watched, despite the smoke and the smell of my own hair burning, my so carefully preserved clothing and body disintegrating; watched as he stumbled over the burning heads, as they rolled beneath his feet, and he lost his balance.

His head bounced off the floor with an audible crack when he fell, and his eyes rolled back in his head.

He couldn't have been out long, not long, not if I still had eyes to see with, not if my composition body had not yet burned like the sawdust, glue, resin, and cornstarch it was.

But when he opened his eyes he could not focus them, and when he tried to get to his feet, he dropped back to his knees and began vomiting, and then he began choking, though whether on smoke or vomit I could not say, and then the smoke was too thick for me to see anything more, but I know that he never reached the door.

So we all burned together: Coppelius with his talent, his skill, his madness, his sadism, burned; and the nameless heads and limbs and torsos burned; and Chatty Cathy burned; and Cassie, whose arms and legs had been swapped, burned; and Linda, whose mouth had been erased, burned; and Rachel, whose skull had been split, burned; and all the permanent collection burned; and I burned, with my slightly mussed ringlets and my cherubic smile and my hazel eyes (the real Shirley's are brown), I burned as well; and the flames took our bodies, all of us who had once been loved.

۞

There is no longer a doll hospital in New York City.

۞

And I? I am no longer a composition 1935 Ideal Toy's *Curly Top* Shirley Temple doll with box and clothing and button, almost like new, worth between $1,000 and $1,400.

I am smoke clogging the air, black grit on your windowsill. I am the grime on the walls, the greasy dust that settles so softly on your skin.

Or perhaps, if you don't mind a bit of philosophy, I am even a lost soul, adrift and alone, waiting for one of my girls to find me.

Homemade Monsters

by John Langan

W as my childhood happy? I'm sorry, I—I don't know how to answer that.

If by "happy" you mean, were my physical needs met, for food, shelter, medical care, then yes, without a doubt. I was never hungry that I can recall (outside of "Where's dinner? I'm *starving*" complaints). My father provided the money, and my mother made certain I was dressed in the latest fashions (however much the photographic record of those outfits makes me cringe). Whenever I complained of any ailment, I was whisked off to the pediatrician's office posthaste (apparently I had had numerous emergency visits when I was too young to remember, for everything from a fall during which I smacked my head on the garage's concrete floor, to a small but mysterious bump that my mother found between my eyebrows).

If, however, "happiness" implies contentment, satisfaction with one's family and surroundings, then I'm less sure. I loved my parents as feverishly, as desperately, as only a small child can, but that love was threaded with fear. I wasn't afraid of them physically; while I'm sure they swatted my butt or slapped my hand when I was a toddler, I don't remember them lifting a hand even in threat until I was a teenager, and, in all fairness, my father's warnings of violence were mostly a rhetorical device to stop me arguing with him. I was their oldest child, the product of seven years' effort at conceiving, and their love surrounded me. Perhaps because I lived in such close proximity to their affection, though, I was sensitive to its daily fluctuations, which, as I grew older and first my younger brother, then each of my sisters, appeared, grew more pronounced. My feelings about those siblings were shot through with ambivalence, the fierce, animal love I had for them alloyed with jealousy and frustration—and guilt, at my conflicted response to them. While our family expanded, our house grew steadily smaller, a structure that had been built for three straining to accommodate twice that number. My parents did their best with the space, converting the original living room into their bedroom, transforming the garage into a new, larger living room, doubling up me and my brother in their former room and my sisters in my old room. But there was nowhere in the house to go for privacy, except the bathroom, and even there, it wouldn't be long before someone would be knocking on the door, telling you to hurry up. It's funny: For all that my siblings and I have gone our separate ways in things like religion and politics, each of us lives in a house that has an upstairs and a downstairs, a place where there's room to be alone.

I'm digressing. The fact is, all the emotions I experienced seemed enormous, much too big for my body. It was as if they roamed the space around me, and every now and again, depending on the situation, stepped into me, filling me to overflowing. I might have been a city in one of the giant-monster films I watched on the 4:30 Movie. One minute, everything was peaceful and calm, the next, a three-hundred-foot-tall reptile was shouldering buildings aside, crushing cars and buses underfoot, breathing jets of flame at the hordes of people fleeing it. Afterward—especially if I had been angry—I felt wrecked, hollowed out by what had inhabited me.

My toys—yes, you're right. I did say that what I wanted to talk about concerns a toy. I was pretty well off, in that department. Most of my toys were what they call action figures today; though I don't remember the description attaching to them at the time. First I had G.I. Joe, twelve inches tall, articulated, with a crew cut and beard made of a soft, fuzzy material that came out in clumps after you took him in the bath with you. I had Eagle-Eye, whose eyes moved from left to right and back again—scanning the horizon, I guess—when you slid a lever set in the back of his head, and Kung-Fu Grip, whose curled hands were cast in a flexible plastic that started to tear along the palms after a little bit of play. They were succeeded by the first generation of *Star Wars* figures, who were a third his size, not half as posable, and infinitely cooler.

They and their vehicles and playsets soon occupied the top positions on my birthday and Christmas lists. What I most wanted, however, was something that, for years, was nowhere to be found outside of the movies. This was a figure of Godzilla, the king of the monsters, whose rampages and battles had been a staple of my imaginative diet since first grade, when I first learned of his existence via several of my classmates, who recounted what I later discovered was an extremely inaccurate version of *King Kong vs. Godzilla* to me. From the start, he interested me much more than his smaller American cousin, King Kong. Perhaps it was because he resembled the dinosaurs with which, I, like every other boy in my class, was fascinated. That he didn't die—at least not permanently—but continued on in a series of adventures that gradually recast him in the role of hero, also appealed to me. I was never much good with tragedy; although, in all fairness, what child is?

In *Godzilla vs. the Smog Monster*, which must have been one of the first Godzilla films I saw, the little boy who was the son of one of the (human) protagonists had a number of Godzilla figures ranged among his toys. The instant I saw them, I coveted those figures as I had no toy before. There was nothing like them at either of the local Kay-Bee Toy & Hobby Shops, and it would be another decade until the first Toys "R" Us appeared in the area. In those pre-Internet days, I knew of no other way to search for a toy I didn't possess. I had a sickening suspicion that the Godzillas were unavailable outside of Japan, or, worse, that they were only props, commissioned for the movie, then taken home by the child-actor.

So desperate did I become for my own figure of the giant monster that, when I was in the fourth grade, I fashioned one myself, repurposing an eight-inch Captain Kirk, whom I'd never found all that interesting in the first place. After stripping him of his accessories, uniform, and boots, I colored him with a green Magic Marker whose ink dried in long smears. Next, I used Scotch tape to affix to his back a row of dorsal plates I'd painstakingly scissored from a piece of cardboard, then to fasten to his butt a tail I'd rolled from a piece of aluminum foil. I'd tried to construct a Godzilla mask out of a couple of cardboard tabs, a pen, and still more tape, but it required a concentrated effort of the imagination for me to view the head as a success. All the same, the figure was the closest I had to an actual Godzilla toy, and I made the most of it.

Using cardboard tubes, the cardboard backs of the legal pads my father brought home from IBM, aluminum foil, and roll after roll of tape, I built playsets for my monster to trample. I borrowed one of my mother's brownie pans, lined it with foil to represent the Hudson River, and put together a passable replica of the Mid-Hudson Bridge. A cookie sheet beside it supported a model of the Mid-Hudson Civic Center, and several of the tallish buildings I remembered from trips into the city of Poughkeepsie. The scale was off, of course, between the monster and the metropolis, but there was something deliriously terrifying and delightful in the image of Godzilla striding through landscapes familiar to me. In my most elaborate creation, I took over half the dining room table to build a model of my house and the houses in its immediate vicinity. I cut up sheets of construction paper into the shapes of our various yards, and taped them together at the margins. The trees that grew thickly around our homes were toothpicks I'd found in the kitchen junk drawer, left over from one party or another. I broke off pieces of an eraser to hold each toothpick upright, and raided the hall closet where we kept medical and cosmetic supplies for a bag of cotton balls, which I separated, dabbed with my green Magic Marker, and slid on top of the toothpicks for the trees' crowns. The houses themselves were a mix of boxes I'd scavenged from around the house and ones I'd put together with cardboard and tape. I went so far as to include the elementary school where I'd attended kindergarten, five buildings up the road, and the swamp behind it. My mother was sufficiently impressed with the final result of a long afternoon's work to insist on photographing it with me standing beside, holding my improvised Godzilla. My brother, who came and went as I worked, standing silently at my elbow until I told him to get lost, pronounced my work cool, but that was mostly because Mom was there, and he wanted to participate in her approval. Neither of my sisters paid my project any notice. By the time my father stepped through the front door, I was well on my way to leveling the neighborhood, much to my mother's regret, but, like my brother, Dad joined in her praise.

I barely heard him. I was caught up in a private movie so vivid it might have been a memory. I was standing in my driveway. To the north, beyond the wide, overgrown field across the road from my house and those of my neighbors, Godzilla occulted the sky. Skyscraper-tall, he appeared to move slowly, ponderously, yet each of his earth-shuddering footsteps brought him fifty yards nearer. All around me, birds rose from the trees in panicked flocks. Behind me, my house creaked as the ground continued to tremble; from inside it, I heard my mother's good glasses ringing as the vibrations jostled them. Trees cracked and splintered as Godzilla's feet pushed through them. He lowered a splayed foot the size of a barn onto the field across the street, and paused. Eyes burning with white light swept the half-dozen houses and the school that comprised my little neighborhood, as if they were a row of strange growths. I could hear the monster breathing, inhaling and exhaling hurricanes of air, and alongside that sound, a low, steady rumble like the earth's plates sliding against one another. Heat poured off Godzilla's corrugated hide, wilting and blackening the tall grass next to him and raising sweat all over me. A smell of burning metal wrinkled my nostrils. When he opened his mouth and roared, I clapped my hands to my ears and dropped to the ground, as if I could slip under the noise that radiated from him, bursting the windows of my house and all the houses on the road. Once more, Godzilla was on the move. The earth shook so hard it bounced me onto my back. He'd corrected his course a few degrees to his right and was making straight for Eddie Isley's house, which was separated from mine by old Mr. Warner's. The monster's left foot swept the front of Mr. Warner's gray farmhouse, shearing it off and causing the rest of the building to sway backward, half-fallen. His right foot came down squarely on the Isleys' two-story blue colonial, bursting the house like a balloon. Siding, Sheetrock, and wood flew in all directions. Nor was that enough. A segment of the back wall and the deck remained standing, as did the small barn behind the house in whose neat interior Mr. Isley kept his tools and his car when the weather was bad. That giant foot raised again and drove down once, twice, with sufficient force to pulverize what was left of the Isleys', not to mention sending the Warners' house crashing the rest of the way to the ground, and bouncing me around as if I were on a trampoline. Godzilla stepped forward and kicked the Isleys' barn, most of which disappeared in a cloud of splinters; although I watched part of its black roof arc high into the sky. He snorted and continued up the street.

How did I feel? I felt *great*. What I was watching—and I swear, that was how it seemed to me, as if I were actually there, witnessing all of this, and not imagining it—the scene playing out, exhilarated me. The sheer terror the presence of this gargantuan monster evoked from me was balanced, maybe exceeded, by the profound delight, the joy, it also produced. For once, my emotions were in proportion to my surroundings. It didn't hurt, either, that Godzilla had visited such utter destruction upon the home of Eddie Isley.

Eddie. I guess he's the reason I'm here talking to you—him and what happened to him. We were the same age, and had been in school together since Eddie and his family had moved into their house when we were in second grade. I'm pretty sure they had come from Arizona, though what had brought them to upstate New York, I don't know. Possibly his father's job: he was with IBM, as was my dad, as was the father of every other kid you asked. (At that time, the Hudson Valley was IBM country, from Wiltwyck down to Ossining, with stops along the way for Poughkeepsie and East Fishkill.) Eddie was shorter than I was by a couple of inches, but he was better proportioned; even before the adolescent growth spurt that would raise the top of my head above first my mother and then my father, I had long arms and longer legs, as if my body were laying in plans for the changes to come. Where my hair was a fine, dirty blond that I wore in no definite style, Eddie's was a thick, shining black that he parted on the right with military precision. A pair of heavy, square glasses defined his face, while my own glasses would wait until I was in fifth grade.

Because we were neighbors and the same age, not to mention students at the same Catholic elementary school, the assumption on the part of our parents was that we would be friends. Our interests were similar enough to place us within the same social group at school, where the more athletically inclined kids and the more academically inclined kids were continuing the process of differentiation and separation that would reach its culmination in high school. Not only did Eddie and I like to read, we liked to read the same types of things: books about older cultures, the Greeks and the Romans, the Vikings and the Samurai. I was fascinated by their myths and legends, Eddie by their history, especially the battles they'd fought. Both of us liked to draw, but my artwork was influenced by the styles of the comic books I pored over: Its figures were big, bold, either engaged in a dramatic act or posed in the immediate aftermath of one. Eddie's pictures showed the effect of the military histories he read: Their figures were small, almost miniature, and there were a lot of them, usually wearing the same uniform, and in the midst of an enormous undertaking, usually a battle. I loved the wealth of detail with which he loaded each of his drawings. He ignored my work, except to pass an occasional snide remark about it.

From the distance of three and a half decades, I can recognize that Eddie's dismissal of my artwork was driven by jealousy. He was intensely competitive—in class, each of us tried to have his hand up first when the teacher asked a question—and he resented anything that was done better than he could, whether a drawing or an essay that the teacher invited me to read out loud. For the three years of school we shared, there was no success I could have, but Eddie had to mock it. Also from this remove, I can't help wondering where he had learned such behavior. He had an older sister, Yvette, but she was five years his senior, and from what I observed, she was as uninvolved with her little brother as she could manage. I don't recall much about his parents, except that they had a rule that you had to remove your sneakers upon entering their house, and that they served celery sticks smeared with peanut butter as a snack. His mother did—she brought them downstairs to their basement, which was furnished and served as a family game-room. She was pleasant enough to me, but I have the impression of her as distracted, as if always listening for the phone to ring or someone to knock on the door. I saw Eddie's father much less frequently; he worked what struck me as much longer hours at IBM than did my dad. I remember him as distracted, too—or, not so much distracted as detached.

It's difficult for me to picture either half of that distant couple unleashing the same withering vitriol on their son that he used on me. But maybe they did.

Whatever its source, from time to time Eddie's verbal nastiness was accompanied by a physical expression of his sentiment. This never happened at school. Even during recess, when the location of the playground monitor might allow you to raise your hand against someone, Eddie did not risk the shoves or sloppy punches of the rest of us; instead, he stalked away from confrontation, a scowl darkening his face. If you ran after him and grabbed hold of his arm to stop him, he flung your hand off with a windmill of his arm and continued on his path. Outside of school, which is to say, in his basement or my room, or either of our yards, or the schoolyard down the road, where we sometimes went to explore the swamp behind it, things were different. Eddie's disdain for a drawing I had completed would be followed by him sweeping his hand across the table at which we were seated, catching the sheet of paper I'd labored over and crumpling it, sending it onto the floor along with a dozen of the Magic Markers we'd been sharing. His envy over a new toy my grandparents had sent me—say, the Colonial Viper from the first *Battlestar Galactica*, which fired a red missile from its nose—would lead to him pleading for me to let him play with it, just for a minute, *please*, and, once I gave in and handed it to him, finding the quickest way to break it: in the case of the Viper, jamming the missile in so far it because stuck and could not be fired. Any reproach on my part was likely to be met with a sarcastic, "Sorry," and a remark about how my drawing hadn't been any good in the first place, or what cheap junk my toy had been.

It's funny: It's not only that I remember how I felt at those moments—a mix of anger, frustration, and resentment that enveloped me in a fiery sphere—but, when I revisit them, I still feel the same emotion, incandescent around me. No matter how much I think I've grown, matured, no matter how many white hairs the mirror shows have infiltrated my beard, the instant I recall that crumpled sheet of paper, that damaged toy, there's a direct route in my mind to my younger self and the feelings that rampaged through it. It's as if I'm still there.

I know, I know. Why didn't I cut ties with Eddie, at least in those locations where he could do most harm? There was a part of me that recognized this as the most sensible course of action. That level of resolve, however, was beyond me. No matter how egregious Eddie's act, it wasn't long before I was at the back door of his house, asking his mother if he could come out to play. When he emerged, he wore a slight smirk that said he knew what he'd done wasn't that big a deal. For a time, he would be on what for him was good behavior, restricting any hostility in his comments to me.

If I couldn't keep away from Eddie, over time, I learned to keep anything that was precious to me out of his sight. This included my improvised Godzilla figure, which seemed guaranteed to arouse the full measure of his contempt. I have yet to work out how he found it. We were in my room, playing Stratego with my younger brother. Eddie and I faced each other while my younger brother looked on, then, after I had defeated Eddie, my brother and I played. Irritated by his loss, Eddie prowled the undersized room. Three moves into the game, I heard him saying, "What's this?"

He was holding my handmade Godzilla. The expression on his face was blank; he might have been trying to identify what the figure in his grip was supposed to be. I opened my mouth to say I don't know what, something that would distract Eddie, call his attention away from the toy, back to me. My brother spoke first. "Hey," he said, "he's got your Godzilla." The name completed a circuit. Eddie's face brightened. He said, "Godzilla?" and with a wrench of his hands, tore the figure's rubber head off and flung it across the room. I scrambled to my feet, one of my sneakers lashing out and striking the Stratego board, clearing it. Eddie shifted his grip to the toy's waist and snapped it in half. He opened his hands and let the pieces of the figure drop to the carpet. "Doesn't seem like the king of the monsters to me."

My brother, in a move both brave and reckless, had wrapped his arms around my legs. Had he not, I would have crossed the room in a heartbeat. I could see myself leaping onto my bed and using the mattress to trampoline into Eddie. I was beyond angry, beyond upset; I was the center of a fury so transcendent that, for an instant, it seemed as if I could stretch out my hand and the rage would pour from me in a white blaze

that would burn Eddie Isley to a shadow on the wall. As it was, my
brother held me in place, and said to Eddie, "You'd better leave."

How I would like to be able to report that the sight of me in my rage
unnerved Eddie, registered on his face as the slightest faltering in the
sick smile that had crept onto it, the faintest lowering of his brows with
concern. It did not. He opened the door to my room, stepped out into
the hallway, and departed the house, all without another word. My
brother held me until we heard the back door *shunk* closed. Then he
released me. I wanted to kick him for what he'd done, but I was more
concerned with sprinting to the back door, hauling it open with enough
force to rattle the venetian blind hung on it, and rushing onto the
porch. Eddie had moved fast, himself, crossing the field between my
house and Mr. Warner's, reaching the pair of enormous evergreens
whose needled skirts marked the edge of the Warners' yard. I don't
know if he heard me throw open the door; he didn't look back, anyway.
I considered tearing after him, but with this much of a head start, he'd
likely outpace me to his house, and if I caught, tackled, and started
pounding him, I'd be doing so in his backyard. I knew how that would
look, to his family and to mine. So I waited until Eddie was out of
sight behind the evergreens, then returned inside, closed and locked
the back door, and retreated to my room to plan my revenge.

There wasn't much to it. The next day, after I came home from
school, I went into the backyard to the spot behind the garden shed
where my father piled the tree branches that the winter snow and ice
had stripped from the trees. He would build that heap as the spring and
summer thunderstorms brought down more limbs, until the fall, when
we would dump the leaves we'd raked on top of the wood and my
father would set the whole thing ablaze. I sifted through the branches
gathered there until I found one that was a little taller than I was,
mostly straight, and not too heavy. I snapped what smaller branches
remained from it and carried it to the porch, where I set it on the
picnic table there. I went into the house for a roll of duct tape and a pair
of scissors. Outside again, I dug my pocketknife out of the right front
pocket of my school pants. My father had bought it for me last summer
vacation, at the gift shop at Fort William Henry, in Lake George. Its

side panel was decorated with an image of the fort in vivid green and brown. I unfolded the blade and taped the hilt to the narrower end of the branch. I used enough of the duct tape to secure the knife reasonably well and, by the end of my efforts, had a decent spear. I didn't bother trying to bring it inside; my mother wasn't fond of the mess such imports made. Instead, I carried the spear to the white metal garden shed, inside whose right-hand door I positioned my new weapon.

No, I wasn't plotting to kill Eddie; this isn't a murderer's confession. I was as furious with him as I had been the moment he'd destroyed my improvised Godzilla; there appeared to be no danger of that emotion fading anytime soon. Yet my rage was mixed with a terrible grief that threatened to send tears flooding down my cheeks every time I looked at the ruin of the figure I had devoted so much time to crafting. My brother had suggested I could repair it, borrow the Krazy Glue and restore it to what it had been. For once, I hadn't told him to shut up, only shook my head from side to side. The pieces of the figure seemed charged with the contempt Eddie had visited upon them. When you're a kid, you internalize the violence that's done to you; you don't know how not to. Someone calls you a name, and it hurts, and part of the reason it hurts is because you fear it might be true. A toy that I had fashioned had been ruined, and I was afraid that it had deserved to be. What I wanted now was to assert myself against Eddie, and in so doing, to refute the scorn he'd inflicted on me.

Yes, it is pretty sophisticated reasoning for a ten-year-old. Of course I didn't frame what I intended to do in those terms. My thoughts were more concrete. In another couple of days, I would tell Eddie I was going on an excursion into the swamp behind the elementary school down the road, and ask if he had any interest in joining me. I had no doubt he would accept my invitation. For one thing, while I hadn't had him back to my house, at school, I'd kept a tighter lid on my emotions than at any point in the past; even when Eddie asked me how Godzilla was doing after his defeat by the Hands of Isley, I smiled tightly and looked down, as if embarrassed. For another thing, Eddie was inordinately proud of his skill at orienteering; I say "inordinately" because, on our previous voyages into the swamp, he hadn't impressed me as any more competent a navigator than I was. Spear in hand, then, I planned to lead Eddie deep into the swamp, much farther than we'd been, until everything around us was unfamiliar. Once we were good and lost, I would demand that he apologize for destroying my homemade Godzilla, for all his acts of wanton violence. I would brandish the spear to reinforce my demand. That I might have to put it to use was a possibility I rejected. Eddie behaved like a bully, and the knowledge I'd aggregated from a host of comic books, TV shows, and movies that dealt with such types told me that they were, finally, cowards, who, if confronted convincingly, would back down. I wish I could convey the trembling pleasure with which I contemplated my plot. Lying in bed at night, on the verge of dropping into sleep, I would picture Eddie, standing knee-deep in the swamp's brackish water, glancing from side to side at the strange trees fencing us in, his lip quivering as he struggled to keep from crying.

That vision was the closest I came to my plan's success. While the early stages went smoothly, by the time we were in the swamp, my design had unraveled with surprising speed. From the moment we stepped onto the dirt ridge that served as a pathway through the swamp's outer reaches, Eddie had kept well ahead of me. Though he hadn't commented on it, he'd registered my spear with a slight widening of his eyes, a jerk of his head. Our previous journeys into the swamp, I hadn't carried anything with me, afraid to lose it in the murky water. For me to have changed my behavior, and to have done so by bringing a weapon with me, had raised Eddie's suspicions—not enough for him to refuse to accompany me, but sufficiently for him to maintain a cautious distance between us. I had anticipated we would travel with our usual leisurely pace; instead, Eddie moved briskly, leaping from the end of the dirt ridge onto the first of the chain of small hummocks that formed the route into the swamp's interior. He hopped to the second while I was still on the ridge. I was well practiced at traversing the network of dirt mounds that thrust their grass-covered peaks above the dark water, but the addition of the spear upset my balance. I miscalculated a couple of my jumps, and paid for it with a sneaker full of cold water. The deeper into the swamp we pushed, the thicker the air became, humid and heavy with the stink of the skunk cabbages that populated the hummocks to either side of us. Sweat glued my T-shirt to my back. Clouds of tiny insects drifted through the air, and when I landed on one of the diminutive islands, the insects swarmed my eyes and nose. Already, we were in new territory. Eddie launched himself onto the trunk of a huge, fallen tree and ran along until he reached the wreckage of its crown, where he dropped onto the first of a new line of mounds leading further into the swamp. I struggled to keep up with him. Ferns of prehistoric size sprouted from the soil of this latest archipelago and flailed against me when I landed on their hummock, as if trying to force me off. Great trees whose trunks were wrapped with ivy and patched with moss enclosed us; from somewhere in their ranks, a bird uttered a stuttering cry like a monkey's call. Throughout, I maintained my grip on the spear, but I was more worried about the object in the right front pocket of my jeans. I had stuffed the decapitated head of my handmade Godzilla there with the intent of confronting Eddie with it during my demand for his apology. The problem was, the pocket was shallow, the jeans a fraction too small, and the figure's head felt constantly on the verge of falling out into the swamp. Nothing was happening as I had imagined it. The fury I'd worked to contain, to channel into my plan for revenge, was leaking from the growing cracks in that plot like radiation from a damaged reactor. It seemed to spill out over my surroundings, making them ripple like a sheet in the wind. In that rage—through it—I was aware of something, a kind of presence, an attention, waiting just out of sight. It was vast as the swamp, alien.

Once Eddie reached a hummock that was sizable enough to host a pair of slender birches, he paused. This, I thought, was my chance if I could take it. I sprang from hummock to hummock, unconcerned when one of my sneakers splashed the water. *Here I come*, I thought. *Here I come.*

He punched me at the moment my feet touched the mound on which he was waiting. It was a shot to the gut that drove the air out of me and sent me backward, my arms flailing as I sought and failed to keep my balance. Butt-first, I fell into the swamp's water. For a terrifying instant, I was sure I was going to go under the water's surface and continue dropping, down into inky darkness. The water, however, was only two feet deep. I was soaked up to my armpits, but I was safe. "Eddie!" I shouted. "What the hell, man?"

"Shut up," he said. He was crouched at the edge of the hummock, his hand outreached to where my spear was floating. I dove for it, but Eddie was faster, snatching it out of the water. As I struggled to my feet, Eddie inspected the spear, his expression somewhere between interest and disdain. "Eddie," I said. He grabbed the spear at either end and brought it down onto his knee. The wood broke with a flat crack. "Hey!" I shouted. He flung the base of the spear to his right, and the top, my pocketknife still taped to it, to his left. The pieces spun off between the trees, each plunking somewhere out of sight.

"What did you expect?" Eddie said. "Good luck finding your way home." He turned and strode to the opposite end of the hummock, where he leapt between the birch trees to another hummock, and the one beyond that, ignoring my cries for him to *wait, wait, come on,* until he was lost amidst the trees.

The fury that burst from me was made worse by the realization that my jeans pockets was empty, the head of my Godzilla figure lost. Big: The emotion dwarfed anything I'd felt before. I was suspended in it, and it extended for miles around and below me, an ocean. For a second time, the swamp rippled, and I was conscious of that vast presence at the edge of my perception.

What happened next began as a thunderclap, a cataclysm of sound that rushed across the swamp toward me, blowing a wall of debris, of leaves and sticks and bark, ahead of it. I ducked to the water's surface, but I already had seen what was following close behind, a wave that rolled through the water and the ground underneath, making the trees shake like grass in a breeze, snapping their trunks. The ground beneath me flexed like the hide of some great beast twitching at an irritant, vaulting me into the air. For a long moment, I hung in space, water around me, and then I struck the hummock on which Eddie had been standing. Winded, terrified, I lay there while trees continued to crack and splash into the water, which slopped and slapped against the hummock.

I was still there hours later, when the first firefighter stumbled across me. Before the earth had ceased shaking, my mother and Eddie's were on the phone to each other, asking if the two boys were at the other's house. They knew we were bound for the swamp, and they were horrified at the thought that the ground had started to move while we were within it. This was well ahead of the seismologists' determination that the epicenter of what they would describe as a substantial seismic event was located in the swamp—by my later estimates, about 150 yards south-southeast of where I'd been standing. In short order, our fathers were called, and not long after that, the police. Although damage to the buildings in the immediate vicinity of the event was in many cases substantial—the ceiling of the elementary school's gym fell in—injuries were remarkably few and mild, allowing the police to devote more resources to a pair of missing fourth-graders than might otherwise have been the case. One look at the wreckage that had been the swamp, and the cops called for whatever backup was available. A steady flow of firefighters, paramedics, and concerned men and women who'd heard the news on their CB's responded to the request. Someone laid their hands on a map of the swamp, and the people who'd gathered in the school parking lot, including my father and Eddie's, were divided into groups and assigned an area of the swamp to investigate. This was how I was found.

Eddie was not. The portion of the swamp I'd watched him heading toward fell, the ground in some places dropping as much as fifteen feet. Apparently there had been a network of caves immediately beneath the swamp, and when the earth shook, they collapsed, birthing a sinkhole that sucked down whatever was above it, including Eddie. Or so the theory went. Despite ten days of searching that included the use of backhoes to excavate select areas of the sinkhole, no body was recovered.

The Isleys moved a couple of months after the search was called off and their son declared missing and likely dead. During that time, they made no effort to contact me, to ask me about Eddie's last moments. I lived in dread that they might, and had invented a tale of Eddie running off for help after I twisted my ankle, in case I needed it. But I didn't have to use it, which was a relief. I wasn't certain I'd be able to maintain the requisite deception.

How did I feel? Relieved . . . and satisfied . . . and guilty. The last of those emotions was the only one to which I could admit. Without the other two, though, it was diagnosed as the survivor's guilt typical of a child who had undergone the experience I had. My parents, our parish priest, the therapist I was sent to, all offered versions of the same counsel: What you're feeling is normal, but what happened was not your fault. Only I knew how true and not true that statement was, and since I couldn't find a way to explain that to anyone, I buried it in my memory.

Time passed, years, decades. I continued to draw, continued to improve at it, made connections, and eventually got a job drawing comic books. I married, had a daughter who's almost finished college now. I left the publisher I'd been working for to join some people I knew who'd formed their own company. Eventually, we secured the rights to do a new Godzilla book. I'm going to draw it. Talk about a childhood dream come true, right? I made sketches, planned the first few issues with the writer. I had this idea that it would be fun to sneak a few of the locations I'd grown up with into the comic, so that when the monster's wading out of the ocean it's onto my favorite beach, that kind of thing. I sat down in front of the computer, called up Google Earth, and started typing locations into the search bar. I haven't been by the house I grew up in since my parents retired to North Carolina, and one of my sisters told me the old neighborhood had changed to the point that she barely recognized it anymore. I entered my childhood address and waited.

My sister was right: The old place was different. The field across the road had been replaced by a sprawling storage facility. Mr. Warner's house had been expanded to the rear, until it was almost twice its former size. There was a large, round pool behind the Isleys' former house. And so on. What drew my notice, however, as I scrolled up the satellite photo, was the swamp behind the school. Following Eddie's disappearance, it had been fenced off, at no small cost to the local taxpayers. But there was no way it was going to be left open, especially when it was right behind an elementary school. No doubt, kids snuck in there; no doubt, stories sprung up about the boy who'd been lost there, consumed by the swamp. Do you know the official description of what occurred that distant afternoon is that it was an atypical seismic incident? Maybe the scientists never studied the satellite images of the area. Or maybe they did, and didn't notice anything: When I called my wife in and asked her what the picture on the monitor looked like to her, she leaned in, squinted, and said it didn't look like anything, just wetlands. She didn't distinguish the shape in what had been called a sinkhole. Thirty-five years later, its outline was still visible: the broad base, the three long channels branching off its top, the shorter channel angling forward on its left. It was the imprint of a foot, the foot of a creature whose head would have towered above my old neighborhood the way mine rises over the garden. I told myself I must be imagining things, imposing design on random destruction. But I could not unsee it, no matter how hard I tried. I leaned back in my desk chair, the head of that old, homemade Godzilla in my hand, and contemplated that shape for a long time.

What? Oh, that's right—I didn't tell you. When the fireman carried me out of the swamp, I had the head I was sure I'd lost clutched tight in my left hand. I have no idea how it came to be there. Afterward, I kept it with me as a kind of talisman, I guess. A few days after I bought my first car, I drilled a hole through the head and threaded it onto my key chain, which is where it's been ever since. Whenever I'm upset, agitated, or angry, I squeeze it. The green marker has long worn off, and the flesh tone underneath has faded to a dull color that my wife says resembles bone. Sometimes, if I'm dealing with a particularly annoying person at work, or if my wife and I are at loggerheads over something, or if my daughter is aggravating me as only she can, I clench that relic of distant catastrophe with such force, I half-expect it to push through my skin. I can almost feel what I did that day in the swamp, a vast presence, waiting.

For Fiona, and in memory of Lucius Shepard

Word Doll

by Jeffrey Ford

Every morning I take the back way to town, a fifteen-mile drive on narrow two-lane roads that cut through oceans of corn. The cracked and patched asphalt is lined on either side with telephone poles shrinking into the distance. Sometimes I pass a hawk perched on a fence post. Every few miles there's a farmhouse, mostly old, like ours. In the winter, the wind is fierce whipping across the barren fields, and I have to work to keep the car in its lane, but in summer, after I get my cigarettes in town and stop at the diner for a cup of coffee and a glance at the newspaper, I drive home and go out back under the apple trees, sit at a little table, and write stories. Sunlight filters down through the branches, and there's always a breeze blowing across the fields that finds me there. Sometimes the stories flow and I don't notice the birds at the feeders, the jingle of the dog's collar, or the bees in the garden just beyond the orchard; and when they don't, I stare out into the sea of green and day-dream into its depths.

In late September, on a Monday's journey to town, I passed this old place at a bend in the road like I'd passed it every morning. It was a Queen Anne Victorian with a wraparound screened-in porch, painted blue and white. The house was in good shape, but the barn out back was shedding shingles and the paint had weathered off its splintered boards. I'd often seen chickens bobbing around on the property, and a rooster at times dangerously close to the road. There were blackberry bushes tangled in a low wall on either side of the entrance to the gravel drive. As I rolled past, I noticed something partially covered by those bushes. It looked like a sign of some kind, but it was faded and I was going too fast to catch a good glance.

On the way back from town I forgot to slow down and look, but the following day I woke up with the thought that I should stop and investigate. Nine times out of ten, I could drive to town and back and never pass another car, and that day was no exception. I slowed as I got close to the place, and right across from the sign, I stopped and studied it—about two by three foot, made of tin, fading white with black letters. It was attached to a short rusted post. The berry bushes had grown up and partially over it, but now that I'd stopped I could make out its message. It said, WORD DOLL MUSEUM, and beneath that, OPEN 10 TO 5 MONDAY THRU FRIDAY.

The next morning I got up and instead of driving to town, I took a shower and put on a white shirt and dress pants. I took a cup of coffee out under the apple trees. Instead of writing, I sat there, smoking and wondering into the heart of the cornfield what the hell a "Word Doll" was. At 10:30, I got in the car and drove toward town. The sun was strong and the sky was clear blue. The corn had begun to brown, it being summer's end. At the bend in the road, without hesitating, I pulled into the driveway of the Victorian. The chickens were in a clutch over by the corner of the house. The place was still. I didn't hear any television or radio playing. I walked slowly to the porch door, scuffing the gravel in the drive in order to let anybody listening know I was there. The screen door was unlatched. I opened it and called in, "Hello?"

There was no reply, so I entered, the screen door banging shut behind me, and walked to the main door of the house. I knuckle-rapped the glass three times and then folded my arms and waited. Fading yellow roses bordered the front porch and gave off a strong scent, and a wind chime in the corner over an old rocker pinged in the breeze sifting through the screen. I was about to give up and leave when the door pulled back. There was a thin old woman, a little bent, with a cloud of white hair and big glasses. She wore a loose, button-up dress, yellow with white flowers.

"What do ya want?" she asked.

"I'm here for the Word Doll Museum," I said.

My pronouncement seemed to momentarily stun her. She reached up and gently grabbed the doorjamb. "Are you kidding?" she asked, and smiled.

"Should I be?" I said.

Her demeanor instantly changed. I could see her relax. "Hold on," she said, "I have to get the keys. Meet me over by the barn."

I left the porch, and the chickens followed me. The entire gray structure of the barn, like some weary pachyderm, was actually listing more than a few degrees to the south, something I'd not noticed from the road. The door was hanging on by only the top hinge. The lady came out the back of the house and walked with the help of a three-pronged cane over the lumpy ground of the yard. As she drew closer, she said, "Where you from?"

"Not far. I pass your place on the way to town every morning, and I saw the sign the other day."

"My name is Beverly Gearing," she said, and held out her hand.

I took it in mine and we shook. "I'm Jeff Ford," I told her.

As she passed by me toward the ramshackle barn, she said, "So, Mr. Ford, what's your interest in Word Dolls?"

"I don't know anything about them."

"Well, that's okay," she said, and opened the broken door.

I followed her inside. She shuffled over the hay-strewn floor. Swifts flew back and forth in the rafters, and the holes in the roof allowed sunbeams to cut the shadows. On one side of the barn were animal stalls, all empty, and on the other there was a wall of implements and tools and a small room built within the greater structure. Over the door to it was a wooden sign with the words *Word Doll Museum* burned in script and shellacked. She fished in the pocket of her dress and eventually came out with the key. Opening the door, she flipped on a light switch, and then stepped aside, allowing me to enter first. The room was painted a light blue. There was a window on each wall that looked out at nothing but bare plywood, and inside, window boxes fixed up with plastic flowers.

"Have a seat," she said, and I sat in a chair at the card table at the center of the room. She worked her way to the other chair at the table and half-sat, half-fell backward into it. Once she was settled, she took a pack of Marlboros out of her pocket and a black lighter. She leaned forward on the table with one arm. "Word Dolls," she said.

I nodded.

"You're the first person to ask about the museum in about twenty years." She laughed, and I saw she was missing a tooth on the upper right side.

"You can hardly see your sign from the road," I said.

"The sign's a last resort," she said. "I have a permanent spot in the *What's Happening* section of three of the local papers. In January, I send them enough to run the ads for a year. Still, no one pays attention."

"I'm guessing most people don't know what a Word Doll is."

"I know," she said, and lit the cigarette she held. She took a drag and then pointed with it at the left wall where there were three beige file cabinets. The middle one had a golden laughing Buddha statue on it. "What's in those nine drawers over there is all that remains of the history of Word Dolls. This is the largest repository of material evidence of the existence of the tradition. When I'm gone, knowledge of it will have been pretty much erased from history. You live long enough, Mr. Ford, you might be the last person on earth to ever think of Word Dolls."

"I might be," I said, "but I don't know what they are."

Beverly put her cig out in a half cup of coffee that looked like it had been on the table for a week. "I want you to know something before I start," she said. "This is serious to me. I have a doctorate in anthropology from Ohio State class of sixty-three."

"Yes, ma'am," I said. "I seriously want to know."

She sat quiet for a moment, eyes half shut, before taking a deep breath. "A 'Word Doll' is the same thing as a 'Field Friend'; they're interchangeable. Their existence is very brief measured in anthropological time and also very localized. Only in the area that's now roughly defined by our county border was this ritual observed. It sprang up in the mid-nineteenth century and for the time in which it ran its course affected no more than fifty or sixty families at the most. No one's certain of its origin. Some women I interviewed back when I was in graduate school, they were all in their eighties and nineties then, swore the phenomenon was something brought over from Europe. So I asked, where in Europe? But none could say. Others told me it originated with a woman named Mary Elder, back in the eighteen thirties. She was also known as the Widow, and I have a picture of her in the cabinet, but her candidacy for the creation of the tradition is called into question by a number of factors.

"Anyway, back in the day, I'm talking the mid–eighteen hundreds on, in rural areas like this, kids, when they reached a certain age, were sent out to participate in the fall harvest. By about age six or seven, they were initiated into the hard work of the fields during that season of long hours well into the night. It was a difficult adjustment for them. There are a lot of writings from the time where farmers or their wives complain about the wayward nature of their children, their inability to focus through the hours of toil. Training a kid to endure a harvest season with no real prior experience appears to have been a common problem. So, to offset that, someone came up with the idea of the Word Doll. The idea, in a nutshell, is to allow the child to escape into her imagination, while her physical body stays on the task at hand.

"Whoever came up with it really could have been a psychologist. They attached a ritual to it, which was a smart way to embed the thing into the local culture. So, in September, usually around the equinox, if you were one of those kids who was to be sent out in the fields for the first time come harvest, you could expect a visit from the doll maker. The doll maker came at night, right after everyone was in bed, carrying a lantern and wearing a mask. As far as I can tell, the doll makers were usually women in disguise. There'd be a knock at the door, three times and then three times again. The parents would get up and answer the call. When the child was finally ushered into the dark room and seated next to the fireplace, the doll maker was already there in her own seat that faced his. Her hands were reportedly blue, and bejeweled with chains and a large ring, its carnelian etched to show an angel in flight. She was wrapped in black velvet with a hood sewn into it to cover her head. And the mask, the mask was a story unto itself.

"By all accounts, that mask was dug up on one of the local farms. It had deep-set eyes, a crooked nose, and a large oval mouth opening bordered by sharp teeth. It was an old Iroquois False Face mask, and could have been in the ground a hundred years before it was plowed up. It was made of basswood and had rotted at the edges. One of the farmers painted it white. I suppose you're starting to see that the whole community was in on this?"

"Everybody but the kids," I said.

"Oh, the tenacity with which the secrets of the doll maker were kept from the young ones then far exceeds what's now done in the name of Santa Claus."

"So they wanted to scare the kids?"

"Not so much scare them as put them in a state of awe. Remember, the promise was that the doll maker was coming to them with a gift. The competing qualities of her aspect and her purpose no doubt caused a heightened sense of tension."

"Do you know anything about the False Face mask?"

"The False Face was a society of the Iroquois tribes. Their rituals dealt with healing. There were two ways to join the society—if you were cured by them or if you dreamed you should join them. It doesn't really have any bearing on the Word Doll tradition. Just an artifact that was appropriated by another culture and put to another purpose."

"Okay, the kid is sitting there next to the fireplace with the doll maker. . . ."

"Well, the parents leave the room. Then, as I was told by those surviving members of the ritual back in my graduate days, the doll maker tells the child not to be afraid. She's going to make the child a doll to take into the fields with him or her, a companion to play with in the imagination while the hard work goes on. The doll maker cups her hands in front of her like this." Beverly demonstrated. "And then leans over so the mouth of the mask is right over her palms. You see?" she said, and showed me.

"The voice was a kind of harsh whisper that none of my interview subjects could hear well or follow completely. The words poured out of the doll maker's mouth into the cupped hands. One woman told me a string of words she remembered her whole long life that came from behind the mask. Hold on, let me see if I can get this right."

While Beverly thought, I took out my cigarettes and held them up for her to see. "Okay?" I asked. She nodded. I lit up and drew the coffee cup closer to use as an ashtray. She held her hands up and snapped her fingers. "Oh, yes. I used to have this memorized so good. It's like a poem. My mind is scattered by age," she said, and smiled.

She was still for a second. Her eyes shifted, and she stared hard at me. *"The green sea, the deep down below the sweep of rolling waves, whales and long eight-legged pudding heads with eyes over which the great ship glides, and Captain Moss spinning the wheel . . .* That's the part she remembered, but she said the whole, what was called 'talking out of the doll,' went on for some time. The average I got was about fifteen minutes. When the doll maker spoke the last word, she rubbed her hands together vigorously and then reached over and covered the child's ears with them."

"You mean as if the words were going inside the kid's head?" I asked.

"I suppose, but from that night on, the child had, in his or her imagination, this Word Doll that had a name and a form and a little bit of history. The more the child played with it during work, the clearer it became, till it had the same detail as dreams or memories. Word Dolls all had a one-syllable name attached to whatever its profession was. So you had, like, Captain Moss, Hunter Brot, Milker May, Teacher Poll. The woman who was given the Captain told me she'd never seen the ocean but had only heard about it from elders and travelers passing through the area. She said the Captain turned out to be a man of high adventure. She followed him on his voyages through her childhood into adulthood and then old age. Another interviewee said he'd been gifted Clerk Fick, but that as he followed the days of Clerk Fick while toiling in the fields, the doll slowly became a glamorous woman, Dancer Hence. He hadn't thought of her in years, he said. 'She's still with me, but I put her away when I left the farm.'"

Beverly grabbed her cane and slowly stood. She walked to the files, bent over, and opened the second drawer down on the left hand side. Reaching in, she drew out an armful of stuff. I asked her if she needed help. "Please," she said. I went over to her, and the first thing she handed me was the white False Face mask. After that she gave me a rusted sickle with a wooden handle. "Okay," she said. She closed the drawer with the end of her cane and we started back.

"I can't believe you've got the mask," I said, laying it down. I put the sickle next to it.

She sat and shoved her pile onto the table. "The mask came easy. A lot of this stuff I really had to dig for." Pulling an old book out of the pile, she opened it, turned a few pages, and took out a large rectangle of cardboard. She turned it over and laid it in front of me. It was a picture of a woman in a high-collared black dress. Her hair was parted in the middle and pulled severely back. Her glasses were circular. She wore a righteous expression.

"The Widow?" I asked.

Beverly nodded and said, "That's a daguerreotype, not a photograph. From the eighteen fifties. She looks like a pill, doesn't she? I used to have it in plastic, but I've slacked off over the years as far as preserving all this. I resigned myself to its eventual demise when I finally resigned myself to my own."

"It's a remarkable story and archive," I said.

"My husband built me this place to house it. He was very supportive and as long as he lived, that kept me going with it. His family farmed all this acreage around here at one point."

"You got a PhD in anthropology at OSU and then married a farmer?"

"I know," she said, and laughed wistfully. "It was true love, but I still had it in my mind to be the next Margaret Mead. I knew I wasn't going to make it to Samoa any time soon, so I looked closer to home and found this." She moved her shaking hands over the things on the table.

We passed an hour with her reading me parts of her interviews, journal entries from dirty old leather-bound diaries, all of which attested to the strength of the image of the Word Doll, a doll that grew as you did, could speak to you in your mind, lead you to places you'd never been. The strangest particulars surfaced. One woman, thirty years old at the time, wrote in her diary that in all the years she'd played with Cook Gray, she'd never seen him naked, but she knew without looking that he only had one testicle. His best dish was roasted possum with cabbage, and she often used his recipes in cooking for her family. One interviewee said that her Word Doll was Deacon Tru, and that her husband's had begun as Builder Cy but somehow transformed into Barkeep Jon and was subsequently the ruination of their love. Among the papers was a letter detailing a farmer's thirty-year argument with his field friend. After he retired, he said he realized that fight had been the one thing that kept him going "through thick and thin."

Eventually Beverly ran out of steam. She lit a cigarette and eased back in her chair. "It's completely mad," she said, then flicked her ash on the floor and smiled.

"What about this?" I asked, and lifted the sickle off the table.

She blinked, pursed her lips, and said, "Mower Manc, that was the end of the whole shebang."

"The end of the ritual?"

She nodded. "In the early eighteen eighties, Word Dolls were still part of the local culture. Who knows how much longer they would have carried on with the twentieth century coming full speed ahead. But in that last year, somewhere around mid-summer, a fire started in the minister's barn one night. The place burned to the ground, and the minister's wife's buggy horse died in the flames. Everyone suspected this boy Evron Simms, who'd been caught lighting fires before. The minister, knowing the boy's parents well, decided not to pursue punishment for the crime. Come the equinox, only a week later, Evron was due a visit from the doll maker, and the doll maker came.

"Some of the folks I interviewed in the sixties knew this boy, grew up with him. He'd told more than one of them that his Field Friend was Mower Manc, a straw hat brim covering his eyes, a laborer's shirt and suspenders, calloused hands, and a large sickle. In other words, the doll maker made Evron a Word Doll whose very job was to toil in the fields. That doll maker, I discovered, was none other than the minister's wife. You can't be sure that her choice for him was malicious or that he didn't change the aspect of what was initially given to him, but if she did knowingly make his only plaything in the fields *work itself*, that would be hard-hearted."

I looked down at the sickle and said, "This doesn't sound like it's gonna end well."

"Hold on," she said, and put her hand out like a traffic cop to stop me. "Harvest starts, and Evron's sent out into the fields with that sickle you see there and is given a huge plot of hay to cut. By many accounts he immediately set to work and worked with a kind of ferocity that made him seem possessed. By sunset the field was mown, and the boy had a violet pallor, froth at the corners of his mouth. Even his father, a severe man, worried about what he'd witnessed. He wrote, 'I never thought I'd see an instance where a boy could work too hard, but today I seen it. My own Evron. I should be proud, but the sight of it wasn't a prideful thing. I'd describe it more as frightful.'

"People passed by the farm frequently after that first harvest to catch a glimpse of the boy mowing hay. They noticed that he had taken to wearing a broad-brimmed straw hat to block the sun. When the minister passed away, among his papers was a sermon he'd written about the boy's mowing. It's a very elegant document for what's there, predictably linking Evron's sickle with the scythe of Death, but halfway down the page the minister runs out of words. There are marks on the paper then, circles and crosses and a simple sun. At the bottom he writes, *Elegast*."

"What was that?" I asked, unsure I'd heard correctly.

"Elegast, an entity from the folklore of the Dutch Low Countries. A supernatural creature, like the field and forest in human form. Only the minister made that connection, though, whereas most of the local folks were convinced Evron was just touched in the head. Three years at the harvest and his look became more distant, his words fewer and fewer. When not working he'd sit perfectly still, eyes closed, and sniff at the wind. During the following winter, he was working on a hay wagon, changing one of the tin-covered wooden wheels, when the axle splintered and the cart fell and broke his left leg. That's when the real trouble started."

"Because he couldn't work?" I asked.

"Exactly. They had to tie him down to keep him from tending to the horses and cows, or shoveling the snow off the path, or keeping a low fire going in the barn during the frozen nights. He struggled to get free. The local doctor prescribed laudanum and told him if he didn't stay put and let the break mend, he'd never make it back out into the field. So they kept him in a stupor for months. Meanwhile, that winter of 1883, a stranger was spotted by more than a few folks, usually off at a distance, limping across the stubbled, misty fields, carrying a sickle and wearing a broad-brimmed straw hat. They swore it was Evron, but on the few occasions someone got close to this mysterious figure, it proved to be that of a wasted and grisly old man.

"One day Evron's father saw the old man moving across the distant landscape, and he saddled a horse and rode out to meet him. In his diary he reports, 'I confronted the grim old fellow and told him he trod upon my field. He wore no coat, though the wind was bitter, but only the summer clothes of a day laborer. I asked what it was he was looking for. He yelled at me in a harsh voice, "Work. I want work." I reminded him it was the dead of winter. He stalked away, dragging his bad leg. By then a fierce snow had begun to fall, and in a moment I lost sight of him.'"

"You've got an incredible memory," I told her.

"I've been waiting to tell somebody all of this for forty years," she said. "I'll jump ahead. I know I've kept you too long already."

"Take your time."

"To make a long story shorter, the minister's wife was found one afternoon, not but a few days later, hacked to pieces in a church pew. Nobody had a doubt but that it was the stranger. A posse was formed, and the men went out into the fields on horseback searching for him. At night they carried torches. Always they would glimpse him in the distance across the vast acreage of a barren field, but when they arrived at that spot, he'd be gone. Still, he struck twice more. A fifteen-year-old girl, who lived two miles down the road from the Simms' place. Her body was found in a horse trough, neck cut so bad that when they lifted her out of her frozen blood, her head fell off. Then a farmer slashed to ribbons, his body still upright in the seat of his buckboard, leaving a long trail of red in his wake as the horses stepped smartly through the snow.

"The younger boys called the killer Mower Manc after Evron's Field Friend. Everyone saw the connection, but it was impossible to blame the killings on the boy, who was in a perpetual daze at home, fastened to his bed. All through the rest of that winter and into the spring, they chased the illusive figure. Sometimes he'd disappear for months, and then there'd be a sighting of him. Once the crops were put in and the corn and wheat came up at the end of the spring, it got still more difficult to track him. Someone would see him cross the dirt road, and then he'd plunge into a cornfield and vanish.

"Harvest time finally came, and Evron was allowed to return to the fields to mow. His leg was still tender, and there was a slight but noticeable limp, but the boy, sickle in hand, went out into the fields to cut wheat. His father, his mother, his sister, the doctor, and a neighboring farmer watched Evron walk into the wind-rippled amber expanse, and that was the last anyone ever saw of him. All they found was that sickle." Beverly clasped her hands, set them in her lap, and sighed.

"He ran away," I said.

"I suppose," she said. "But all through the end of the nineteenth century, through the twentieth, and into the twenty-first up to today, folks have continued to farm this land. Geologists call it the Ohio Till Plain, one of the most fertile spots in the country. In all that time, every so often someone peering from a second-floor window of a farmhouse spots a strange figure in a distant field moving through the corn. A shadow with a hat. A loping scarecrow with a sickle. People nowadays refer to this phantom simply as the Mower. If you live here long enough, Mr. Ford, and you get to know the farmers well enough, you'll hear someone speak of it. It's said that certain nights in deep winter, below the howl of the wind, you can hear him weeping for want of work. If you wake on a cold morning and find your garage door open when it wasn't the night before, it means the Mower has taken refuge from the cold in there."

Beverly got up and took her papers and old diaries and daguerreotypes to the filing cabinet and put them away. I carried the False Face and the sickle. She took the mask from me and stored it, but when I handed her the tool, she said, "No, you keep that."

After all she'd told me, I wasn't sure I wanted it, but eventually my sense of politeness kicked in and I thanked her. She walked with me to my car, and before I got in, we shook hands. "You're the last one," she said before I drove off. When I got home, I immediately looked around for a place to stow the sickle. Crazy as it was, I shoved it down into the big freezer in the garage underneath the layers of frozen vegetables from the garden. I figured I'd freeze the creep out of it.

The Word Doll Museum and old Beverly Gearing stuck with me for a week or so, and I'd sit out under the apple trees and stare off into the corn to see if I could spot a shadowy figure passing amid the rows. Nothing. Just as it started to get too cold to sit out there, and Farmer Frank had the combine going, harvesting corn, I got an idea for a story about a religious painter who's sent out by a prelate on a journey to find and paint a true portrait of the Devil. It was a relatively long piece, and it consumed my imagination. By the time I finished a first draft the fields were barren, and I was forced to move inside. The revisions on that story turned out to be extensive, and I didn't finish it until the middle of winter.

The very night I was finally satisfied that the piece was ready to send out, the coldest night of the year, I had a dream of Mower Manc. In it I got out of bed and went to the window. It was night, and the light in the room was off. There was a full moon, though, and I saw, out in the barren field past the orchard and the garden, a figure moving through the snow, curved blade glinting as it swung like the pendulum of an old clock. Across that distance, I heard the weeping clear as a bell, and its anguish woke me.

When I went out to get my cigarettes the next morning, I came around that bend and saw that the gray barn and home of the Word Doll Museum had at some point since the day before collapsed into a smoldering pile of rubble. Orange flames still darted from the charred wreckage and smoke rolled across the yard and fields like a storm cloud come down to earth. I thought instantly of Beverly's habit of flicking her cigarette ash on the floor of the place and just as quickly of Evron's penchant for lighting fires. Then I saw her, on the snow-covered lawn in front of the house, cane nowhere in sight, in a long blue nightgown and dirty pink slippers, white hair lurid in the wind. There was a cop car in the drive-way, and the officer stood next to her with a pen and pad as if waiting to take down her statement. She was just staring into the distance, though, her grief-stricken expression pale and distorted like the False Face mask, and as I passed I realized that what I was seeing was the end of it—a fellow doll maker, all out of words.

About the Authors

Richard Bowes has won two World Fantasy Awards. He has published six novels, including the 2013 Lambda-nominated *Dust Devil on a Quiet Street*. Many of his more than seventy short stories have been published in four short story collections, the most recent two being *The Queen, the Cambion, and Seven Others* and *If Angels Fight*.

He's recently had reprinted and original stories published in *The Time Traveller's Almanac, Handsome Devil, The Mammoth Book of Gaslit Romance, The Book of Apex: Volume 4, The Revelator, Best Gay Stories 2014,* and *Tor.com*.

Pat Cadigan is the author of fifteen books, including two nonfiction titles, a young adult novel, and the two Arthur C. Clarke Award–winning novels *Synners* and *Fools*. She has also won the Locus Award three times and the Hugo Award for her novelette "The Girl-Thing Who Went Out for Sushi." Pat lives in gritty, urban North London with the Original Chris Fowler and Gentleman Jinx, the coolest black cat in London. She can be found on Facebook and tweets as @cadigan.

Her books are available electronically via SF Gateway, the ambitious electronic publishing program from Gollancz.

Award-winning horror author **Gemma Files** has also been a film critic, teacher, and screenwriter. She is best known for her Weird Western Hexslinger series, *A Book of Tongues, A Rope of Thorns,* and *A Tree of Bones,* and has published three collections of short fiction, *Kissing Carrion* and *The Worm in Every Heart,* as well as two chapbooks of poetry. Her most recent collection, *We Will All Go Down Together: Stories About the Five-Family Coven*, was published in 2014.

Jeffrey Ford is the multi-award-winning author of the novels *The Physiognomy, Memoranda, The Beyond, The Portrait of Mrs. Charbuque, The Girl in the Glass, The Cosmology of the Wider World,* and *The Shadow Year.*

His short fiction has been published in numerous journals, magazines, and anthologies and has been collected in *The Fantasy Writer's Assistant, The Empire of Ice Cream, The Drowned Life,* and *Crackpot Palace.*

Stephen Gallagher, a Stoker Award and World Fantasy Award nominee, and winner of British Fantasy and International Horror Guild Awards for his short fiction, combines the life of a novelist with a career creating and working in prime-time miniseries and episodic television.

He created the modern science thriller *Eleventh Hour,* starring Patrick Stewart in the United Kingdom and Rufus Sewell in the CBS remake, and is the creator/showrunner of ABC's *Risen.*

He is the author of fourteen novels, including *Valley of Lights; Down River; The Boat House;* and *Nightmare, with Angel. The Bedlam Detective* continues the exploits of ex–Pinkerton man Sebastian Becker, first introduced in *The Kingdom of Bones* and slated for a further appearance in *The Authentic William James.*

Stephen Graham Jones is the author of fifteen novels and five story collections. The most recent are *The Least of My Scars, After the People Lights Have Gone Off, Once Upon a Time in Texas,* and, with Paul Tremblay, *Floating Boy and the Girl Who Couldn't Fly.*

Jones has some two hundred stories published, many reprinted in best-of-the-year annuals. He's won the Texas Institute of Letters Award for fiction, the Independent Publishers Award for Multicultural Fiction, and an NEA fellowship in fiction. He teaches in the MFA programs at CU Boulder and UCR–Palm Desert.

He lives in Colorado and really likes werewolves and slashers and hair metal.

For more information: demontheory.net or @SGJ72.

Richard Kadrey is the *New York Times* bestselling author of the Sandman Slim noir fantasy novels. The sixth book in the series, *The Getaway God*, was published in 2014.

His other books include *Butcher Bird*, the dark YA novel *Dead Set*, *Metrophage*, and the graphic novel *ACCELERATE*.

Mary Robinette Kowal is the author of *Shades of Milk and Honey*, *Glamour in Glass*, *Without a Summer*, and *Valour and Vanity*. In 2008 she received the Campbell Award for Best New Writer; in 2011 her short story "For Want of a Nail" won the Hugo Award for Short Story; and in 2014 "The Lady Astronaut of Mars" won the Hugo Award for Best Novelette. Her stories have been published in *Asimov's*, *Clarkesworld*, and several best-of-the-year anthologies.

Kowal, a professional puppeteer, also performs as a voice actor, recording fiction for authors such as Elizabeth Bear, Cory Doctorow, and John Scalzi.

She lives in Chicago with her husband, Rob, and over a dozen manual typewriters. Visit www.maryrobinettekowal.com.

John Langan is the author of two collections, *Mr. Gaunt and Other Uneasy Encounters* and *The Wide, Carnivorous Sky and Other Monstrous Geographies*.

His first novel, *House of Windows*, was published in 2010, and he is currently working on a second. He coedited the anthology *Creatures: Thirty Years of Monsters* with Paul Tremblay.

He lives in upstate New York with his wife, younger son, and menagerie.

Tim Lebbon is a *New York Times* bestselling horror and fantasy writer from South Wales. He's had almost thirty novels published to date, as well as dozens of novellas and hundreds of short stories. His most recent releases include the apocalyptic novel *Coldbrook*, *Alien: Out of the Shadows*, *Into the Void: Dawn of the Jedi (Star Wars)*, and the Toxic City trilogy from Pyr. Forthcoming novels include *The Silence* and *Endure*.

Lebbon has won four British Fantasy Awards, a Bram Stoker Award, and a Scribe Award. He recently started his own Dreaming in Fire Press to publish his back catalog as e-books.

Twentieth Century Fox acquired film rights to The Secret Journeys of Jack London series (coauthored with Christopher Golden), and a TV series of his Toxic City trilogy is in development. In addition, his script *Playtime* (with Stephen Volk) is currently being developed in the United Kingdom.

Find out more about Tim on his website: www.timlebbon.net.

Seanan McGuire is an avid doll collector, and she shares her room with several hundred blank, soulless eyes. In addition to her doll problem, she has a small writing problem, and she publishes an average of four books a year under both her own name and the pen name Mira Grant.

When not writing or curating her private museum of the creepy, she travels, visits haunted corn mazes and Disney parks, and hangs out on the Internet. Seanan is rumored not to sleep. The rumors are probably true.

Find her on Twitter as @seananmcguire, or at www.seananmcguire .com.

Joyce Carol Oates is one of the most prolific and respected writers in the United States today. Oates has written fiction in almost every genre and medium. Her keen interest in the Gothic and psychological hor- ror has spurred her to write dark suspense novels under the name Ro- samond Smith and to write enough stories in the genre to have published several collections of dark fiction, the most recent being *Give Me Your Heart: Tales of Mystery and Suspense*, *The Corn Maiden and Other Night- mares*, *Black Dahlia and White Rose*, and *Evil Eye: Four Novellas of Love Gone Wrong*, and to edit *American Gothic Tales*.

Oates has won the Bram Stoker Award, the National Book Award, the Pulitzer Prize for fiction, the O'Henry Award, the PEN/Malamud

Award, the PEN/Faulkner Award, and the Rea Award for the Short Story, and she's been honored with a Life Achievement Award by the Horror Writers Association.

Oates's most recent novels are *Mudwoman*, *Daddy Love*, *The Accursed*, and *Carthage*. She teaches creative writing at Princeton.

Veronica Schanoes is associate professor in the Department of English at Queens College–CUNY. Her novella "Burning Girls" won the Shirley Jackson Award and was a finalist for both the Nebula and the World Fantasy Awards. Her most recent fiction can be found on *Tor* .com. Her first book, an academic monograph on revisions of fairy tales entitled *Fairy Tales, Myth, and Psychoanalytic Theory: Feminism and Retelling the Tale*, was recently published by Ashgate Press.

Miranda Siemienowicz lives in Melbourne, Australia. She has published fiction in literary journals such as *Overland* and *Island* and in speculative fiction magazines, including *Aurealis* and *Black: Australian Dark Culture*.

Her short stories have been reprinted in *The Best Horror of the Year* and *Australian Dark Fantasy and Horror*.

Lucy Sussex was born in New Zealand. She has edited four anthologies, including *She's Fantastical*. Her award-winning fiction includes books for younger readers and the novel *The Scarlet Rider* (reissued in 2014).

She has five short story collections: *My Lady Tongue*, *A Tour Guide in Utopia*, *Absolute Uncertainty*, *Matilda Told Such Dreadful Lies* (a best of), and *Thief of Lives*. Her latest project is *Victorian Blockbuster: Fergus Hume and the Mystery of a Hansom Cab* (forthcoming).

Genevieve Valentine's first novel, *Mechanique*, won the 2012 Crawford Award. *The Girls at the Kingfisher Club* was published in 2014; her third novel, *Persona*, is forthcoming in spring 2015.

She's also written for DC's *Catwoman*.

Her short fiction has been published on *Tor.com*, *Clarkesworld*, *Strange Horizons*, *Journal of Mythic Arts*, *Lightspeed*, and other websites, and in anthologies, including *Federations*, *After*, *Teeth*, *The Cutting Room*, and *Nightmare Carnival*.

Her nonfiction and reviews have appeared on *NPR.org*, *The A.V. Club*, *Strange Horizons*, and *io9*.

Her appetite for bad movies is insatiable, a tragedy she tracks at genevievevalentine.com.

Carrie Vaughn is an Air Force brat who survived her nomadic childhood and managed to put down roots in Boulder, Colorado.

She's the author of the *New York Times* bestselling series of novels about a werewolf named Kitty, the most recent installment of which is *Kitty in the Underworld*.

Vaughn has also written several other contemporary fantasy and young adult novels, as well as upward of seventy short stories, and is a contributor to the Wild Cards series of shared-world superhero books edited by George R. R. Martin.

Her most recent nonseries novel is about a superhero and is titled *Dreams of the Golden Age*.

Visit her at www.carrievaughn.com.

About the Editor

Ellen Datlow has been editing science fiction, fantasy, and horror short fiction for more than thirty-five years. She currently acquires short fiction for *Tor.com*. In addition, she has edited almost one hundred science fiction, fantasy, and horror anthologies, including the annual *The Best Horror of the Year*, *Lovecraft's Monsters*, *Fearful Symmetries*, *The Cutting Room*, and *Nightmare Carnival*.

Forthcoming is *The Monstrous*.

She's won multiple World Fantasy Awards, Locus Awards, Hugo Awards, Stoker Awards, International Horror Guild Awards, Shirley Jackson Awards, and the 2012 Il Posto Nero Black Spot Award for Excellence as Best Foreign Editor. Datlow was named recipient of the 2007 Karl Edward Wagner Award, given at the British Fantasy Convention for "outstanding contribution to the genre," was honored with the Lifetime Achievement Award by the Horror Writers Association in acknowledgment of superior achievement over an entire career, and recently won the World Fantasy Life Achievement Award.

She lives in New York and cohosts the monthly Fantastic Fiction Reading Series at KGB Bar. More information can be found at www.datlow.com, on Facebook, and on twitter as @EllenDatlow.